Emperor's Lion

Alex Gough is an author of Roman historical adventures. The Carbo Chronicles, including *Watchmen of Rome* and *Bandits of Rome*, was written as a result of a lifelong obsession with ancient Rome, and the culmination of a lot of research into the underclasses of the time. He has also written a collection of adventures following Carbo and other characters from *Watchmen of Rome*, where you can learn more about their rich lives.

For reviews of Roman fiction, and articles about Roman history go to www.romanfiction.com

Also by Alex Gough

Carbo and the Thief
Who All Die

Carbo of Rome

Watchmen of Rome
Bandits of Rome

The Imperial Assassin

Emperor's Sword
Emperor's Knife
Emperor's Axe
Emperor's Spear
Emperor's Lion

ALEX GOUGH

EMPEROR'S LION

CANELO

First published in the United Kingdom in 2022 by

Canelo
Unit 9, 5th Floor
Cargo Works, 1-2 Hatfields
London, SE1 9PG
United Kingdom

A CIP catalogue record for this book is available from the British Library.

Print ISBN 978 1 80032 901 0
Ebook ISBN 978 1 80032 900 3

Printed and bound in Great Britain by Clays Ltd, Elcograf S.p.A.

1

MIX
Paper from responsible sources
FSC® C018072

Chapter I

Rome, 214 AD Martius

Silus watched the procession approach along the Via Sacra, the hysterical cheering from the crowd already deafening, and whispered to himself, 'Fuck!' The expletive was born part of awe and part of disgust. It was the first Imperial Triumph he had witnessed, and for all his discomfort with the reasons for the celebration, it was undeniable that Caracalla knew how to put on a show.

Rome was garlanded in flowers of all colours and varieties. Roses, hyacinths, violets and narcissi bedecked the temples, shops, public buildings and private dwellings. A vast crowd thronged the streets, so Silus was shoulder to shoulder with jostling onlookers. Not the tallest, despite his Celtic ancestry, he had to stand on tiptoes to get the best view.

The screaming around him rose to an even higher pitch and volume as the first riders passed, officers of the Praetorian Guard, resplendent in polished armour, immaculately behaved mounts groomed so not a hair was out of place. And Silus thought he would be deafened when they caught the first glimpse of Caracalla.

The Emperor rode in a gold chariot, a quadriga drawn by four perfectly white horses side by side. He was dressed in the traditional purple robe of Jupiter, with his face painted red to emulate the ancient statue of the king of the gods. Behind him, a slave held a laurel wreath above the Emperor's head, but all the time he was whispering in Caracalla's ear. Silus knew the tradition. The slave was reminding Caracalla that he was a man, not a god. Silus wondered if Caracalla believed that.

The Emperor held the reins loosely in one hand, while with the other he waved indulgently to the adoring crowd. Beside him stood his stepmother, Julia Domna, dressed in a white stola with a purple palla covering her head and shoulders. She bore a thin, almost pained smile, which neither Caracalla nor the onlookers noticed or heeded. At one point Silus thought she looked directly at him, but then her gaze drifted onwards, and he decided he had imagined the moment of connection.

Behind the chariot came the trophies and spoils of war. Sacks overflowing with gold and silver coins. Cups and bracelets decorated with precious jewels. Fine weapons. Martial symbols taken from the battlefield. Large placards bearing illustrations of scenes of battle and pictures of the conquests of the German campaign, captured rivers and forts and forests and mountains. Marching behind these, row after endless row, came the legions, the praetorians leading the way, then the other legions that had taken part in the campaigns, or at least as many as could be spared from guarding the borders. These were followed by dancers, flautists and trumpet-players.

And in the rear, weighed down with chains and guarded by spear-wielding praetorians, a long train of prisoners marched. Some had their heads down, flinching as stones and rotten fruit hurled by the crowd hit them. Others stared back defiantly, even growled and lunged if one of the crowd dared to dart forward to strike them. Silus' stomach clenched at the sight. Some of these were unrepentant enemies of Rome, Chatti and other Germanic tribes who wanted nothing more than to flood across the borders, tear down the temples and burn the homes of the Roman citizens who lived peacefully in the German and Gallic provinces. But others were Alemanni, allies until Caracalla turned on them and betrayed them. Silus wondered if they knew that this was their final march, an ignominious death at the hands of the official executioners awaiting them at the climax of the show.

He had heard the reasons for the betrayal over and over, from Atius, from Oclatinius, from the legionaries he talked to in the bars and taverns, and he understood, on an intellectual level. The Alemanni were organising into a confederation large enough to threaten Rome, just like the Maeatae and Caledonians had in northern Britannia. Caracalla had ruthlessly eliminated the threat before it had become a problem. But that had been at the cost of the lives of so many. Some that Silus had counted as friends.

And Atius had known of the impending betrayal and done nothing to stop it; had gone to great lengths to keep it secret, even from his closest friend, Silus.

Friend no more.

Silus had avoided Atius as much as possible after that day. Atius had tried to approach him, to repair the rift. Oclatinius had tried to mediate, though Silus had little time for the old spymaster any more. Silus had declined all attempts at reconciliation. Eventually, Oclatinius had sent Silus away on a minor and unimportant spying mission, just to prevent violence breaking out between the two Arcani.

Silus had spent the winter in Rome, bored out of his mind. He wished he had Atius' appetite for gambling, drink and casual sex, but in fact they did little for him. And when Caracalla had appeared with his legions at the Porta Triumphalis and asked the Senate for a Triumph to celebrate his victory over the Germans, he had felt a thrill of anticipation, a desire for the action and excitement that had been so lacking in his life.

As the last of the procession passed, Silus became aware of his aching legs and the crick in his neck as he had been straining for the best view. He had been there for hours, he realised, and the March sun was well past its zenith. The crowd began to disperse, not to their homes but in search of whatever free entertainment had been put on by the triumphant Emperor. Silus shifted his weight from foot to foot, and wondered what next. The excited feeling in his belly was fading as the procession receded into the distance in the direction of the forum. He sighed and steeled himself for another pointless night wandering around Rome looking for any excitement that could substitute for the thrill of the battlefield.

A low voice, emanating from a mouth right next to his ear, said, 'We need to talk.'

Silus turned abruptly and looked into the aged, stern features of Marcus Oclatinius Adventus, head of the Arcani. And despite himself, that feeling of anticipation surged up in him once more.

-

Oclatinius led Silus through the streets of revellers. Though Oclatinius was no longer as sound of body as in previous decades, Silus marvelled at the way he cut through the crowds like a sharp knife through a rotten pomegranate. Most who caught sight of the spymaster moved aside without protest. Those that didn't found that a surprisingly firm two fingers into a sensitive area made them leap aside with a yelp.

Ignoring Silus' queries, which were escalating to demands, Oclatinius took him to a bookshop on the ground floor of an insula just north of the Forum Boarium. He strode in through the front door, past the shelves lined with scrolls, parchments and tablets, past the surprised-looking slave who ran the shop on behalf of his absentee master, and out of the back, an irritated Silus in tow.

The back room was gloomy, with no windows, just a couple of flickering oil lamps on a shelf, and it took a moment for Silus' eyes to adjust. As he became used to the dark, he saw wooden crates full of more books, a table with three chairs, a figure occupying one of the chairs. The man leant forward, moving out of the shadows so his face became illuminated by the dull orange glow from the lamps.

'I've got nothing to say to that man,' Silus spat, and turned to leave.

'Silus, wait,' said Atius, rising to his feet and reaching a hand out as if he could pull him back. Silus didn't turn, but Oclatinius was blocking his exit. Silus considered pushing him out of the way, but he didn't feel confident that Oclatinius wouldn't break his arm if he tried anything physical.

'Sit,' said Oclatinius, and it wasn't a request.

Reluctantly, Silus settled himself in the seat furthest from Atius, and Oclatinius took the middle chair. Atius looked across the table at Silus, his face full of regret and remorse. Silus looked away, eyes drifting over the scroll-filled shelves, jaw clenching and unclenching.

'Silus...' began Atius, but Oclatinius held up a hand and Atius closed his mouth and sat back.

Silus waited for the spymaster to speak but he said nothing. After a few moments of increasingly uncomfortable silence, the door leading to the front of the shop opened and the slave entered, bringing three cups of wine. He set them down on the table, bowed respectfully, then hurried back out.

Oclatinius picked his cup up, and held it in front of him. Silus folded his arms. Oclatinius glared at him. It was a stare that set icy fear in the hearts of most on the receiving end of it. But Silus knew Oclatinius well. He knew he was not in real danger. He also believed that he could best Oclatinius in a fight, though he wasn't completely sure of that, and he knew he would have no hope if Oclatinius and Atius combined forces against him.

Atius reached out for his cup, then paused, stiffened, a grimace of pain flashing across his face.

'What is it?' Oclatinius asked in concern.

'It's nothing.'

'Tell me.' Oclatinius' voice brooked no argument.

'It's my shoulder,' said Atius, working his arm in a circle. 'When I was captive, they had my arms tied above my head for a long time. I think it did me some permanent injury. But it's fine. It doesn't stop me fighting.'

Silus swallowed involuntarily, remembering the horrors his friend had been through while prisoner in Germania.

Oclatinius returned his icy stare to Silus. Silus sighed and picked up his cup.

'What are we toasting?' he said testily.

'Fidelity, loyalty and keeping oaths.'

Silus grimaced. 'Not a toast to Caracalla then.'

Atius stiffened, but Oclatinius put a gentle hand on his forearm.

'We aren't discussing the policies of our Emperor here. We are talking about deep ties. Bonds forged in shared hardship. Sacred oaths sworn on all we hold dear. I'm talking about loyalty to the Arcani. And that is my toast. The Arcani.'

Without waiting for a response, he drank deep. Atius followed suit. Silus hesitated. For all the disgust he felt towards Caracalla's actions in Germania, and the way Oclatinius and Atius had facilitated him, he still believed in the oath he swore to Oclatinius when he was first inducted into the Arcani. And he still loved Atius, even as he hated what he had done.

Silus picked up the cup and drank. Oclatinius nodded his satisfaction. Atius' features betrayed profound relief. It made Silus realise how much he had been hurting his friend by keeping his distance. After all they had been through, they were closer than brothers. A sudden feeling of emotion welled up inside him. To cover it, he reached out and squeezed Atius' shoulder. When he trusted himself to speak, he said, 'This doesn't make what happened right.'

'We never said it was,' said Oclatinius evenly. 'Just that Caracalla, correctly or incorrectly, thought it necessary. And our jobs, our duties, were to support him.'

'There are limits to duty,' said Silus, but his defiance was gone. He drank again. 'So, that's what you dragged me here for? To make nice with this idiot?'

Atius grinned, knowing the insult was a sign of affection.

'This was a necessary preliminary,' said Oclatinius. 'The Emperor wants a meeting with his finest operatives.'

Silus and Atius glanced at each other.

'It surprised me too,' said Oclatinius, 'but apparently he means you two. And I couldn't have you two at each other's throats in the Imperial presence.'

'So what's this about? Another inviting opportunity for probable death?'

'I have an idea it is related to some intelligence I presented him with. But we will find out at the meeting. Which, incidentally, is one hour from now. So freshen up, fast.'

–

Caracalla clearly hadn't been idle in the months since Silus saw him last. Some people tucked themselves away for the winter, out of the cold, and ate enough to put on an extra layer of fat to stay warm. If anything, Caracalla looked leaner, and with that permanently furrowed brow, meaner. He was dressed in military uniform, seated on his throne, deep in conversation with his advisors. Silus stood patiently at attention, Atius by his side, waiting for Caracalla to acknowledge his presence.

The discussion revolved around the logistics of a grand expedition, Silus gathered. His attention wandered at the talk of how many modii of fodder were needed per day for the wagon oxen, and how many amphorae of wine to keep the legionaries from revolting. He tried to put names to all the serious-looking, important faces present.

Seated on Caracalla's right was Julia Domna, also looking thinner since Silus last saw her, and a little paler too. Everyone else was standing. Oclatinius was there, of course, and Festus beside him. Silus also recognised Macrinus, who he recalled was some sort of bureaucrat and an important lawyer. Macrinus was around fifty, with a long curly beard and short cropped grey hair, receding around the temples. He had a tan complexion, and unusually sported a gold earring, a hangover from his Mauretanian heritage. He was flanked by two men that Silus thought he had seen in Caracalla's wider entourage before, but he had no idea of their names. Behind Caracalla, in a position that allowed him to both whisper advice and serve the Emperor's needs and whims, was the round-faced eunuch, Sempronius Rufus. The two praetorian prefects, freedmen called Epagathus and Theocritus, stood together to one side.

Also present was Helvius Pertinax, the son of the former Emperor Pertinax, who had been elevated to the purple by the praetorians, the same body of men who had been guilty of the murder of his predecessor, Commodus. The son of a freedman, Pertinax senior had risen from nothing. But he had served with distinction in previous Parthian wars and had ascended to the rank of urban prefect before being thrust onto the throne. Sadly his reign only lasted eighty-six days, before the avaricious praetorians decided to make some more cash by selling the throne to the highest bidder. Much good it did his successor, Didius Julianus, who was murdered by followers of Caracalla's father, Septimius Severus, sixty-six days later.

Caracalla's father had deified Pertinax, and Caracalla had kept faith with his father's respect for the former Emperor by recently admitting his son to his advisory council. Helvius Pertinax had briefly been declared Caesar, as son of the Emperor, some twenty years ago, despite being the grandson of a timber merchant. Now an old man himself, he carried the resentful air of one who had been promised a great prize, only to have it snatched away.

And finally, there was Flavius Maternianus the urban prefect, tall enough that he looked down on everyone else with a certain aloofness. Silus gathered from the conversation that he would be left behind to govern the city when Caracalla left for whatever campaign they were planning.

Silus' bored gaze returned to Julia Domna. How old was she now? Certainly over fifty, but still looking magnificent. No doubt having the best maidservants in the Empire attending to her skincare, hair and make-up helped, but there were plenty of older women in Rome who tried their best to look like nubile young Roman girls with limited success. Domna wasn't trying to appear young, but just accepted help to accentuate her natural beauty, and maybe cover up the worst excesses of ages. Still, despite that, he noticed her cheekbones were a touch more prominent, and now he looked, her forearms where they protruded from her stola a little thinner. He wondered how much care and worry, grief and regret she carried within her, stepmother and lover of the Emperor, who had killed her son while she held him in her arms.

Domna looked up suddenly, and caught Silus staring at her. Silus reddened, looked down, looked back up. She was still looking at him, her lips curled in an amused half-smile. Silus bowed his head, then lowered his gaze respectfully. He felt Domna's eyes on him for some time after, but the next time he dared to glance up, her attention had moved on, and she was giving her opinion on the itinerary of Caracalla's progression. The Emperor nodded, listening intently to her advice, and all the other wise and powerful men present were silent when she spoke, despite her sex. It suddenly struck Silus what an unusually powerful woman she was. It spoke well of her intellect and personality, since no woman had had as much power in Rome since Agrippina the Younger, mother of Nero.

When Domna had finished speaking, Caracalla held up a hand, and everyone waited intently for his words.

'Thank you all for your advice. There is a lot still to discuss, a lot of planning to do. But now I wish to pause proceedings to make an announcement.' He looked around him, eyes resting one by one on those assembled, letting them all know this was a moment of importance. When Caracalla's eyes reached him, Silus was sure that he gave him a wink, then immediately dismissed the idea as foolish. But a brief surge of anger rose in his belly as the Emperor's recent betrayals came back to him once more.

'Since my friend Marcellus went to Numidia as governor, my loyal freedmen, Theocritus and Epagathus here, have been acting as praetorian prefects, and doing a fine job. But with my journey to the East imminent, and the demands this onerous position brings, I have decided to expand the role. Theocritus and Epagathus will become joint supreme praetorian prefects, with ultimate authority over the Praetorian Guard, and any other commands that I see fit to give them. But I am also creating two new posts.

'The laws of Rome have held our people together since the time of the kings, and no one is above the law. In order that I should have the best legal advice available to me at all times, I am promoting a lawyer to the rank of praetorian prefect. Macrinus, approach.'

Macrinus stepped in front of the Emperor and dropped to one knee.

'Macrinus, you have given my father and me sound advice for years, not least when I introduced the Constitutio Antoniniana and made all Romans equal citizens. As a reward for your service and in order to have you near at all times, I pronounce you praetorian prefect. In addition, you are to command the Second Legion Parthica.'

Macrinus bowed his head deeply, then stood and kissed Caracalla's outstretched hand.

'I am deeply grateful for this honour, Augustus, and I vow to be loyal and faithful to your Imperial greatness.'

Silus tried not to roll his eyes at the sycophancy, though he knew that nothing less was required.

Caracalla waved him away.

'But laws are nothing without the might of our soldiers to enforce them throughout the Empire. So the second praetorian prefect position goes to a military man. A man who has done more than any of you know for the Senate and people of Rome, and for her Emperor. Step forward, Oclatinius.'

Oclatinius looked up in surprise, blinking rapidly. Silus smirked. The promotion was clearly unexpected, and the old man's shock was unfeigned. Silus doubted that Oclatinius had sought, or desired the position. He was not one to wish to stand in the glare of the public eye.

Nevertheless he moved to stand in front of Caracalla, and dropped, slowly and stiffly, to one knee.

'Marcus Oclatinius Adventus. Your service to me has of necessity rarely been publicly acclaimed. But now, in thanks for your long years of loyalty to my father and to me, and in expectation of many years to come, I promote you to praetorian prefect. You will be by my side in the forthcoming campaign, so I have access to your wise advice at all times.'

To Silus' ears, it almost sounded sarcastic, but that was probably just him. He knew that hyperbole was expected in these sorts of pronouncements. Oclatinius seemed to take it at face value. He bowed his head.

'Infirm and aged as I am, Augustus, I will do my utmost to serve you to the limits of my endurance.'

'Bullshit,' muttered Silus under his breath. He thought no one had heard, but Domna's eyes swivelled back to him sharply. Her brows drew together and Silus' heart stuttered in his chest. Then she smiled and turned her attention back to Caracalla and Silus let out a breath he hadn't realised he was holding. Atius elbowed him subtly in the ribs by way of rebuke.

Caracalla extended his hand for Oclatinius' kiss, then the old man slowly got to his feet. Silus was pretty sure he was exaggerating the stiffness in his joints for the audience. The old spymaster always preferred to be underestimated. Which suggested there were people present that he didn't trust. Silus scanned the room, wondering who was under the cloud of the Arcani master's suspicion. He wouldn't want to be in their place.

Caracalla sat back and surveyed the room. 'Thank you everyone for your time. Everyone is now dismissed except Oclatinius, Macrinus, Festus… and you two.'

He waved a hand in the direction of Silus and Atius, who both stiffened at the sudden attention from the Emperor. A few resentful glances were thrown towards them by those leaving the room, no doubt wondering why these two nobodies deserved the honour of time in the Imperial presence.

When the room was emptied of all but those that Caracalla had named, the Emperor stood and started to pace, his muscular chest pushed forward, hands behind his back.

'Oclatinius, tell everyone what you told me.'

Oclatinius looked around the room uncertainly, but didn't question the Imperial directive.

'I have received some important intelligence. Regarding the Governor of Numidia. His life is threatened.'

Silus clenched his jaw. He had liked Marcellus, and his quirky son Avitus and even his crazy wife, Julia Soaemias, Julia Domna's niece. He didn't like the idea of them in danger. And quick on the tail of that thought was a realisation of the reason he was here. He glanced at Atius, whose eyes had lit up. Silus sighed. Still a stupid kid, excited at the thought of action. Although – he had to admit to himself that there was a little part of him that wanted something to relieve his own boredom. He waited to hear more.

'One of my spies sent me a report. An assassin is being dispatched from Rome. Imminently.'

Silus felt a sudden surge of jealousy that Oclatinius had others that he relied on besides Atius and himself, even though he knew that was entirely irrational, especially as he had given the old man the cold shoulder for the last few months.

'By whom?' asked Festus. 'Who is the assassin? What is the reason behind all this?'

Oclatinius held his hand out. 'If I may continue? I don't know who the assassin is, and I don't know who hired him. And I can only speculate as to the reason.'

'Then speculate,' said Caracalla.

'I understand that you are planning to recall Marcellus to Rome, and make him consul.'

Caracalla stopped pacing and stared intently at him.

'And how did you come by this information?'

Oclatinius looked abashed. 'Forgive me, Augustus. My network is extensive, my sources manifold. I would prefer not to speak of them, although if you command me, I will of course reveal all.'

Caracalla waved a dismissive hand. 'No matter. Continue.'

'Marcellus is a loyal ally of yours, Augustus. He will not be turned from your side, not by promises of money or power.'

'How do you know?' asked Macrinus.

Oclatinius shrugged. 'Because I tried. My agents tempted him in a number of ways. He is completely steadfast. And that is well known. So bringing him back to Rome will bolster your power and make any conspiracies against you harder to bring to completion.'

'And there are conspiracies?' asked Caracalla.

'Augustus, there are always conspiracies.'

Caracalla looked around the room, then to the door through which the rest of his council had just departed. He stroked his beard and frowned, the creases in his forehead growing even more crevasse-like.

'So, I need Marcellus by my side. Yet he is far away, and someone wants him dead.'

'That is the situation, Augustus, yes.'

'And your solution is these two?' Caracalla waved his hand at Silus and Atius.

'You know how well they have served us in the past.'

'Do you not feel we place too much reliance on these two?' put in Festus. 'They have had Fortuna on their side, it's true, but she can turn her face away at any time. And have they had their loyalty tested, as Oclatinius tested Marcellus?'

Caracalla looked Silus straight in the eyes as he said, 'Their loyalty is not in question.'

Silus suppressed a shiver. He knew that Caracalla was reminding him of the vulnerability of Tituria, still in exile in Lipari. Concern for her welfare emboldened him.

'It is as you say, Augustus. We are absolutely loyal to you, and ready to take on any mission you command. And though I have no right to ask for anything, nevertheless, may I request a favour?'

Silus could tell Atius was holding his breath, and Festus looked outraged. Oclatinius shook his head in disappointment. But Caracalla just inclined his head indulgently.

'Ask.'

'You know there is a girl who has been in my care, who is important to me. She is in exile because of the misdeeds of her father, but that man is now long dead.' At the hand of Silus' colleague, in fact, right before his eyes, and the girl's eyes too.

'And you wish me to recall her?'

'If you feel she is no longer a threat to you, yes, Augustus, I would be very grateful.'

Caracalla raised his eyebrows. Silus wondered if he had gone too far, implying that he was fearful of a girl. But the Emperor laughed.

'Very well. Festus, make it happen. She will be brought into Rome, and I will ensure she is adopted into a good family. Equestrian rank. She will grow up and marry in safety. And you will do your duty.'

Silus did not miss the obvious link between Caracalla's last two sentences.

'Of course, Augustus.'

'So, Oclatinius. Make sure these men get to Marcellus, and bring him back to me. You may all leave.'

They all bowed deep and turned to leave in order of seniority. Macrinus led the way, then Oclatinius, then

Festus. As Atius and Silus reached the guarded doorway, Caracalla spoke again. 'And, Silus – make sure the boy stays safe, too.'

–

The two Arcani hurried after Oclatinius, who was striding angrily away from the meeting and out of the palace. Silus nearly had to break into a run to catch him as he headed downhill towards the Forum.

'Congratulations,' said Atius cheerily.

'Congratulations? For a promotion I didn't ask for and didn't want, that will only hinder me in my work.'

It struck Silus how little he actually knew about what Oclatinius did.

'How do you know about the plot against Marcellus?' he asked.

'If I didn't tell the Emperor, why should I tell you?'

'Oh, maybe because Atius and I are your finest operatives.'

Oclatinius stopped and turned on Silus, making Silus halt so abruptly that Atius walked into the back of him.

'Who told you that?'

'You said…'

'I told you the Emperor said that. Caracalla doesn't know the extent of my network, who works for me, or what their quality is.'

'Neither do we,' said Silus, quailing a little under Oclatinius' firm gaze, but holding his nerve. 'Don't you think we should? You never tell us anything. Who else is in the Arcani? How long has the organisation been around?'

Oclatinius looked about him, spied a stone bench outside a small temple. He gestured to it. 'Sit.'

Silus and Atius complied obediently.

'There is a reason the workings and personnel of the Arcani remain secret. Threats against the Empire and the Emperor can come from anywhere, from friend or foe, colleague or adversary. History has shown us this time and again. Do you know at least eight Roman Emperors have been assassinated since the reign of Caesar Augustus? Maybe more, depending on who you believe.

'When we lost the great Marcus Aurelius, it was obvious his son would need help to cling to power. Commodus directed me to form the Arcani, and I created a secret network of spies, enforcers and assassins who have been serving the Emperor ever since.'

'Wasn't Commodus assassinated?' asked Atius, and Silus winced at the typically blunt question.

Oclatinius rubbed a hand over his face. 'He was. We failed that day. I failed. Although we had saved his life on many occasions before that. But we learned, and grew. Some of my operatives are more visible than others, like you two. Some work in the shadows, gathering secrets in exchange for money, or other rewards. Slaves placed strategically in important households, junior officers in the legions, freedmen in the civil service. All reporting to me.'

'So one of these men told you about the plot against Marcellus.'

'A freedwoman, actually. She earned the money to buy her emancipation working for me, then married her former master, an important equestrian. She supplies me with a steady stream of valuable intelligence, but this has been her most important.'

'So she told you that someone plans to kill Marcellus? Who? Why?'

'I told the Emperor the truth. I don't know who is behind this plot, nor why, only that it is real. But I think it is just the first move in a carefully planned strategy. Someone wants to kick away the supporting timbers, to make it easier to demolish the house.'

'Marcellus is that important?' asked Atius.

Oclatinius took a moment to reply. 'Caracalla is a powerful emperor. The soldiers love him, they think he is one of them. But the elites, the men who make up the Senate and the senior ranks, they care for him much less. Marcellus is a powerful man in his own right who is nevertheless completely loyal to Caracalla, through his own personal morality and through family ties – he is after all married to Julia Domna's niece. With Marcellus by his side in Rome, giving him legitimacy, smoothing things over with the Senate and keeping the praetorians loyal, Caracalla is all but unassailable. His absence emboldens those plotting against Caracalla.'

'So there is a real conspiracy against Caracalla? You weren't just speculating?'

Oclatinius nodded. 'The conspiracy is real. And immensely powerful. But well hidden. My people have had very little success infiltrating it.'

'And what about Caracalla's other allies? Macrinus? Festus? You? Don't you all protect Caracalla from his enemies?'

'None of us are noble-born. Marcellus comes from a good equestrian family, and has married well. He is respected, even loved, by all the strata of Roman society. Caracalla was foolish to ever send him from his side, in my opinion. But he is doing the right thing by recalling him. It will strengthen his position immeasurably.'

'If he makes it back to Rome alive,' said Atius.

'And that's where you two come in,' said Oclatinius.

Chapter II

Atius sat on a stool in the corner of Silus' Suburan apartment, four floors above a malodorous fishmonger, while Silus stuffed a small bag with travel essentials. A spare tunic. A leather sheet to make a tent – Atius carried the pole and ropes. A multipurpose copper pot with a short wooden handle. A cup. A small coin purse. He looked around his apartment. Was that it? All he had to show for all his work and service?

He was not a poor man, and in fact had a considerable sum deposited with a couple of bankers in Rome. But he hadn't done anything with it. He wasn't interested in art or theatre. He didn't drink much, didn't chase women. Had no interest in acquiring a big property. A sudden, chilling thought hit him. When had he become so boring?

He glanced across at Atius, who was shelling a handful of nuts, tossing them up into the air and catching them in his mouth. As Silus watched one of the nuts went down too far, and Atius doubled over, coughing explosively until a nut shot out across the room.

'Mithras' balls,' muttered Silus. 'You can't even eat a nut without endangering yourself. How have I managed to keep you safe these years?'

Atius grabbed a cup of water and swallowed, coughed then swallowed again. 'I think it's usually been you that put me in danger in the first place,' said Atius when he had recovered his voice. 'After all, who was it who gave me these nuts?'

Silus tutted, slotted his knife into his belt and gave one last look around his apartment. There was nothing else he wanted to take, nothing that he cared about leaving behind. Damn this life he led. Once, he'd had something. A wife, a daughter, a place that he called home. All that was gone, as a direct result of his own actions. Maybe that was why he was avoiding building up anything that he could call his own, whether it was possessions or a relationship. Was he scared of losing it all again?

He pulled the drawstring on his travel bag closed, hefted it onto his back, and opened the door.

'Let's go. We need to collect our horses from the cursus publicus stables and get to Ostia by dawn.'

Atius picked up his own backpack and walked through the doorway, then waited for Silus to lock the door.

'Oclatinius could have organised us a berth on a ship at a more civilised time,' complained Atius. 'It's way too early to be up. In fact, this would be a perfect time to go to bed after a good night out.'

'I got the impression there was some sort of urgency,' said Silus, and watched the irony go straight over his friend's head.

They descended the long rickety staircase to ground level. Silus glanced around him to check he wasn't being observed, then placed the thick iron key to his apartment under a rock in front of the fishmonger's shop. The fishmonger knew he was away for a while and Silus had asked him to keep an eye on the place. Not that he had any particular attachment to the place, nor any of its remaining contents.

They set off in the direction of the Circus Maximus. The private stables of the White team were used to supply mounts for those eligible to use the state courier service known as the cursus publicus. The extra income no doubt helped made up for their failures on the track.

As usual the streets were choked with the wheeled traffic that was banned during the day. The average speed of the vehicles was little faster than a toddler could crawl given the amount of congestion, but occasionally a gap appeared, and a frustrated mule or cart horse driver would whip his beast into an uneven canter. At those times, any pedestrians in the way would have to fling themselves to one side to avoid being mown down. Broken limbs and cracked skulls were common results of a nocturnal stroll through Rome, and that was just from the traffic accidents. Add to that the risk of falling masonry from the shoddily constructed insulae, detritus tossed from top-floor windows, twisting ankles in potholes or being mugged by professional criminals or high-spirited drunk youths, anyone walking through the city at night took their life in their hands.

Silus and Atius trudged along the pavements, making a vain attempt to avoid being covered by muck splashed up from the gutters by the iron-rimmed wheels. They reached the Forum Romanum, which was as busy at night as during the day, but with a different set of businesses. At night, the air was full of the cries of fast-food sellers, cheap wine merchants and prostitutes vying for custom.

Silus and Atius walked on without either making attempts at conversation. There was still a marked awkwardness about them. Since Oclatinius had forced them into each other's company, they'd had no time to sit and have a drink and clear the air. Would getting drunk, shouting at each other, then hugging and laughing together be enough?

They reached the Forum Boarium which had similar merchants and tradespeople to the Forum Romanum, but if anything more cheap and sleazy. A young girl, no older than Tituria, grabbed the hem of Silus' tunic, entreating him to come with her to a nearby alleyway. Silus pushed her roughly away, feeling sick, a sudden image of Tituria being forced into this degradation coming to him unbidden. The child sprawled on her back, and tears sprung to her eyes, trickled down her face, where they streaked the heavy kohl through the white lead on her cheeks.

Atius gave Silus a sidelong glance, and Silus sighed, feeling like the worst kind of bully. He reached into his bag and took out his purse, tossed the girl a silver denarius. She gasped when she saw the value of the coin.

'Go and find somewhere nice to stay for the night, away from the street.'

The girl got slowly to her feet and backed away from him, clearly thinking he was some sort of madman. Then she turned and ran over to a skinny man on the far side of the square who had been watching her. She gave him the coin and pointed to Silus and Atius, talking rapidly. The pimp shrugged, pocketed the coin, then sent her back out to work, making sure to direct her to a different part of the square from the crazy, foreign-looking pair.

Atius patted Silus on the shoulder, and turned him away before his friend could do something stupid. Silus let himself be guided away despondently. They left the market behind and took the road leading south that would carry them to their destination. As the street curved left, they came to a stop at the sight of an overturned cart, its load of vegetables strewn across the road. The donkey was still attached to the shafts either side of its body, and the poor creature was suspended in the air, legs flailing parallel to the ground, letting out distressed cries. The carter tried desperately to detach the donkey's harness without cutting the leather, while at the same time chasing away the urchins and destitute who had crowded around to steal as much of the fallen produce as possible.

Silus and Atius stopped to watch the chaotic scene, amused and irritated by the hold-up in equal measures. A cabbage kicked by an old man with a withered arm rolled across the ground towards the two Arcani. A child chased after it, then stopped and looked behind them, mouth forming an O, eyes widening.

Neither man hesitated. Simultaneously, they pushed each other hard, propelling themselves sideways forcefully, rolling in opposite directions across the street. Two knives slashed the space they had occupied half a heartbeat before.

Silus and Atius were back on their feet in an instant, weapons already drawn, ready to face the threat. Four men stood behind them, two at the front, both short and wiry, bearing short daggers, the two at the back larger and holding thick clubs with nails protruding from the ends.

A thrill of excitement shot through Silus, even as awareness of the mortal threat hit him, and with it knowledge of how close to death he had just come. Atius was grinning.

The club men hung back. It looked like their purpose was to prevent escape, while the two smaller assassins did their work. They had been surprised by the failure of their first attack, but had recovered quickly and now moved into a knife fighter's stance, crouched, knife held low, ready to slash upwards.

Silus and Atius advanced together, squaring off against one opponent each. Silus kept his eyes locked on his own target. The knife point was in the periphery of his vision, but he would know when the strike was coming. The eyes always showed it first.

Sure enough, something in the parting of the eyelids, the widening of the pupil – Silus didn't even know consciously what it was – indicated a strike coming. The knife slashed forward, but Silus was already twisting to one side, letting the blade pass harmlessly by. He didn't counter this time, getting the measure of his adversary. An amateur would have pressed again, hoping his opponent was off balance from the first attempt. This man was no amateur.

There was no space in the street to circle each other. A space had formed in the crowd, with the six fighting men in the centre of a large rectangle, bounded by shuttered shops on two sides, and fascinated onlookers on both sides. The ambient light was dim, but a little moonlight and some oil lamps hung on the stalls of sellers of pies and sausages meant they weren't fighting in pitch darkness, and the onlookers could make out enough of what was going on to pick sides and start to cheer. Most supported the underdogs, the outnumbered Arcani, but a few, maybe wishing to have the tedium of the night broken by bloodshed and murder, were clearly on the side of the thugs and yelled vociferous encouragement at them.

Silus ignored them, the way the finest gladiators tune out the noise of the crowd baying for their blood. All his focus was on the man before him, except for a small portion of attention directed to the contest between Atius and his opponent. The two Arcani had fought as a team for a long time now, and so often that they seemed to move as one body, one mind. The two would-be assassins opposing them were skilled fighters, but moved independently. They feinted, lunged, unaware of what their colleague was doing, almost clashing at one point.

No words passed between the two Arcani, maybe not even a conscious signal. But they knew, at some deep instinctive level, exactly what to do when the moment arose.

One of the attackers lunged towards Atius' middle. As Atius twisted right, Silus, to Atius' left, flicked his knife sideways. The edge of his blade sliced across the back of the attacker's hand, lacerating tendons. The man's fingers went limp, and his weapon fell to the ground. Silus dodged left as his own attacker tried to take advantage of Silus' shift in focus. Atius, now facing an unarmed opponent, lunged to his left, thrusting his knife up into the side of Silus' foe, the blade slipping easily through tunic, skin and muscle, lodging in liver. Atius twisted and withdrew, a gout of blood following the knife's exit.

Silus kicked the stuck attacker in the side of the knee and he went down, bleeding heavily and clutching his side. Atius turned back to his own attacker, who was clutching his hand and staring at Atius in sudden fear. Atius stepped up close, put his arm around his attacker in a companionable embrace, and slipped his knife between the ribs to penetrate the great chambers of the heart.

Atius lowered the would-be killer gently to the ground as he withdrew his knife, then wiped it on the dead man's tunic. Silus' attacker was still breathing, lying on his side, eyes open, but the extensive pool surrounding him showed he would not be alive much longer. Silus looked up at the two thugs standing a dozen feet back. They showed no inclination towards joining the fight. Cheap muscle, hired as back-up for the real killers, he supposed. They looked completely out of their depth.

Silus took a sudden step forward, and they flinched back. He shook his head.

'Fuck off,' he said, tone dripping contempt. They turned and fled.

Atius was already searching the bodies – the bleeding man had now expired – but they wore no jewellery, sported no tattoos, didn't even have any distinctive birthmarks.

'Professionals,' said Silus. Atius stood and nodded his agreement.

'Arcani?' The word was almost a plea. *Gods, no. Not that.*

Silus let the thought sink in for a moment, the awful implications. Could Oclatinius really have set their brothers against them? The Arcani network was extensive, and most of the assassin-spies were unknown to each other. If Oclatinius had turned against them, they were really screwed.

But why? It made no sense. He dismissed the idea.

'The Arcani aren't the only shadowy group operating on behalf of the Emperor, at least ostensibly. There are the Frumentarii, the Peregrini, the Speculatores, the Evocati, the spies of the Commander of the Sacred Bedchamber…'

'Festus,' put in Atius.

'Festus, yes. Then there are praetorians, vigiles, private clients of important men. These could have worked for just about anyone.'

Atius looked down on the dead men. 'So, what now?'

'Well, this didn't look particularly random, did it?'

Atius nodded to the overturned cart and raised his eyebrows. Silus shook his head. 'No, that was just luck. They took the opportunity when it arose. They were probably following us, just waiting for the moment to strike. But someone sent them to stop us.'

'To stop us saving Marcellus,' said Atius. 'The same bastard that wants Marcellus dead.'

'Bastard or bastards, yes. We were careless, friend. Just because we are in Rome, rather than in Caledonia or Germania, doesn't mean we should be any less alert. It seems wherever we go, people are out to get us.'

'Friend?' Atius was grinning.

'Did I say friend? I meant arse. Come on, let's get to that ship.'

-

Caracalla wasn't sure of the hour when he entered Domna's bedchamber. It was nearer to sunrise than sunset, but he had slept fitfully, and it was difficult to judge how much time had passed when short dozes were interrupted by coming suddenly wide awake, gasping for breath like a fish dangling on a line.

Domna didn't stir, but her maid who slept on a mat by her bedside opened her eyes, then sat upright and clasped her hand over her mouth. Caracalla put his finger to his lips, then nodded to the door. Quietly, the maid slipped out. Caracalla eased himself onto the bed beside Domna, lay on his side behind her, and slid his arms around her waist. She moved a little, took his hand in hers, but didn't wake. Caracalla felt himself relax. This woman had been his comfort and his rock for so long now. It amazed him, that despite everything, they were still there for each other.

The death of his father, her husband. The slaying of her son, his half-brother, at Caracalla's own hands, in her arms. How could she still care for him, after that?

Yet she knew that it had been self-defence, that Caracalla had had no choice. And ultimately, their love for each other had won out. They remained confidantes, friends, companions, lovers.

Although 'lovers' was largely a historical relationship now. Caracalla found it increasingly hard to perform with her, these days. He had thought the problem would pass, as the horror of Geta's death receded. But if anything it had got worse, to the point that whenever he thought of being sexual with her, a crippling anxiety rose within him, overwhelming all pleasurable thoughts.

And more recently, she too had become more distant, less physical in bed. Maybe it was just her age. Maybe his poor performance had tired her, and she no longer felt an urge to try. Much as he tried to reassure her that the problem was his, and nothing to do with a lack of desirability on her part, he knew that she must take it as a consequence of her increasing years.

It wasn't true, of course. She was still beautiful, and he was still very attracted to her. He very much wished to be intimate with her. But it was true that he could still satisfy himself with someone of no importance, whose feelings he had no regard for. A dancer or actress. A high-class courtesan. The wife of a senator he particularly disliked.

He was hopeful that his upcoming campaigns in the East would give him the opportunity to visit a variety of shrines, temples to the gods of healing, priests and sages and physicians. Someone who could restore to him what he had lost with his beloved Domna. He had been visited by a Greek doctor only the day before who had provided him a potion that he promised would restore his virility, but he had noticed no effect yet.

He stroked his hands down her legs, feeling the smoothness of her skin underneath her silk shift. His fingertips stroked the inside of her thighs, moved a little higher. The half-sleeping Domna moved her hips, pressing forward against his touch. He pressed more firmly and she let out a little sigh.

He felt himself getting harder. A thrill rose inside him. Maybe the Greek's concoction really worked. He ground himself against her and she moaned. He placed one hand on her breast.

Froze.

Domna suddenly came wide awake, pulled herself away from him, drew the blanket up to her neck and sat clutching it, lips parted, breathing shallowly, pale in the dim illumination of the flickering night light.

'Julia,' said Caracalla. 'What was that?'

-

'You underestimated them.'

'You underestimate how difficult it is to assemble a team of assassins at short notice.'

'I thought that was your job.'

The sun was rising over the city, shafts of light protruding through the infrequent gaps in the tall buildings, the magnificent temples and ramshackle insulae. The two men stood in the shadow of the Baths of Caracalla, as they were being informally called in the city, even before their completion. Commissioned by Septimius Severus, work had started while the old Emperor was campaigning in Britannia, but Caracalla had revised and extended the plans, to create something truly magnificent. Even surrounded by rickety wooden scaffolding, swarming with builders, stonemasons and sculptors, it was obvious that the finished structure would be awe-inspiring, as well as a great boon to the populace, for whom bathing was one of the greatest pleasures in life.

The baths complex covered over sixty acres, and the main building had already reached a height of over a hundred feet, without the roof yet added. Cartload after cartload of tuff, pozzolana, basalt, quicklime, bricks and marble rumbled in, were emptied, and trundled away back towards the docks to be refilled. Two thousand tons, every day, to keep the five thousand workers on site occupied.

'What a waste of time and money,' said the second speaker, pulling his toga tighter round him to keep out the early morning chill.

'Vanity and popularity with the rabble,' said the first speaker. 'All this Emperor desires.'

The second man looked around him. No one was paying them any attention. Still, a shiver ran down his spine which had nothing to do with the cool air. 'You still need to guard your words, friend. Even when you think we are alone.'

The first man nodded, though showed no contrition. 'So, what now? We failed? That's it?'

'Of course not.' The second man snorted his derision. 'You know I am not the sort to put all his eggs in one basket.'

'I see. Care to enlighten me?'

'Not really. It wouldn't help, would it? And why share secrets more widely than is necessary?'

The first man pursed his lips. 'Fine. But don't forget how important is it that Marcellus is put out of the way.

And that meddling wife and the little bastard. Caracalla's support must be cut off before we can make a move. And we certainly don't want a direct descendant with powerful family support ready to inherit his position. That would put everything we are trying to achieve in jeopardy.'

He turned back to look at the vast structure, rising towards the gods, testament to the power and resources of the Empire, and the man who ruled it absolutely. A thrill of excitement rose within him. What a challenge. And what a prize. To think that he, whose father had been a nobody, could have the purple almost within his grasp. He clapped his companion on the shoulder, and they parted, walking away in opposite directions, merging unobtrusively back into the throng.

Chapter III

Silus dismounted heavily and handed the reins to a slave, giving him instructions to return it to the nearest cursus publicus stables. Atius sprang from his horse, gave it an affectionate pat on the neck, then passed it to another waiting slave.

Silus sneered, rubbing his backside. Fucking horses. His idea of a punishment from the gods for the worst of crimes was being posted to the cavalry. What could be worse than spending all day, every day, sitting on one of those demonic, uncontrollable, horrifically uncomfortable beasts? He hefted his pack on his shoulder, and turned towards the ship that awaited him. His stomach gave a pre-emptive churn. Oh, that's right. The navy would be worse.

Atius clapped Silus on the shoulder and started up the gangplank. Silus slouched after him, like a reluctant schoolboy on his way to a tutorial for which he knew his lack of preparation was going to get him beaten. When he reached the deck, Atius was standing with his shoulders back, taking in deep lungfuls of salty air.

'So good to be back at sea,' he said, beaming with satisfaction. 'There's nothing like it, is there?'

Silus sniffed cautiously, his nose filling with the overpowering aromas of fish, tar and the strange smell at the back of your throat that you only got from the sea or after a lightning strike. The boat rocked as a large wave hit it broadside, and Silus staggered, arms out to keep his balance.

'Yeah, nothing like it.'

'Come on, let's find a spot to stow our stuff.' Atius made to move but a wiry, white-bearded man blocked their way.

'Who are you?'

'I'm Atius, this is Silus. Who are you?'

'I'm the captain of this ship. What are you doing here?'

Atius and Silus glanced at each other.

'We have passage booked. To Numidia.'

'We aren't going to Numidia.'

'What!' Silus gasped. 'Look here. We have berths on the *Minerva*, booked and paid for. We are Arcani, on a mission from the Emperor of Rome himself. Now are you going to take us to Numidia or…'

'This isn't the *Minerva*.'

'Or do I have to… what?'

'Umm, Silus,' said Atius, tapping him on the shoulder and pointing.

'What is it?' snapped Silus. He looked in the direction Atius was indicating. 'Oh.'

At the next berth on the dock was a Liburnian, a fast bireme. It had two banks of oars, a ram at the front, and a large white sail with a wide-eyed owl painted in the middle, and the name, '*Minerva*', emblazoned underneath.

'It seems there has been a bit of a…' began Silus.

'We should maybe…' said Atius at the same time.

They turned and shuffled back down the gangway as the captain watched them go, hands on hips, the sound of the laughter of the crew echoing behind them.

'Why did you get on that ship?' hissed Silus. 'I just followed you.'

Atius shrugged. 'It had a picture of a crow on the sail. Isn't that Minerva's sacred animal?'

'No, that's the owl, you idiot!'

'Well, it's all pagan mumbo jumbo to me.'

Silus cursed him in lengthy and vivid detail as they walked up the gangplank of the *Minerva*. They were greeted by a plump, middle-aged man, bald on top but with white tufts of hair sticking out above his ears, and a long white beard. He had a broad grin on his face, and it was clear he had witnessed their humiliation on the neighbouring ship.

'I'm Adonibaal, captain of the *Minerva*. Silus and Atius, I presume?'

Silus glowered at the obvious enjoyment the man was showing in their discomfort. He vowed to get his own back on Atius for this.

'Come on, I'll show you to where you can sleep.'

He led them along the deck, to the aft. The deck was incomplete, with boards extending to roughly a third of the width of the ship on either side, leaving a gap in the middle. Silus could see down, past the banks of oars, to the bottom, from where an overpowering smell of bilge water and sweaty human wafted up.

Adonibaal pointed to an area near the stern on one side of the decking. 'You can bed down here.'

'Don't we get a cabin?' asked Atius.

'There are only two cabins on the ship. One is mine. The other is for important passengers. You don't qualify. You can put up a tent overnight if you have one, but take it down during the day or you will be in the way.' Silus nodded. The basic two-man tent they carried between them, just a leather sheet, a pole and some ropes, would nevertheless keep the rain off.

'Feel free to wander around the ship,' continued Adonibaal. 'Warm broth is served once a day and we have an almost unlimited supply of hard tack. There is wine but I don't allow drunkenness on my ship. Any questions?'

'How long until we reach Cirta?' asked Silus.

'Depending on how long it takes us to reprovision at Caralis, about nine days.'

'Can you do it any quicker?' asked Atius.

'Can you make the winds blow faster?'

Atius considered for a moment. 'If I think of anything, I'll let you know.'

Adonibaal let out a snorting laugh. 'Listen, usually a journey like this takes weeks. We go down the Italian coast, cross the straits to Messana, hug the north coast of Sicilia, then brave a short stretch of open ocean to get to Carthago. From there we cruise along the north coast of Africa until we get to Cirta. And we stop every night to reprovision.

'But someone is in a hurry, so we are heading in a straight line south-west to Caralis, then from there straight to Cirta. It's a lot of open ocean, and I don't like it. And we have had to pack in extra supplies so we don't have to stop each night for stores. That meant cutting down on our complement of marines and our supplies of ammunition.'

'Is that a problem?' asked Silus, suddenly concerned. He remembered being chased down and attacked by another ship on a previous voyage.

'Not really. The *Minerva* can outrun anything on the water. It's not ideal, but as long as you boys aren't spoiling for a hand-to-hand fight, all will be as fine as summer's day in Baiae. Now get yourself settled. We set sail within the hour and I have to attend the sacrifices. Pray they are favourable or the crew won't leave.' He left them, heading forward.

Silus looked down into the bowels of the ship. The rowers were already in place, hands resting lightly on the oars. Silus marvelled at their forearms and chests, muscles bulging, veins wrapping around them like thick vines. Their skin tones, hair colour and facial features suggested a variety of provincial origins – Celtic, Germanic, African and Eastern races were all represented. They were all bare-chested, wearing only loincloths, and were already grime-smeared before the journey had begun.

Interestingly, there was not a slave brand, tattoo or collar in sight. Silus had never understood what motivated free men to volunteer for such a life. The pay couldn't be that good. The chance to see the world? Joining the legions was much less arduous, and less risky. He caught the eye of a bulky Asian rower who had glanced upwards, and nodded to him. The man grunted, then cracked his knuckles with a sound like a snapping branch. Silus swallowed.

'I'm going for a walk,' he said to Atius.

The *Minerva* wasn't as big as the old-fashioned quadriremes and quinqueremes and even bigger ships, but since the threat of all-out naval warfare had receded, those lumbering beasts had been replaced in recent times by the smaller and quicker triremes and Liburnians as the mainstay of the Roman fleet. But she was still about a hundred feet stem to stern, and there was plenty of space for Silus to stretch his legs.

He watched the sailors scurrying about their last-minute preparations. Supplies were still being brought on board, but this was not a cargo ship, rather a fast, light ship for skirmishing and getting places around the empire quickly, so loading was quick and efficient. Adonibaal was shouting orders to some sailors who were doing something complicated with ropes and knots related to the sail.

A man came to stand beside Silus.

'So you are one of my fellow passengers?'

Silus glanced at him. Tall, dark-haired, with a jutting, dimpled chin, the newcomer held himself like a man who knew he was handsome. He was dressed in a well-laundered, tight-fitting tunic which suggested a body well-toned by hours put in at the gymnasium. Silus instantly despised him. He put his hand out. After a moment's hesitation, the man took it, and squeezed with unnecessary firmness. Silus saw that, unlike his own, the man's hand was clean, and free of calluses or dirt-engrained cracks.

'Lucius Granius Claudius, pleased to meet you.'

'Gaius Sergius Silus.'

'And what are you doing on this fine vessel?'

'Official business. I'm here with my colleague, Atius. You?'

'Official business too. I'm a frumentarius. On my way to Numidia.'

'Oh. What's your mission? You have some wheat to pick up?'

Granius narrowed his eyes at the jibe. The role of the frumentarius had originally been as a wheat collector in the provinces, but since this involved meeting farmers, merchants and other natives, their local knowledge was soon put to use for activities such as mapping and spying. Now they were the best-recognised branch of the intelligence networks, and generally enjoyed instilling fear in those they encountered. Clearly Granius didn't like being taken lightly, but he replied as if nothing was amiss.

'I'm just transporting some routine messages to Numidia. Nothing exciting. What branch of the government did you say you represent?'

'I didn't,' said Silus. Even if he had any desire to be open about his occupation and mission, this annoying man's secrecy and superior air had put Silus right off.

'Right.'

There was an awkward silence.

'Well,' said Silus, 'I'll be off. I want to look around the ship.'

'It won't take long,' said Granius. 'It's not exactly a quinquereme. Listen, apparently they serve some warm slop soon after noon. The other passengers will be there. We could all get to know each other.'

'Other passengers?' Silus thought about this. Oclatinius had booked them passage at short notice on a ship that was already preparing to sail. It must have had other duties than hanging around waiting to see if any random Arcani needed a lift. And this sort of vessel carried little cargo. So there would likely be others onboard on 'official business'. He should warn Atius to keep his mouth shut. He nodded to Granius and went back aft to their designated space on the deck.

There he found Atius sitting on the floor with a full cup of beer, drinking deeply and laughing with another man.

'And then Oclatinius said, if you want to be an Arcanus, you need to know when to keep it under your tunic and when to shove it up some fucker's arse!'

The other man squealed a high-pitched peal of laughter, slapping his thigh and spilling his own beer into his lap. Silus sighed. So much for Atius keeping his mouth shut. That really was too much to expect.

Atius looked up. 'Silus! This is Calev. Calev, this is Silus, centurion in the Arcani.'

Calev stood abruptly, got his feet tangled in a coil of rope, and waved his arms around as he lost balance. Silus reached out a hand and grabbed his arm to steady him. Calev grinned boyishly. 'A pleasure to meet you.'

'Well, you know my name and position, apparently,' said Silus. 'Can I ask what brings you onboard?'

'I'm being sent out to be the assistant to the under-procurator responsible for the water supply in Numidia.'

'That sounds like a very important position.'

'Oh, it is,' said Calev earnestly. He was a young man, with Eastern Mediterranean features, who looked like he would blow away in a stiff breeze.

'Well, it's good to be in such illustrious company. If you would excuse me, I need to talk to my colleague.'

'Of course,' said Calev, and clasped his hands in front of him, looking down at the wooden planks.

'Alone,' said Silus.

'Oh, yes, yes.' Calev hurried away, sloshing beer from his cup as the boat rocked.

Silus sat next to Atius and put his arm around him.

'Been getting to know the other passengers, eh?'

'Yeah, he seems really nice. He is from Jerusalem. He has actually been to lots of the places that the Christos went. He even knows the hill of the skull, where God's son was crucified.'

'Imagine that,' said Silus, trying to sound impressed for his friend's sake, but knowing he was failing hopelessly.

Atius frowned. 'What did you want to talk to me about?'

'Well, you know this mission we are on?'

'Of course.'

'This secret mission.'

'Yesss.'

'Do you think it would be a good idea if we didn't tell everyone who we are and who we work for?'

Atius looked at him like it he had genuinely never thought about it.

'I didn't tell him what we were doing.'

'Just that we were secret spies on a secret mission.'

'I didn't put it quite like that.'

'All this time in the Arcani, and you still haven't learnt that if you have a secret to keep, you must first keep it a secret that you have a secret.'

Atius pulled back, a dark look crossing his face, and Silus cursed himself. Atius had been tortured in Germania, and had still kept the secret with which he had been entrusted.

'I'm sorry, I shouldn't have said that,' he said more gently. 'But come on, Atius. Let's try to be a bit more discreet.'

Atius nodded. 'Fine.'

'I just met this odd guy, a frumentarius. He's taking some messages to Numidia.'

'Another spy. Coincidence?'

'Maybe. Or maybe he is taking instructions to an assassin?'

'We need to find out.'

'I agree.'

'So what's the plan?'

'Why does it always have to be me that comes up with the plan?'

There was a shout from Adonibaal to cast off, which was repeated and relayed around the ship. The ropes were unwound from their moorings and pulled in, and a light breeze in the sail carried the ship far enough away from the dock for the rowers to engage. With heaves on the oars coordinated by the beat of a drum and rhythm-heavy song, they manoeuvred the ship out of the harbour and into the Tyrrhenian Sea. Sunbeams shone over the port to the east as the sky began to lighten.

'Let's just get some rest. We had an early start. This afternoon we can meet the other passengers when they serve the broth. And then we can work out how to get a look at Granius' messages.'

'That sounds like a plan.'

Atius stretched, then lay down on the hard oak deck, using his pack as a pillow, and fell instantly asleep.

-

Hot food was served on the poop deck at the rear of the ship. Silus and Atius queued with their bowls and spoons at the ready. Silus had already eaten a couple of the hard biscuits, which were tough enough to break teeth, but had sated him a little. Still, he was ready for something warmer. The early spring winds, though blowing in their favour to speed their journey, were flapping the large lateen, a triangular sail that could catch the wind from either side, allowing the ship to tack, and penetrating right through his tunic. He wished he had packed some of the woollen underwear he had routinely worn in northern Britannia, but hadn't thought he would need it in Numidia.

Already they were out of sight of land, the Italian coast far behind them, the island of Sardinia ahead.

Silus presumed the sacrifices before they had sailed had produced favourable omens. The squawks of the chickens and the bleating of the kids that Silus had heard over the chanting of the captain before they were silenced by a sharp knife suggested that the sacrificial victims didn't agree.

The rowers had been served their meals at their stations. There wasn't room for them to mill about the decks. In fact, they worked, ate and slept at their oars, only being allowed up intermittently to stretch cramped legs and answer the call of nature over the side of the ship. The half-dozen marines, a much smaller complement than usual, their bored-looking centurion, and the sailors, carpenters and other workmen that kept the ship functioning and afloat, waited resentfully for their turn behind the captain and the passengers.

When the cook was satisfied the pottage had been boiled sufficiently long to remove all flavour, he ladled a generous portion into Adonibaal's bowl. A semicircle of folding wooden chairs with linen seats had been arranged at the rear of the poop deck, and the captain took the one in the middle. He beckoned the passengers over after each had collected their meal, and soon the full manifest had joined him to eat. Silus and Atius were last, and found themselves at the edge of the semicircle. The wind, the rattle from the sails and the splash of the oars muffled voices, so even when people spoke loudly, Silus had to strain his ears to follow the conversation.

An elderly man, stoop-shouldered, a fine rim of white hair around his freckled pate, blew on his spoon and then sipped, working at the small morsels of tough meat concealed in the broth with a gummy mouth. Beside him, straight-backed, sat a beautiful woman with the complexion and dress of an Egyptian. She looked around thirty years old, but Silus suspected that without her heavy make-up, her real age would be at least ten years more. She glanced at the old man as he ate with ill-disguised contempt.

'Gaius Dillius Vocula, how is your food?' asked Adonibaal, addressing the old man.

Vocula looked up, and his brow creased. He cupped his hand to his ear. 'My what now?' he said in a wavering voice.

'Your food,' said Adonibaal, shouting. 'How is it?'

'Oh, yes, my food, yes. Perfectly acceptable, yes indeed.'

'It's disgusting,' said the Egyptian woman.

'Now, Khnum-Aa,' said Vocula placatingly. 'It isn't too bad. We can't expect luxury on this sort of trip.'

'I don't expect luxury, but this so-called food is not even fit for Korinna here.' She indicated her attendant slave, a plump, matronly Greek, who bowed her head in acceptance of her mistress's words.

'Well, dear, don't forget you were a slave yourself once.'

Khnum-Aa's features drew into a mask of fury, and Vocula shrank back.

'I only meant… since I freed you and took you as my wife we… I mean. Oh dear.' Vocula turned his attention back to his broth and didn't look up.

Adonibaal watched the pair with open amusement for a moment, then turned to Granius and Calev, who were seated together.

'And you two are settling in well, I trust. Found your sea legs yet?'

'This isn't my first time at sea,' said Granius dismissively. Calev, however, was looking into his bowl and breathing heavily, his cheeks puffing out. It may have been the rolling motion of the deck, or the strong smell of garlic, onions and fish sauce emanating from the broth, but whatever the cause Calev dropped his bowl with a clatter, spilling the gloopy liquid over the deck, as he rushed to the side rail to vomit loudly, not quite getting there in time. Adonibaal sighed and gestured to a sailor to bring over a mop and bucket. The sailor efficiently slooshed the deck clean and returned to his station. Calev came back, red-faced, retrieved his bowl and spoon and took his seat again.

'Would you like a refill?' asked Adonibaal. Calev shook his head hastily. Adonibaal smiled.

'Silus, Atius? You found somewhere to rest?'

'Yes, thank you, captain. Very comfortable.' Silus also felt nauseous, and though he'd managed a little sleep, the cramped and uncomfortable conditions and the sudden motions of the ship as it crested a wave or rolled in a swell had frequently woken him. He refused to complain at the conditions, though, partly because of the displays by the Egyptian woman and Calev, but also because he had endured far worse, and in fact in the bigger picture, not sleeping rough in the rain or snow in enemy territory, with a ready supply of warm food and no threat from rampaging barbarians and wild beasts, was something of a blessing.

Atius mumbled something incoherent, then wiped his chin clean of the broth that had spilt out of the corner of his mouth. Silus rolled his eyes.

Adonibaal then spoke to the final passenger, a tall, well-built, dark-haired and dark-skinned man with a tightly curled black beard. But the words were not Latin or Greek, and all the other passengers looked at them in puzzlement. After a few moments of this exchange, Adonibaal noticed the others' stares and spread his hands.

'My apologies. Bomilcar hales from Africa Province, the same as me, and we both speak the old language.'

'Punic?' asked Granius.

'Well, I think there is a lot of Latin mixed in with it these days, but yes, it is the language our ancestors spoke, before the Romans.'

'But you do speak Latin, right?' Granius directed his question at Bomilcar.

Bomilcar gave him a steady stare, then nodded once.

There was a long silence, punctuated by the cawing of a gull and the crack of the sail as it filled out with a strong gust of wind. Silus turned to Vocula.

'So what takes you to Numidia?' he asked loudly.

'Oh, Numidia. Yes. That's where we are going.'

'I know,' said Silus patiently. 'But why?'

'Yes, well, I'm not as young as I once was. You may have noticed.' He gave Silus a gappy smile, and Silus couldn't help but smile back. 'My physician said the air in Numidia might benefit my health. And my darling wife here thinks that the climate in Rome is dreadfully cold.'

'It rains all the time, and I have to wear five layers of clothing to stop from freezing, even in the summer,' said Khnum-Aa firmly. Silus wondered what she would make of Britannia.

'I see. And you, Bomilcar?'

Bomilcar regarded him for a moment, then said, 'Going home.'

Nothing more was forthcoming, and conversation dropped to occasional comments on the weather and the journey ahead, until all the bowls were empty.

Khnum-Aa stood. 'Come on, dear. We shall retire to our cabin.' She held out her arm for Korinna to take. Vocula struggled painfully to his feet, and followed along behind them. They all disappeared into the tiny, cramped room which on this ship constituted the luxury accommodation.

Granius stood too, and stretched. 'Well, I guess I will wander around the deck for a little. Unless anyone can think of anything better to do.'

Atius shot Silus a quick look, then said, 'Hold on, Granius. I've got some dice in my bag. Fancy losing some money?'

Granius smiled broadly. 'Now you're talking.'

'Let's find somewhere quiet where we can play undisturbed.'

'I'll just get my purse, it's in my bag.'

'No need,' said Atius quickly. 'We'll keep a tally. I'm sure you are good for it.'

He put his arm around Granius' shoulders and led him along the deck towards the prow. As soon as they had gone, Silus stood and excused himself. He hurried past the sailors towards the bow, glancing down into the depths of the ship at the heaving banks of rowers.

There were only a few places where the passengers could situate themselves for a rest, away from the hustle and bustle of the crew. He found a small pack which appeared to double as a pillow. There was no mattress, but there was a small statue next to the pack that Silus recognised as a representation of Tanit, the Punic goddess. Bomilcar's resting place, then.

Calev's bed was near to where Atius and Silus had slept, so the remaining bedding and pack, a little further forward, had to belong to Granius. There was a mattress rolled up, similar to Silus' own, so thin it would have done little to cushion the body from the hardness of the floor. A small wooden engraving of Mithras slaying the bull confirmed this was a soldier's berth. There were few adherents of the Mithraic mystery cult outside the military.

Silus gave a hasty look around. There were few places on the ship that were truly private. He was in the line of sight of the lowest rank of rowers. But there were no passengers around, no non-rowing crew, and the oarsmen had their eyes set forward, lost in their own worlds of muscular ache, the unceasing repetition of pull, raise, push, dip, pull, an endless, hypnotic rhythm.

Silus turned his attention to the bag. It was cloth, with a simple drawstring. He knelt, undid the bow that held the string closed, and rummaged inside. His searching fingers identified the usual miscellaneous items that accompanied any traveller – spare tunic, a knife, a cooking pot, a carved wooden board, probably laid out for a game of tabula. Right at the bottom he felt three rolled pieces of papyrus. He drew out the first and inspected it. It was closed with a wax seal, stamped with a wolf suckling the founding twins. Silus drew out his knife and ran it under the edge of the seal, expertly lifting it off the papyrus without damaging it, just the way Oclatinius had taught him.

He unrolled the scroll and hastily scanned it. He deciphered the scrawled words one by one, his lips moving as he read.

> *From Titus Paulinus, office of the urban prefect, to Marcus Curtius Mellitus, procurator's office, Cirta, greetings.*

The last grain shipment from Numidia was five thousand modii less than we agreed. As you know, the prompt and adequate supply of wheat to Rome is essential to keep the citizens pacified. I have heard no reports of harvest failures, so I cannot understand the shortfall. I do hope that no produce is going missing along the way, maybe sold to another party for some extra profit. It would be tedious for me to have to organise an investigation of your accounts, with all the unpleasantness that entails. Please make sure the missing wheat reaches Rome as soon as possible.

Silus couldn't quite suppress a smile. So the scary, self-important frumentarius was just transporting messages about wheat after all. Using some spit, he smoothed the edge of the seal back into place. Close inspection would easily show it had been tampered with, but it would hold for the time being, and hopefully the fact that it had been opened would only become apparent much later. He repeated the process for the other two scrolls, as swiftly but as carefully as he could. One was a personal letter, a declaration of love from what appeared to be a moderately wealthy woman to a minor official in the province, with admonishments to keep their love secret, lest her husband divorce her and leave her destitute. The final letter was from a priest in the temple of Castor and Pollux to his opposite number in Cirta, a reply to a request for advice on the interpretation of certain dreams and unusual omens seen in the entrails of recent sacrifices. Silus skimmed through them, then sealed them up again and replaced them at the bottom of the bag.

So Granius was exactly as he seemed? Just a frumentarius transporting messages of questionable importance across the vast reaches of the Empire? Maybe there was a code in one of the letters, but if so, it was beyond Silus' abilities to decipher. Maybe the frumentarius had another mission besides messenger boy, but there was nothing in the letters that would indicate this, or what it might be.

Well, if it was paranoia, it was healthy. He had learnt to trust no one. Almost no one. He put the bag down and looked up.

Bomilcar was watching him with a steady, expressionless gaze.

'This isn't my pack,' said Silus weakly, and strode off towards his own berth. Bomilcar watched him go.

-

Silus lay on his back, listening to the nocturnal sounds of the ship. The waves smacked against the wooden hull, the wind flapped the sails. The bilge water slopped gently back and forth. The beams and planks groaned and creaked as they bent, resisting the forces that Neptune threw their way. The north-westerly wind was brisk but far from stormy, so Silus' seasickness was largely under control. The leather tent kept the weather at bay, but it was flapped open so he had a view of the deck and the night sky. When the clouds parted, as they just had, he could see the stars clearly, the Via Lactea stretching across the middle of the heavens.

Most of the rowers were asleep at their stations, the snores and farts adding to the noises of the ship and sea. A few of the crew were awake, steering, manipulating the sail to make the most of the breeze. One of the marines walked up and down the deck intermittently, but spent most of his time at the rail on the deck, leaning on his spear, probably hoping to appear on watch, but more likely half asleep. Progress was slow without the propulsion from the oars, but the timesaving aspect of this route didn't come from sailing night and day, but from the much shorter distance that travelling direct instead of hugging the coast entailed. It wasn't common or popular because of the difficulty of making the victuals last, and the dangers from storms, gusts and freak waves in the open water. But when speed was of the essence, it was worth the risk.

Atius rolled over next to Silus and muttered a few incomprehensible words, then the name 'Silvia' in a whisper, then some moans. Silus wrinkled his nose. He really didn't want even that partial glimpse into Atius' dreams. He closed his eyes, hoping for sleep though he was wide awake, and Somnus seemed very distant. But soon he found himself drifting, thoughts that always kept him awake, like memories of Velua and Sergia, his wife and daughter, of Odo and Daya, of Tituria, of blood and fire, retreating into a gloomy haze.

He heard footsteps approaching, and something about the tread made him come instantly back to alertness. He remained still, not even turning his head, but he opened his eyes, looking left and right, trying to locate the source of the sound. The soft steps came nearer, pausing, treading carefully to stay as inaudible as possible. But noiselessness was impossible on the ship, the boards squeaking and groaning each time they took any weight, no matter how carefully applied.

When the approaching person was only a few feet away, they stopped. Silus could make out a tall, male figure, his peripheral vision actually providing more detail in the dark than if he had looked at the man directly. Silus' heart was hammering in his chest, and he inhaled and exhaled through his mouth so as not to alert the intruder with stertorous noises from his nose as he breathed heavily.

What was he waiting for? Silus tensed, muscles ready, every fibre straining for action. It took immense willpower to remain still, but he had to choose his moment, find out for sure if this man was hostile, and take him unawares when he attempted whatever he planned.

There was a smooth noise, sliding metal on leather, a glint in the starlight.

Silus jumped up with a loud cry, the explosion of noise and movement calculated to alarm and disorient. The intruder took a step backwards in surprise. Silus lunged.

Atius sat bolt upright. 'Silvia?'

Silus kicked Atius in the head as he leapt for the intruder. He flew forward, heading for the planks of the deck even as he reached out. He grasped the tent pole, which brought the tent down, covering Atius and entangling Silus' legs. The intruder turned to flee and Silus managed to grab an ankle. The big man stumbled, threw his arms out for balance. Something fell, made a clattering sound. The man steadied himself, then ran, heading forward.

Atius struggled out of the leather sheet's grip, and lay, propped up on his elbow, groaning and rubbing the side of his head. 'What the fuck did you do that for?'

'Get up,' Silus hissed and got back to his feet. Something on the floor, gleaming in the starlight, caught his attention. He picked it up, a long, thin, wickedly sharp knife. 'Come on.'

Silus hurried in the direction in which the man had fled, a grumbling, half-asleep and slightly stunned Atius following behind.

The commotion had woken the entire ship, the oarsmen sitting up, shouting to each other. As they made their way forward, they came across other passengers, Calev and Granius, wiping sleep from their eyes, asking concerned questions. Khnum-Aa emerged from her cabin and demanded to know what was going on, while Vocula snored loudly behind her, his deep sleep undisturbed. Trying not to trip over packs, supplies or ropes in the darkness that was so sparsely lit by oil lanterns, Silus and Atius scurried forward.

Calev reached out for Silus from his mattress – he had no tent and had been sleeping on the open deck. 'What's happening?' Silus ignored him. Bomilcar pushed his head out of his own tent and watched them pass, frowning, but saying nothing. Granius was up, pulling his belt tight around his waist and cursing.

The marine on duty came hurrying aft, staggering with the deck's motion beneath his feet. He saw the knife in Silus' hand, and fumbled with his spear. Silus stopped and waited patiently until the soldier had brought it to bear, pointing it at Silus' chest.

'Drop it.'

Silus made a show of opening his hand, so the blade fell to the floor. Atius stood by Silus' shoulder, an intimidating presence, and the tip of the spear wavered. The marine had clearly not expected any disturbance on the ship, his presence, and his comrades', mainly a deterrent to opportunistic piracy. He opened his mouth, then closed it uncertainly, his training leaving him completely unprepared for this situation.

Adonibaal appeared behind the marine and reached out to gently press the tip of the spear downwards.

'Stand down.' The marine complied, lowering his weapon and stepping backward, clearly grateful that someone was taking charge.

'Silus,' said Adonibaal. 'Would you like to explain why you have woken the entire ship in the middle of the night?'

Slowly, making no moves to threaten the marine, Silus reached down and picked up the knife, passed it handle-first to the captain. Adonibaal took it, turned it over in his hands, then looked at Silus quizzically.

'Someone came at us with this in the night. Fortunately I was awake and frightened him off.'

Some of the other passengers had gathered around, and there was a chorus of sharp intakes of breath and muttered notes of alarm.

'Did you see who it was?'

Silus shook his head. 'It was too dark. A man, taller than Calev here, but not as big as Atius. It could have been one of the crew, one of the marines, Bomilcar, Granius. It could even have been you, captain.'

Granius protested when his name was mentioned, while Bomilcar just pressed his lips tightly together. Adonibaal cocked his head on one side in apparent amusement. 'You think I am creeping around my own ship at night looking to stab someone?'

'I didn't say that,' said Silus. 'Just that somebody is, and I don't know who. And it looks like Atius and I are the targets.'

'Maybe it was just someone sleepwalking,' said Calev, but the suggestion sounded weak, and he dropped his head when no one commented.

Adonibaal looked up at the stars. 'Well, it's a few hours yet until dawn. I'll ask the marine centurion to double the watch and make sure they patrol properly.' He glanced at the duty marine, who hung his head in embarrassment. 'Everybody else, get back to your berths. And try to get some sleep.'

Chapter IV

The sunrise was a deep crimson, reflecting off the underneath of a thin layer of clouds. The crew exchanged comments about the bad portents of a red morning sky. Silus knew the significance from the folk wisdom of farmers back in Britannia. It was no mere superstition, but an indicator of stormy weather. For now, though, the wind was moderate and steady, and the threat of rain seemed distant.

Silus had a headache, a stomach that claimed to be both nauseous and hungry at the same time, and his eyes itched from lack of sleep. He had stayed awake for the rest of the night after the disturbance, both to keep watch and because sleep would have been impossible. Atius had offered to take a turn as lookout, but when Silus had told him it wasn't necessary, the big Arcanus had fallen asleep instantly. He woke now, sat up, stretched and yawned, looking like he had spent twelve hours in a feather bed, rather than an interrupted night on damp, cold, wooden floor. Even after all this time together, Silus couldn't help but be surprised by his friend's resilience and nonchalance.

'No more assassins in the night then?' asked Atius.

'A couple,' said Silus. 'But you were sleeping like a dog, so I didn't want to disturb you.'

'Very considerate,' said Atius. 'I'm starving. What's for breakfast?'

Silus dipped into his backpack and brought out some hard tack and some nuts. He shared them with Atius, who consumed them with delight, as if they were delicacies from Trimalchio's banquet. After washing them down with water from Silus' bottle, they climbed the ladder to the deck and relieved themselves next to each other over the side of the ship.

'So what's the plan, boss?' asked Atius.

Silus and Atius both nominally held the rank of centurion, but it hadn't always been so, and even without it being explicitly stated, it was usually assumed that Silus was in charge. Silus shrugged. 'We ask around, I guess. Maybe someone saw something.'

Atius nodded. 'Would be good to find out who this bastard is. We have a long journey still to go, and it will be irritating to have to sleep with one eye open every night.'

'We'll take it in turns, one of us awake at all times. We can catch up on sleep during the day if necessary. We have bugger-all else to do on this ship.'

'Oh, I don't know. I was rather enjoying taking money off Granius. He is really shit at dice. And that Egyptian woman, the old guy's wife, Khalum-something?'

'Khnum-Aa.'

'Yeah. She makes for nice scenery when I get bored of looking at the horizon.'

Silus sighed. 'Come on, let's see what we can find out.'

They split up, partly to cover the ground quicker, partly so they weren't intimidating people by having two rough-looking men gang up on them.

Silus began with Granius, who was exercising on the foredeck. Silus watched as the frumentarius, wearing only a loincloth, performed squat jumps, press-ups and lunges.

He was well-toned, and a fine sheen of sweat appeared across his skin as he exerted himself. Silus waited patiently until he had finished.

Granius took a swig of water and wiped himself with a towel. 'I don't usually have an audience. Did you like what you saw?'

'I've seen better,' said Silus. 'I'm more interested in what you saw. Last night.'

'I saw two clumsy Celts charging around the boat and waking everyone up.'

'That's all?'

'I certainly didn't see your mysterious attacker. If he exists.'

'If he exists? Why would I make something like that up?'

Granius shrugged. 'Some people like to be the centre of attention.'

'Just so you know, if someone saw my very real attacker last night, and tells me it was you, you will be over the side of the ship before you can get out a prayer to Mithras.'

Granius looked at Silus curiously. 'How do you know I worship Mithras?'

Silus snorted. 'You're a soldier. It's not exactly a wild guess.' He gave Granius a contemptuous look up and down, then went to seek out Bomilcar.

The big Carthaginian was seated cross-legged underneath the sail, his back against the mast. His eyes were closed and he was breathing deeply and steadily. Silus poked his leg with one foot, and instantly the man's eyes flew open, though he didn't move a muscle in the rest of his body. When he saw it was Silus, he closed his eyes again, and continued with his meditation.

Silus poked him again, and this time when the Carthaginian opened his eyes there was a flicker of irritation.

'What?'

'I just want to know if you saw anything last night.'

Bomilcar shook his head.

'You didn't see anyone run past? You didn't hear anything?'

Bomilcar regarded Silus steadily, as if he had already answered the questions, and had nothing to add. Silus sighed and went in search of Calev.

The young Jew was rather more loquacious than Bomilcar, to the point where Silus found it hard to get a word in.

'What happened?' asked Calev breathlessly. 'Do you know who it was? Why were they trying to kill you and Atius? Are you on a secret mission? Are you fugitives with a bounty on your head?'

Silus calmed him down gently. 'I don't know who it was or why they were after us. That's what I'm trying to find out. Do you know anything?'

'Well, I wasn't asleep the whole night. At one point I went for a pee-pee, and I saw Granius walking up and down the deck.'

'Granius? I thought it must be...'

'Then when I came back, I saw Bomilcar's berth was empty. I don't know where he was. And heard Vocula and Khnum-Aa arguing. She was calling him names that would have made some of the rowers here blush.'

'So Bomilcar was...'

'And the centurion of the marines got up to oversee the watch change. And the captain was up and about at one point, talking to the helmsman about the course.'

Silus shook his head. This much information was as bad as none at all.

'Thanks, Calev. If you hear or see anything else, let me know.'

'Of course. Would you like me to spy on anyone? Maybe follow someone around?'

'No, no,' said Silus in alarm. 'Please, just keep it all to yourself. We don't want to tip anyone off that they are under suspicion.'

Calev nodded conspiratorially. 'You can rely on me.' Silus seriously doubted it, but he smiled his gratitude, and headed off to catch up with Atius.

He found his friend lounging next to Khnum-Aa, propped up on one elbow, chatting easily to her, while she covered her mouth and giggled coquettishly. Khnum-Aa was lying on a mattress on the deck and eating grapes passed to her in small bunches by Korinna, presumably from some private supply. Vocula sat on a stool next to them, concentrating intently on the contents of a scroll, ignoring his young wife's blatant flirting.

'Atius.'

Atius looked up and smiled. 'Silus, come and join us. I was just telling Khnum-Aa about that time we were in Alexandria and you nearly started a riot by drowning that cat.'

'That was you!' Silus gasped.

'Was it? So it was. But the cat survived, right?'

'It did,' said Silus. 'No thanks to you.'

Khnum-Aa put a hand lightly on Atius' forearm. 'I'm sure you didn't mean to,' she said, and left her fingers there a few heartbeats longer than was necessary.

'I hope the commotion last night didn't disturb you too much,' said Silus.

'At least there was some excitement to break up the tedium,' said Khnum-Aa. 'It's only the second day of our voyage, and I'm so bored!'

'I'm sure we could come up with some ways to entertain ourselves,' said Atius.

Vocula glanced up briefly from his scroll and with a shake of his head, muttered, 'It wouldn't be the first time.' Then he lifted the scroll higher to block his wife from his line of sight.

'When there is no entertainment at home, it must be found elsewhere,' said Khnum-Aa, raising her voice pointedly so her husband didn't miss a word. Vocula didn't respond, but he gripped the edges of the scroll tighter, so the papyrus took on a fine tremor.

'You're Egyptian?' asked Silus, trying to steer the conversation away from a full domestic row.

'Does it show?' Khnum-Aa batted her green-painted eyelids, outlined with dark kohl in a pattern with the traditional lateral horn. Her lips shone a glossy red, and her cheeks were whitened with a lead make-up that was reputed to not only blanch the skin to prevent one gaining the appearance of a sun-tanned worker, but also to have magic properties that kept away acne and other skin infections. She wore a stola, the neckline of which verged on the immodest, and she sported ornate gold earrings, bracelets and necklace. She was undoubtedly a beauty, and Silus could see why Atius couldn't take his eyes off her, though his own tastes ran to the less gaudy.

'A bit,' said Silus. 'Native Egyptian, not Greek, right?'

'I'm from Memphis,' she said with evident pride. 'The ancient capital of the country, before those upstarts in Alexandria claimed the title.'

Upstarts, thought Silus. Alexandria was founded by Alexander the Great some five hundred years previously. It was comments like this that brought home how truly ancient Egypt was, a proud kingdom at the height of its power long before the founding of Rome, if the Egyptian priests and priestesses could be believed.

'What took you to Rome?' asked Atius.

'I suppose you could call it abduction. Sold by my father to a Roman slaver. Taken to Rome to be a lady's slave. Until her husband divorced her and freed me, deciding that I would make a better wife than a slave, and a fine replacement for one who was getting past her best.' She spoke loudly, making sure her deaf husband could hear every word. 'Surely a match that your Cupid would have been proud to make.'

Silus glanced at Vocula, but the only sign that he was listening was an increase in the whistling noise his breathing made through his hairy nostrils.

'Well,' said Silus, and then couldn't think of anything else to add. So he just said, 'Well,' again.

Atius got to his feet and stretched. 'I feel like a walk along the deck. Khnum-Aa, would you like to accompany me? If your husband has no objection, of course? Vocula?'

'Eh?'

'May I take your wife for a stroll?'

'Yes, yes. Don't hurry back.'

Atius held out his hand to Khnum-Aa, who took it and rose elegantly. The two of them walked off arm in arm, like a newly courting couple.

Vocula watched them go, then turned to Silus. 'When we get to Numidia, I am going to divorce her. Let's see how she affords her make-up and jewellery then.'

Vocula's voice was pitched at the high volume of all elderly deaf people. Silus glanced quickly at the retreating back of Khnum-Aa to see if she had heard, but she gave no sign, just letting out a light giggle at some no doubt dirty quip from Atius. Silus hoped that the noises of ship and sea had drowned Vocula's words out. He patted the old man on the arm and left him to his reading.

–

It was late afternoon when the storm hit them. It started with a sudden darkening of the sky, a gusting wind, a noticeable increase in the swell of the waves, and a few heavy drops of rain. But within half an hour it had turned into a full gale. The rain merged with the sea spray to create an almost horizontal deluge of water that drove into the faces of the crew as they hurried around, manipulating the sail, tying down anything that moved and heaving away at the bilge pump.

Silus and Atius clung to wooden struts as the ship rolled heavily, one way then the other. It didn't take much of this motion before Silus was heaving, the afternoon's broth splattering into the bilge. He retched over and over again until he had nothing more to bring up, then retched some more. Freezing salt water stung his eyes and soaked through his tunic so thoroughly that he felt he had just been dragged fully clothed out of the sea. They had taken their tent down, as had the other passengers – in this force of wind, the sheets would have been quickly blown away.

The ship crested a huge wave and came crashing down with a bone-crunching impact that produced alarming cracking noises from the ship's timbers. There was a cry, and one of the crewmen who was reaching out towards a piece of loose rigging was swept overboard. One moment he was there, the next he was gone beneath the waves, not a trace of his existence left behind. The other crew members muttered prayers to Galene, the goddess of calm seas, and made signs to ward against evil, but did not pause in their labours.

Adonibaal stood near the rear of the boat, shouting instructions to the helmsman who, with the help of two marines, heaved on the steering oars to keep the ship pointed away from the wind. The oarsmen rowed with immense power, though they were barely able to hear the beat of the drum keeping them in time over the howling noise of the storm. Silus wondered how long they would be able to keep up that effort, and would they fail before the wind blew itself out? He knew nothing about sailing, but he figured that a ship that had lost its main motive force would find itself helpless against the forces of Neptune and his consort Salacia.

One of the crew took a moment to sacrifice a chicken, chopping off its head and sending a plea of mercy to the powerful sea god Aegaeon. Silus didn't know whether that would help, but for the short time it had taken the sailor away from his duties, he decided it was worth the attempt.

But the gods were not listening to the crew's prayers, at least not yet, and if anything the storm intensified. Wave after wave broke over the side of the ship, overwhelming the capacity of the bilge pump, no matter how hard the sailors worked the handles. The bilge level rose higher and higher, until they were up to their knees. Packs and crates floated on the surface and crashed dangerously from side to side as the ship rolled, pitched and yawed. Adonibaal gave an order to one of his men that Silus couldn't hear, but soon after buckets were being distributed to everyone not involved in rowing or sailing the ship.

'Captain's orders,' said a sailor, tossing Atius a bucket. 'Start bailing.' He then organised the other passengers and the other marines into a bucket line that led from the rapidly rising water level inside the hull, up the ladder to the deck and to the side railing. Silus found himself at the end of the line, nearest to the rail. Huge waves rolled past him and broke against the side of the ship, drenching him even more than he thought possible. He gasped and coughed, vainly wiping the water from his eyes with all the success of Sisyphus. Then he felt Granius, who was next in line, thrust a full bucket into his hands. He emptied it over the side, then tossed the empty bucket back down into the hull.

More buckets followed rapidly, one after another in an endless line, the exact reverse of the bucket lines he had seen the vigiles use to extinguish fires in Rome, this time attempting to subtract water from the environment rather than add it. The ship pitched, rolled and yawed beneath his feet, and he staggered, trying to keep his balance while still bailing as fast as the buckets reached him. There was a cry as someone fell off the ladder, and there was a momentary pause in the bucket supply. He turned to see there was a corresponding chain on the other side of the ship, another line of passengers, marines and any crew that could be spared frantically passing buckets hand to hand, though half of the contents slopped back into the ship. But the waterline inside the hull was creeping upwards despite the bailing and pumping.

Another bucket appeared at the bottom of the ladder and made its way up to him. As he reached out for it, he saw his counterpart at the end of the other chain, a marine, suddenly stagger, when a wave smashed through the deck rail, a swinging piece of timber catching him in the temple. He crumpled to his knees, both hands clutched to his bloody head. The next in line shouted a warning, and as the marine looked up, a wave swept along the deck. The marine reached out to grab the railing as the wave struck, but the wood broke off in his hand and he was borne away. Briefly a head and waving hand could be seen in the water before it vanished from view.

Silus froze, the full bucket grasped in his hands, staring at the spot where the marine had been. He had stared death down many times, but this was the most terrified he had ever felt. He was helpless in the power of a force beyond anything a man could resist. Not even the Roman empire could resist the might of the gods, as the inhabitants of Pompeii at the time of the eruption of Vesuvius, or of Antioch during the earthquake, could have testified, albeit briefly.

And he suddenly became acutely aware that a man who could have been his mystery attacker from the previous night was standing beside him. One well-timed nudge, and Silus would be gone, and none would even be able to prove Granius had done anything wrong. He stared at the frumentarius who wiped his eyes and grimaced back.

'What are you doing, Silus? Bail, for fuck's sake, or we will all be joining that poor bastard under the waves.'

Silus swallowed a mouthful of saline, then turned to throw the contents of the bucket overboard.

Something powerful hit him in the back, and he was thrown against the side rail. The rail splintered, gave, and Silus pitched forward. He instinctively took a deep breath, but the air was punched from his lungs as he hit the water.

The roar of the wind, the shouts of the crew, the protests of the timbers, all silenced.

Deathly quiet.

Icy cold.

Panic.

The freezing temperature triggered a reflex to inhale, and Silus fought it down, knowing that taking a breath would be fatal.

He kicked hard upwards, gripped by mindless terror, animal desperation making him fight for survival even while part of him was telling him it was all hopeless, futile. *Spend your last moments making peace with the gods, Silus*, it said. *Get ready to meet Sergia and Velua again.*

He broke the surface and was immediately buffeted by the wind, the waves, and the hammering rainfall. He was just feet away from the side of the ship, but it might have been a mile. He paddled hard in a clumsy, weary stroke, trying to regain safety, but it was as if he was swimming in honey. He felt the undertow sucking at him. He gasped another breath as he was pulled under again, still struggling.

Bubbles escaped him as he kicked and flailed.

A hand grasped his wrist, gripped tight. Silus clutched desperately. He could see nothing through the impenetrably turbid seawater. He wondered if this was real. Was it a dead hand, guiding him to Hades or Tartarus or heaven or whatever lay beyond? Maybe it was Velua reaching out to him, pulling him to her embrace.

Then there was a tug that almost dislodged his grip. He held on tighter, feeling his air running out, his strength ebbing.

The next tug hauled him back into the maelstrom. But this time he did not get pulled back under. He blinked hard, and saw Granius gripping him tightly.

'Pull, you bastards,' yelled Granius. 'Harder!'

Slowly, the team of sailors and marines drew Granius out of the sea by the rope he had tied around his waist. Silus dangled at the end of his wrist, feeling like his shoulder would be dislocated as the sea attempted to retain its hold.

The two men were dragged unceremoniously over the side of the ship and dumped onto the deck. The sailors and marines instantly dropped the rope and returned to their duties, working desperately on the ship's survival. Silus lay on his front, his cheek against the decking, moving weakly like a beached whale, coughing and vomiting up seawater.

Atius had shoved everyone aside and sprinted up the ladder as soon as he realised what had happened to Silus, and arrived just as he was being hauled on board. He dropped to his knees by Silus' side, turned him onto his back.

'Silus, Silus. Christos. Are you alive?'

In answer, Silus retched a mouthful of water into Atius' lap. He squeezed his friend's forearm, too weak to speak.

'Holy God, I thought I had lost you.'

'I'm fine too,' said Granius wryly, sitting up and inspecting the scrapes and bruises on his legs and chest where he had been dragged against the barnacles on the ship's hull.

'Granius, I don't know how to thank you. You saved his life.'

'I can be stupid like that sometimes,' said Granius.

'You lot!' yelled Adonibaal. 'If you can speak you can bail. Stow that lucky bastard somewhere safe, then get back to it.'

Granius and Atius used the rope to strap Silus to the mast, then returned to the bucket line. Silus lolled against his bindings, rocking this way and that at the ship's violent motions. He started to shake, from the cold, from the reaction to surviving a certain death. His teeth chattered, and he pulled his legs up to his chin and hugged them, trying to still the convulsive tremor unsuccessfully.

Eventually the shaking stopped, and a little feeling and strength returned to his limbs. But fear prevented him from untying the rope and rejoining the others in their battle to save the ship, even as he saw the water level creeping up in the hold, the vessel sitting lower and lower in the water, each wave threatening to finally swamp and sink the ship.

But the efforts of the crew, the oarsmen, the marines and the passengers was just enough. The storm began to blow itself out, the rain slowed to a drizzle, the wind to a firm breeze, the waves stayed outside the ship. The pumping and bailing slowed the encroachment of the water line, stopped it, reversed it.

The captain did not let anyone rest until the ship was once more riding high in the water, the bilge level an inconvenience rather than a threat. Then he ordered the rowers to take breaks in shifts, the crew to start makeshift repairs on the most dangerous aspects of the damage, and the marines and the passengers to distribute strong wine and hot broth to everyone.

Silus plucked up the courage to untie himself, but did not move from the spot. Atius brought him a cup of soup, and despite his nausea, he ate hungrily, feeling the warmth of the thick liquid the cook had hastily brought to the boil descend into his stomach and heat him from the inside. Atius settled down beside him and swigged wine from a cup, then offered Silus a drink.

They sat together as the clouds cleared, the moon and stars appeared, and the ship sailed through the night as if nothing untoward had happened.

–

Silus watched two sailors lower the gangplank to the dock, while others threw ropes to the dockhands, shouting instructions to tie off and make fast, until the *Minerva* was secured. He let out a wet cough, then sneezed and wiped his nose on the sleeve of his tunic. As soon as the gangplank was in place, he pushed to the front of the queue of passengers waiting to disembark and hurried down the narrow, slowly rocking strip of wood, not looking down towards the gently lapping waves. When he reached the dock, he dropped to his hands and knees, kissed the filthy ground, mired with animal faeces and spilt vegetable produce, and offered a fervent prayer of thanks to Neptune for sparing his life.

Atius put a hand on his back, then helped him to his feet when he had finished his prayers.

'Tavern?'

Silus nodded gratefully. Then he saw Granius shoulder his pack and walk on. He drew breath to shout to him, but it set off a coughing fit. He gestured towards the frumentarius, and Atius understood his intentions.

'Granius. Care to join us for a couple of drinks of something strong to warm your innards?'

Granius turned, hesitated, then gave a half smile and nodded assent. The three of them left the Minerva behind and set off for the interior of the port city.

Caralis was an ancient settlement, founded by Phoenicians, then taken over by Carthage before they lost it to Rome after the first Punic war. There was little trace of its Punic origins after four centuries of Roman rule – though the Romans had built their first fortified community to the east of the old city, the two settlements had soon merged, with Roman culture and construction rapidly obscuring the venerable foundations.

So Silus, Atius and Granius walked past temples mostly dedicated to the Roman pantheon, although some Greek and Eastern deities were also represented, past traditional Roman multistorey housing, past market traders and fast-food sellers and barbers and carpenters and all the usual businesses and entertainment venues that were ubiquitous throughout the urban communities of the Empire. Any traces of worship of Melkart, Tanit or Ba'al were either well-concealed, or had vanished completely.

Atius spotted a tavern with a sign of a dolphin emerging from the waves.

'How about this one?'

Silus gave him an incredulous glance. 'Are you kidding? Haven't you had enough of everything marine yet?'

'Come on, it's a good portent. It shows our respect for the seas.'

'You're a Christian. You don't care what Neptune thinks.'

'Listen, when you are at sea, you pray to whoever will get you to a safe harbour.'

Silus shook his head. He didn't really understand Atius' beliefs. He thought Christians were supposed to believe in only one God – or was that the Jews? Christians believed in three gods, didn't they? Atius had tried to explain it, but given even he was hazy on the details, it had made no sense to Silus. In any case, he was sure Atius was not supposed to honour any other gods but his own, yet he seemed happy to toss a coin into a well sacred to Fortuna when he was about to spend the night dicing, or make a sign to ward off evil when he came across something ill-omened.

Granius had already sat down at a table on the pavement and dumped his pack on the floor, up against the wall, away from the ordure running down the centre of the street. Atius joined him, then looked up at Silus. Silus sighed and sat beside them.

Strangely, the solid ground seemed to be moving, rocking slowly back and forth, and closing his eyes accentuated the feeling. It wasn't his first time at sea, so he was familiar with the fact that getting accustomed to the motions of the waves somehow led to the sensation that you were still at sea, even when you were back on dry land. His nausea, which had largely settled, returned. He snapped his fingers at a serving slave.

'Get me something hot and meaty, and a big cup of strong wine.'

Atius and Granius ordered too, and when the drinks arrived, Granius poured a small amount of wine onto the floor and moved his lips in an inaudible prayer. Silus did likewise, beseeching Neptune, Salacia and Nodens, the British god of the sea, to let them complete the rest of their journey with a fair wind and gentle waves. Atius closed his eyes and prayed, then dipped his finger into his cup and drew the sign of the fish on the table.

Superstition and religion were as commonplace as eating and breathing, but there were times when they became all-important. Being at sea, especially in a storm, took away all sense of control of one's own destiny, and left one with the certainty of being at the mercy of forces vastly more powerful than oneself. It was a feeling Silus hated, and he wished their voyage was complete, rather than just at the halfway point. He felt a sudden, almost irresistible urge to get up and run into the depths of the city, disappear, away from the threat of the water, his mission, his duty to the Emperor and Oclatinius and the Arcani.

Of course, he didn't do that. Instead he drank his unwatered wine, savouring the sensation as it ran down his throat and warmed him from the inside. When a large hot sausage slathered in onions and garum arrived, stinking enough to stimulate even his catarrh-dulled sense of smell, he devoured it hungrily, and mopped up the sauce with some sweet-tasting fresh bread.

When Granius reached into his purse to put some coins on the table, Silus held out his hand to stop him.

'This is on me.'

Granius nodded and put his money away. 'Very kind.'

'Really, it's the least you deserve.' He looked Granius straight in the eye. 'Why did you do it? Take such a risk for me. You don't know me.' They had been at sea for two days and two nights since the storm, and Silus had spent most of that time huddled in his berth, throat and lungs in agony from their inhalation of salt water, eyes and nose streaming with fluid as he was seized by a powerful cold. He had thought about seeking out Granius to express his thanks, but he had used his illness as an excuse to himself to avoid the frumentarius. In truth, the brave man reminded him too keenly of the terror he had felt.

Granius looked embarrassed. 'It was the right thing to do. You would have done it for me.'

Would he? Silus wasn't sure. 'I hope I would have. But no one knows how they will react in such a situation.'

'I know,' said Atius. 'You would have dived in without hesitation.'

Silus was grateful for Atius' faith in him, and he wished he shared it. But his near-drowning had frightened him more than he would admit, even to his best friend. It was the most certain he had ever been that he was about to die, and he couldn't shake the sensation that fate was not yet finished with him.

When they had finished eating and drinking, Atius suggested they explore Caralis further. Silus tried to express his reluctance but was interrupted by a bout of hacking coughs, so Atius clapped him on the shoulder and set off deeper into the city, a curious Granius and a grumbling Silus in tow. Atius had a nose for, as he called it, the more interesting parts of a city. That usually meant the seediest, grubbiest and most dangerous quarters. After the journey they had had so far, Silus would have been quite happy with sightseeing in the boring parts, or even better getting an early night, but that was never going to be a possibility with Atius.

Atius' found them a suitably sordid establishment for them to start the evening, with gaming boards carved into the tables, cheap strong wine, and rooms that could be hired by the half hour, along with male or female companionship. Ignoring Silus' suggestion that they keep their heads down, Atius introduced himself to a small group of labourers – freedmen and slaves – who were playing knucklebones, and asked if he could join them. Their initial reticence was overcome when he showed them the contents of his purse, and when they invited him to play, he beckoned Granius and Silus over too.

Silus played a few rounds, but quickly lost enough money to sour his mood even further. He sat back and watched Atius in his element, entertaining Granius and the locals with jokes and anecdotes, giving them tips on how to improve their gameplay, despite which he kept winning. Atius had a genuine skill at these sorts of contests, being successful way more than chance should permit. Another less charismatic opponent may have been accused of cheating, with the degeneration into arguments and violence that that always entailed. But Atius had them marvelling at his talent, and grateful for the secret techniques he shared with them.

When Silus insisted it was time to retire for the night, and he was leaving with or without Atius, his friend collected his winnings, then paid the tab for everyone's drinks. Though they were sorry to see him go, the other gamblers slapped him on the back and dubbed him a genuinely generous fellow who was welcome back any time. They gave them directions to a boarding house that they swore had clean rooms, good food, decent prices and beds with largely acceptable levels of bedbugs, lice and fleas. Atius wished them all well, and the three of them went out into the night. An unnoticed figure observed them from the shadows across the street.

Chapter V

It was pushing midnight, and the cloud-covered sky provided no illumination. No lighting was emitted from the shuttered windows of the houses lining the street. Granius carried a small oil lamp which allowed them to see a couple of yards beyond their noses. They fumbled along the pavement, using touch as much as any of their senses to find their way.

The knife thrust that dropped Atius came literally out of the darkness. Silus whirled round as his friend sank to the floor with a cry, clutching his side. A figure loomed up, Granius' oil lamp casting an eerily large shadow against the nearest wall. Then the lamp was dashed to the floor, the flame spitting for a moment as the oil spilt from the bronze vessel into the watery mud in the gutter, before sputtering out completely.

The swishing noise of a blade was just audible over Atius' curses, then there was a wet, gurgling sound. Silus heard Granius drop to his knees, then fall supine, feet kicking, bubbling breath sounds growing loud, then ceasing.

Silus' own knife had been in his hand the moment Atius cried out, and he had instinctively dropped into a defensive crouch. He swung his blade in a rapid arc in front of him, straining his eyes to make out the figure of the attacker in the darkness, trying to hear his steps, the rustle of his clothing, his respiration, anything that would give an indication of his location.

A shadow to his left.

He twisted fast, pain flashing across his upper arm. A trickle of warm blood ran down to his elbow and dripped to the ground.

It wasn't deep, didn't impair the limb's function or fighting ability. But it was a warning.

Another glimpse of the shadow in his peripheral vision. The slightest movement in the air. It was enough to alert Silus, so he could leap backwards, the knife thrust that would have gutted him stabbing harmlessly into empty space.

His antagonist was clearly seeing better than himself. He realised that the dim light from the oil lamp that he had been relying on was enough to impair his night vision. Their attacker must have been preserving his, maybe keeping one eye open to follow the little flame that revealed their position, the other shut to see better when the lamp was extinguished. Silus' eyes would adjust too, so he would be able to make out shapes and movement in the tiny amount of available light. But it would take time. Time he didn't have.

Silus had once seen a gigantic blind wrestler called Polyphemus. Most people who watched him fight for the first time assumed it was some sort of contest staged for comedy value, like making a hunchback with a wooden sword fight a pig. Most were surprised when they found out that bets were being taken at what seemed like a forgone conclusion. These people were even more surprised when they lost their money.

Polyphemus always struggled at the start of a bout, when his contestant would stay out of reach and strike from unexpected angles, feet, fists, knees and elbows landing flurries of blows, which Polyphemus could do nothing but take. But eventually, and inevitably, Polyphemus would get a grip somewhere on his opponent's body, whether it was a wrist or an ankle, or a handful of hair. And then his superior size and strength would tell. His opponent would be pummelled or crushed or smashed to the floor, the end result always being submission, often accompanied by major injuries.

Silus closed his eyes and went still.

He couldn't tell which of his senses detected the motion. It could have been smell or taste. All he could say was that he knew where his opponent was when he next struck. And this time, instead of dodging or weaving or ducking, he stepped forward.

He didn't throw himself suicidally onto the blade, though. He twisted, leading arm low, protecting his advancing side. The attacker's knife glanced off his forearm, scored the skin and muscles of his midriff, then passed on. Silus gripped the arm wielding the knife with both hands, lifted it, then slammed it across his knee. There was a satisfying shattering of bones with an accompanying bellow of pain. The knife fell to the ground.

It was not the end. His opponent was strong, stronger than Silus, and he still had some tricks. He fired a punch towards Silus' throat with his free hand. Silus dropped his head, catching the force of the blow on his chin. His jaw clashed shut, and he saw stars briefly. But he kept a tight hold on the broken arm, and the attacker lacked the strength to free himself, even if he could have borne the agony that that would entail.

The other man punched hard into Silus' side, and Silus exhaled a whoosh of breath. He yanked the broken arm he held, and the other man cried again. Silus twisted, and the man could not resist. He contorted his body to try to take the pressure off the injury, and fell to his knees. Silus kicked him hard in the head, and he tumbled backwards. Still holding onto the limp arm, Silus dropped onto his chest, elbow first, the classic wrestling move. The bony point of his joint caved in the ribcage with a sickening crunch. The body went limp.

Only now did Silus release the shattered arm. He crawled over to Granius' body, found his pack nearby where it had fallen, and rummaged rapidly through until he found the dead frumentarius' fire-striker, a horseshoe-shaped piece of steel that made sparks when struck against its companion piece of flint. He felt around on the muddy ground for the lamp until his fingers closed gratefully on the cool metal. A small pool of oil had remained in the bottom, and after a few strikes of the lighter, he managed to coax the lamp to produce a small flame.

The first thing he did when he had light was to hurry over to Atius. His friend was slumped with his back against a wall, his hands clasped to a rent in the side of his tunic over his abdomen. A large quantity of blood had poured out despite Atius' own pressure, but in the faint lamplight, it was too dark for Silus to tell if the volume looked like it would be fatal.

'Who…?' whispered Atius, teeth gritted against the pain.

'No talking,' said Silus curtly. 'Move your hands.' Atius did as he was told, and more blood flowed forth. Silus lifted the tunic up to expose the wound. Low on his right side, it had clearly penetrated deeply. A sick feeling settled in Silus' stomach. If the blade had punctured one of those slippery ropes of intestines that people kept inside themselves, his friend was dead, and no potion or ointment or prayer would save him. But if it was only the muscles of the body wall that were damaged, he had a chance, as long as he didn't bleed out first.

He put Atius' hands back over the wound and told him to press down hard. Then he tore two strips of cloth from Atius' tunic. One he stuffed into his friend's mouth.

'Bite down hard, and when I say, take your hands away again. Ready? Now!'

Atius clamped down hard on the cloth between his teeth and lifted his hands, and instantly Silus stuffed the second strip into the hole. Atius roared, the noise muffled against the material in his mouth. Silus tore up more clothing to make bandages, and wrapped them tightly around his friend's waist. When he was satisfied he could do no more, he sat back.

Atius spat out the cloth in disgust.

'Christos, Silus. This one hurts bad.'

'I know, mate. But you've had worse.'

'Granius?'

Silus shook his head sorrowfully.

'Fuck. He was all right.'

'Yeah. More than all right.'

'So who was the bastard?'

'No idea. Hold on.'

Silus took the lamp the short distance to where the body of the attacker lay. One arm was stretched out sideways, an unnatural bend halfway down the forearm, where no bend should be. The sternum was caved inwards, and a bloody piece of rib had torn through skin and tunic and was poking into the air. Silus moved the lamp to the man's face.

'It's Bomilcar,' Silus called to Atius.

'That Punic fucker. What was his problem anyway?'

'I don't think it was personal, Atius.' Silus made his way back over to his friend. 'Whoever tried to stop us in Ostia obviously managed to get Bomilcar onto the boat as a passenger.'

'Somebody knew way too much, Silus.' Atius tried to sit up, then let out a groan and slumped back.

'Take it easy. Let's get to this boarding house. It can't be far now. Worrying about who is trying to kill us can wait until the morning. Here, put your arm around me. That's it. I've got you.'

The boarding house was a mercifully short distance away. When they reached it, just where the gambling workmen had said it would be, Silus pounded on the door. The tavernkeeper opened a small shutter, saw the state of Atius and closed it rapidly.

'I don't want any trouble,' he called out.

'Then open up, and you won't get it,' said Silus, and his tone held sufficient threat that after a moment, the door swung open.

The boarding-house keeper was a weaselly little man with white stubble and narrow-set eyes. He ushered them inside, and stared at Atius in alarm. The better illumination from the lamps inside the atrium showed Silus the extent of Atius' blood loss, his clothing soaked red, and Silus marvelled that his friend had got this far, even with Silus' help.

'Is he going to die?' asked the housekeeper. 'It's bad luck if he dies here.'

'Do you know a physician? A medicus? Someone who can help us.'

'No one who would answer their doors at this time of night. But my daughter knows a few things about healing. Her mother passed a lot of knowledge to her, before she…'

'Help me get him to a bed, then send your daughter to us. You will be paid for the lodgings and for your daughter's help.'

The housekeeper and Silus, one on either side, helped Atius slowly and painfully up a single flight of stairs to a small bedroom, separated from the landing by a grubby curtain. Silus eased Atius down onto the bed, and Atius lay back, eyes closed, breathing rapid and shallow. The housekeeper disappeared, pulling the curtains closed. Silus sat on the edge of the bed and held his friend's hand, feeling helpless.

A young female voice came from the other side of the curtain.

'Masters, I'm Zephyra. My father sent me.'

Silus drew back the curtain to reveal a young woman wearing a plain tunic, dark, unstyled hair framing her unmade-up face.

He stepped back and indicated the bed. Zephyra approached Atius, leaning over him, placing a hand delicately against his cheek. Atius half-opened his eyes, then he lit up with a broad smile.

'Well, hello there,' he said. 'Who are you, sweetheart?'

Silus rolled his eyes. Even as he stood on the banks of the river Styx, he couldn't help flirting with a pretty lady. Mind you, Silus thought that Zephyra's looks could probably revive the dead.

'I'm Zephyra. I'm a healer. Can I look at your injury?'

'You can do what you like with me,' said Atius. The young woman pursed her lips. Silus sighed.

Zephyra handed a lamp to Silus, then lifted Atius' tunic. Atius' face went taut, and he couldn't stifle a groan as she rolled him gently to get a better look.

'Bring the light closer,' she instructed Silus. He did as he was told, and got his first proper glimpse of the sticky, congealed red-brown hole in his friend's flank. Zephyra leant down, inhaling a long, slow breath through her nose. She stood up, and Silus scanned her expression for clues.

'I can smell no putrefaction. I think his guts are still intact.'

Silus let out a sigh of relief. It was still a deep enough wound to kill Atius, if it developed an infection. But it wasn't an automatic death sentence.

Zephyra took a bowl of warm water and used a cloth to bathe the wound, removing the gunk contaminated with the dirt of the road. When she used a spatula to slather honey into the hole, Atius cried out in pain, jaw clenched, the veins in his neck standing out like ropes. Ignoring him, Zephyra took some cobwebs from a pouch and layered them over the honey. Finally, she got Silus to help Atius sit up, and she wrapped some clean bandages around his midriff.

They lowered him back to the bed. Slowly, Atius' harsh breathing slowed, he closed his eyes, and lapsed into something between unconsciousness and sleep.

'What do you think?' Silus asked Zephyra, voice low to avoid waking Atius, but dripping with concern.

'I think he is strong. He has every chance.'

'Shouldn't the wound be sewn closed?'

'No, that just traps the evil inside. His best chance is with frequent changes of the bandages, and lots of honey to tempt the bad spirits out. But he must not be moved. There is a lot of healing to be done.'

'Our ship sails tomorrow morning!'

'Then it will sail without him. If you don't want to be burying him at sea.'

Silus looked at his friend. 'Damn you, Atius. Just as I was getting used to having you around again.' He turned back to Zephyra. 'Fine, as you say. Can you keep him here until he is better? I may be gone a few nundinae.'

'The longer the better. Injuries like that don't heal overnight.'

'I'll leave money with your father for his care and keep, but if it's not enough, I will settle up any outstanding debts when I return. Anything he needs, he gets. Understand?'

'Of course.'

Silus perched himself on the edge of Atius' bed, and ruffled his sleeping friend's hair.

'I'll bed down here tonight. Fetch me a mattress and some food and wine.'

'Certainly. But I shall visit often too, to tend to his needs.'

'Thank you.'

Silus prepared himself for a long night.

-

Silus spent much of the next three days at sea on his own, staring out across the waves. At first the seascape appeared to be unchanging, out of sight of land as they were, not passing even the smallest of islands on their route from Sardinia to Numidia. But the more he watched, the more he noticed the subtle details, the way the shade of green or blue changed with the depth of the seabed, the variation in the shape and size and direction of the waves, the foam-flecked peaks that, if he squinted and tilted his head, looked like horses galloping at the front of chariots, or mythical beasts – the Hydra, Cerberus, Medusa. The motion of the boards beneath his feet became familiar, a reassurance like the rock of a baby's cot.

It was calming. His life had held so much trauma and terror, recently and as far back as he could remember. Now, with the assassin on the boat who had threatened them dead, his mission on hold until he reached land, he could lose himself in the present. Was he really starting to enjoy travelling by ship?

Of course nothing could really remove all his anxieties. If the ship lurched suddenly with a particularly full swell, his heart raced and his throat closed, and he was beneath the waves, clawing for the surface, and his breathing raced uncontrollably. At moments like that, he bent at the waist, holding the deck rail, gasping until he regained control and began to breathe normally again. If he sensed someone behind him, he whirled, reaching for his knife, ready to fight for his life. The crew and passengers quickly learned to clear their throats or make their footsteps particularly loud when they approached Silus.

His mind flicked back to Caralis, where he had left Atius in the care of Zephyra. His face had had a touch more colour than the previous night, and he had been back to flirting with Zephyra, much to his nurse's disgust. Atius had wished Silus the best for his journey and promised to pray to Christos for the success of his mission. Silus had hugged his friend, and had resolved to make offerings for Atius' health. The injury could still kill him, and when he hugged Atius and bade him goodbye, he wondered if he would ever see his friend again. Losing Atius would surely be more than he could bear.

A shout went out around the ship that the broth was ready. Silus' stomach growled. Now his nausea had gone, his hunger was trying to compensate for his previous inappetence. He took one last look across the water, then pushed himself away from the rail and strolled in the direction of the cook's pot, the odour of garlic and onion getting stronger in his nostrils.

The ship's complement of passengers had dwindled substantially. No Granius, no Bomilcar, no Atius. When Silus had returned to the ship, Adonibaal had demanded to know where they all were. Silus had feigned ignorance of the fate of Bomilcar or Granius, and had simply said that Atius had become unwell and didn't feel up to the next leg of the journey. Adonibaal had been momentarily perturbed, and then had shrugged, commenting that they had all paid in advance so it wasn't his problem.

So the only passengers in front of Silus in the queue for food were Calev, followed by Vocula, Khnum-Aa and her slave Korinna. The ill-matched couple seemed to have formed a truce since they had come back on board after an overnight stay in Caralis. Now, Khnum-Aa held Vocula's elbow, supporting him when the ship rolled beneath their feet, and helped him fill his bowl. She accepted a couple of ladles' worth of the broth for herself, and then guided Vocula to one of the vacant seats on the poop deck, settling herself on the other side. She made sure Vocula was settled, that he had a good grip on his bowl and spoon, and then watched him eat with the attentiveness of a nursemaid supervising a newly weaned infant. Calev joined them.

Silus sat on the other side of Vocula, next to Adonibaal, and devoured his broth. He finished before anyone else, licked his spoon clean, then ran his finger around the inside of his bowl and sucked the last of the sauce off. He dropped the spoon into the bowl, then looked around him. The crewmen and marines were dividing up the last dregs from the cookpot between them. Calev was just finishing his own meal. Khnum-Aa had more or less finished her own small portion. Only Vocula was still eating, blowing on each spoonful, gummily masticating the soft meaty portions, then swallowing hard before dipping his spoon once more.

He noticed Silus looking at his three-quarter-empty bowl and proffered it to him. 'I couldn't eat another mouthful.'

Khnum-Aa laid a concerned hand lightly on his arm. 'Gaius, you should finish it. You need to keep your strength up.'

'Now, my sweet, you are kind to look out for me, but alas my appetites are not what they were when I was younger.'

Silus thought he detected an expression on Khnum-Aa's face that said something like *you're damned right there*, but it was only fleeting. 'Please, my love, it will do you good. Restore your energy.'

'If he says he is full, he is full,' said Silus, whose stomach was still growling. He held out his hand, and Vocula passed the bowl over. Khnum-Aa's protests died away as Silus quickly finished the remains before his forceful wife could change his mind. He looked at her triumphantly as he passed the empty bowl back to Vocula, and was surprised to see a look somewhere between concern and resignation. He excused himself, and went back to his post by the deck rail and watched the sun descend towards the gently curved horizon, eyes unfocussed as he listened to the sound of the sails, the waves, the drumbeat, and the dip of the oars in the water.

-

Silus woke suddenly in the night to find his heart thumping frantically in his chest. He had been dreaming of a storm, waves inundating the ship, bailing frantically, while somewhere behind him a faceless man with an unfeasibly long blade made his slow, inexorable way against the flooding waters towards his exposed back.

He panted, deep and hard, reassuring himself that it was just a dream, that the panic and the symptoms that went with it would recede as he got control of himself. But if anything, his heart rate accelerated. He sat up, gasping, clutching his belly. He looked up, and the stars above rotated like they were painted on the wheels of an ox cart. As he stared, the stars moved out of their position, rearranged themselves into a face. A familiar face.

Caracalla stared down out of the heavens, bearded, scowling. He extended a finger towards Silus, and his deep voice boomed out. 'Bow before me, Arcanus!'

Silus rolled onto his hands and knees, but when he tried to stand his legs buckled. He tried to call out, but his mouth was as dry as the Parthian sands, and he couldn't seem to form words. A splitting pain resonated inside his skull.

From somewhere he heard a high-pitched scream, but he couldn't tell if it came from Caracalla or someone on the ship. There was a commotion, and someone yelled out, 'He's dead.'

Was it him? Had he died and just hadn't realised it yet? His eyelids started to twitch, then his fingers. He rolled onto his back, spasmodically kicking his legs and flailing his arms. Spittle ran from the corner of his mouth, and his bowels and bladder released their contents at the same time. Darkness fell.

–

Silus awoke to the raucous sound of seabirds wheeling overhead, and found himself lying on a comfortable mattress in the captain's cabin. He tried to sit up, then sank back down again, clutching his head as a sharp pain ricocheted around behind his eyes.

It was daylight, early morning judging by the orange hue that bathed the timberwork and fittings, but even that dim dawn light hurt his eyes, forcing him to squint.

Adonibaal was looking at an unrolled chart, his back to Silus. Silus tried to speak, worked up a little spit to moisten his dry mouth, and managed to emit a small croak. Adonibaal turned.

'So. You made it. That was touch and go, I would say.'

'What…'

'I'm not sure you are up to hearing stories right now.'

'Tell… me.'

Adonibaal rubbed his hand over his eyes. He looked tired. 'We are a few hours from docking in Cirta. I have things to do. Just lie here. Drink some water.' He indicated a jug that had been placed beside Silus. 'I'll be back to check on you in a while.' Adonibaal patted his shoulder and then ducked out of the low door.

Silus lay still, taking stock. His heart rate seemed normal now, but every muscle in his body ached, like each one had individually attempted to outdo Philippides' famous run from Marathon to Athens. His tunic had been changed – the one he wore now was clean but ill-fitting, more suited to the captain's figure. By moving slowly, he managed to get into a seated position, and he sat with his back to the hull, unable and unwilling to attempt to get to his feet. He sipped at the water, and some semblance of humanity slowly returned.

Presently, Calev came to check in on him. The small Jew smiled when he saw Silus awake.

'You made it.'

'Why does everyone seem surprised by that?'

'Because not everyone survived the night.'

Silus sat upright now, clenching his jaw against the throbbing inside his skull.

'Who? What happened?'

Calev shook his head. 'Vocula. When Khnum-Aa woke this morning, she found him dead next to her. I'm surprised her screams didn't wake you.'

'Vocula?' Silus was still groggy. 'What… how did he die?'

Calev spread his hands. 'Who knows? He was old. It happens, right?'

'But so suddenly. He had no symptoms last night, did he?'

'When he went to his cabin, he said he had cramps in his abdomen. And I saw the body this morning. He had spit all round his face, and he had messed his nightclothes. It looked like he didn't go easy. Now I think about it, it's surprising that didn't rouse Khnum-Aa.'

Silus thought of his own symptoms – what he could remember, before the fit took him. It was just too coincidental.

'Help me up,' he said. 'I need to see the captain.'

Adonibaal was berating a sailor for the cleanliness of the decks.

'It's not just about appearances,' he was saying firmly. 'If you let the slime and grime build up, people slip, and when people slip, they crack their skulls or fall overboard. Now get on your knees and scrub. Yes, what is it?'

This last was snapped at Silus.

'Captain, I need to talk to you.'

'Not now. Go and get some rest. We can talk after we have docked.'

'It will be too late then.'

Adonibaal looked at him with a mix of frustration and curiosity. The latter won out.

'Fine. Speak.'

Silus looked around. Calev was the only other person in earshot, and Silus had already concluded he was harmless enough.

'Vocula and I were poisoned.'

Adonibaal's eyes narrowed. 'How is that possible? To poison both of you and no one else?'

'We ate from the same bowl. I finished off Vocula's meal last night. But he ate most of it. I guess that's why I lived and he didn't.'

'Who would want to kill Vocula? And why?'

'Well, I think it's safe to assume he was the target and not me. No one could have known I would finish off his meal. And there is only one person on board who could have a personal reason for getting rid of him. Vocula told me he was going to divorce Khnum-Aa and leave her destitute. She must have found out.'

Adonibaal fiddled with the tufts of hair at the side of his head. 'I can't accuse Khnum-Aa without evidence. She is the widow of a respectable Roman noble.'

'She has a slave,' commented Calev.

Silus opened his mouth to protest, but Adonibaal jumped on the suggestion. He flicked his fingers and called over the marine centurion.

'If you please, get two of your men and bring Korinna the slave to me. But do it discreetly.'

Silus wasn't clear who was above whom in the chain of command between the captain and the marine centurion, but the centurion agreed without conflict. Moments later, Korinna was before Adonibaal, standing between two burly marines, her face as white as a freshly laundered toga. The soldiers held her arms by the elbows, and they had to support her weight, as her knees trembled weakly.

Adonibaal regarded her for a long moment. When it looked like the slave was about to pass out in terror, he spoke. 'It would be better for you if you tell us everything, without me having to ask.'

She looked from stern face to stern face, the marine centurion, the captain, Silus and Calev.

'Please, masters, I've done nothing.'

Adonibaal sighed. 'On this boat, as captain, I have the power of life and death. I can order you flogged until you are half dead, then have weights tied to your feet and have you tossed over the side.'

'Please,' she whispered.

'Speak!'

'It wasn't me. I just purchased it in Caralis for her.' The terrified slave's words came out in a rush. 'She found out he was going to divorce her. She made me seek out the apothecary and buy the poison. She knew exactly what herbs she needed, and how much it would take to kill him. But she bought extra, in case her first attempt failed. She needed to be sure. She told me she wasn't ever going back to being poor. She still has some of the poison in her cabin. You can search it if you don't believe me.'

Adonibaal looked at the marine centurion, who nodded once, sharply. The captain beckoned one of the marines holding Korinna to accompany him, and marched towards the guest cabin. Silus and Calev followed closely behind.

Adonibaal knocked on the cabin door, and called out, 'Domina, would you please come out? I need to speak to you.'

There was a pause, then the reply came. 'Let me ready myself.'

Long moments passed. Adonibaal was in the process of lifting his hand to knock again when she emerged, dressed in her finest clothes, make-up immaculate. She looked at Silus, who was, if not exactly well, most definitely alive. Her shoulders dropped, just a fraction, but Silus caught it, along with the look of resignation that settled in her eyes.

'We are getting ready to dock soon, I understand, captain. Is there some preparation I need to make?'

She obviously hadn't given up yet, maybe still hoping she could brazen it out, bluff her way through. Then she caught sight of Korinna further down the deck in the company of a marine guard, and her composure nearly broke. But she was tough. Silus wondered if her previous life as a slave had hardened her to adversity. She straightened her back and looked Adonibaal straight in the eyes, raising a questioning and supercilious eyebrow.

'Domina,' said Adonibaal, still respectful, his tones measured. 'This is very awkward, but some information has come to my attention about the death of your husband. May we search your cabin?'

'No you may not!' she gasped with indignation.

Adonibaal sounded sad as he replied, 'I'm afraid I must insist.'

'How dare you? What manner of insolence is this?' She took a step forward as if to strike him, and the marine stepped in, catching her wrist. She struck with the other hand, raking sharp fingernails across the marine's face and drawing blood. He grabbed that hand too, and held her firm.

Silus caught the captain's eye and gestured towards the cabin. Adonibaal nodded, and Silus slipped inside, the curious Calev just behind.

The cabin was tiny – space was very much at a premium on the ship. Nevertheless, it had been made as luxurious as possible for the journey. A small dressing table held a comb, a mirror and a variety of perfumes, make-ups, ointments and unguents, together with the paraphernalia needed to apply them. Against one wall was a large bed big enough for two, with a feather mattress and clean sheets and blankets that had obviously been changed since Vocula's messy death. At the foot of the bed was a large travel chest.

Silus opened a drawer in the dressing table, and found some ornate and expensive-looking jewellery and some writing implements – wax tablet and stylus, as well as some papyrus and Vocula's seal. The papyrus had a half-written letter in cramped cursive handwriting that was hard to decipher, but seemed nothing more than a request to a merchant for various items to decorate Vocula's new residence in Numidia. The wax tablet had a partially erased attempt at what Silus presumed was poetry, though he knew little about such matters.

He flipped open the chest's heavy oak lid and rummaged through the various items the rich couple had thought important for the journey. He presumed that their other possessions, the furniture and busts and the bulk of their wardrobes was packed in crates in the hold, or was to follow on another ship, or had perhaps even been sent ahead so their new accommodation would be homely for when they arrived.

He found beautifully dyed stolas and pallas, a heavy woollen toga, men's boots and ladies' sandals. There was a small bronze statue of a lar, one of the household gods, holding a cornucopia. Vocula clearly hadn't wanted to trust the god of his home to another's care. Much good it had done him.

Then Silus' fingertips touched a small cloth bag, closed with a drawstring, its contents dry and crisp. He pulled it into the light, opened it. Inside were dried roots and leaves, chopped and crushed. Silus sniffed, and even through his cold-numbed sense of smell, the sharp, bitter odour they gave off made him wrinkle his nose. His Arcani training had given him some expertise in poisons, and though he could not identify this one with certainty, he suspected it was belladonna or something similar. If so, there was enough there to have killed Vocula several times over.

Silus threw the bag to Calev, who held it as if it could kill him by the merest proximity. He went back outside and gestured to the bag Calev held. Adonibaal sighed, as if he had personally been let down.

All the fight left Khnum-Aa. She fell to her knees, gripping the hem of the captain's tunic, and tears streamed down her face in black lines of kohl.

'You don't understand. You don't know what he was like. Being married to him was awful. But I couldn't leave him. Without him, I had nothing. I couldn't go back to being a slave again. I wouldn't!'

Adonibaal reached down and firmly removed her hand from his clothing.

'Marine, take her back to the cabin. Put her slave in there with her. Keep guard until we dock, then we can hand her over to the authorities at Cirta.'

'What will happen to them?' asked Calev, his voice quavering.

'I would imagine the slave will be crucified,' said Adonibaal. 'I'm not sure how they will treat Khnum-Aa. She is technically a free woman, but she is a poisoner who killed her husband. Beheading? Tied to a stake in the arena and have the lions set upon her? Tied in a sack with a monkey, a snake and a dog and thrown into a river?'

Khnum-Aa began to shake violently, her babbling pleas now incoherent. The marine took her by the elbow and dragged her inside the cabin, her resistance feeble now. Adonibaal waved to the marine guarding Korinna and he brought the slave over to them. Korinna too trembled like a mouse before a cat.

'You understand what will happen to you?' asked Adonibaal.

The slave didn't reply, just wrung her hands compulsively in front of her belly.

'When we reach Cirta, you will be tortured for your evidence, so that your mistress can be convicted. Then you will be executed, painfully.'

Silus frowned. It seemed an unnecessary cruelty to rub in the horror of their impending punishment. Was Adonibaal taking pleasure from their terror?

Adonibaal held out his hand to Calev. For a moment, Calev didn't seem to understand his request. Then comprehension dawned and he passed him the bag of poisonous herbs. Adonibaal in turn gave it to Korinna, who took it, staring at it as if she knew it contained her doom.

'Go and keep your mistress company. Say your prayers to the gods. Comfort each other. Presently, I will have some hot broth sent to you. I'm afraid it is plain fare. It may need some…' he looked at the bag the slave held, '…seasoning.'

Korinna didn't thank him. That would be too much. But to Silus, it seemed that her shaking eased a little. Or was that just wishful thinking? The marine led Korinna inside the cabin, then closed the door and stood guard, spear by his side. The other marine who had held Khnum-Aa stood guard beside him. From behind them came the heart-rending sounds of two women sobbing uncontrollably.

Silus felt suddenly sick of the whole affair. He wondered if he should have brought his suspicions to the captain at all. If he hadn't mentioned that he had eaten from the same bowl as Vocula, Khnum-Aa may have got away with it. Instead, she and her slave – accomplice but no doubt without choice in the matter – would now die the unpleasant death of the poison, if they were brave enough, or a far worse death if they weren't.

He wandered disconsolately along the deck to the place he had made his berth, and made sure everything was packed. Tent, clothing, bedding, saucepan and bowl were all stowed in his pack or on his person. Then he sat with his legs straight out before him, and as he waited for the coastline of Numidia to finally come into view, he patiently and methodically sharpened his knife on his whetstone.

Chapter VI

Silus had commandeered a fast horse at the dock in the port city of Russicada and ridden straight to the city of Cirta as swiftly as his mediocre equestrian skills would allow. He had been tempted to walk, allowing himself time to process all that had happened since he had left his apartment in Rome. But if anything, the attempts to stop him had emphasised the urgency of his mission. And it would have made the efforts of Adonibaal and his crew, including those who lost their lives in the storm, pointless if he had squandered the extra time that the hazardous open ocean route had brought him.

The air was hot and dry, and the horse's hooves beat on an arid dirt track as it cantered, scuffing up clouds of dust. Dark flies buzzed around, attempting to alight on anything moist – the horse's eyes, Silus' still-running nose.

He had bid goodbye to Adonibaal at the dockside, and expressed his gratitude for his skill and sacrifice in bringing them to Cirta so swiftly. Adonibaal had shrugged off the thanks. Then he had said farewell to Calev who, Silus realised with a jolt, was the only one of the passengers to make it to port. To Silus' surprise, it had been Calev who had volunteered to go and check on Khnum-Aa and Korinna after enough time had gone by for the poison to do its work. He had come out, and grimly pronounced them both dead. When they docked, the three bodies

– Vocula, his wife and his wife's slave – were taken away, wrapped in shrouds, before any passengers disembarked or cargo was unloaded. The crew would not hear of the corpses remaining on the ship any longer than was necessary. They already believed the ship was unlucky, and Silus had heard murmurs of several planning to abscond once they were in Cirta rather than risk a return journey on a vessel that Fortuna had so clearly turned her face from, and Poseidon had some grudge against.

Silus himself was greatly relieved to leave the ship and the sea behind, and tried not to think about the journey back to Rome that he would have to undertake at some point. Before then, though, he had a mission to carry out, and he forced himself to concentrate on this. His first job was to warn Marcellus of the plot against him. His second job was to protect Marcellus from whichever assassins were sent against him. It crossed his mind that Bomilcar may have been tasked with both stopping Silus and Atius from delivering their warning to Marcellus, and killing the governor himself. It would be efficient, and Bomilcar clearly had skill and training, maybe provided by whoever he worked for in the same way Oclatinius had trained up Atius and Silus.

In fact, it was almost as if Oclatinius had trained Bomilcar himself. Could he be an Arcanus? He fought like one. And Oclatinius rarely revealed the names of other Arcani, preferring them to know as little about each other as was feasible outside the pairings or cells they worked in.

Was it possible? Could Oclatinius be part of a conspiracy to destabilise Caracalla? And be willing to sacrifice Atius and himself along the way? Silus dismissed the idea as soon as it occurred to him. He trusted Oclatinius with his life. Didn't he?

Still, someone with inside knowledge had arranged the ambush at Ostia, and the presence of Bomilcar on the *Minerva*. The list of suspects wasn't long. Macrinus, Festus and Oclatinius were the only ones present at the meeting with Caracalla at which they had been given their mission. So, one of them, or someone they had spoken to. When he returned to Rome, he would need to make sure of Oclatinius, and if he was certain the old spymaster was blameless, they would need to attempt to find out who was behind the plot. It wouldn't be easy – whoever it was clearly had some skill at spycraft.

But for now, Marcellus was his priority. He arrived at the city gates, and announced to the guard that he had an important message for the governor. The guard gave him directions to the governor's provincial palace, and Silus set off at a trot.

Cirta was very different in character from Rome. It was a city of around 50,000 inhabitants, so Silus had been informed by Adonibaal, so many times smaller than the Eternal City, but a similar size to Londinium, the capital of Silus' home province. But many things were familiar. The small city boasted temples and taverns, a forum and a market, fountains and statues to the gods and the Emperors, with Septimius Severus, the first Emperor of African origin, particularly prominent. The streets were narrow and filled with animal manure and rotting carcasses of dead beasts of burden. Feral cats and dogs mingled amongst the pigs and chickens and goats.

Silus was used to seeing darker-skinned individuals in the ethnic melting pot that was Rome, and it wasn't uncommon to see people from North Africa or the East even in Londinium, such was the interconnectedness of the Empire. Most of the population here, though, were more heavily pigmented than himself, and he felt conscious of the sun on his bare skin, wondering how long it would take him to burn.

Merchants called out to him as he passed, trying to persuade him to eat and drink in their taverns, buy their clothes and shoes and other goods. Silus managed not to run any of them down, despite the almost suicidal bravery with which they leapt in front of his horse in an attempt to make a sale.

The governor's palace dominated the district in which it was situated. Marble steps led up to Doric columns, behind which huge bronze doors embossed with mythological beasts guarded the interior. Silus handed his mount off to an attendant slave, and swiftly ascended the steps.

The duty legionary took in his attire, filthy from travel by sea and road, and angled his spear to block his passage.

Silus was a little breathless from the ride and the steep steps. He swallowed and spoke clearly.

'My name is Gaius Sergius Silus. I am here to see the governor, Sextus Varius Marcellus. I have an important message for him.'

'The governor is not granting audiences today,' said the guide. 'Give me the message and I will see that it is passed along in good time.'

Silus took a deep breath, let it out slowly through his nose, calming down before he got himself in trouble for losing his temper with the guard.

'I have come from Rome. My message is direct from the Emperor, Imperator Caesar Marcus Aurelius Severus Antoninus Pius Augustus Britannicus Maximus Germanicus Maximus and is for the governor's ears only.' Silus had tried to memorise Caracalla's titles to help emphasise Silus' own importance as his messenger and servant, though he was sure he had forgotten some. Wasn't there a Magnus and a Parthicus in there somewhere?

The guard looked uncertain. He turned to the legionary next to him, who stroked his wiry beard. 'Best ask the centurion,' he suggested. 'I'll keep him here.'

The guard puffed out his cheeks in irritation, then disappeared inside the palace. Silus lounged against a column, watching the citizens plodding about their business, trying to stick to the shade to avoid the direct glare of the early afternoon sun. Presently the centurion appeared, a world-weary veteran with an ugly scar across his prominent chin. He quizzed Silus briefly about his business, then, sufficiently satisfied, escorted him inside to a large atrium, where Silus was instructed to sit and wait.

Silus found a stone bench and settled himself in. His knee jiggled up and down and he twiddled his thumbs in circles around each other, frustration gnawing at him, to be held up after all his previous haste at the last hurdle. He distracted himself by looking around the ornate room, open-ceilinged, with a central pool and fountain. Large golden fish swam in lazy circles. The walls were decorated in bright frescoes depicting the Italian countryside. A huge statue of Caracalla dominated, staring straight at Silus in a look of anger and disapproval. Despite having seen that look on the Emperor in the flesh on more than one occasion, the statue was sufficiently life-like that Silus had to resist the urge to get to his knees before it and beg forgiveness, though for what, he didn't know.

Although the guard had told him that the governor wasn't seeing anyone, half a dozen others waited in the atrium with Silus. It was obviously a stock answer to put off all but the most persistent, or important, visitors. A tall, gangly youth sat with his back to the wall, legs extended, crossed at the ankles, an air of nonchalance about him that he had probably worked hard to affect. A man sat with his heavily pregnant wife, one hand on her swollen abdomen, whispering soothing words in her ear. A finely dressed merchant paced up and down, shaking his head, looking up anxiously whenever he thought he heard someone approach. An official-looking slave or freedman waited patiently, arms full of papyrus scrolls. An old man sat with his head in his hands, shoulders shaking, emitting occasional audible sobs.

A freedman entered the atrium, straight-backed, with a serious expression.

'Gaius Sergius Silus?'

Silus raised his hand.

'The governor will see you now.'

'What!' The exclamation came from the merchant. 'I have been waiting for hours. This man just arrived.'

'You were told there would be a long wait, if indeed the governor has time to see you at all today,' the freedman replied patiently but firmly.

'But I need that export licence straight away. My goods won't last long in this damned heat.' He wiped his perspiring brow to emphasise his point.

'Most merchants don't leave this sort of detail until the last minute. Especially when it is something that requires the governor's personal attention. Silus, please come with me.'

Silus gave the merchant an apologetic smile, and followed the freedman deeper into the palace. He was taken to Marcellus' tablinum. The freedman knocked on the double doors, and after a few moments, a voice bade them enter.

Silus was ushered inside, and finally found himself face to face with Sextus Varius Marcellus. Two years had passed since they had last parted company, but if anything the Numidian governor looked younger. Once he had quelled the incipient rebellion in the province, which he had initially been appointed to deal with, he had turned to making the country run more efficiently and more productively. The work seemed to agree with him. Certainly it was less stressful than when he was caught up in the struggle between Caracalla and his brother for power, or when his son had been kidnapped for reasons that Silus thought were probably still unclear to him.

The powerful man was looking down at a wax tablet, his lips moving as he attempted to decipher the scrawled, handwritten report.

The freedman announced Silus in an affected, sing-song voice. 'Gaius Sergius Silus to see you, master.'

Marcellus looked up from the tablet, and his face lit up. He leapt to his feet, took three long strides across the study and gripped Silus in a bear hug, tight enough for the breath to whoosh out of Silus' chest.

After a moment, Marcellus stepped back, both hands on Silus' shoulders, and studied him.

'You look terrible.'

'It's good to see you, too, sir,' said Silus. But he was sure Marcellus was right. His broken nose was red from the heavy cold he was still trying to shake, and he was grimy and dishevelled from a long journey, not to mention the numerous scars and other minor disfigurements he had accumulated over the previous couple of years since they had last seen each other. Marcellus by contrast had put on a little weight, but mainly muscle, in all the right places.

His skin sported a healthy tan and his hair was thick and lustrous.

'Maybe I could have stopped to bathe,' Silus conceded. 'But it really was important that I came to see you urgently. I've come on a fast Liburnian direct from Rome with a message from the Emperor. People died to get me here this fast. And… people died trying to stop me.'

Marcellus' expression became sombre, his mouth pressed into a tight line.

'Let's hear it, then.'

Silus licked his dry lips, wishing he had asked for some water while he had been waiting.

'I have been sent to warn you of a plot against your life.'

Marcellus didn't react apart from a barely detectable narrowing of his eyes. He waited patiently for Silus to continue.

'Oclatinius doesn't have details. We don't know who the assassin is, or who sent him, or why. Though we can guess the last bit.'

'Speculate for me, then.'

'There is a conspiracy afoot against Caracalla.'

'Nothing unusual there.'

'Maybe not. But I think this one is more advanced than most. And I personally believe there are people close to the Emperor involved. They knew about my and Atius' mission, sent multiple people to stop us.'

'Atius is well?' asked Marcellus sharply.

'I believe so. He was injured during an assassination attempt on the two of us. A frumentarius who was with us died during the fight. I left Atius to recover in Caralis.'

'Give my clerk the name of the frumentarius. I will see that his family is compensated.'

'Thank you, sir.' Silus was reminded why he liked this man. Not many nobles would think about the welfare of the men who did them good services the way Marcellus did. Most just believed it was no more than their due.

'So persons unknown high up are trying to kill Caracalla. And these same people want me dead?'

'Yes, sir. Oclatinius believes that your loyalty is so unshakeable, and your power strong enough, that you need to be… um… disposed of, before they can make their move.'

Marcellus rubbed his hand over his cheek.

'I see. Thank you for your warning. How is Oclatinius, by the way? The old man is still alive then?'

'He is well. He has just been promoted to praetorian prefect.'

Marcellus let out a short laugh.

'Oh, he won't have liked that. So, were there any suggestions as to what I should do with this information?'

'You are to return to Rome, where the Emperor can better protect you, and of course where you can likewise protect him. Oclatinius has ordered me to accompany you and to protect you and your family.'

'You think my family is in danger?'

'I don't know. But Caracalla specifically told me to look out for Avitus.'

'Did he now?' Marcellus looked thoughtful. Silus too had wondered about that. There were rumours that Avitus was in fact Caracalla's son, rather than Marcellus'. But that didn't need to be brought up now.

'Caracalla has no heirs. Your son might have a claim to the throne through his mother. She is niece to the Empress after all. Maybe the conspirators think it would be best to be rid of him as well.'

Marcellus showed the first sign of anger now, jaw clenched, fist balled. Regardless of whether Marcellus had any suspicions about Avitus' parentage, Silus had seen first-hand how much Marcellus loved the boy. It was as well he still had no idea of his wife's role in Avitus' kidnapping two years previously. Silus suspected Marcellus' retribution on Soaemias and her lover Gannys would have been severe.

'Thank you for the warning,' Marcellus said tightly. 'I will double my personal bodyguard and alert the centurion of the guards to a possible threat. He can organise extra patrols or whatever he sees fit. We will arrange passage to Rome as soon as possible. But I have affairs here to conclude first. You saw all the people waiting for my attention in the atrium, and they are just the few who pleaded or bribed their way past my clerk. There is so much left to do here, and I suppose much of it will have to remain undone, or at least taken up by my successor.'

'I would recommend you hurry, sir. It's not safe here.'

'I understand. But even so, arranging suitable transport for my family and possessions is no quick task. Still, I shall try to expedite it as quickly as possible. We will aim to leave within the next few days. Now you have alerted me to the threat, we should be safe.'

'I hope so, sir. Every hour you remain in this province is an hour you and your family are in danger.'

Marcellus nodded. 'I can fight if needed. I'll make sure I remain armed, with my bodyguard near me at all times. But Silus, I need you to do something for me.'

'Of course, sir. I was sent to serve you.'

'Protect my son. He is very precious to me.'

Silus swallowed. 'You don't need to command me to do that. I'm fond of him myself.'

'Thank you. Now go and get yourself a bath. My clerk will find you fresh clothes and accommodation in the palace near to Avitus' rooms. I have much to do, and much to think about.'

Silus bowed and went in search of Marcellus' freedman assistant.

-

Silus walked through the marketplace, a respectful two paces behind the young lad and his mother. Every so often he reached down to caress the reassuring hilt of his sword, a well-balanced gladius supplied to him by the centurion of the palace guard.

Avitus was dressed in an androgynous tunic made of red-dyed silk that reached down to his ankles and swished as he walked. It could easily have passed as a stola. He wore long, dangling gold earrings in each pierced ear, and his powerful perfume floated back in the air to penetrate even Silus' mucus-clogged nostrils. Two slaves, a young boy and an older woman, both African in appearance, hovered close by to act as human shopping baskets if required.

Their reunion the day before had been emotional for Silus. Children change a lot in two years, and Avitus, now around ten years old, had lost some of the puppy fat around his waist and cheeks, and grown a few inches. Silus had realised with a pang that his own daughter, Sergia, would be nearly the same age as Avitus, if she had lived.

Avitus for his part had been delighted to see Silus. He had recognised him straight away – Silus obviously hadn't changed as much as Marcellus had implied, although maybe the bath and fresh clothes helped – and had rushed over to hug him around his waist as soon as he set eyes on him. His mother Soaemias had been more reserved. Their previous encounters had been strained, to say the least. Nevertheless, his actions in concealing her plot from her husband had spared her life, and she was grateful for it. Many times since, he had wondered if he had done the right thing, allowing Soaemias to go on living unpunished, hopeful that she was truly repentant and would no longer be a danger to her son – rather than denounce her, see her executed, and her son deprived of the mother he adored, and who clearly adored him.

Watching the two of them together now, browsing jewellery stores, holding up earrings against each other's lobes, trying on necklaces, smiling and giggling together, vindicated his decision, he felt. In fact, he was warmed and comforted by their easy companionship and love for each other. He had caused many bad things to happen in his life, by action or inaction. Surely saving Avitus' life and sparing his mother would help give some weight to the other side of the scales when he came to be judged.

Still, he had a job to do, and he remained fully alert, even as he took vicarious pleasure in their relationship. Over there was a youth with buck teeth and spots, lounging against a statue of Dea Africa, the Romano-African goddess, without the invocation of whom it was said that Numidians would do nothing. The boy was watching Avitus a little too closely, and it made the hair on the back of Silus' neck prickle. But then the lad was distracted by a cat rubbing against his legs. He picked up the mangy creature and wandered off, stroking it between the ears.

Two large, dark-skinned women, plump in breast, belly and backside, one carrying a basket of laundry, the other two loaves of bread and some eggs, gossiped loudly, but one of them seemed to keep one eye always on Avitus. Silus stepped near to his wards and said in a low voice, 'Maybe it is time to move on.'

'Really, Silus,' said Soaemias. 'What danger can there be to us here on a crowded street in broad daylight?'

Silus raised an eyebrow, and Soaemias had the good grace to look abashed. After all, she had engineered the kidnapping of her own son in a similar situation in Syracuse.

Avitus squeezed his mother's hand. 'If Silus says we should go, then we should listen.'

'Of course, darling. Do you want to visit any other stalls in the market?'

'No, I think we should return to the palace. It is nearly time for prayers to the Lord Elagabal and I need to prepare for the service.'

So Avitus was continuing his role as priest of the Syrian god? Silus wasn't sure how he felt about that. Fanaticism about Elagabal was what had caused all the trouble in Alexandria. But it was clearly important to the child, maybe even central to his identity, so he kept his thoughts to himself.

As they walked back towards the crossroads where they had left their litter, Silus saw a familiar face, framed by tufts of white hair sticking out above his ears.

'Adonibaal,' Silus called out. The captain of the *Minerva* turned from the merchant with whom he had been involved in a heated negotiation.

'Silus. Enjoying Cirta? I hope your mission was successful?'

'So far. You haven't set sail yet?'

'No,' Adonibaal said emphatically. 'We will be in port for some time. The ship needs extensive repairs, the crew and rowers need time to recover from their efforts, and we currently have no urgent missions.'

'I might need passage home soon. With some important people. A slow, safe route this time.'

'When do you need to depart?'

'Later than I would like. A few days.'

Adonibaal considered it. 'At a push we could have the boat and crew ready in three days.'

'That would be ideal. Consider yourself requisitioned. Emperor's business.'

'Very well. But please, can this journey be less eventful than the last?'

'That is in the hands of the gods.'

Adonibaal gave a pained half-smile. 'Sailors know that better than anyone. By the way, I made a report of what happened on board to the port officials. I take it you informed your superiors too?'

'I told the governor, yes.'

Adonibaal raised his bushy eyebrows. 'You have friends in high places, I see. Will it be the governor joining us for our little cruise?'

'I can't tell you that, not yet.'

'Did you show the poison to an apothecary? I would be interested to know what was the nature of those herbs.'

'What do you mean? I don't have the poison.'

Adonibaal's mouth twisted in confusion. 'Well, it wasn't on board after you had disembarked.'

'Did Khnum-Aa and her slave consume it all?'

'Surely there was way too much of it for them to have finished it off. Besides, the bag the herbs were in was gone too.'

Silus ran his hand through his hair. 'Calev went into the cabin alone, didn't he? I think I had better find out if he knows what happened to that stuff. It's a bit dangerous to have it out there somewhere. Someone might put it in a stew by mistake.'

'Silus!' called out Soaemias, who was inside the litter with Avitus now. 'Are you going to accompany us home, or are you going to hang around on the street gossiping like an old woman?'

Silus gave Adonibaal an apologetic look. 'Duty calls.'

Adonibaal glanced across at Soaemias. 'Rather beautiful duty, though.'

'Keep those thoughts to yourself. That's the governor's wife! I'll see you in three days at the docks.'

–

The under-procurator for the water supply of the city of Cirta was a man in his fifties, balding at the temples, with a drooping mouth that gave him a perpetually melancholy air. Silus was shown into his presence by a disrespectfully informal slave, but the under-procurator seemed too harassed to reprimand or even notice. Silus had slept soundly the night before, despite all the troubling thoughts circulating inside his head. By the time he had dropped Avitus and Soaemias at the palace, and reported to an anxious Marcellus, the sun was low in the cloudless sky. The slave had tried to tell Silus they were closing, but Silus would not be put off.

'Visitor for you, boss,' said the slave, and wandered off. Silus looked around the under-procurator's tablinum. It was utilitarian in decor, whitewashed walls devoid of frescoes or tapestries, a bust of the Emperor in one corner the only item that wasn't purely functional. A large map was unrolled on the table in the centre of the room. Although upside down from Silus' viewpoint, he could see it illustrated the aqueducts, baths and largest fountains of the city. Various points were marked and annotated, and Silus presumed these were areas where repairs or upgrades were required.

'Yes, what is it?'

'I'm centurion Gaius Sergius Silus,' said Silus. 'Sorry, your name is…?'

'Gnaeus Cluntius. What do you want? I am rather busy.'

'I won't take up much of your time. I just need to see your new assistant.'

'My who?'

'Your new assistant. He just arrived from Rome. Calev. Little Jewish fellow?'

'An assistant. Pah. As if.'

'I'm sorry?'

'Look, Numidia is a hot, dry province. Water isn't just a luxury for bathing and washing here. It's about survival. The aqueducts keep the livestock that feed us and transport us alive. They irrigate the fruit gardens. They are where we get the very water we drink. And if they fall into disrepair, it would be disastrous. But do I get the respect my office deserves? Of course not. All the glory goes to the governor's staff, or the officials responsible for games and festivals. Not the likes of me, who keep the city alive.'

'I understand what you do is important, but…'

'And how many times have I petitioned for extra help? I sit in this office from daybreak to sundown, trying to organise the slave gangs working on the repairs, the supplies of bricks and tiles and cement, the lead for the pipes. But do they send anyone? Of course not. Cluntius, you're doing a great job, they say. Keep it up. Of course we will try to get you an assistant, but funds are tight this year.'

'So you're saying…'

'I'm saying that I have no assistant, and you asking after one rather rubs that in my face.'

'And there is no Calev working in this office. In any capacity?'

'No. He must work in a different department. Have you tried the under-procurator for sewers and drainage?'

'He was very clear, he was due to report here.'

'Then you have been misled, young man. Now if you will excuse me. The piping to the fountain of Saturn has burst, and there is a new river running down the Via Severa.'

Silus bowed his head, then hurried back to the governor's palace, a feeling of anxiety growing in the pit of his stomach.

-

The palace guards admitted Silus straight away, now he was officially on the governor's staff. His mind was whirling, turning over the facts, not liking where they were leading him. The poison was missing. Calev was the last one to have access to it. Calev had lied about his job.

He broke into a run, heading straight for the kitchens, and found the head chef. He grabbed him by the collar of his tunic, making the refined Greek cry out in indignation.

'Have you served the evening meal yet?' Silus demanded.

'Take your hands off me, you thug.'

Silus grasped the chef's chin and squeezed, forcing the man to look directly into Silus' flashing eyes.

'Answer me right now or I will start breaking you.'

The chef's superior, defiant air disappeared like a pricked bladder.

'The cena is still being prepared. The governor is entertaining some local dignitaries tonight, so the meal will be more elaborate than usual.'

Now he had the man's cooperation, he released his grip. 'What are you preparing?'

The chef looked defensive now. 'The governor has simple tastes. He would not allow me to use the full range of my skills. Nevertheless, I think the repast I am preparing will be pleasing.'

'Go on.'

'Well there will be a course of figs stuffed with flamingo liver. Then there will be some goat's cheese drizzled in royal jelly. The main course will be fresh-caught turbot served with artichokes and olives, and drenched with my special fish sauce.'

'What's in the sauce?'

Recovering some of his previous haughtiness, the chef said defensively, 'It's a secret family recipe, passed to me by my father, and his father before him.'

'Do I look like I am planning to set up in business against you? Just show me the sauce.'

The chef presented Silus with a large pot full of a creamy liquid. Silus sniffed hard, conscious that his cold might dim his ability to detect subtle odours. Still, he could detect onion, garlic and other herbs he couldn't identify. There was no hint of the bitterness of the poisonous roots and leaves he had encountered on the *Minerva*.

But could it have been hidden by the other flavours? The poison hadn't been obvious when he had consumed it in the remains of Volcula's meal.

'No food is to be served until it has been tasted by you personally. I take it your palate is refined enough to detect any ingredients that shouldn't be there.'

'Naturally,' said the chef. 'But what is this about? Is there some danger? Should I ask one of the serving slaves to taste the food? After all, the governor wouldn't want to risk a valuable asset like myself.'

'Do as you are told. And if the governor or anyone else is poisoned by your food, you will be tortured and executed. That should be enough incentive for you.'

The chef paled. 'Of course. It shall be done.'

'Good. One more thing. Have you had any new staff in the last couple of days? New slaves in the kitchen?'

'There is one. One of my pot-stirrers was taken ill, and I was able to arrange a temporary replacement from a slaving company with headquarters in the forum.'

'Bring this new slave to me now.'

'Well, she is right here.'

The chef indicated a tall, thin, black woman, who looked over at Silus, puzzled at being singled out.

'Not her. There is no one else? I'm looking for a Jewish man called Calev, though he might not have used that name.'

'I think I know my kitchen staff. There is nobody...'

'Master,' said a lad holding a vegetable knife, his apron stained green. 'I'm sorry to interrupt but I couldn't help overhearing.'

'How many times must I tell you that you are only to speak when you are spoken to?' said the chef, raising a hand to strike the boy.

'Wait,' said Silus. 'What were you going to say, boy?'

'There is that new wine-server. He just arrived today. Said he had just been purchased by the governor's wife.'

'What did he look like?' asked Silus sharply.

'Short, skinny. Kept his head down a lot, like he didn't want anyone looking at him.'

'Oh, by Saturn's balls,' Silus said in a whisper. 'Where is the governor now?'

'I believe he is in the triclinium, receiving his guests.'

Silus set off at a headlong run, shoving palace civil servants and attendant slaves aside as he rushed to the dining room. He burst through the double doors to find Marcellus reclining on the head couch, Soaemias by his right side, Gannys on his left. Two other couches were occupied by togate men, each accompanied by a finely dressed wife or mistress. All eyes turned to him as he made his dramatic entrance.

Marcellus was holding a silver cup to his lips, and frozen in the act of drinking.

'Silus, what is the meaning…'

Silus hurdled the nearest couch, his trailing foot kicking a grey-haired woman in the head, lunged for Marcellus, and knocked the cup from his hands. It crashed down with a clatter. A tiny amount of wine trickled from it onto the mosaic floor.

'Silus, have you gone mad?' gasped Marcellus.

Silus knelt down, heart sinking. So little liquid had split. That meant…

He dipped his finger into the wine from the floor, dabbed it onto his tongue. Even that small amount tasted incredibly bitter, the flavour identical to the odours he had smelt from that bag of poison he had encountered aboard the *Minerva*. He looked up at Marcellus.

'How much did you drink?' he asked, fearing he knew the answer.

'Almost a cupful, until you dashed the last sip from my lips.'

'Didn't you taste how bitter it was?'

'The slave boy said it was flavoured with special herbs, that it was an acquired taste, but one worth persisting with.'

Silus stared, aghast at the governor's stupidity. He looked to Soaemias, who had realised exactly what was going on. She put a hand on her husband's arm, and despite her past behaviour Silus could see there was genuine affection there, as her eyes filled with tears.

'Silus, what's going on?'

Silus shook his head sadly, unable to find the words, to break the news. Soaemias was more proactive. She summoned a slave boy and sent him to fetch a physician at the run. She ordered everyone present to put down their cups, and sent a guard to bring the palace centurion to her immediately.

Realisation had dawned on Marcellus, and he looked from Silus to the dented cup on the floor and back again.

'How... how long do I have?'

'The physician will have a cure,' said Silus weakly, not believing it.

'And if he doesn't? How long?'

'It depends how much you consumed. I think there was a lot. So, maybe an hour or two.'

Marcellus nodded. He looked around at his guests. 'Did anyone else drink the same wine?'

One of the men raised his hand hesitantly, and the young wife of one of the other dignitaries gasped and put her hand to her mouth.

'Let us all wait for the physician,' said Marcellus calmly.

The centurion arrived, red-faced and out of breath.

'Centurion, guard every exit from the palace. No one is to leave, and no one is to enter except the physician. Start a room-by-room search for anyone who you don't recognise, and have them brought to me.'

'When did you last see him?' Silus asked Marcellus.

'Not many moments ago. He hovered near me for a while, asking if the wine was to my liking, whether I wanted any more. I guess he was waiting to see if I drank it.'

'He may not have got far,' said Soaemias. 'Silus, you can do no more here. Find him.'

Silus nodded, bowed his head to Marcellus, and then raced out.

The palace was already in commotion, slaves and servants shouting questions, guards rushing about, tearing open doors and ripping apart curtains. Four guards stood at attention at the palace entrance.

Silus took a moment to gather his thoughts. If Calev was still inside the palace, the guards would find him quickly. He would have had to flee as soon as he was sure the job was done. But he wouldn't be able to escape through the heavily guarded front gates. There were no windows within the palace that viewed the outside. That meant his most likely escape was through the gardens and over the wall.

Silus put his head down and sprinted to the rear of the palace. He hadn't explored the grounds fully, and twice he took a wrong turn into a blind corridor and had to ask for directions from startled and panicky servants. But quickly he found the garden doors, and burst into the daylight.

The gardens were too extensive to be called a peristylium, extending for a couple of hundred yards to the rear of the palace. The nearest area sported a colonnaded walkway with mosaics, ornately topiaried shrubs and fragrant flower beds. Further, the garden was bounded on three sides by a ten-foot wall, lined with brightly painted statues of gods and animals, the style more pastoral, with small fruit trees and naturally shaped bushes. The furthest boundary consisted of a thorn hedge against a low wall.

Silus' eyes adjusted to the light – though it was late afternoon, it was still brighter outside than in. He squinted around, then in his peripheral vision caught the movement of a small figure halfway down the garden, walking swiftly with head bowed. Silus broke into a run, trying to keep quiet so he didn't alert his quarry. But the man heard the footsteps on the mosaic tiles. He turned, and instantly seeing he was discovered, sprinted towards the hedge.

Silus broke into a run. He didn't waste breath shouting at him. When had that ever stopped anyone? The figure – Silus could clearly tell now from the man's build that it was Calev – charged straight into the thorn bush. Barely slowing, he forced his way through to the wall behind, leapt and dragged himself over.

Silus' lips moved in a silent curse, and moments later, he plunged into the bush himself. Sharp thorns torn his clothes and his skin, raking his flesh like an angry wild cat. He pressed his palms to his face, and deep gouges opened up on the backs of his hands. Better there than his cheeks and eyes, he consoled himself.

Then he was through, and up against the low wall. He jumped, grabbed the top with both hands and winced as he realised the top was lined with jagged, flinty rocks to deter intruders. He held on and swung a leg up, hooking his foot over to enable him to lever himself upwards. His tunic sprung more holes as he rolled over the sharp boundary and the jags scored more bloody lines along his belly. He hit the ground on the other side of the wall with his skin on fire.

He was in a broad street running along the back of the palace, mainly residential. Judging from the architecture, it was an affluent area. No crumbling, teetering insulae here like in the poor parts of Rome, not the scaffold-covered wooden structures you found in the slums of the provincial cities. These houses sported fluted columns, bronze gates, marble statues painted bright reds and yellows and blues. Growling dogs chained near the doorways and tough-looking porters guarded the properties. They were no safe haven for a fugitive.

Sure enough, Silus quickly spotted Calev charging down the street towards the more crowded city centre. Silus set off in pursuit.

Cirta was a sizeable provincial capital, but it was no Rome when it came to population density. Streets that in the eternal city would be packed shoulder to shoulder, slaves and the urban poor jostling with the bodyguards of senators trying to clear a path for their charges, were here more sparsely sprinkled with men, women and children on their business. He ran past a group of children sitting cross-legged around their tutor, who goggled at him, styli held loosely in their hands, wax tablets forgotten in their laps. He rounded a corner and had to swerve to avoid the front pair of slaves sweating under the effort of bearing a corpulent man draped in silk and gold. He hurdled a mangy dog that shot out from under the stall of a spice seller in pursuit of a squealing piglet.

Calev was fast. He was light-framed and could accelerate and dodge with more alacrity than Silus. His leaner build would probably give him an edge in endurance over Silus too. But Silus' superior musculature meant that he could outsprint the little poisoner. So the gap between them shortened and lengthened with the character of the environment, Calev extending his lead where it was busier and the streets were windier, Silus closing when he could get his head down and make a straight run.

But overall, Calev would have outpaced Silus before long, had he not made a mistake. Glancing back to check the distance from his pursuer, Calev failed to spot a particularly deep pothole in the paving. He pitched forward, throwing his hands out to break his fall. He even managed an impressive shoulder roll, allowing him to spring straight to his feet. But as he set off again, his forward momentum barely impeded, Silus saw that he was limping, and realised that he had twisted his ankle. He quickly gained on his quarry, and Calev clearly knew that he would soon be caught.

To their right was a large theatre, multiple stone arches leading inside. Calev darted in one of the entrances, straight past the startled merchandise sellers, and pushed his way through the latecomers to the show. Silus shoved and jostled his way in, chasing Calev down the corridor between the semi-circular stepped stone seating, and straight out into the pit before the stage.

Some sort of pantomime or musical comedy was being performed. The stage held a dozen performers, a chorus of singers, pipers and cymbal players, two half-naked dancing girls and two male actors prominent at the front, one dressed as a large-busted matron, a hefty iron pot held threateningly in one hand, the other on his knees, hands clasped, apparently playing her wayward son. The raucous laughter from the crowd died as Calev desperately mounted the stage, looking for a way out, and the actors and entertainers stared in disbelief at the interruption.

Foot dragging now, Calev headed towards the exit in the wings, but before he could get halfway across the stage, Silus was on him, barrelling into his back, bundling him to the wooden floorboards.

Calev twisted beneath him, struck out, extended fingers seeking Silus' eyes. Silus turned his head just in time, taking the impact painfully but harmlessly on his cheekbone. He grappled for Calev's wrists, sitting astride the small man, pinning him down with his greater weight. Killing him would be easier, but Silus wanted to know who had sent Calev on his deadly mission. To find out who was really responsible for what would surely turn out to be the murder of Marcellus.

The crowd, who had initially been silenced, started to cheer and boo. They seemed careless as to whether this was part of the scheduled show or an unexpected bonus, but enjoyed the spectacle of the two wrestling men for whatever entertainment it provided.

Calev bucked and struggled, fighting like a cornered wild cat, and Silus boxed him hard in the side of the head in an attempt to subdue him. The blow had little effect, and as Silus reached again to pinion his wrists, Calev sank his teeth into Silus' forearm, making him yell out. The crowd cheered and clapped.

Pain and anger threatened to overwhelm Silus, and he reached for Calev's neck, gripping it with both hands and squeezing hard. Calev grasped Silus' arms, trying to prise them apart, to ease the pressure choking off the blood to his brain. Silus was far stronger than him, though, and

Calev's face turned red, his eyes bulging, spittle on his lips. At that moment, Silus wasn't sure he could stop himself from killing him.

Something heavy thumped into the side of his head with a metallic clang, knocking him sideways from Calev. Silus looked up into the furious face of the big-bosomed actor, who was holding the iron pot with which he had previously been menacing his fictional son, and with which he had just clubbed Silus.

'Nobody upstages me!' yelled the actor, his booming voice projecting all the way to the back of the theatre. 'That was my big scene!' The audience hooted with laughter, and missiles of soft fruit and vegetables pelted the stage. Silus held up his hands to protect himself in case of another blow, and from the corner of his eye, saw Calev struggle to his feet.

'No,' said Silus, trying to focus despite the loud ringing in his ears, and the stars darting in front of his eyes. 'You don't understand…'

'I'll have you whipped through the streets for this, you… you fiend!'

'He's getting away.'

Silus tried to prop himself up on one elbow, but sunk back when the actor lifted the pot high, threatening to bring it down hard again. Calev limped off towards the wings to cheers from the crowd. He turned and saluted Silus, then gave a deep bow to the audience, whose cheers echoed around the theatre as they applauded the victor of the unscripted tussle. Calev winked at Silus, then disappeared.

Dizziness and nausea overwhelmed Silus. He turned his head and vomited on the actor's sandals.

Chapter VII

The cremation of Sextus Varius Marcellus took place in the ustrinum, the part of the cemetery set apart specifically for that purpose. He lay on a plush, upholstered couch, arms by his side, atop the pile of oil-soaked wood that was ready to be lit. The funeral itself was a strange hybrid affair. Marcellus was not a devout adherent of the religion of his wife and son, the cult of Syrian mountain god Elagabal, but he had certainly paid lip service to the worship, to keep his home life peaceful if for no other reason. He had also been an important Roman statesman, with all the tradition, ceremony and worship of the official Roman pantheon that that entailed. So representing the eastern religion was the young Avitus, dressed in his ceremonial priestly robes, with attendant flautists and lyre players and dancing slave girls and boys, not to mention the strange, black, conical rock, a facsimile of the original which represented the centre of worship of Elagabal in the god's home town of Emesa. Representing the western, Roman religion was a stern-faced priest of Apollo, who looked sideways at the eastern representatives with evident disapproval. Two legionaries from the Third Augusta, their uniforms and arms polished to perfection, stood at stiff attention, both guards and representatives of the military arm of Rome in which Marcellus had been highly ranked.

The priest stepped forward and gave a loud, short prayer to Apollo, Jupiter, the deified Emperors and a few others for good measure, then expertly dispatched a bullock as a sacrifice, felling it with a hammer blow between the eyes before cutting its throat. His part of the ceremony completed, he retreated to the furthest part of the funeral party, where he could glower at the rest.

Avitus knelt before his father's pyre, while Soaemias, supported by Gannys, wept and cried aloud, tearing her dark dress. The young priest intoned a prayer to Elagabal, and anointed the pyre with incense and other perfumes. Silus admired his composure. So mature for one so young. So dedicated to his calling, even when it was his own murdered father whose funeral he was conducting.

The crowd of onlookers comprised professional mourners – those paid to weep and tear their hair and gnash their teeth and cry out to the gods, the familia of Marcellus, and a large number of curious locals, interested in seeing the final passage of an important man, and hopeful that there would be entertainment and maybe even some gifts handed out. The familia was smaller than would usually be expected for such an important man, but that was because he was far from Rome. Of immediate family, there was only Soaemias and Avitus. Avitus had had a younger brother, who they maintained was with them in spirit, but he had died, like so many Roman infants, at a tender age. The familia of course comprised the whole household of the father of the house, so there were many slaves and other servants present, some looking genuinely grief-stricken. The chef that Silus had threatened was at the forefront, crying out that it should have been him taken, not Marcellus, and while Silus privately agreed with him on that, he didn't think

Soaemias would actually take any steps to punish the chef. It wasn't really his fault that the wine had been adulterated.

Silus had returned from his unsuccessful pursuit of Calev to find Marcellus in the advanced stages of intoxication. The others who had drunk the poisoned wine were already dead. Despite Marcellus appearing to be in great pain, and on the verge of being taken by convulsions, he had summoned Silus to his side, and dismissed his distraught wife and son.

'Silus,' he whispered with an effort. 'Thank you for your efforts. For me, and my family. Now and in the past.'

'It was my simple duty,' said Silus solemnly. 'I am so sorry I failed you.'

'No,' said Marcellus, then arched his back as some spasm took him. He breathed heavily, tears running from the corners of his eyes, then swallowed and managed to speak again.

'Not failure. My wife and son are still alive.' He looked straight into Silus' eyes. 'You must believe me a very naive fool, Silus.'

'What? No, of course not.'

'Don't lie to a dying man. Well, maybe I am a fool. But not a naive one. I know about the relationship between my wife and Gannys. And I know that Avitus is probably not my son.'

'Governor…'

'Don't protest. Time is too short. You knew it, didn't you? You know who his father is?'

Silus hesitated, then nodded.

'The thing is, Silus, I love him, like he was my very own. Just as much as his poor departed brother, who I think really was mine. And I love Soaemias too. It's why I have tolerated so much from her. Tell me one thing, though. All this…' He waved a hand over his stricken body. 'It wasn't her, was it?'

'No, governor. The plot originated in Rome, I'm sure of it.'

Marcellus seemed to relax. He lay back, closed his eyes, and his breathing slowed. Silus wondered if this was the end, and whether he should call Soaemias and Avitus back. Then Marcellus clutched his hand, and lifted his head.

'Care for them, Silus. Now that I won't be able to do it myself. Protect them. Swear it.'

What could Silus do? Turn down a dying man's request? Besides, he had already been ordered to look out for Avitus by Caracalla himself.

'Of course. I swear.'

Then Soaemias and Avitus, unable to keep away any longer, had returned, and kept vigil over Marcellus for the short time until he breathed his last.

Now, the brave young boy faced the gathering, and opened his mouth to address them. Young as he was, he had demanded the right to the funeral oration, refusing to allow his mother, or a priest or professional, to take over as substitute.

His voice was high-pitched, and it wavered with his grief, but it rang out so those at the back of the gathering could hear every word.

'Sextus Varius Marcellus was a true Roman. He served the Emperor and the people and Senate of Rome with loyalty, devotion and unstinting hard work. In his time, he held the posts of procurator centenarius of the water supply, procurator ducenarius of Britain, procurator trecenarius of the private purse, a praetorian prefect, urban prefect, senator, prefect of the military treasury, commander of the Third Legion Augusta and finally Governor of Numidia.'

Either the boy had an amazing memory, or he had followed his father's career closely, thought Silus. Or maybe he had just practiced his speech assiduously. Any of the possibilities were worth admiring. Silus listened attentively as Avitus continued.

'But more than this. He was a loving father. Strict when he needed to be, kind when he could be. And he was a loving husband. My mother could not have wished for better.'

Silus glanced at where Soaemias was clutching the arm of Gannys, her paramour. He wondered whether Avitus knew of their relationship. He wouldn't be surprised if his mother had told him, and persuaded him that it was moral and acceptable in the eyes of Elagabal. Marcellus was the only one in that family who had been even slightly normal.

'And now, he ascends the mountain, on the path that all the devoted will one day tread. Up to the peak, to gaze on the face of the Lord Elagabal. And our Lord will receive him with open arms, and keep him safe, until the day I join him.'

Avitus broke off abruptly, as if his throat had been closed by a powerful fist. He seemed to be struggling for breath, and for a terrible moment, Silus thought he was showing the delayed effects of some new toxin. But then Avitus took a deep, choking gasp, leant forward and started to weep.

Silus looked around to see who would support the grieving child. But Soaemias, fully occupied by her own dramatic public display of grief, at least some of which he thought was unfeigned, made no move, not even seeming to notice that the eulogy had ceased. The rest of the mourners looked at each other uneasily, not knowing what to do. A priest should not behave like this, but a priest would not usually be delivering his own father's eulogy. Nor was it usual that such a young boy should give the oration at the funeral of his father. It was acceptable for a Roman man to show his distress at the passing of a beloved relative, but he would not expect to be shown pity or mercy, and his period of mourning would be short, lest he be accused of being unmanly.

So Avitus stood, bent at the waist, arms folded in front of his belly, bawling like a baby, tears and snot dripping from his face, alone.

Silus, just a few paces away, cursed and stepped forward. He put his arm around the young priest, and hugged him gently, letting him cry into his chest. He patted his head awkwardly, then realised that the mourners were all looking at him expectantly. Oh no. Surely they didn't want him to…

'Thank you, Silus,' whispered Avitus through his tears. 'Father could have no one braver to speak for him.'

Brave? Silus stared at the faces turned towards him. Still, patient, for now. Suddenly his heart accelerated, thumping in his chest like the hind legs of a startled rabbit. He opened his mouth to speak, and found that not only could he not find words, he could not even formulate thoughts. A sweat broke out on his forehead, and the hairs on the back of his neck prickled. He took a deep breath, then another, though the air seemed thin and insufficient. The mourners shuffled their feet and gave each other sideways glances.

'Marcellus was a Roman,' he said, and his voice sounded to his own ears thin and tremulous. 'A good

Roman.' *Jupiter, Mithras, Elagabal and Christos, get me out of this.*

He couldn't believe the drivel coming out of his mouth, but the mourners were nodding agreement to his words. 'He served. He lived… well.' He was feeling dizzy now, and had the sudden certainty that he was about to pass out. Every instinct was telling him to turn around, to run, to an extent he never felt even in battle. This was like when the cold sea waters had closed over his head and choked off the air. He had to get this over with.

'He was a good friend to… people. He was a good father and husband.' A moment of inspiration as something in his brain clicked. 'He was someone we would all be proud to be.'

The mourners cheered and clapped. Relief washed over Silus. It was over. It hadn't killed him, though he wasn't sure how he had survived. Avitus hugged him tightly, then turned back to the crowd. He had recovered his composure, though he was still sniffing and rubbing his eyes with little balled fists.

'As my friend Silus says,' said Avitus, 'he was someone we would all be proud to be. And now, we must bid him farewell.'

He nodded to one of the attendant slaves, who stepped forward holding a lit torch. Avitus took it, and thrust it deep into the kindling at the base of the pyre. The oil and dry wood quickly took, sizzling and crackling. Perfumes soaked into the wood heated and evaporated, a sickly-sweet smell combining with the odour of the woodsmoke. Avitus stared into the flames, apparently enchanted by the flickering orange shapes that danced across and between the logs. The temperature built to an uncomfortable intensity, and Silus wanted to move back, but Avitus remained, seemingly oblivious to the fierce heat. Silus wondered for a wild moment whether he was preparing to throw himself onto the pyre and immolate himself with his father. He tensed, ready to grab the boy.

But Avitus, with one final glance at the peak of the pyre, where his father's body was being shrouded in smoke and flame, stepped away, and moved back to his mother.

The mourners watched in respectful silence as the body was consumed. Silus whispered a quiet prayer to Marcellus' ancestors, the words consumed by the crackling and spitting from the fire.

The mourners started to drift away. Silus stood on Avitus' right side, one arm around his shoulder. It likely broke with tradition, Roman and Syrian, but Silus didn't care – though he was rapidly growing up, Avitus was still a young boy in Silus' eyes, a young boy who had just lost his father, and needed a hug. Soaemias stood on Avitus' other side, but she seemed lost in her own misery, no doubt uncertain as to her future without her important husband, and she leant heavily against Gannys who was on her left.

The fire burned down, the wood and Marcellus' earthly remains mingling into a coarse ash that glowed orange. The mourners had now almost all gone, with only Silus, Marcellus' household, the priest of Apollo and the two legionaries remaining. Silus' feet were starting to throb from the long period of standing, and for all the sadness and solemnity of the occasion he was thirsty and hot. He hoped Avitus and Soaemias would want to leave soon, but he wouldn't prompt their departure. They could take as long as they liked.

The priest was more impatient. He had already been clearing his throat for some time, and now he stepped forward, and with a tone that dripped with insincerity, he asked, 'May I collect the ashes for their return to Rome now?'

Soaemias looked like she was about to make an angry retort, but Avitus laid a hand on her forearm, and nodded to the priest. 'We will do this together.'

The priest looked ready to protest, but presumably realising that would only lengthen the ceremony, agreed. He produced a small silver trowel, and the two priests of the two vastly different religions, kneeling before the still smouldering embers, took turns scooping the ash into a beautifully painted earthenware pot. Silus glanced sideways. Soaemias eyes were cast down, and Gannys was focussed on her. Silus returned his attention to Avitus, wondering if Gannys would now become his father figure, and if that was a good thing or not.

There was a strange grunt from behind Silus, then the sound of something falling. He whirled, senses coming to full alertness, understanding something was wrong before he could even consciously work out what.

One of the legionaries was pulling his bloodied sword out of the chest of his comrade, who lay prone in the dirt, blood pouring from his open mouth. Without pausing, weapon to the fore, the legionary lunged for Avitus.

He was quick, but Silus was quicker. With no time to draw his own sword, he leapt, arms outstretched, and grabbed the legionary around the chest. His momentum knocked the soldier over backwards, and his sword flew free from his hand. With the man beneath him taken by surprise and momentarily stunned, Silus managed to land two solid punches in the middle of his face, bone and cartilage breaking beneath his fist with a satisfying crunch.

Then the soldier bucked and twisted, throwing Silus to one side.

Silus rolled, coming swiftly to his feet. The soldier levered himself up, but the stunning blows from Silus and his heavy armour slowed him. His mail shirt would help protect against a knife thrust, but it was no help when Silus leapt and kicked him with two feet in the centre of his torso. The legionary went down again like he had been hit by a charging bull. Before the felled legionary could move, Silus stamped down hard on his head. He felt the bones of the skull crack. The legionary's eyes rolled into his head, and blood mixed with a clear fluid leaked from his ears and nose.

Silus put his hands on his knees and panted heavily, regaining his breath. He admonished himself for finishing off the legionary, allowing no chance for questioning, but his self-flagellation wasn't too severe. He worked on the principle of safety first. Make sure the immediate threat was eliminated, then see what benefit could be accrued from what remained. Well, the threat was gone, but there was no benefit to be gained from the dead soldier. It probably didn't matter; he doubted the lowly killer knew much.

He looked around. Gannys had his arm around Soaemias protectively. Avitus stood with his back to the pyre, still as a statue. Beside him the priest was trembling, the sudden, unexpected brutality so shocking and out of his experience. The average citizen of the Empire was inured to violence at a distance, whether it was executions, gladiatorial displays or the carnage of a chariot race. But the only blood this priest encountered close up was from the animals he sacrificed in his duties.

Silus paid the priest no more attention, and went first to Avitus. He bent his knees so he was at eye level with the boy, put one hand on each of the lad's shoulders and looked with consternation into his eyes.

'Are you hurt?'

Avitus swallowed, seemed to genuinely consider the question, then shook his head.

'You're safe. I won't let anyone hurt you.'

He just couldn't stop himself making these impossible promises, could he? He turned to Soaemias and Gannys. Soaemias' face was pale and Gannys' jaw set; his mouth was a thin line.

'You're both well?' asked Silus, more brusquely than he intended. Maybe he was irritated with them for their inactivity when Avitus was in danger. But Soaemias redeemed herself, at least partially in his eyes, by rushing over to Avitus and wrapping her arms around him and hugging him tight. Silus scanned the surroundings. There was no one else nearby. He strode over to the priest.

'Get your ceremonies finished, and the ashes collected. You have until the time it takes to count to a hundred, then we are leaving.' He approached Avitus, more considerately. 'It's time to say your goodbyes, little friend. Don't worry, the ashes will come with us to Rome.'

'We're going to Rome?'

'Yes, we are. It's the best place to keep you safe.'

At least, it was the only place he could think of off the top of his head. And Silus needed to get back to Rome to report the murder of Marcellus, and he wanted Avitus by his side until he was someone else's responsibility.

He rested his hand on the hilt of his sword and scanned the surrounding terrain, checking for any movement from behind the tombs that crowded the cemetery. In the distance some slaves were unloading a funerary stele from a wooden cart, cursing as the slave holding the ropes slipped and the solid stone crashed into the dirt and toppled over. In a different direction, an old man was on his knees, pouring libations of wine and milk onto a grave, while a young boy, presumably his son, played with a cat that was rubbing around his shins. Nothing threatening, but the attack out of the blue had unsettled him, and he shifted from foot to foot, chewing his cheek as the priest went around his final duties with as much sense of urgency as a kitchen slave who knows when he has finished cleaning the pots, he must start sweeping the floors. Eventually, Silus' patience ran out.

'Time's up,' he said, and grabbed the priest by the collar of his tunic, hauling him to his feet. 'Let's go.' The priest yelped, grabbed his incense burner and sacrificial knife, then allowed himself to be marched back to where Avitus, Soaemias and Gannys were waiting.

'What now?' asked Gannys.

'Now we get out of Africa as soon as possible.'

–

Adonibaal watched open-mouthed as the slaves went up and down the gangplank of the *Minerva*, carrying statues, urns, chests of drawers and dining tables. Silus smirked as the captain confronted the steward who was organising the loading of the household possessions. The steward waved his hands around animatedly, while Adonibaal pointed to various items and artefacts, shaking his head emphatically. Behind him, Gannys helped Soaemias out of the carriage that had conveyed them from Cirta to the port, followed by Avitus who leapt down on his own.

It was hard to be sure there were no threats around on a busy dock, and despite his brief amusement at Adonibaal's exasperation, his nerves felt on edge, and he jumped at every noise – a dropped amphora, a barking dog, the cry of a carpenter hitting his thumb with his hammer. But the loading continued without any more conflict than that between the captain trying to keep the ship afloat and the steward refusing to leave anything of value behind. The last thing on board was a large chest, balanced on two poles and carried by two porters who were sweating and swearing at the weight. Silus idly wondered what essential items the steward had loaded in there. Maybe the brickwork from the hypocaust that supplied the underfloor heating to the governor's mansion, judging by how much the slaves were struggling.

At last the ship was loaded and household slaves, crew and rowers were on board. Under Silus' watchful eye, Gannys, Soaemias and Avitus ascended the gangplank, Avitus holding the delicately carved marble funerary urn into which his father's mortal remains had been transferred. The centurion of the palace guard had accompanied them from the palace, and he now stepped forward towards the gangplank. Silus stood in front of him and put a hand out. The centurion frowned.

'What are you doing?' he asked, more puzzled than irritated.

'You're not coming,' said Silus.

'What are you talking about? Get out of my way.'

Silus stood his ground. 'Centurion, I am taking responsibility for Avitus' well-being on this voyage. And after what happened at the funeral, I judge that it is safer that we don't have your men on board.'

The centurion's jaw dropped in disbelief. 'But... but...'

'Centurion, do you have absolute confidence in the loyalty of your men?'

'Of course I do,' he said, turning red.

'And did you have absolute confidence in your men at the funeral yesterday?'

'Yes, I… well, no…'

The centurion was damned whatever his reply. If he said no, then he was negligent for allowing them to be close to the governor's family; if he said yes, then he was incompetent for not knowing his man had been corrupted. But Silus was not out to condemn him, he knew it really wasn't the centurion's fault. Money, blackmail, threats, few were fully immune to them, and it was easy to find one man in a group who was susceptible to one of those ways of compelling them.

'Look,' said Silus, 'I'm not blaming you. But whoever is behind all this has a long reach, and a big purse. I can't take the risk with the boy's life.'

'How do I know that you aren't in on the conspiracy?'

'Really, centurion. You know how I saved the boy's life at the funeral, and tried to save the governor. And this is my wish and command.'

'Well who put you in charge?' The centurion was still defiant, uncertain.

'The late governor, and the Emperor. Both charged me with the boy's safety.'

There was not much the centurion could say to that. He tried a different tack.

'What about pirates, if you have no marines on board?' Adonibaal had not taken on any legionaries in the expectation that the governor would provide his own guard.

'This thing can outrun any pirate vessel, even loaded with all this junk from the palace.'

The centurion's shoulders slumped, and Silus could see the argument was over.

'I had been looking forward to seeing the old city,' he said wistfully. 'It's been years. I've got a kid there, you know. A lad, about the same age as young Avitus.' He clapped Silus on the back. 'Look after the boy.'

'You're not the first person to ask me that. I'll do my best.'

Adonibaal was waiting at the top of the gangplank as Silus boarded, and he put a hand out. 'Where are the soldiers?'

'Decided they wanted a bit more of the Numidian sunshine before heading home.'

Adonibaal didn't look pleased, and seemed about to say more, but Silus forestalled him. 'Trust me, it's better this way.'

'You may say so, but the North African coast is swarming with pirates right now.'

'We aren't going the long route. I want to be back in Rome as soon as possible to inform the Emperor what has happened here, and get the kid somewhere safe.'

'Are you having a joke with me? Back across that sea, after what happened last time?'

Silus conceded he didn't like the idea either after his near-death experience, but speed remained of the essence. Who knew what was happening in Rome, or even what might happen in Numidia with the governor dead, and his deputy now in charge of the third legion? 'The weather will be a bit better, won't it? This much further into spring?'

'Marginally. But that's like saying would you rather be run down by an elephant than a rhinoceros.'

'You're up to it, I have confidence. By the way, have you taken on any new crew or any new rowers for the homeward journey?'

'One new rower, and one deckhand. Why?'

'Where did you find them?'

'The rower was found for me by an agent. For a handsome payout. They are hard to find, you know, and a strong, well-trained one is rare as cow's bollocks.'

'And the deckhand?'

'Found him hanging around the docks, looking to work his passage to Rome. What's all this about?'

'I'm sure you heard there was an attempt on the life of the governor's son, at his own father's funeral. I'm concerned there may be more. I doubt any of your crew from the outbound journey would be involved, although it's not impossible for someone to have got to one of them. More likely, though, they try to plant an assassin amongst your crew.'

'Filthy dogs,' spat Adonibaal. 'If I find out he isn't who he says he is, I'll throw him overboard myself.'

'Can you take me to him?'

The new crew member was clearly a veteran sailor. When Silus reached him, he was hauling on a rope and tying it fast with expert ease. Still, that didn't prove anything. His name was Kyriakos, a Greek, and he stopped his work and looked at his feet as the captain approached.

'Kyriakos, this is Silus. He has some questions for you. Answer them fully and completely, as if I had asked them myself. Understand?'

'Yes, captain.' His accent was strong, and his Latin poor. Silus considered speaking to him in Greek, but Silus' own Greek was hardly perfect, so that might not have improved the situation. He persevered in Latin.

'You're Greek?' he asked. 'From which city?'

'From Athens, boss.'

'How long have you been a sailor?'

'Since my twelfth year, boss.'

'How old are you now?'

'Don't know, boss. Not been keeping count.'

From someone else the reply might have come across as sarcastic, but Kyriakos seemed sincere.

'How did you know the *Minerva* needed crew?'

'Ships always need crew. Sailors retire, or die, or run off with a woman. Or man. Or goat.'

Now Silus knew he was being funny, even though there was no change in his tone or expression.

'And why did you choose the *Minerva*?'

'I want to go to Rome. There is a girl in a tavern there. Been too long since I saw her. And *Minerva* looks like a good boat. Seaworthy. Not like some of these wrecks.'

Well, he was either telling the truth or he should be on stage acting Euripides. Actually scratch that, he should be proclaiming in the courts. Actors were so terrible you could tell their words were fiction, while lawyers could claim white was black and make you believe them. Still, Silus wasn't in the mood to be trusting. He would keep a special eye out for this one. Though he would be watching the rest of the crew, too. In his eyes, no one was above suspicion any more.

He left the sullen sailor and sought out Avitus and his family. They had taken the special guest cabin next to the captain's quarters, of course. Silus knocked on the door and Soaemias' called to him to enter. He ducked under the low door frame, and found himself in the cramped room that he had last seen occupied by the unfortunate Vocula and Khnum-Aa. The place smelt of vinegar and brine, but the cleaning it had received didn't quite disguise the underlying odour of vomit, faeces, and death. He wondered if its new occupants could smell it too, or if it was more obvious to him because of his knowledge of what had transpired there.

The cabin was tight for two, cramped for three, and with Silus intruding, it felt like there wasn't enough space to breathe. Gannys and Avitus looked up at him expectantly, but it was Soaemias who spoke.

'What do you want, Silus?'

'Don't you think we should talk?'

'About what?'

Silus narrowed his eyes. 'How about the murder of your husband and the attempted murder of your son? We can get on to the weather later if we run out of conversation.'

'Watch your tone, boy. Remember your place.'

Boy? She must be around five years his junior. It was the style used to address a slave, and she was making it clear where she stood in the pecking order, and that it was way above him. She was right, of course. In theory. In practice, he had saved her life, kept her mad secret to save her from disgrace, and saved the life of her son more than once. He felt that earned him a little respect.

'Domina,' he said, bowing so deep his forehead almost touched the bed. 'With your permission, may we discuss the difficult situation in which we currently find ourselves?'

She inclined her head, though her cold expression showed that his exaggerated deference bordering on insolence was not lost on her.

'I was sent from Rome to warn your husband of a threat to his life. There is a conspiracy against the

Emperor, and the conspirators wanted Marcellus out of the way, as one of Caracalla's key supporters.'

'So you failed.' Her words were emotionless, yet the repressed anger in her eyes chilled him. He was tempted to say that technically his mission had been successful, in that he had arrived in time to warn Marcellus of the danger. But he knew that was sophistry. Marcellus was still dead.

'Yes. I failed in that part of my task. And for that, I am truly sorry. I hope that you and young Avitus will find it in your hearts to forgive me one day.'

Soaemias regarded him steadily, saying nothing. Gannys looked at the floor. Avitus' gaze darted between Soaemias' and Silus' faces, like they were two parents arguing in front of their child, who just desperately wanted them to be friends. After the silence had hung in the air long enough for it to be uncomfortable, Silus went on.

'But there is another part to my mission. I have been commanded to look after your son. By your husband and his father.'

Gannys looked up sharply. Soaemias blushed. Avitus did not appear to notice that Silus' statement could refer to the same person, or two different men.

'Very well,' said Soaemias eventually. 'Though I doubt you can protect us from the whims of the gods of the sea.'

'I can only do what is possible for man, Domina. Before you know it you will be in Rome, and then the Emperor himself, and the Empress Julia, your aunt, will take responsibility for your well-being, and you can be rid of me.'

'Elagabal speed that day,' said Soaemias.

'Indeed,' said Silus, and took his leave.

-

The weather was fair, the sea calmer than his previous experience of the crossing to Caralis. A clear moon shone a dappled streak of quicksilver across the waves, and a moderate breeze flapped the sails. Silus had pitched his tent within direct line of sight of the door to Marcellus' family's cabin, with the flap open so he could maintain surveillance. He still wasn't sure about Kyriakos, and had followed him around discreetly earlier in the day. The new crew member had done nothing suspicious, going about his duties assiduously enough, but that didn't prove anything to Silus. Nor could he trust the rest of the crew completely. At least there were no other passengers for him to worry about.

On an impulse, he got off his mat, left the tent, and walked around the deck. Below, most of the rowers were sleeping at their stations, just a few pulling to maintain speed and direction. Most of the crew were asleep too. The helmsman rested against the tiller, eyes half-closed, the lookout was slumped against the forward railing, and a couple of deckhands lounged around. Nothing out of the ordinary. No cause for alarm. But the hair on his arms prickled.

He went back to his tent, determined to keep a close eye on the cabin. His eyelids felt heavy, and he closed them for a moment, just to rest them.

He jerked awake suddenly with a quiet gasp. Damn it. He would have been crucified if he had fallen asleep on sentry duty when he was an auxiliary in the legions. But he was only one man, and he knew it would be impossible to stay awake for all twenty-four hours of the day, for the whole length of the voyage.

What was it that had woken him, anyway? He peered out of the tent flap, concentrating on his peripheral vision which he knew was better for detecting movement, especially in the dark.

There.

Just a flicker, and when he turned his attention to it, with the poorer night acuity of his central visual field, it disappeared. He looked away again. Nothing. Then another moving shadow, darting from behind a crate on the deck, to where some sacks of grain had been stowed. It was obviously not someone going about the ship's business.

Silus eased himself onto his hands and knees, keeping out of sight in the tent, and drew his sword, slowly so it slid out of its scabbard noiselessly. He watched as the figure came nearer. Was it Kyriakos? He couldn't be sure. The figure drew near. It was definitely approaching the cabin. Soon it was within a few steps of the cabin door. It gave a furtive glance around, and its gaze lingered on Silus' tent for a long moment. Silus froze, but it was impossible for someone outside the tent to see inside with that level of darkness. Apparently satisfied, the figure turned its back on Silus, and approached the door.

Silus eased out of the tent, the creaking in his knees sounding to him like the loud crack of a bone under a dog's teeth. But the figure didn't react. Silus crept up behind him, and as the figure reached out for the handle, he touched his blade gently to the side of the man's neck.

'Put your hands out to the side,' said Silus quietly. The figure did as he was told, and Silus saw there was a knife clutched in one fist.

'Drop it.'

The fist opened and the knife fell to the floor, the clatter splitting the quiet.

'Now turn around, slowly.'

The figure slowly turned, while Silus kept the sharp edge of the blade in continuous contact with the great vessels of the neck. Silus found himself looking into the smirking visage of…

'Calev! How the fuck did you get on board? Did you catch a ride with a dolphin?'

'No need. I was carried on by the governor's own slaves.'

Silus thought back to the strangely heavy chest he had witnessed being loaded and felt acutely foolish. This cunning assassin had smuggled himself onto the ship right under Silus' gaze.

'Who pays you?' asked Silus.

Calev sneered. 'Who says I do this for pay?'

'Oh, don't tell me you're an idealist. Are you a descendant of one of the rebels from Masada or something? Or are you fighting for the restoration of the Republic?'

'Fine, I do it for the money. And because I am good at it. Better than you, in fact, Centurion Silus of the Arcani.'

'Really? Whose neck has a sword pressed against it?'

'Where is the man you were supposed to be protecting right now?'

Silus gritted his teeth. This little worm was really starting to get under his skin, and he felt his grip tightening on the hilt of his sword, even though he knew it was the exact response the little assassin was looking for.

'You are going to die for the murder of Marcellus. The only question is how. What would you prefer? Quickly now, with a sharp edge, or slowly under the hands and tools of Caracalla's torturers?'

There was a flash of uncertainty in Calev's eyes. Only momentary, but Silus caught it, and saw his barb had struck deep. But Calev was obviously not one to break easily.

'There is a long journey from here to Rome. If you intend to keep me alive that long, I think I will take my chances of a third option coming my way.'

Silus ground his teeth in frustration. He could tie Calev up and torture him himself, but there was no guarantee he would survive the journey if he did that, and if he revealed any names to Silus and then died, he would have no proof of the conspirators' identities when he got back to Rome. He hesitated, unresolved. He was itching just to cut this dangerous man's throat and be done with it, but he knew how much trouble he would be in with Oclatinius if he killed him without at least trying to get some information.

Then the decision was taken out of his hands. The cabin door flew open, thumping Calev in the back. Instinctively, Silus took his blade away, not yet certain enough that he wanted Calev dead. It was all Calev needed. Despite being knocked off balance by the blow to his back, as soon as a gap appeared between his neck and the sword edge, he threw himself in the opposite direction, reaching out to grab the knife on the floor, rolling neatly and coming to his feet.

Silus shifted his stance into a fighting pose, sword to the fore.

'Nice move. You haven't been hanging out with Oclatinius, by any chance?'

'That old man? Maybe if I want to be taught how to piss my bed at night.'

Oclatinius could probably still beat both of us in a fight with one hand tied behind his back, reflected Silus, but he didn't comment.

‘What is this?’ gasped Gannys. ‘I was just going to relieve myself.’

‘Do you have a sword?’ asked Silus.

‘Somewhere in my luggage. I didn’t see the need to…’

‘Just go and wake up the captain.’

Gannys sidled around behind Silus and then ran the short distance to the captain’s cabin and pounded on his door, shouting for him to come out.

‘So what now?’ asked Silus. ‘We are many miles from land. There may not be marines on this ship, but I’m here, and the crew look pretty tough too. Think you can take us all on?’

‘I don’t need to do that. Just take the helmsman hostage and get him to steer us to the nearest land.’

‘We are a good day’s sail away from the African coast. Think you can keep it up that long?’

‘Don’t you worry about my ability to keep it up.’

Adonibaal emerged from his cabin, bleary-eyed but alert.

‘Silus. What is all this?’

‘It’s our old friend Calev. It turns out he was the one who murdered the governor, and he was on his way to finish off the governor’s son. Now he is threatening to take the helmsman hostage.’

Adonibaal sighed. ‘I’ve really had enough of all this nonsense.’ And with that he disappeared back inside his cabin. All eyes watched him go in astonishment. Then Silus and Calev turned back to each other, facing off, alert, waiting for the other to make the first move.

But Adonibaal had not abandoned them to their own devices. He had merely gone to fetch something. A moment later, he re-emerged, holding something long and weighty in his hand. With a swiftness that was impressive, before anyone could react, he drew it back and threw.

The heavy spear hit Calev squarely in the centre of the chest. The impact sent him tottering backwards. The back of his legs hit the side railing and he teetered, arms flailing, staring down in disbelief at the weapon penetrating his torso. Then he tumbled backwards over the rail, and disappeared under the waves with the barest splash. He didn't come back up.

Silus stared at Adonibaal in disbelief. The captain gave a little shrug of his shoulders. 'I used to be in the legions before I got transferred to the navy. I was always handy with a pilum.' He looked over to the froth in the water, drifting away as the boat passed, under which Calev had vanished. 'And no one threatens my ship.'

He gripped the handle to the door of his cabin. 'If the ship is sinking, or Neptune comes to ask for a cup of wine, wake me up. Otherwise, don't disturb me until dawn.' He closed the door firmly behind him.

Silus looked down at the sword in his hand, suddenly redundant, then over to Gannys, who looked shocked by the whole chain of events.

'Well, I guess I'll turn in too,' said Silus, and headed for his tent. 'Sleep well.'

-

In Caralis, Silus retraced his steps to the boarding house where he had left Atius. They had docked just after noon, and Silus had helped Avitus and his family find suitable lodgings in the city, making sure they weren't followed, at least as best he could. Though with Calev dead, he didn't think there was anyone who knew where they were at that time, or who could send anyone their way with mischief in mind. Gannys had sniffed at the guest rooms that Silus found, but Soaemias had snapped at him to stop being so stuck-up, and had thanked Silus for his help.

He had left them to settle into their room, but waited for a while across the street, in sight of the entrance to the tavern above which the rooms were situated. After some time, confident that no one else was watching surreptitiously, he left them with promises to return before night.

He hammered on the boarding house door, and it was opened by the housekeeper. He looked down his nose at Silus, and said sniffily, 'We're full.'

'I'm here for Atius,' said Silus.

The housekeeper's face darkened. 'I see. Well you are welcome to him. Come in and take him away from here.'

He stepped aside and held the door open for Silus, nodding upstairs when Silus entered. Silus ascended the rickety staircase to the first floor. There were two doors at the top, and Silus hesitated, unsure on which to knock. Then he heard noises, the sound of furniture crashing, a grunt, a woman's cry. Silus lifted his foot and kicked the door so hard it flew off his hinges. A woman screamed as he burst into the room.

Atius had his back to him, looking over his shoulder in surprise and alarm. Between him and the wall was a woman, with her legs around his waist and her arms around his neck, her jaw open in shock. The side table was overturned where her flailing legs had caught it, a clay oil lamp smashed on the floor.

Atius lowered the woman to the floor, and Silus recognised her now as Zephyra, the housekeeper's daughter who had been nursing him. The naked Zephyra dived for the bed and disappeared under the covers while Atius adjusted his tunic.

'Feeling better, then?' asked Silus drily.

'Christos, Silus. Don't you know how to knock?'

'I thought there was a woman in trouble in here. I can see I was right.'

Zephyra's head appeared from under the blanket long enough to spit out a long stream of curses in Silus' direction. Silus held up his hands.

'Say your goodbyes, Atius. The *Minerva* sails at dawn. I'll see you on board.'

'Hold on. What news from Numidia?'

Silus shook his head. 'Nothing good. I'll fill you in tomorrow. Settle your affairs here.'

Silus left through the shattered doorway, stopping before he left the boarding house to apologise for his friend, and pay for the damage. Then he found his way back to the establishment in which he had lodged Avitus.

The family were dining in the public bar area, which made Silus uncomfortable. He had no reason to believe anyone of danger to them knew they were here, but he decided he would keep them company to err on the side of caution. He wasn't sure of anything right then.

Avitus waved him over to join them, and an elbow in the ribs from Soaemias sent Gannys to fetch a chair for Silus. Silus bowed to Soaemias and Gannys, ruffled Avitus' hair, and sat down.

'Is Atius still alive?' asked Avitus bluntly.

'Very much so,' said Silus, suppressing a smirk.

'Good,' said Avitus. 'He is a good man, despite his beliefs.'

'I guess so.' Silus turned to Soaemias. 'How is the food, lady?'

'Not fit for pigs,' spat Gannys.

'Perfectly acceptable,' said Soaemias.

Silus called over a serving slave, and ordered the same as the others, and some cheap wine. The food when it arrived was fine, tending towards the luxurious in Silus' experience. Boiled eggs, asparagus, some cured ham and some delicate pastries filled with some sort of pâté. The wine wasn't too bad for the price either, and Silus took a deep draught, hoping it would obscure the fresh image of Atius' arse that was seared into his brain.

'What happens when we get to Rome?' asked Soaemias.

'We go straight to Caracalla, report everything.'

'I think we should go to Syria,' said Gannys. 'We don't know that Caracalla isn't behind all of this. We have friends and contacts in Emesa. It's the safest place.'

'If Caracalla wants you dead, nowhere within the frontiers of the Empire is safe. Between the various different intelligence services, the military, the Arcani, and the amateurs willing to sell their own children for a few sestertii, your chances aren't good. Even outside the Empire, there are plenty of allied princes and minor royalty who would jump at the chance to curry a bit of favour with Rome by handing over a traitor.'

'Traitor?' gasped Gannys.

'If Caracalla doesn't like you, that makes you a traitor.'

'We aren't going to Syria,' said Soaemias, calmly but firmly. 'You're right, Silus. It looks like we are running away. But tell me, as far as you know, are we out of favour with the Emperor?'

'As far as I know, you are not. I don't have the Emperor's ear. But he did seem concerned for young Avitus' welfare.'

Gannys glanced at Soaemias but her face did not betray emotion.

'Good,' said Soaemias. 'Then there is no need for further discussion. When we arrive in Rome, you will escort us to the Imperial presence, to make sure there are no mishaps along the way. And then we will be in the Emperor's care.'

'And at his mercy,' muttered Gannys.

Avitus had been daintily finishing his meal while the adults talked, looking from one to the other with interest, but without comment. Soaemias too ate the last of her dish, and dabbed her lips with a cloth.

'Silus, would you be so good as to entertain my son for a while? I have a headache, and I need to retire and lie down. Gannys, would you attend me?'

Gannys had a mouthful of meat pie. He tried to speak, and crumbs flew out of his mouth. He tried again. 'But I haven't finished eating.'

'Gannys, would you attend me?' said Soaemias rising. The tone brooked no debate, and Gannys stood, looking regretfully at his half-eaten meal. Soaemias held out her hand, and Gannys took it respectfully.

'I must close my eyes for around an hour. You can bring Avitus to my room after that time.' She looked at Gannys who had just seemed to understand what was happening and was starting to look excited. 'Actually,' she said. 'It will probably be more like half an hour.'

She left the table, Gannys in tow, and Silus regarded Avitus, who was watching them leave, head cocked to one side. When they were out of earshot, the boy said, 'They are going to make love, aren't they?'

Silus had been halfway through a deep glug of wine when Avitus spoke these words, and he nearly choked, managing with an effort not to spray liquid across the table. Avitus regarded Silus expectantly, waiting for an answer.

'I... well, I wouldn't know. It's none of my business. Nor yours!'

Avitus shrugged and pointed at the table. It had lines carved into the wooden surface to make a grid of eight rows by twelve columns. 'Shall we play latrunculi?'

Silus was taken off guard by the sudden change of topic, but quickly realised it would be a good distraction for however long it took Gannys to assist Soaemias in her recuperation from her headache. He asked the slave serving drinks if he had any counters for the board, and the slave returned with a set of terracotta pieces, thirteen painted white and thirteen black, twelve soldiers and a dux for each side. Silus ordered a cup of milk for Avitus and some more well-watered wine for himself, and they began to play.

Silus was no expert in the game, but neither was he a beginner, and he had won his fair share of copper coins with victories on the board. But it quickly became clear that Avitus was his superior in strategy and tactics. Before he even realised it was happening, Avitus had pinned Silus' dux, surrounded on three sides by Avitus' men, and on one side by Silus' own man, who could not be moved in time to rescue him. Silus sat back in surprise and frustration.

'You've played this a lot, boy?'

Avitus frowned. 'You should really be calling me master, or high priest.'

'Should I, boy?' Silus was taking something of a risk. Avitus was technically correct, but having just been humiliated on the board, he didn't feel like making himself subservient to this little lad. Avitus gave him a stern look, then laughed. 'Call me what you want, Silus. You have earned it. I only ask that you show me the appropriate level of respect when we are in public.'

Silus smiled. 'I can do that. Boy. So tell me. You play this game often?'

'I've played it twice before, I believe. One of Father's soldiers taught me the rules, and let me win the first time. The second time we played, I beat him, and he refused to play me again.'

So the boy was a genius? At least at this kind of mathematical game. He wasn't so sure about his real-world intelligence.

'Do you think I will be Emperor one day?' asked Avitus abruptly.

Silus glanced around him nervously, but no one seemed to have overheard.

'If you talk like that, you won't live long enough to find out,' he hissed.

Avitus thought about that, then nodded. 'Very well, I will be discreet. But I still want to know what you think.'

'Why do you think you should be Emperor?'

'Mother thought I should be. And Gannys. Caracalla sent you to look after me, so maybe he has plans for me too.'

'Maybe,' said Silus. 'But I think it's very dangerous to speculate.'

'I believe I will be Emperor one day. And when that happens, I will reward my friends. Are you my friend, Silus?'

'Of course. Your friend and protector.'

'I'm glad,' said Avitus. 'Do you want to play again?'

'Not really,' said Silus, and sat back in his chair, waiting until he could return Avitus to his mother, and then get some sleep in a comfortable bed himself.

–

'Get ready to cast off,' yelled Adonibaal.

'Yes, captain,' came the reply from one of the dock hands, preparing to untie the thick rope that bound the Minerva to its mooring.

Silus looked anxiously out from his position at the port railing. Where the fuck was he? The stupid bastard. Every single time – when he saw him he would...

A bulky figure emerged from the throng of dock workers and sailors, shoving men aside as he thrust his way toward the ship.

'Wait. Wait for me!'

Silus rolled his eyes and tapped Adonibaal on the shoulder, pointing out Atius. Adonibaal shook his head, but held his tongue, waiting until Atius had reached the gangplank before giving the order to the dock hand to release the ship.

Atius staggered up the wooden plank onto the ship, threw his backpack onto the deck and bent double, hands on his knees, breathing heavily. Silus waited until he had recovered, which took a surprisingly long time. Eventually, Atius straightened, gave a half smile and a sloppy salute and said, 'Reporting for duty, centurion.'

Silus raised an eyebrow. 'One last fuck, was it?'

Atius didn't even have the grace to look shame-faced, let alone deny it. 'You know how it is.'

'I wish I did,' said Silus, then put his arms around his friend and hugged him hard. Atius gasped, and Silus stepped back, looking with concern into Atius' pained features.

'What is it?'

Atius hesitated, then lifted his tunic. An ugly scar swept across the side of his lower abdomen, poorly healed, dark red and moist in places, oozing a turbid fluid.

'Saturn's balls,' whispered Silus. 'After all this time, it still isn't healed.'

Atius let the tunic drop back down. 'The wound was deep. And I must confess, maybe I didn't rest quite as much as I should have.'

'Been going for little jogs like Phillipides?'

'In a manner of speaking.'

Silus picked up Atius' bag. 'Come on, let's get you settled in. You can spend the remainder of the voyage recuperating, and when we are in Rome, we will see about finding you a decent healer. In the meantime, I need to get you up to date.'

He put his arm around his friend's shoulder, and guided him to their berth, where their tent awaited them.

Chapter VIII

Rome, 214 AD Aprilis

A dinner party did not seem the best situation for Silus to relay bad news, but if the Emperor commanded it, what choice did he have? Oclatinius had told him it was Julia Domna's suggestion in any case, to throw a banquet in honour of the return to Rome of her niece and great-nephew. To some extent the celebration was a family affair. Reclining on the top couch, Caracalla was flanked by the Empress Julia Domna and her older sister Julia Maesa. Julia Maesa's husband Gaius Julius Avitus Alexianus was on the couch to the Emperor's right, flanked by his two daughters, Julia Soaemias and the younger Julia Mamaea. On the other side of the Emperor's couch were Avitus and his young cousin, the six-year-old Alexianus, son of Julia Mamaea. Gannys sat between them, present on the pretext of being unofficial guardian to Avitus.

Feeling far more like an intruder at this family event than Gannys, Silus lay on his own on a couch furthest from the Emperor, but within conversational distance of Avitus. Not even Macrinus, Oclatinius or Festus had been invited. Silus had already given his full report to Oclatinius, and his heart had sunk when his superior had told him that Caracalla wished him to attend this dinner, where he could also relay all his news. Apparently it had actually been Soaemias' request that Silus be present, and Caracalla had decided to combine business with pleasure by hearing Silus out.

So far, Caracalla had studiously ignored Silus, which was only proper given the importance of the other guests. He had greeted Soaemias warmly with a hug and a kiss on both cheeks, then seemed to start when he had set eyes on Avitus for the first time in a couple of years. The boy had indubitably grown, his round face still that of a child, but a child on his way to becoming a man. Caracalla looked at him with his stern brow wrinkled and his eyes narrowed for a long moment before shaking his hand formally and welcoming him back to Rome.

The talk until now had been idle chatter. Domna had asked Soaemias about the weather in Numidia, and whether she found the local customs very alien compared to Rome and Syria. Marcellus' absence was like a huge pothole in a major road, which the traffic of the conversation had to navigate around, from time to time getting congested as it tried to avoid the obstruction, a cart wheel occasionally teetering momentarily on the edge.

Caracalla casually informed Alexianus that he would be taking up the post of Governor of Dalmatia which had recently become vacant. Julia Maesa looked shocked, no doubt angry that she would have to leave Rome with her family, or stay behind and lose her husband for a protracted time, but she held her tongue, and Caracalla at last turned his attention to Silus.

'Talking of vacant governor posts, perhaps, Silus, you could tell us what news you bring from Numidia.'

Silus swallowed, the flamingo tongue pasty before him no longer looking appetising. Caracalla stared at him with piercing eyes, his features as stern as ever.

'Well, sir, Imperator. It is my sad duty to report the death of the governor, Sextus Varius Marcellus.'

There was a silence, which Caracalla allowed to persist, and Silus wondered whether he should continue. But Caracalla spoke again.

'Remind me of your mission to Numidia.'

'My mission was to protect Varius Marcellus and bring him back to Rome. And to keep young Avitus safe.'

All eyes in the room swivelled to Avitus, who was sipping oysters from their shells, oblivious of the sudden attention. Silus wondered if he had overstepped the mark. Technically, keeping Avitus safe had been an unofficial side mission, one that Caracalla maybe didn't want too much focus on. But he also wanted to point out that he hadn't completely failed.

'Well, I see Avitus, but not Marcellus.'

'I regret to say that the governor was poisoned by an assassin. But that assassin is now dead.'

'And you interrogated him? You know who sent him?'

Silus held the Emperor's gaze, intimidating as it was. 'He died before he could reveal that information.'

'So how would you rate your mission, Arcanus?'

Silus gave a pointed glance towards Avitus, who was whispering in Alexianus' ear and making the little boy giggle. 'I would say, partially successful.'

'I see.' Caracalla sighed. 'I can't say I am not deeply disappointed, and saddened by the loss of my dear friend, not to mention the husband of the Empress' niece. But your past service speaks highly of you, Silus, and I know that, given the other ties that bind you to me, you will have tried your best.'

He was talking about Tituria, of course. And Caracalla knew he would always have Silus' loyalty, as long as Tituria was within his reach. And his reach extended, as Silus had pointed out to Gannys, anywhere within the Empire, and most places outside it.

Silus bowed his head. 'Always, Augustus.'

'Do you have anything else of value to tell me?'

'Just that the conspiracy against you is real, and well-organised. Or at least, there were strenuous efforts to prevent Atius and myself from carrying out our task. We were attacked before we even boarded for Numidia. And there were two assassins on the ship, already present before we arrived. Someone had a lot of foreknowledge about our movements.'

Caracalla stroked his beard thoughtfully. 'I had guessed as much, though not the extent of the infiltration of your mission. The person or persons behind this are well-informed, and also highly organised. They planned carefully, multiple actors in case one failed, and they knew exactly where you were going, when and why. Given these challenges, your failure can perhaps be understood.'

'You are gracious, Imperator. Although, I would say, partial failure.'

There was a moment's breathless silence, as all present wondered how the Emperor would react to being corrected. But Silus had judged correctly. *Thanks be to Fortuna*, he thought. Caracalla let out a barking laugh.

'Partial failure. Very well. Anyway. There are a limited number of people who have access to the information and the resources to have done this.'

'Limited, but not small enough to draw any conclusions, unfortunately. There were several people present when I was given my mission, and any of those could have mentioned it to several others. That makes the circle of suspects very wide. I discussed this with Oclatinius…'

'Ah yes. Oclatinius. You notice he is not here. Did you wonder why?'

'Well, I presumed, as it was family, and I…'

'Yes?'

'I don't know, Augustus.'

'Your loyalty, Silus, is I think beyond doubt. Both because of your obligations to me, and how you have demonstrated your service over the last few years. Even on this mission, it was clear that you were targeted and could have lost your life, which means that you are not part of the conspiracy. Everyone else here is family.' He gave a sideways glance at Gannys. 'More or less. I don't doubt the loyalty of anybody on these couches.'

It was fortunate he wasn't aware of the full extent of Soaemias' machinations in Alexandria. Silus doubted Caracalla would have been as confident of her loyalty, or Gannys', if he knew what she had planned. But Silus was sure that that madness was behind her now. Reasonably confident, anyway.

'Anyone who is not present tonight,' continued Caracalla, 'let's just say I have concerns.'

'Oclatinius?' Silus blurted out. 'Surely not.'

Caracalla just regarded him steadily. Silus' mind whirled. Oclatinius? It wasn't possible. The old man had been steadfastly loyal, and had proven his loyalty over and over again. But loyalties could shift. Had something happened to Oclatinius to change his mind? He was sure that Oclatinius would not be corrupted by money, nor the thought of power. He had all the wealth and influence he needed, and had never shown any desire for more. The only thing that would turn him against the Emperor he swore an oath to was if he considered that man was a threat to the Empire. Despite his treacherous behaviour in

Germania, Caracalla was not that. Whatever you thought of the man and his deeds, he was an excellent general, who had proven himself time and again in battle, and was running the Empire competently, if not with the brilliance of the first Augustus, or Hadrian or Marcus Aurelius.

'No,' said Silus, more firmly. 'Not Oclatinius. He is loyal.' Silus was sure of it. But he hated the fact that Caracalla had put a doubt in his mind.

'I hope you are right, Silus, but at the moment, no one who is not present today is above suspicion.'

He turned his attention to his family, and Silus breathed more easily as soon as he was out of the dagger stare of the Emperor.

'We must consider the safety of Julia Soaemias and her son,' said Domna. 'They were also targets.'

Caracalla twiddled a finger through the curls of his beard. 'I wonder why that would be.'

No one replied, but the question hung in the air. The obvious conclusion was that Avitus was a potential heir, and an obstacle to someone else's ambitions to take the purple. But Avitus' official lineage was a little tenuous to be an automatic choice to inherit the throne – he was the grandson of the Emperor's stepmother.

Of course, Caracalla was childless, and adoption in the past had been the route to ensuring a nominated successor took power. Tiberius, the stepson of Augustus was the obvious example, not to mention the young Octavian himself, grand-nephew of Gaius Julius Caesar. In later years, adoption had become a way of nominating a suitable successor even when there was no family connection. Trajan's succession after being adopted by Nerva was a notable example of this method working admirably to the benefit of the Empire. Even Septimius Severus had taken on the name of his predecessor, Pertinax, despite not being formally adopted, in order to increase his legitimacy.

It was generally more acceptable to the legions and to the people, though, if a new Emperor had a legitimate connection to the old, the closer the better. And the son of the current Emperor was best of all. Hence why Avitus' parentage mattered. If he was indeed the son of Caracalla, he was his most likely successor.

But that brought up some embarrassing questions. It would not reflect well on the Emperor, to have impregnated the wife of one of his closest friends, especially now the man was dead and would be lauded as an exemplar of Roman fidelity, dignity and authority. Nor, though of lesser concern, would it look good for Julia Soaemias, cuckolding her respected husband. And finally, of the least importance, it brought young Avitus' legitimacy into question.

Which may be why Caracalla came to the decision he did.

'Julia Soaemias,' he said, and his tone was not harsh but it was firm. 'You are to return to your home town of Emesa with your son. You may take Gannys with you, to act as the boy's guardian until he is of age, together with your household, and any possessions you wish to take. You are to remain there until I judge it prudent to allow your return.'

Soaemias mouth was a straight line, though she inclined her head in gracious acknowledgement. It sounded like exile, this indefinite vacation, and maybe it would have been if it was to any other city or province in the Empire. But this was Emesa, home town of the Bassianus family, from whom Julia Domna, Maesa, Soaemias and Mamaea were all descended. Home also of the mountain god Elagabal, to whom Avitus had inherited the position of high priest. In Emesa, she would have power, respect, familial support, and the honour of being mother of the high priest. So it was likely a two-edged sword, as far as she was concerned.

But was it safe?

'Augustus,' ventured Silus, emboldened by the latitude the Emperor had shown him so far this evening.

Caracalla did not seem pleased that the first spoken response was from the lowly Arcanus, but he gestured an impatient hand to Silus to allow him to speak.

'May I accompany the lady on her journey?'

Caracalla looked surprised, and in truth, Silus himself was a little taken aback by his own words.

'Why would you want to do that?' He sounded genuinely puzzled.

'I swore an oath to the boy's father to protect him.' The ambiguity surrounding Avitus' parentage worked in Silus' favour here, since he had in fact promised both Caracalla and Marcellus he would look after him.

'You have a greater oath, to your Emperor.'

'Which is why I ask your permission, Augustus.'

Caracalla considered briefly, then said, firmly, 'No.'

Soaemias was looking at Silus with interest, but she remained silent. Domna spoke up, however.

'Augustus,' she said, ever respectful, at least in public, 'we know there is some threat to my niece and her son. You are confident of Silus' skills and loyalty. Maybe it would be prudent to lend him to them. For my peace of mind, if nothing else.'

Caracalla turned to the woman by his side, and Silus saw an emotion in his eyes that he never saw when the Emperor looked at anyone else. He wondered if his love for the woman was as obvious to everyone else.

Caracalla put a gentle hand on Domna's arm. 'I do agree, but I have other plans for Silus.'

That familiar sinking feeling appeared in the bottom of his stomach. What now?

'But we must ensure their safety,' said Domna.

Caracalla considered. 'Silus, where is your friend? The one who is usually attached to your hip. What's his name?'

'Atius, Augustus? He was injured by one of the attempted assassins. He is still recovering. He isn't currently fit to serve in the Arcani.'

'But is he well enough to act as a bodyguard? He wouldn't have to do much, after all. He is a big man, his mere presence would be an effective deterrent, and you can vouch for his loyalty, I'm sure. Is he up to it?'

'I think… yes, Augustus.'

Was he dumping his friend in the shit? He thought not. The actual threat to Avitus and his family was hopefully low if they were being sent far from Rome. And though travelling a long distance was something of a strain, he would be doing it in luxury in the company of these wealthy and important people. With help from Apollo and Fortuna, he would have plenty of time to heal up.

'Very well. Atius will accompany Soaemias to Emesa, with a small detachment of legionaries that you can pick, Silus.'

'Yes, Augustus. And me?'

'What about you?'

'You said you had other plans for me.'

Caracalla waved a dismissive hand. 'That's for another day. Now onto other business.'

And the conversation moved on. Silus pecked unenthusiastically at his fabulously elaborate meal. When he looked up, he saw Soaemias regarding him with a slight smirk. She was quite beautiful, he realised. Then a thought struck him. He was sending Atius away with this newly widowed woman of uncertain virtue.

Oh Atius, for Jupiter's sake, please don't fuck her!

–

The domus of Tituria's new adoptive family did not have quite the grandeur of her father's palatial dwelling, though it was in the same district on the Esquiline. Nevertheless, it demonstrated clearly that the owner had more wealth than Silus could ever aspire to. The Greek statuary in the atrium certainly looked authentic and antique to his inexpert eye. The ancestral masks around the walls also spoke of a respectable lineage rather than some parvenu freedman who had made a fortune trading olives or slaves. And the ornamental carp in the impluvium that swam in lazy circles, mouths gaping in the hope that morsels would be tossed their way, suggested money to spare on luxuries.

Silus looked down at a particularly curious fish that was watching him. He bent over and mimicked it, making his mouth into an O and opening and closing it with popping sounds.

'Am I interrupting?'

Silus spun round, already flushing with embarrassment, but before he could speak, Tituria had charged into him and wrapped her arms around him. Silus was not a short man, but Tituria had grown considerably since he had last seen her. The top of her head clunked painfully into his chin and he winced, but he kept a grip on her, hugging her tight for a long moment before putting his hands on her shoulders and taking a step back to get a good look at her.

'Wow, look at the size of you.' It had been a long time since he had last seen her. 'How old are you now? Eleven?'

'I had my twelfth birthday last month.'

Twelve. Of marriageable age, potentially. He hoped that she was given a chance to grow up before being given to a man. In his eyes she was still a child, little older than his daughter Sergia would have been, had she lived.

He swallowed. His eyes were becoming moist, and he found himself facing the sudden dilemma of wiping them, or risking the tears overflowing down his cheeks, making his emotions obvious in either case. He was saved by the *yip-yip* of an excitable little dog. A young female slave had entered the atrium with Issa in her arms. Her face was turned away, nose wrinkled in disgust at the remarkable smells emanating from the tiny pet. Issa wriggled, and she hastily put her down. Issa ran over to Silus and jumped up at him, her feet resting on the top of his shins. He reached down and picked her up and cuddled her, stroking her between the ears while she rubbed her head on him. She really did stink, from both ends. She was grey and her eyes were cloudy with cataracts. She had to be fifteen years old now, but she was still full of life and character.

'She's missed you,' said Tituria.

'I've missed her too,' said Silus. 'And you.'

Tituria smiled. 'Good. Are you staying for dinner?'

'Am I invited?'

'I think that could be arranged.'

–

The atrium of a domus was often the only part of a house that people saw. It was where the man of the house, the paterfamilias, received his clients in the morning, doling out favours and cash as was the duty of a patron. It was the place, too, where any business was done, if he had to dirty his hands with mucky financial affairs. And it was the place where important guests, the paterfamilias' own patron for example, would be received, at least initially. So if funds were limited, the atrium was the place where any opulence would be concentrated. That meant less for the rest of the house.

Silus thought the triclinium felt tired. The couch he reclined on was threadbare, and some of its stuffing was protruding through a couple of holes. The frescoes had faded, and there was a large crack down one wall. The fare was sumptuous, to someone of Silus' humble background, but he recognised it lacked the finesse of an expensive chef, or the rare, costly ingredients that might be found on the table of the most affluent.

Titus Petellius Facilis fitted right into the decor. His face was lined, his grey hair thin, and his lower eyelids drooped in pendulous bags. The corners of his mouth were perpetually turned down, like the jowls of a mournful hound. Like the decor, life seemed to have worn him down.

'So what do you do with your life, young Silus?' he asked. His voice was slow, low, with a hint of a croak.

Young? It was a long time since Silus had felt young. 'I serve the Emperor,' he said, intentionally vague.

'Don't we all?' said Facilis, turning to his wife beside him with an ironic smile. She ignored him and sniffed suspiciously at a piece of cheese that she held between finger and thumb like it was a dead mouse. 'But specifically, in what way do you serve?'

'In the military,' said Silus, and when Facilis waited expectantly, he expanded, 'In the intelligence service. I'm not supposed to speak about my work in any detail.'

'I see, I see, quite right, quite right. Then tell me, what is your connection with my lovely new ward, Tituria here?'

Tituria looked at Silus sharply, a flash of concern in her eyes. Silus opened his mouth, then gave a little cough and took a sip of water to give himself time to think. He really should have been prepared for that question. He didn't think Facilis would be impressed with the truth – that Silus had been part of the team that had killed her entire family; that he had spared her and killed his own team member in a sudden fit of conscience.

'I was a friend of her family.'

It was a mistake. He knew it as soon as the words were out. Tituria looked down, and her hand clenched around her bronze goblet, the knuckles whitening. He cursed himself for his clumsiness and lack of forethought. For all his closeness with Tituria; for all he had done for her and sacrificed for her; for all that, at least until now, he had been her only friend in the world, there would never be a way of getting past the horrific trauma of their first encounter.

Facilis continued, oblivious to Tituria's reaction. 'Poor old Titurius. I knew him too, somewhat. Our social circles occasionally overlapped. What a tragedy. You poor dear, Tituria, to lose your whole family in a fire that way. I blame the vigiles. If they did a better job of enforcing the fire laws…'

'Be quiet, Facilis,' said his wife. Facilis looked at Tituria, who was staring down, lips pressed together, tears flowing down her cheeks. Silus wanted to jump up and hug her right then, but even if that had been acceptable under these social conditions, he wasn't sure how Tituria would react.

'Yes, of course. Apologies, my dear, Tituria. How insensitive of me.'

Tituria swallowed and waved away the apology, but obviously didn't trust herself to speak. Silus' heart ached at the sight of her, and he felt suddenly sick.

'Would you excuse me, Facilis?' he asked. 'I need to… you know, relieve myself.'

'Certainly.' He clicked his fingers towards the slave who had been serving them, a tall blonde woman with long hair tied back in a simple ponytail. She was currently waiting patiently with a jug of wine in case she was required. 'Slave…' He looked blank and turned to his wife. 'Apollo, my memory. What is that Armenian girl's name?'

'Juik, dear,' said Facilis' wife with barely concealed irritation. 'She has been in our household for over a month, you know.'

'I preferred the last one, Greek lass, Aristomache. Good, solid woman. Shame about the accident.'

Silus cleared his throat.

'Yes, Juik. Please show Silus here to the latrine.'

Juik set her jug down. 'Please follow me, sir.'

Silus rose from his couch and followed the slave out of the back of the triclinium and down a short corridor to a small room. The domus was luxurious enough to have its own latrine with flowing water to wash away the effluent, and there was even a clean sponge stick in case that was needed. But Silus just needed a moment to compose himself, which he did by taking some deep breaths, and then having a satisfying piss. When he emerged from the latrine, Juik was waiting for him.

'Thank you,' he said, 'I think I can find my own way back.'

'As you wish, sir. But first, I must pass on a message.'

Silus stopped abruptly, suddenly alert. 'A message. From whom?'

'From the person who arranged for Aristomaches' accident and for my position in this household.'

Silus' heart started to race. He knew where this was going.

'I am to remind you that you have a duty, and a loyalty to the Emperor. The Emperor trusts you. But I am here, to make sure that trust is not misplaced.'

'Just say what you mean.'

Juik looked at him as if she was explaining a simple maths problem to a child.

'If the Emperor dies, for any reason, I will slit Tituria's throat while she sleeps. Enjoy the rest of your evening, sir.' She walked away, leaving him staring after her. Then he bent over and vomited his meal onto the cracked tiled floor.

–

'A partial success,' said the first man.

'Only partial? You think?' said the second. They knelt side by side, at the back of the Temple of Castor and Pollux in the Forum Romanum, and spoke in low voices. A young priest swept the floor behind the altar, and threw irritated glances at a derelict cripple who was leaning against a column and snoring loudly.

'Yes, partial. The boy lives. And his ambitious mother.'

'They are nothing without the father. And the Emperor is diminished, too, by Marcellus' death.'

'True, and the circle of people he trusts shrinks. But he grows more paranoid. And the whole operation was very costly, in terms of valued personnel. Men like that don't grow in fields like cabbages, you know.'

The second man nodded. 'I know you sacrificed a lot of resources for this result. But I am happy with the outcome.'

'His paranoia could become dangerous.'

'Maybe, but it can be a double-edged sword. He might think he is being more cautious and protecting himself from threats, but he risks turning friends into enemies. It is something we might exploit.'

'Perhaps. Cautiously, and discreetly.'

'Indeed. There is no rush. In time, the opportunity we need will present itself. And when we strike, we will have the Senate behind us. You only have to talk to Cassius Dio to know how much the senators resent the way he sidelines them from government, while bleeding them dry of their cash.'

'I don't fear the Senate. But he is loved by the army. They won't react well to anything blatant and obvious.'

'Then let's not make it obvious. An accident would certainly be preferable.'

The second man nodded. 'I'll think about what can be arranged.'

'Do that. Shall we sacrifice to the twins, for their aid in our quest?'

'If you believe it will help. I'll go and purchase something suitable.' He stood stiffly, and approached the seller of sacrificial animals who plied his trade at the temple door.

'I don't suppose you have a lion we could slaughter?' The sacrifice seller just looked at him blankly. 'Fine. Just a couple of doves, then.'

–

Silus stared at the beast lying next to Caracalla's throne, twitching its tail, amber eyes flicking around the room, as if watching for sudden movement that would make it pounce. Though it was only a small specimen, a juvenile, Silus was pretty sure he knew what it was, even though he had only previously seen adult versions, fighting gladiators in the arena or disembowelling tied-up criminals.

So the rumours were true. Caracalla had a pet lion.

He wasn't sure if it was a male or female version. If it was male, it was too young to have grown its mane yet. But Caracalla, with his thick curly hair and thick curly beard, had plenty of fur around his head for the both of them. The lion cub probably thought the shaggy Emperor was one of his own species. It was everyone else in the room that was a potential meal.

Arrayed behind Caracalla and along the sides of the room were tall, broad-chested, long-haired guards, wearing cuirasses, swords belted at their waists, and holding long spears vertically. Though they all stood at attention, there was something sloppy about them, a back not straight enough, a spear not vertical, two feet turned outwards instead of pointing neatly forward. These were not legionaries, certainly not praetorians. These were recruits from the Celtic and Germanic countries, Germania, Iberia, Gaul, Galatia and Britannia. Silus knew who they were. These were the Leones, Caracalla's newly formed bodyguard.

Caracalla's trust of the praetorians and the other bodies traditionally associated with safeguarding the Emperor must have waned considerably. Silus couldn't blame him. The praetorians didn't have a great record of protecting past Emperors from assassination. Just off the top of his head, Silus knew the praetorians themselves had murdered Caligula and Commodus, and failed to prevent the slayings of Galba, Vitellius and Domitian. And of course in living memory, the praetorians had auctioned off the Empire to the highest bidder, the short-lived Didius Julianus, ultimately replaced by Caracalla's own father. And with the recent evidence of more conspiracies afoot, even the most stable of rulers would be forgiven for a touch of paranoia. Silus watched Caracalla stroke his lion cub between the ears, and reflected on the Emperor's stability.

'Gaius Sergius Silus,' said Caracalla.

That sounded ominous. Like when he had been naughty as a child, and his mother had used his full name at the start of a chastisement.

'Yes, Augustus.'

'Your father was a Roman?'

'He was, Augustus.'

'And your mother? A Briton?'

'Yes, Augustus.'

'Celtic, then. Do you consider yourself Roman or a Celt?'

'Roman of course, Augustus.' Where was this going? Was Caracalla about to accuse him of some sort of native British plot?

'And yet the blood of the Celts runs in your veins.' He looked Silus up and down, stroking his beard thoughtfully.

'You aren't a big man. Not like a pure Celt or German. Still, you will do.'

Do?

'Kneel.'

Silus swiftly dropped to his knees and bowed his head.

'Gaius Sergius Silus. I am inducting you into my personal bodyguard, the Leones. You will attend my person, and follow any and all orders given to you by myself, or the commander of the Leones, Athaulf here.'

Caracalla gestured to the man to his right, a grizzled veteran with long, shaggy hair and a scar across the side of his face that incorporated the orbit of his white, sightless right eye. The man's good left eye regarded Silus through narrowed lids, and Silus felt he was being stripped naked under the unblinking gaze.

'But Augustus…' Arguing with the Emperor was generally suicidally stupid, but Silus had got away with it in the past.

'Yes, Silus?' Caracalla raised an eyebrow, and Silus couldn't decide whether he looked amused or irritated.

'I am an Arcanus, Augustus. Under the command of Oclatinius.'

Caracalla waved a dismissive hand. 'If Oclatinius has need of you, he can ask Athaulf for you to be detached. Your primary duty will be with at my side, ensuring the safety of my person. Athaulf can you brief you in more detail.'

Silus bowed deeply. 'I am yours to command, Augustus.' What else could he say? The message from the slave in Facilis' household made more sense now. His job was no longer just to seek out and prevent plots against the Emperor. His job would be to throw himself in front of the assassin's knife.

He looked at the cub again. Now Silus too was one of Caracalla's lions.

-

'I guess times are hard, Silus, if you need to hold down two jobs.'

Silus grimaced at Atius. His friend was making light of the situation as usual, but he knew as well as Silus how difficult it would be being both an Arcanus and one of the Leones.

'This is your punishment for being too good at what you do,' said Oclatinius, and Silus didn't appreciate his commander – or, he corrected himself, one of his commanders – joining in the levity.

Oclatinius must have taken note of Silus' sour expression, because he put a hand on Silus' shoulder.

'Listen, it's not that bad. Your first duty is to the Emperor, but you can still serve me and the Arcani well in this position. Not only can you physically protect him, but you are ideally placed, at the centre of the Imperial circle, to gather information about the conspiracy. That is clearly still active, despite their partial failure in Numidia.'

Silus nodded, grudgingly accepting the logic of Oclatinius' statement.

'But I swore another oath, too,' said Silus. 'I promised to protect young Avitus.'

'Well, as I understand it, you took care of that by asking the Emperor to decree a proxy.'

Atius glowered at Silus, who felt a moment's chagrin. He quickly dismissed the feeling. 'I thought maybe you needed two jobs too, to fund your drinking and gambling. No, no, don't thank me. In any case, some light guard duty in warm climes will do you the power of good.'

'Losing you two to other tasks does leave me short of experienced operatives in Rome,' said Oclatinius with a sigh. 'But Fortuna throws what obstacles she wills in our path, and we must overcome them as best we can. Wine?'

The three of them sat in Oclatinius' dining room, reclining on couches around a table laid out with Spartan fare – nuts, bread, cheese and a jug of well-watered, vinegary Posca, the cheap wine more commonly drunk by the masses. Oclatinius was never one to be seduced by the lure of riches and luxuries. More than once Silus had reflected on what really motivated the old man in life, and he had concluded it was either a real sense of love and duty towards Empire and Emperor, or a love of wielding power from the wings of the stage. Most likely, both.

Oclatinius himself poured the jug to fill Silus' and Atius' cups. Most households would have slaves to do this work, even at private meetings where confidential matters were being discussed. The punishment for a slave giving away his master's secrets were so severe, the risk was normally dismissed as negligible. But Oclatinius was too cautious to take even that small chance, and no slave was ever present when he was discussing business.

Silus picked up the cup, went to drink, then hesitated. Memories of Marcellus' death agonies returned with vivid immediacy, mingling with Caracalla's suspicions. He felt Oclatinius' gaze boring into him, and took a deep swig, swilling the liquid around his mouth to see if he could detect any out-of-place flavours before swallowing. When he looked up, Oclatinius' face bore a trace of a smile. Silus cursed himself. Nothing got past the old man, and Silus had given away the fact that Caracalla's paranoia was rubbing off on him.

Oclatinius seemed happy to let it pass, but Silus knew this piece of information was now squirrelled away in the depths of his mind, along with all the pieces of gossip, leaks, denunciations and other intelligences that made him one of the most dangerous men in Rome, even without counting the team of highly trained spies and assassins that he commanded.

'Are you ready for the Emperor's departure?' he asked.

The next day, Caracalla was leaving Rome for the East, taking with him a vast entourage of advisors, senators, civil servants and palace slaves, as well as an army consisting of the praetorians, speculatores, the second legion, detachments drawn from across the western provinces, and Mauretanian and German cavalry. At a meeting of his military advisors, at which Silus had been present in his role as one of the Emperor's Leones, Caracalla had declared his ultimate objective as being a campaign to defeat Rome's old nemesis, Parthia. But before he could achieve that, he needed to secure the Pannonian and Dacian frontiers, to recruit more cavalry to counter the formidable Parthian horsemen, to take control of Armenia, and to create a brand-new unit of men that he claimed would be effective against the Parthian cavalry, though at that stage he gave no details. Silus knew that he faced a long period of campaigning, and it may be years before he returned to Rome. He had already said tearful goodbyes to Tituria, marvelling at the notion that the child might be an adult by the time he next saw her. And also an emotional goodbye to little Issa, who was already in her dotage, meaning there was a strong chance she would not be around when he returned.

If he returned.

'I'm always ready,' said Silus, with little enthusiasm.

Oclatinius noticed his glum demeanour. 'Well, you may not have the pleasure of Atius' company on this journey, but you will be glad to know I will be accompanying the Emperor.'

'That's a great comfort,' said Silus, and Oclatinius laughed.

'In all seriousness, the Emperor will be in serious danger from enemies within as well as without, all the time these conspirators remain at large. We need to keep alert. Something will give them away. We must be ready.'

Silus nodded. Caracalla's safety was vital, both for the Empire and for those that Silus held most dear The responsibility felt overwhelming. How easy it would be, for a man of his skills, to simply slip away, find himself a small town in the sticks somewhere far from Rome, and live off his savings and his wits, completely anonymous, with only himself to care about.

Of course, he was not that man. Curse the gods who made him the way he was.

He realised that he must soon bid farewell to Atius, too. Life seemed suddenly even more terrifying with the prospect of being without his friend at his side. He hoped Atius would keep out of trouble. Parting from Atius was going to be emotional. He was fairly sure Atius would cry. He took a long drink of wine, putting off the moment a while longer.

-

Caracalla sat on the edge of the bed, his face in his hands. Domna edged forward to sit beside him, a wool blanket held across her chest. She put an arm around his waist.

'It doesn't make you less of a man, you know.'

He tensed at the words, as if he had been struck. He tried to move away from Domna, but she held him tight, and as his resistance faded, he sunk into her embrace. They lay side by side on the bed, and Caracalla stroked his hand down her side. Domna searched his eyes earnestly. 'What are you worrying about?' she asked.

'You really need to ask?'

'Well,' she said, 'I can't do anything about that. What else?'

'Nothing else. Barbarians threats, conspiracies to murder me, the general business of ruling the world, they don't matter compared to this.'

'That's not true, my love. Those things matter greatly. To you and to the Empire. This? This is a small thing. Decreed by the gods that it must be so.'

'Then it is to the gods that I shall appeal. I will find an answer. I am the Emperor. I will demand the gods listen to me!'

Domna caressed his face gently.

'The gods will do as they wish, love. As they always do.'

Chapter IX

Raetia, Iunius, 214 A.D.

The city of Augusta Vindelicorum was the capital of Raetia, the province on the river Danuvius that nestled between Germania Superior and Noricum, and was the current centre of the Roman world, by virtue of the presence of the Emperor and all his court. That court, of course, included Silus, but he had precious little opportunity to do any sightseeing. Most of his waking hours involved attending the Imperial person, whatever the Emperor happened to be doing, whether it was adjudicating legal cases, exercising or taking a bath. That meant extensive periods of inactivity and tedium which had Silus grinding his teeth in boredom.

Fortunately this morning had provided some much-needed entertainment to rejuvenate Silus' atrophying will to live. Caracalla had decided to go on a wolf hunt in the forests surrounding the city, and the Leones had accompanied him. Though Silus was never fully comfortable on horseback, he had spent a considerable amount of time in the saddle since leaving Rome, and he had become rather attached to his mount, Delicatus. The bay gelding's name meant Pretty Boy, and he did have a certain way of holding himself that suggested he knew he was beautiful to behold. The grooms seemed to play up to this, and always took extra care to make sure that he looked his best. When the scruffy Silus mounted up, he could feel Delicatus' disdain at the unkempt appearance of his rider.

Still, they had bonded over time, and Delicatus was well-behaved and courteous, which was ideal for one to whom riding didn't come naturally, like Silus. That was the same whether they were trekking endless miles out of Italy towards the north-eastern frontier, or dodging through the trees, spear in hand, with a bunch of bloodthirsty Germans and an Emperor screaming crazily in a blonde wig, a half-grown lion bounding along beside him, while they chased down a wolf the size of a mythical beast.

Silus shot the Emperor occasional confused glances. It wasn't the first time he had seen Caracalla wearing the wig, but it was hard to become accustomed to, when one was used to seeing the Emperor's tight, short, brown curls. The wig was long and magnificently coiffured, and he wore trousers and a silver surcoat along with it, all in German style. The Leones loved it, and had cheered madly the first time he had appeared before them dressed as one of them. The important Romans, senators and military commanders and the like had been less impressed, and Silus had overheard Dio Cassius muttering that the whole charade was demeaning to the office of the Emperor, a comment that Silus had duly passed on to Oclatinius. The Arcanus commander had received the information with a perfunctory thank you, adding that Dio was always moaning and it meant little. The senators had been thoroughly fleeced for cash in order to fund this expedition, and though successfully defeating the Parthians might produce a wealth of gold and silver, most of that would flow into the Imperial coffers, leaving the senators out of pocket. The general dissatisfaction with Caracalla from the noble elite might be dangerous in the round, but one man's private grumbles did not constitute a clear threat. Still, Silus had been commended, and ordered to continue to keep his ears open.

The wolf, unaccustomed to being hunted rather the hunter, did not have the cunning of a fox or the graceful stealth of a deer, and though it temporarily evaded them, one of the hounds soon picked up its scent and started baying loudly. The wolf broke cover as the rest of the pack took up the cry, and Caracalla urged his horse forward. The big black stallion responded in an instant, springing forward and leaving Silus flapping at Delicatus' reins in an attempt to keep up. The other attendant Leones were spread out, seeking the prey in order to claim the kill for themselves, an achievement in which Silus didn't have the least interest, and was too far away to be involved with in any case. The only other to join the chase was the young lion who bounded along beside Silus with the youthful exuberance of a kitten racing after a mouse.

The wolf was fast, agile, and in its natural environment. It weaved between the trees, darted through undergrowth that impeded the bulkier horses, and took advantage of every piece of cover. The dogs kept their distance. Now they had located the quarry, their job was done. Though the wolf could rip any one of even these formidable hounds apart, the pack together would make short work of him. But they had been trained not to go for a kill which would deprive the huntsmen of their sport. What was the point of a hunt, if it was just to follow animals around so they could kill each other? The test of a man's strength and courage was in taking on the beast himself.

Caracalla clearly wanted to be the one to make the kill here, to show off his prowess and impress his trusted guards. Silus wanted to make sure that it wasn't Caracalla himself that became the prey, and as the Emperor opened up the distance between them, Silus became increasingly anxious. The wolf disappeared around a rocky outcrop, and soon after, the pursuing Caracalla vanished from Silus' view. Silus urged Delicatus onwards, and the haughty horse, seeming to read the worry in his rider, redoubled its efforts to catch up.

There was a loud cry, then a thump. Silus rounded the rocks, and took in the scene in one glance. At the far end of a clearing, Caracalla lay in the long grass. The wolf stood on his chest, slavering jaws inches from Caracalla's throat. The Emperor tried to reach for his spear but it had fallen out of reach. There was no sign of his mount, and Silus presumed that the wolf had ambushed the Emperor, leaping from cover to knock him off the horse, which had bolted riderless.

Caracalla was a big man, muscular and athletic, and he trained hard with his men. But this was an alpha male, weighing at least as much as the Emperor, and having the advantage of position and teeth set in powerful jaws, while Caracalla was supine and unarmed, completely helpless.

Silus understood all this in the briefest moment, realised he was too far away to reach Caracalla before the wolf ripped his throat out. He had one chance.

He steadied himself, gripping Delicatus' sides tightly with his thighs, drew back his spear arm, threw.

Just as Delicatus stumbled.

It was only a small depression, maybe something begun by a rabbit or fox and abandoned, not deep enough to snap the horse's leg. But enough to make him dip on one foreleg, throw his head to counterbalance, break stride just for a couple of paces.

The spear flew short, thudding into the grass three feet before the wolf. The wolf turned to glance dismissively at the missile, then turned back to Caracalla and opened its jaws.

A blur of golden fur, teeth, claws and pure muscle sailed through the air. The undergrowth that had concealed the young lion parted like the surface of the sea through which a dolphin had leapt, and the feline was the equal of that sea creature in grace and power. He hit the wolf full in the side of the chest, and the pair rolled sideways, snapping and biting and growling and tearing. Juvenile lion and mature wolf were matched in size, but where one had the courage and energy of youth, the other had the experience and confidence of age. The wolf would have seen off many competitors for the position of alpha in its years, while the pet lion had only instinct to guide it.

Experience quickly began to tell, and the lion cub, for the first time in its short life, found itself on the receiving end of a real mauling. Silus urged Delicatus forward, and to its credit, the dainty horse broke into a gallop towards two furious examples of its natural predators. But Silus was armed only with short sword now, of little use from horseback, and he prepared himself to leap down and defend the Emperor on foot.

But Caracalla had regained his feet. He took two strides towards the spear that Silus had thrown, now lodged point-first in the damp earth. He yanked it free, turned to the battling animals, feline and canine. The wolf was on top of the lion now, which was desperately fending off the jaws with its front feet. Caracalla broke into a sprint, spear lodged firmly under his arm. The wolf, absorbed in its own battle, sensed the threat too late. It turned, prepared to leap at Caracalla, just as the Emperor's spear caught it in the side of its vast chest and ran it through.

With a pitiful cry, the wolf rolled onto its side, attempted to snap at the spear shaft, then fell back, breathing heavily. Silus arrived and dismounted, drawing his sword to dispatch the fallen beast. Caracalla stopped him, held out a hand for his weapon. Silus passed the gladius to him, hilt first. Other Leones were arriving on the scene now, summoned by the noises of the epic battle. They were just in time to watch their Emperor thrust the point of the sword through the wolf's neck.

Blood spurted, the wolf convulsed and was still, and a great ululating cry went up from the Leones, raising weapons to the sky, and cheering the heroism of their commander. Silus looked around at their faces. They were lit up with adoration and pride. The most powerful man in the world dressed like them, rode with them, fought with them, treated them as comrades and equals. He was as strong and brave and skilled in the martial disciplines as the best of them. In that moment, Silus understood why the Leones loved Caracalla, and why he loved them. In spite of Silus' own mixed feelings towards the Emperor – his treachery towards the Alemanni, his threats to Tituria and the hold he had over Silus as a consequence – he felt himself caught up in the moment. He pumped his fist in the air, and joined in the cheering.

The Germans among the bodyguard started to call out, 'Donner, Donner!' The Germanic god of thunder, Silus knew, equivalent in some ways to the Roman figure of Hercules. The Leones dismounted, surrounded the Emperor, and Silus found himself in the middle of the celebration, chanting with the rest, as they clapped the Emperor and each other on the back.

Caracalla held up his hands for silence, and the cheers reluctantly died down.

'This wolf was a powerful adversary.'

It was true, thought Silus, looking at the still body. It must have been the biggest example of the species he had ever seen.

'And it is right that a man's enemy is of sufficient strength to be worthy of the battle. Rest assured, there will be many battles to come over the next few months and years, as we secure our borders in preparation for the ultimate test, war against the Parthians!'

The Leones broke out in roars of approval once more, and Caracalla let them have their voice for a few moments before continuing.

'But remember, though I am Emperor, though I am descended from gods, though one day I may be deified myself, I am but a man. When I ride in a triumph, a slave stands behind me and whispers in my ear, *remember you are mortal*. So hail me as Imperator, as Germanicus or Britannicus, as Father of my country. But do not hail me as a god. I am one of you.'

The cheers from the bodyguard were deafening now, and Caracalla soaked it all up, wearing a beatific smile. Silus marvelled at the ease with which the bluff, fierce ruler connected with the common soldier. And his words were well-chosen. Not only had he avoided being hailed as a god, with all the expectations that involved, he had reminded his bodyguard of the vulnerability of his flesh, and that it was their job to keep him safe.

The lion cub limped over to Caracalla, and he bent down to fuss it behind the ears.

'Aureus, you fought bravely, and you saved my life,' he said. He inspected the cub's injuries. To Silus' untrained eye, they seemed mostly superficial – grazes, cuts, puncture wounds – but there was a large gash in the cub's shoulder that showed torn muscle beneath. 'We'll get you patched up when we return to the city, boy.' Aureus rubbed his head against Caracalla's side, looking for all the world like an affectionate cat.

Caracalla asked Athaulf for his knife, and he dutifully handed it over. The Emperor then began to skin the wolf expertly.

Athaulf said, in a voice so low only Silus could hear, 'Why did the Emperor face danger alone?'

Silus turned to him in surprise. 'I was right behind him.'

'Not near enough to aid him.'

'I was a lot nearer than you, you stupid German cow-fucker. Where were you?'

Athaulf stiffened, but Silus had inadvertently raised his voice, and they were attracting attention. Athaulf kept his voice quiet and calm. 'My horse pulled up lame. I expected you to be by his side.'

'Well, unfortunately, the Emperor is faster than me on horseback. I did my best.'

'Hmm. Just remember, the Emperor's life is in our hands. I will not have anyone in the Leones who is not up to the job, however well-regarded they were in their previous positions.'

Silus felt anger surge within him, and he gritted his teeth.

'Maybe you and I could spend a little time alone together. I think we would quickly find out which of us was up to the job.'

There was a moment's silence, then Athaulf laughed, and slapped Silus hard between the shoulders.

'I like you, Silus. But I love the Emperor. Never forget that.'

Caracalla finished his work and draped the skin over Aureus' back like a trophy. One of the other Leones had located his horse, and rode back, leading the black stallion by the reins. Caracalla mounted, waved his hand in the air to call his guard to follow, and set off back towards the city.

–

When they arrived back at the governor's palace that Caracalla had requisitioned for his temporary headquarters, Macrinus was waiting for him, flanked by the frumentarii commanders, Ulpius Julianus and Julianus Nestor. The two Juliani were not related, as far as Silus knew. Presumably somewhere in the distant past, their ancestors had been adopted or freed by a Julius. The two could not be more dissimilar, though they were of a comparable age, probably in their late thirties. Ulpius was broad and short, more muscular than fat, while Nestor was tall with spindly arms and legs and a pot belly that looked like he was hiding an exercise ball under his tunic. All three wore serious looks upon their faces.

'Augustus,' said Macrinus, bowing low. 'Your outrider said you had had a fall. Are you well? Do I need to summon a physician?'

Caracalla waved a dismissive hand. 'No, no, I've suffered no damage. But Aureus is injured. You, Nestor – make sure he is seen by a veterinarius.'

The tall frumentarius looked shocked. 'I, Augustus? But…'

Macrinus shot him a warning glance.

'Of course, Augustus. At once.' Nestor bowed and hurried away.

'If you are sure you are well, Augustus,' said Macrinus, 'you have an important visitor.'

'Don't keep me in suspense, Macrinus. You don't need to use your lawyerly rhetorical devices on me.'

'Yes, Augustus. Gaiobomarus, the chief of the Quadi, has arrived in Augusta Vindelicorum in response to your summons.'

'Excellent. Make sure he and his entourage are properly looked after. I will bathe and eat, and then receive his embassy.'

Macrinus bowed, and rushed off with Ulpius in tow. Caracalla beckoned Athaulf and Silus to accompany him, and marched briskly to his private quarters within the palace. Attendant slaves fussed about him as he entered, taking off his surcoat and removing the wig to reveal his short, tight curls beneath. A young, Greek-looking slave boy pressed a silver goblet of wine into Caracalla's hand, and a matronly woman led the way to the bath complex. Athaulf and Silus accompanied him every step of the way, and took up position either side of the entrance.

Caracalla allowed the slave woman to strip away the remainder of his clothing, and then walked into the central pool. It wasn't the first time since becoming one of the Emperor's bodyguards that Silus had watched him bathe, but still he never knew whether he was supposed to look away at this point. The slave woman had no such compunction, pulling her tunic off and entering the bath with him, holding a jug she could fill with the hot water to pour over his head and back. There was no eroticism involved. The plump woman, though naked, carried out her task without embarrassment, and Caracalla paid her no more attention than if she was a sponge or a towel.

Silus' gaze was drawn more to the Emperor's naked body than the bathing slave woman. The chest was almost as hairy as the head and face, looking like it was covered in tightly curled wire. The pectoral muscles bulged, as did the upper arms and thighs. This was a man who exercised regularly and hard, whether it was marching with his troops or working out in the gymnasium. Whatever else you thought of Caracalla, he was a soldier's emperor.

After bathing, Caracalla was given a massage and a rub-down with oil and strigil from a well-built Gallic-looking slave, who also anointed the scrapes he had received on the hunt with honey. Finally, he was helped to dress, this time in his military uniform. It was rare for Caracalla to wear a toga when he was with the army.

At last, Caracalla was ready, and he flicked his fingers for Silus and Athaulf to accompany him as he strode out of the baths.

The governor's office had been turned into the throne room, and the palace slaves had worked hard to convert it into a place suitable for an emperor to receive important guests. The frescoes on the walls had been refreshed and repainted, the mosaic floor relaid, authentic antique Greek statues of mythological heroes and beasts lined the walls. Silus took up his place behind and to the right of Caracalla's marble throne, aware that unlike the Emperor, he had not been given the opportunity to bathe or even change since the hunt, and that he must look a complete mess.

Caracalla settled himself into the throne, and at a command, Aureus the young lion was brought to him, led by an anxious-looking Nestor on a long lead. The lion limped slightly, ducking its head each time it placed one of its front paws down, and it had had its shoulder wound bathed and stitched. Caracalla gestured for Nestor to release him, and the lion padded over, then laid on its back, feet in the air, rubbing its head against the base of the throne, before suddenly becoming distracted by one of the tassels of the silk cloth that covered the seat.

'You may admit our visitor,' said Caracalla, and two praetorian centurions escorted Gaiobomarus in. The Quadi king was a typical German in build and appearance, with long blonde hair, all his own rather than a wig, Silus reflected. He was flanked by two advisors; tough, scarred veterans – unarmed, of course. He approached Silus, and dropped briefly to one knee, his companions following his lead, before standing again, hands clasped behind his back. Caracalla acknowledged him, but did not signal for the king to stand, so he had to remain on one knee, craning his neck to look up at the Emperor.

'King Gaiobomarus,' said Caracalla, inclining his head.

'I came as soon as I received your summons, Augustus,' said the king in a loud, clear voice.

Silus didn't pretend to understand the politics and diplomacy between Rome and the Germans. Their tribes were so numerous, and the alliances constantly shifted, so today's ally might be yesterday's enemy, and maybe tomorrow's enemy as well. As far as he knew, the Quadi were currently loosely allied to Rome, but it was a balancing act between showing his men he was subservient to none, while keeping the peace with Rome.

Caracalla nodded, and Silus was surprised at his discourtesy. No formal greetings, no gifts. This wasn't a normal reception for an allied king. Silus had a bad feeling about this. He glanced at Oclatinius, who stood with Macrinus, both of them garbed in the resplendent uniform of a praetorian prefect, Macrinus wearing it with pride, Oclatinius looking distinctly uncomfortable in the military regalia. Oclatinius caught Silus' furtive look, gave a slight shake of his head, and returned to staring straight ahead.

'King Gaiobomarus, you gave assurances to my emissaries to support Rome in her military endeavours.'

'Yes, Augustus, to the best of our ability.'

'War is coming. Are you prepared to fulfil your obligations under our treaties? Will you lead your army against Rome's foes?'

Gaiobomarus spread his hands.

'Of course, Augustus. But many of our men are tending the fields at the moment. The harvest last year was not what we hoped, and they work hard to make sure there is food in our bellies come the winter.'

'It is as I thought,' said Caracalla. He motioned towards Macrinus. 'Prefect, please read the charges.'

Gaiobomarus gaped. 'Ch…charges, Augustus? I don't understand.'

Macrinus stepped forward, unrolled a scroll, and using his best oratorical tone, read aloud.

'It is alleged that you, King Gaiobomarus of the Quadi, are conspiring with the enemies of Rome, the tribe known as the Vandals.'

'That is outrageous,' cried Gaiobomarus. 'Who slanders me this way?'

'Oclatinius?' Caracalla indicated the old man. Oclatinius nodded, and said loudly, 'Admit Vangio.'

A younger German strode in, flanked by two praetorian legionaries. Gaiobomarus stared at him.

'Nephew? What are you doing here?'

Vangio avoided Gaiobomarus' gaze, keeping his eyes fixed on Caracalla. He dropped to both knees, bowed his head, and stayed there until Caracalla told him to stand.

'Augustus,' said Oclatinius, 'this is Vangio, Prince of the Quadi. He came to me bearing grave intelligence.'

'Speak, Vangio. What have you to say?'

'Augustus,' said Vangio, and Silus was sure he could detect a sense of distaste in the prince's tone. 'It is my sad duty to report what I observed with my own eyes.'

'Go on.'

'I was at a meeting between my King, Gaiobomarus, and the Vandal King Gunderic. They discussed an alliance against Rome. They plan to form a confederacy of the tribes, and invade Gaul, before striking into Italy, and towards Rome itself.'

There were gasps from around the throne room, and Gaiobomarus cried aloud, 'That's a lie! Vangio, what are you doing?'

'And what are your feelings towards Rome, Prince Vangio?' asked Caracalla.

'Rome is a glorious Empire, the most powerful in the world, and it is an honour for the Quadi to be allied with you. I believe it is treason for a Quadi king to conspire against Rome's enemies.'

Caracalla stroked his chin, as if deeply considering Vangio's words, though it was obvious to Silus that this was all a prearranged show.

'It is with heavy heart that I must agree with you, Vangio. Gaiobomarus is guilty of treason. I hereby strip him of his title of king, and pass it to you, King Vangio.'

'You do not have the authority!' roared Gaiobomarus, stepping forward, fists balled. Silus moved to interpose himself between Caracalla and the angry barbarian, placing his hand threateningly on the hilt of his sword. Gaiobomarus stopped in his tracks, but continued to shout. 'This is not legitimate. I am King of the Quadi. You have no right!'

'King Vangio, you have the sad duty of passing judgement on your uncle. In the matter of treason against the Quadi, and against Rome, how do you find Gaiobomarus?'

'Guilty,' said Vangio, a little quaver in his voice.

'And what is your sentence?'

He hesitated, looked at Gaiobomarus, who stared at him, face pale.

'Death,' he said.

Gaiobomarus lunged towards Vangio, arms outstretched. Silus was nearest and reacted first, diving onto the deposed king's back, wrapping his arm around his throat. The large barbarian thrashed and yelled, trying to dislodge Silus, who clung on with arms and legs wrapped around him. Athaulf was there a moment later, and the two Leones restrained Gaiobomarus, gripping an arm each until a praetorian reached them with rope and tied the struggling man's arms behind his back.

Other praetorians pointed spears at Gaiobomarus' advisors until they too were bound.

'Take this man out, and administer the punishment decreed by his king,' said Caracalla.

Silus looked around for a moment, until he realised that the Emperor meant him. His heart sank. *Oh no, not again.* He had been the Emperor's executioner once before, and had made a terrible mess of it. He looked to Oclatinius in mute appeal, but the Arcani commander just gave him a small apologetic shrug.

Silus and Athaulf dragged the struggling Gaiobomarus from the room, and out of the palace to the courtyard in front of the building. The praetorians marched the condemned man's advisors along behind, and all three were forced to their knees. Caracalla and his council gathered in a solemn semi-circle around the prisoners. Silus looked to Oclatinius, who gave him a small nod of encouragement, then to Caracalla.

'Proceed,' said the Emperor.

Silus drew his sword. He had been given no warning of this, no time to prepare himself, and no instruction as to how he was to do the deed. Decapitation was the obvious way, but the gladius was not the right weapon for that – it didn't have the weight to ensure that one swing would swipe the head clean off. A stab through the liver into the chest was a certain death, but a slow one. He elected in the end for the gladiator's blow. Taking the hilt of his sword in both hands, with no preamble, he thrust the blade down between neck and collarbone. It was clean and instant, and Gaiobomarus slid off his sword and lay still on the flagstones, blood spreading out from the wound.

The praetorians slit the advisors' throats and thrust their bodies forward to lie face down on the stone. Silus looked around for something to clean his bloody blade on, found nothing, so wiped it on the dead king's cloak. He looked up, and saw Vangio looking on, shaking and looking like he might faint. Caracalla wore an amused expression. Silus sheathed his blade and stepped back.

'King Vangio, come with me. We have much to discuss. I hope you will join me for dinner.'

Caracalla put his arm around the new ruler of the Quadi, and guided him into the palace. Silus looked at the cooling corpses, and followed his Emperor back inside.

Caracalla rode at the head of his army, mounted on an elephant, his lion trotting by his side. Caracalla had decreed that the lion would not accompany him into battle, but the elephants were another matter. The Emperor had brought a number of the huge beasts with him, imported from India. Most rode in the rear, with the less skittish pack animals, rather than with the highly strung cavalry horses in the front and on the flanks. But Caracalla, as in most things he did, had a double purpose, both projecting power and getting the war horses accustomed to the terrifying animals. Delicatus for one threw the elephant suspicious glances, and Silus could tell from his pulled-back ears that he was ready to bolt if the elephant so much as looked at him in a funny way.

Silus rode on one side of the Emperor, Athaulf on the other, and a double column of Leones came up behind them, glowing with the honour of marching at the front. Less impressed were the praetorians, relegated to second position, and Silus thought that their uniforms were polished to an even higher level of perfection than normal, maybe to compensate for their injured pride. Silus wondered if Caracalla's preferment of the Germanic and Celtic Leones over the Roman praetorians was wise. He understood how the praetorians were not entirely to be trusted, but spurning them might make them even more likely to rebel.

He glanced back. The Roman army on the march was always awe-inspiring, and this one was vast, with units drawn from across the Empire. Cavalry and infantry, legionaries and auxiliaries, all marched with purpose and a restrained excitement. The imminence of battle gave them all a chance for glory and personal enrichment, and after a long period that involved drills, route marches, practice with wooden swords and long hours of boredom, they were itching to be in the fight.

Many would be veterans of course, and Silus wondered if they had managed to instil any sense of realism into the green troops. Battle was not all thrill and excitement. It was hard, tiring, dangerous, terrifying. If they didn't die, it was likely friends of theirs would. But maybe the veterans too had forgotten what it was like, and were bursting with desire to be back in action once more. Silus had heard that many women quickly forgot the pain and horror of childbirth and desired to be pregnant once more, only for the realisation of the awfulness of the experience to come crashing back once their labour began. Maybe it was like that for veterans in battle. As for Silus, he never forgot. He had seen too much pain, death and loss for it ever to be far away.

It was a long march from Raetia to Pannonia, via Noricum, but Caracalla had made it clear he wanted them to arrive as quickly as possible. He had a long campaigning season in mind. His ultimate aim was Parthia. What a prize that would be, to add the territories of Rome's ancient enemy to the Empire! Julius Caesar himself had planned to wage war on the Parthians, until assassination cut short the possibility. Caracalla's father, Septimius Severus, had had limited success against the Empire to the east, and had even taken the title Parthicus Maximus, but to Silus' understanding, the wars had been far from conclusive. Parthia, of course, was the successor to the old Persian Empire, so Caracalla could emulate his hero Alexander by defeating them. Maybe that would make him the greatest Roman general of all time.

But he had not achieved his successes so far through impulsiveness and lack of preparation. Hence why the entire eastern frontier would be subdued, pacified, and stripped of resources before he would take on the might of Rome's powerful neighbour. He would not make the mistakes of Crassus or Mark Anthony. That wasn't to say that this preliminary campaign would be a walk in the park. These Danubian tribes, the Dacians, Sarmatians, Carpi and the like, were tough as old leather boots, and vicious as wolves.

The days were long, so there were plenty of light hours to march in. There would be no stops in cities, no baths, taverns with hot food and warm girls, not even a comfortable and clean bed. Just tents behind the palisade that was erected every night and dismantled the next morning. Still, the weather was good, and at least he would have a mattress, and a sheet above his head to keep out the elements, and he would be surrounded by the might of the legions. A far cry from his time alone in the wildernesses of Germania or Caledonia. He should thank Fortuna for small mercies. Being Caracalla's bodyguard, barring the occasional unpleasant duty like performing an execution, was turning out to be a rather relaxed posting. Maybe it was something he could get used to. Maybe he would have a long happy career in the Leones.

As long as his Emperor remained alive.

Chapter X

Iulius, 214 AD

It was Silus' third battle in the last month, and he was quite frankly fed up with it. His chest felt like it had been worked on by a blacksmith's hammer, his inner thighs chafed from gripping desperately to Delicatus as they dodged and weaved in and out of the mayhem. Half-healed cuts along his shins and forearms reopened and oozed sanguineous fluid from beneath sticky scabs. If he had thought being one of Caracalla's personal bodyguards was a good way to keep out of danger, he was very mistaken.

The Emperor was at that moment charging madly after a group of fleeing barbarians, standing upright in his war chariot as his driver urged the horses on, whooping and waving his spear in the air. Silus bent low and held onto Delicatus' neck as he let his mount have his head. Intermittently, arrows, slingshots and javelins whistled past, and he ducked at each ominous sound, conscious that he would probably never hear the one that took him down.

A bare-chested barbarian warrior riding a wiry bay pony, unsaddled, steering expertly with his heels, closed in on Silus' flank. He brandished what looked like a Roman pilum, maybe looted from a dead legionary, maybe illegally traded. Its provenance wouldn't matter if it found its way to Silus' heart.

The barbarian drew his arm back, steadied himself, threw. Silus kept his eyes fixed on the missile as it arced towards him, and he prayed that Delicatus would keep steady. With perfect timing, born part of instinct, part of long practice, he swept his shield around and batted the pilum aside. The barbarian shouted in rage and drew a long sword from its scabbard.

Delicatus raced onwards, hooves throwing up great clods of mud as he tried to match the pace of the two magnificent geldings drawing the Emperor's chariot. Silus gauged the speed of the barbarian rider. In a straight race, he thought Delicatus would have the edge. But Silus had to constantly adjust his trajectory to match the Emperor's sudden course changes as he veered wildly towards a running barbarian to hurl one of the javelins stacked at the front of the chariot into the unfortunate man's back, then swerved back to rejoin the pursuit of the routed herd of warriors.

Silus cursed and drew his own sword, the long spatha that had started as a weapon for the auxiliary cavalry, but was rapidly becoming adopted by the foot soldiers of the legions for its superior reach when thrusting into enemy ranks.

The barbarian approached from behind and to Silus' right, seeming to inch towards him, as their speeds, though rapid, were so closely matched. He came close enough that Silus could see his yellow teeth and matted beard as he raised his sword.

Silus yanked on Delicatus' reins, dragging him to the right. He knew that Delicatus hated him being heavy-handed on the bit, and would often resist overly forceful commands, but the wily beast also knew there was a time and place to defy his master, and this was not it. He darted across the path of the enemy horseman, his meaty shoulder impacting the slighter barbarian pony's neck and barging it off course. The barbarian was forced to abandon his sword swing and clutch at his mount's mane to avoid falling, his ability to balance on the animal's back lessened by the lack of a saddle. Silus didn't know if it was bravado or lack of resources that made his opponent ride bareback, but he was happy to take any advantage, whatever the reason for it.

As the barbarian struggled to stay upright, Silus took a back-handed swipe at him. The warrior ducked, avoiding the blow, but dangling even further over the horse's side. Delicatus raced the enemy pony, flank against flank, pushing hard to dominate his speed and direction. Silus drew his sword back, ready to swing again, but it was difficult to reach the unbalanced barbarian from this angle. Instead, he swept the blade down, and severed the barbarian's reins.

For a moment, the barbarian clutched the leather straps, staring in confusion as he tugged on them in a vain attempt to stay mounted. Then Delicatus gave the enemy mount a shove, and the enemy horseman toppled off to hit the earth with a crunch of bones. His pony, now unguided, slowed his pace and moved away from the larger warhorse that had been bullying him.

The barbarian warrior would likely survive the fall, at least in the short term, but it wasn't Silus' job to kill enemy combatants. His only aim was to keep the Emperor alive. And Caracalla was making it difficult for him.

He finally managed to bring Delicatus abreast of the Emperor's chariot as he neared the pack of routed warriors. Caracalla looked over to Silus and waved his javelin, and his lips were drawn back in a feral grin. Silus wouldn't have been surprised if he had seen blood dripping from the Emperor's canines, so bestial did he appear in that moment.

Then they were amongst the terrified, vanquished barbarians, and Caracalla was flinging javelins left and right, skewering torsos, puncturing necks, impaling skulls. Athaulf and one of the other Leones, a recently recruited giant called Maximinus Thrax, had managed to keep pace with their ward, and they joined in the slaughter, slashing down with their spathas at any too slow to get out of the way. Silus contented himself with guarding Caracalla, only striking out if an enemy rounded on the Emperor.

One of the barbarians, a little ahead of the pack, and being hustled away by two other warriors, stopped and turned, and held his sword upright in front of his face. His expression was resigned, ready to face his fate. The warriors berated him, urged him on, but he shrugged them away. It was obvious to Silus that this man was a chief or a noble, and his bodyguards were desperately trying to keep him alive. Just like he was doing for Caracalla.

A javelin thrown by Athaulf took one of the barbarian bodyguards through the shoulder, tumbling him backwards. Thrax, mounted on a huge stallion that was one of the few horses able to bear his bulk, rode at the remaining guard and with one powerful, perfectly timed blow, swept his head off. It rolled across the earth, open eyes blinking once before rolling upwards, as the body sank to its knees and fell sideways, blood pumping from severed neck vessels.

Athaulf picked up another javelin to finish the chief, but Caracalla roared a command to halt. Athaulf stayed his hand, and Caracalla leapt over the side of the chariot, landing heavily but with perfect agility on both feet. He drew his own spatha, and held it before his face in salute. The chief nodded, weary, defeated, but ready to fight one last time for his honour, and the honour of his vanquished people.

Though most of the retreating warriors continued their headlong flight, relieved at the breathing space this spectacle brought them, some stopped, turned and cheered on their chief. Silus and the other two Leones formed the apices of a large triangle around the two combatants, but Caracalla commanded them to stay back.

With a roar, the chief charged at Caracalla, his sword raised high, ready to bring it down in a blow that would cleave the Emperor's head in half. Caracalla waited until the weapon was falling before darting adroitly to one side, letting the blade swish through empty space to lodge in the hard earth. He didn't attempt to counter, but allowed his opponent to haul his weapon free, and shake off the clods of mud that clung to it.

The chief took a deep breath and charged again, this time sweeping a horizontal cut towards Caracalla's midriff. Caracalla countered it with his own sword, turned the blow aside, then slashed back, making the chief jump out of the way.

It was not a fair fight, of course. The chief was a big man, but he wore no armour, only a pair of woollen trousers. Silus could see the grey hair on his scarred, tattooed chest, curly and stained with blood – his own or someone else's, Silus wasn't sure. He was exhausted, too, from combat and his flight on foot, while Caracalla had waited until the battle was won before entering the fray. Caracalla wore a cuirass of segmented armour and an ornate, feathered helmet, and carried a round shield on his left arm. He would need little help from the gods to win this bout.

Nevertheless, there was real danger here. This was not Commodus, fighting in the arena against gladiators armed only with wooden swords. A lucky strike in a vulnerable point, armpit or neck or groin, could be fatal, and Silus watched nervously, itching to intervene, but knowing the wrath it would bring down on him if he did.

Caracalla was clearly enjoying himself, and though he treated his opponent with respect, he was prolonging the encounter as much as possible. Silus presumed at first that this was to lengthen the exciting experience, but as others of the Roman army caught them up, Leones and praetorians, legionaries and auxiliaries, and began to cheer and salute their martial Emperor, Silus realised that, as was so often the case with Caracalla, he had more than one goal in mind. To experience the thrill of battle was the first part, but to demonstrate to his men his bravery, his skill with a sword, and most of all that he fought and endangered his body just as they did, was just as important. Caracalla relied on the army absolutely for his power, hated as he was by the Senate, and he needed them to adore him.

And adore him they did, roaring and clapping and urging him on.

Caracalla engaged the chief in some interchanges of swordplay, showing off some skilful moves that would not have been out of place in a top-class gladiatorial fight. But the chief was clearly tiring, and soon it would become less of a contest and more of a torment.

The chief had clearly come to the same realisation. He took a step back, gathering his breath for a moment, then rushed forward, sword extended, no attempt at subtlety or defence. Caracalla tossed his shield aside and used two hands to sweep his own sword against his opponent's. The weapon arced out of the chief's grip and lodged, point down, in the earth, quivering like the shaft of an arrow in a target. The chief looked to it helplessly, then into Caracalla's eyes. Caracalla nodded to him, then thrust forward.

The weapon skewered the chief's chest, the tip bursting out from his back. He grasped the blade, then his legs gave way and he fell heavily and was still.

A moan went up from the barbarians who had bravely stayed to watch, which was quickly drowned out by a huge cheer from the Roman audience. Caracalla retrieved his sword, and handed it to Athaulf, who passed it to Silus to clean. The Emperor raised his arms to acknowledge the adulation of his soldiers, then spoke loudly.

'This is how those who oppose me end!'

The volume of the soldiers' cheers increased even further.

'And those who fight with me will be forever my friend, and will be rewarded. Now, go and finish these dogs off.'

The Romans, foot soldiers and cavalry, elite praetorians and Leones, lowly auxiliaries, all set off to pursue and slaughter as many survivors as they could find. This was Caracalla's way. He was not one to leave an enemy to regroup and fight another day, if he could annihilate them there and then. Some called it merciless. Some called it prudent.

Silus pulled out a cloth and wiped the Emperor's sword clean as best he could. The armourers would need to work on it later in any case, to sharpen it and file out the notches that marred its edge. When he had finished, he handed it to Caracalla's driver, who stowed it in the front of the chariot.

Silus looked around him now, taking in the day's work for the first time. Scattered across a wide field of battle were the bodies of the unlucky, the dead and mortally wounded. Most were barbarian, but many were Roman, their shields bearing the colours of their units, detachments drawn from across the Empire and recruited locally in Greece, Germania, Pannonia, Raetia and Noricum. Already, the scavengers were moving in, human and animal. Crows and ravens fought over chunks of meat and offal, while local civilians scurried between bodies, looting coins, trinkets and weapons, scattering like vermin when warned away by angry soldiers.

He wasn't entirely sure where they were. Somewhere along the Pannonian border, he thought. And the barbarians? Well, that had got a bit confusing as well. Caracalla had decided to secure his frontiers before tackling the Parthians. He was no fool as a general, and was well aware of the possibility of rebellion and invasion if he threw all his resources into a campaign without crushing all threats to his rear first. As a consequence, the summer had been a blur of marches, skirmishes and full-on battles, with a variety of opponents and allies that seemed to shift more quickly than Silus could keep up with.

Today's enemy had been a mix of Sarmatian and Scythian tribes from east of the Danube that Caracalla had provoked into an invasion of Pannonia with some diplomatic skulduggery or other. Another potential danger crossed off his list.

The Quadi had been a valuable aid in today's battle, fighting on the right flank alongside the Osroene cavalry;

the two allied nations that showed that Caracalla's diplomacy produced friends as well as enemies. The Quadi king Vangio had fallen loyally into line since the execution of his uncle Gaiobomarus, and provided men to swell the ranks of the legions, as well as units that remained nominally under Quadi command but fought on the Roman side. The kingdom of Osroene, a formerly hostile region of Armenia, had been annexed without a fight after Caracalla had summoned and arrested their King Abgarus, and their mounted archers had proven their worth time and again. No doubt Caracalla was learning a lot from them, too. The ultimate goal of this campaign was the defeat of Parthia, but their missile cavalry had humbled Rome more than once in the past. Defeat of this historic enemy was going to take more than overwhelming force. Strategy and tactics, on and off the battlefield, would be paramount.

Athaulf and Thrax approached Silus.

'Did you have fun today?' Silus asked Thrax.

The bulky bodyguard grunted. He really was a vast slab of meat, broad and tall, with a face that could make grown men vomit.

'Another victory,' said Athaulf. 'I think the men are coming to expect them.'

'Let's hope it doesn't breed complacency,' said Silus.

'Perhaps it will. But they have good reason to be complacent. Caracalla has built a force here that Rome has not seen for many a year. Maybe not even his glorious father could have bettered what our Emperor has achieved here. Trained, battle-hardened, loyal, a formidable mix of abilities, and you can't doubt Caracalla's generalship.'

Silus doubted a lot of things about Caracalla, but his ability to lead troops in battle and achieve resounding outcomes was not among them.

'It's not enemies on the battlefield that Caracalla needs to fear, anyway,' said Athaulf.

Silus stiffened. 'What have you heard?'

'Nothing specific, of course. Otherwise we could take action. But the senators are always complaining and moaning. That Cassius Dio should be dealt with, for one. I heard he was saying to any who would listen that this campaign was a waste of men and resources.'

'That's because he is being asked to pay for it,' said Thrax, his accent thick and Germanic.

Silus looked at the big man in surprise. He hadn't known he was able to speak.

'Speaking out isn't the action of a man who intends treachery. It's the quiet ones we need to watch out for.'

'Well,' said Silus, 'if you hear anything, tell Oclatinius.'

'Pah,' said Athaulf. 'I trust him as little as anyone. I command the Leones, I am the Emperor's closest and most senior bodyguard. It is on me to see him safe.'

This was reassuring to hear. Silus had much riding on Caracalla's continued existence, and knowing the competent and formidable Athaulf was responsible for the Emperor's well-being went some way to assuaging Silus' anxiety. Still, he would be even happier if Caracalla behaved more like his more recent predecessors and stayed well away from the frontline in battle.

His mind suddenly focussed on the other thing Athaulf had said. He didn't trust Oclatinius? Was that just a general caution about the powerful and somewhat mysterious spymaster, or did he know something specific? But before he could pursue the subject, Caracalla strode up to them, helmet under his arm.

'My Lions,' he said, clapping Athaulf between the shoulders. 'What a glorious day!'

Silus took in his broad grin, gleaming eyes, the flecks of blood spattered across his cheeks, and realised that in action – the battle, the hunt, the chariot race – and the immediate aftermath was the only time that he ever saw the Emperor truly happy. In council with his advisors, ruling over lawsuits, in diplomatic meetings, even at banquets and parties, he wore the same stern frown, eyes narrow, forehead furrowed. Soldiers were generally not the most subtle of men, but even they were able to tell when a man genuinely enjoyed sharing their triumphs and trials. Caracalla was in no danger of a revolt by his own men, Silus was sure.

'Another great victory,' said Athaulf, and Silus thought that rather than spouting platitudes to his ruler, he probably meant it. And it might be the first time the Emperor was getting full credit for his victories. Though he had won many battles in Caledonia, that was his father's campaign. Though he had more success in Germania than any Emperor for a generation or more, it was marred by his treatment of the Alemanni, with his detractors saying he won by treachery rather than bravery and skill, the way a true Roman should. But in this campaign, though he employed various underhand tricks and stratagems, there could be no doubt that his victories were coming on the field, and he was at the centre of the action throughout, not waiting until the end before riding in on the back of an elephant the way Claudius had nearly two centuries prior when he had conquered Britannia while sitting on his backside in Rome.

‘What next, Augustus?’ asked Silus, hoping the answer would be rest, a good meal, and a soft bed.

‘We finish mopping up any remaining resistance here. Then onwards. Dacia and the Getae are waiting for us. But first I have something else to do.’

Silus hoped he remained outwardly impassive. Because his inward voice had just screamed loudly, ‘Fuck!’

-

The shrine was small and unassuming, but nevertheless had a long stream of visitors queueing for entry. Only Silus and Athaulf accompanied Caracalla, all three mounted. Caracalla wore his Gallic cloak, head drawn up to disguise his features. Oclatinius and Festus had both asked to attend the Emperor, but their requests had been dismissed with a wave of the Imperial hand. Oclatinius had taken Silus aside at that point, and asked, with a note of concern in his voice that Silus had rarely heard, whether Silus felt that he, Oclatinius, was out of favour with the Emperor. Silus had thought of Athaulf’s comments, and his own doubts, but had honestly replied that he had no evidence that the Emperor doubted the old spymaster. Oclatinius had not seemed particularly reassured.

This particular holy site was one of a long succession that Caracalla had visited on his travels across the Empire since leaving Rome, and Silus had attended him on most of those side trips, leaving the legions to their march while the Emperor and his chosen companions went on these little pilgrimages. Always the sites were dedicated to one of the healing deities, mainly members of the Roman pantheon, but sometimes local deities, or those odd fusions of local and Roman gods that had arisen over the years, such as Mars Belacutadrus, the war god that had been commonly worshipped by the locally recruited soldiers in Silus' home of northern Britannia.

Rumours abounded throughout the legions and the civilian camp followers as to the purpose of Caracalla's visits. He certainly appeared to be in the rudest of health, strong and fit and active. Some said he hadn't been able to get it up since he had murdered his brother, but comments like that often led to violence from the loyal legionaries, offended by any impugnation of the virility or morality of their beloved Imperator. Silus himself wondered if Caracalla suffered from some hidden illness, maybe a disorder of the mind. Certainly, the joy of battle rapidly faded, to be replaced by brooding and fits of temper that left any near enough to witness his displays of anger shaking and in fear for their lives.

This particular shrine was dedicated to the daughters of Aesculapius, the god of healing and son of Apollo, himself a god of medicine. Oclatinius had given Silus a brief lesson in the genealogy of Apollo's line, and the roles of his descendants. While Aesculapius was regarded as the most important of the deities concerned with health, he was assisted by his five daughters who helped with various aspects of his duties. Panacea was the goddess of universal health, Hygieia was the goddess of cleanliness, Iaso was the goddess of recuperation from illness, while Aceso aided the healing process. Aglaea, not to be confused with the similarly named Grace who was the daughter of Jupiter, was the goddess of beauty and the glow of health. The names of Hygieia and Panacea were invoked in the oath of Hippocrates that was taken by reputable followers of the Greek style of medicine.

It was all very confusing, and Silus could see why people were drawn to the simplicity of the message of Atius' god, Christos. But Caracalla had no interest in Christianity, and set his faith in the old gods. Though he seemed to be growing increasingly frustrated with their lack of aid in whatever matter ailed him.

Silus let his eyes roam over the queue of supplicants and pilgrims waiting for admittance to the shrine, to meet the priest and sacrifice at the altar. They really were a revolting, pitiable bunch, he reflected. Like someone had swept the most afflicted beggars of the streets of Rome up with a big broom and deposited them here. One young woman had a face covered with weeping pustules. A fat man leant on a slave, keeping the weight off his ulcerated leg. A young mother carried a small, painfully thin child, who regarded Silus with wide, sad, unblinking eyes.

'Get rid of them,' said Caracalla.

Silus sighed inwardly. The order was not unexpected – it had been the same at every other shrine they had visited, and obviously Caracalla wanted complete privacy. Still, it was an unpleasant task. He tied the reins of the horses to a tree, then strode to the front of the queue with Athaulf and raised his voice.

'The shrine is closed.'

Groans of dismay and shouts of confusion and anger rose from the sickly supplicants.

'Go home. Leave this place. You may return tomorrow.'

'Please sir, don't make us go,' said the mother of the emaciated child. 'My daughter is dying.'

'I'm sorry,' said Silus.

'I've been waiting here for hours,' shouted an older man, his arm around a woman with a bright yellow hue to her skin.

'Who do you think you are?' cried the fat man, stepping forward, then yelping as his sore leg took his considerable weight.

Athaulf unsheathed his sword, slowly and deliberately, the sound of the metal on the scabbard ringing clearly through the air.

'I'm going to count to ten,' he said. 'When I get there, if there is anyone not hurrying away from here as quickly as your sickly bodies can take you, you will receive healing from the edge of my blade.'

And with that he started to count loudly.

The poor supplicants hesitated, attempted to argue, but Athaulf continued the count, his face impassive, sword dangling loosely from his hand. By the time he had reached five, most of the crowd had turned and begun to shuffle and limp away, and when he had finished all were well in retreat apart from the young mother with her dying daughter. She stared defiantly at Athaulf, trembling, the tiny girl clutched tight in her arms.

Athaulf looked to Caracalla, who nodded for him to enter the shrine first. Athaulf turned and went up the steps and into the small marble temple. Caracalla regarded Silus for a long moment. Silus had a horrible, sick feeling in his stomach. Was Caracalla really going to ask him to kill this desperate young woman? That he thought it possible, even probable, spoke volumes to Silus about how he viewed the Emperor.

But Caracalla seemed to be in a mood for mercy, or at least, had other things on his mind. 'Come,' he said, and followed Athaulf.

Silus let out a breath he hadn't realised he had been holding. He approached the woman and spoke quickly. 'Go and hide, out of sight in that copse over there. He won't be long. When you're sure we are gone, take your daughter to the priest.' He looked at the little girl. 'I pray you find what you need here.' Then he hurried after Caracalla.

The interior of the tiny temple was dimly lit with candles. A strong smell of incense pervaded the air. The walls were painted with symbols – the sun representing Apollo, a rod with a snake entwined around it to represent Aesculapius. At the far end of the room was an altar, carved with similar symbols. On it rested a silver goblet with a snake around the stem, its head raised and looking down into the cup, presumably representing one of the daughters, though Silus wasn't sure which. Before the altar, seated on a cushion, was the priest of the daughters of Aesculapius. He wore a long robe with a pointed hood drawn up, from beneath which crept light, wavy hair. As Silus approached, he saw the man was surprisingly young, not much older than twenty years, with a smooth, shaven chin. Most of the priests in these places had been ancient, wrinkled and white-bearded.

He seemed calm and unperturbed by the entrance of Caracalla and the two armed men. He gestured to Caracalla.

'Approach in humility, and receive healing.'

Caracalla walked forward, uncharacteristically hesitant, even shy. He knelt before the priest, pulled his hood back and bowed. The young lad laid a hand on the Emperor's curly-haired head, closed his eyes, and intoned some words of prayer. When he had finished, he put his hands on his knees, and looked directly at Caracalla.

'What brings you to seek succour from the sacred sisters?' he asked.

Caracalla opened his mouth to speak, then remembered the presence of Silus and Athaulf.

'Wait outside,' he growled at them.

The two Leones bowed, and retreated back into the bright light. Athaulf closed the temple door, and they stood with their backs to it, alert to any threats, unlikely as they seemed.

'What do you think it is?' asked Silus.

'What do I think what is?'

'His… problem.'

'I don't know and I don't care. It's none of my business, and none of yours.'

Silus closed his mouth.

They stood in silence for a while, the afternoon sun beating down, birds singing in the nearby trees. A herd of goats munched on some thorny bushes. It was an idyllic, bucolic scene, so far from the horrors of battle. It made Silus want to lie down in the grass and sleep.

He took a deep breath of the clean air and sighed it out. A feeling of peace grew from somewhere within him, spreading out through his limbs, a sense of relaxation that he had not experienced for so long, maybe for years.

An angry yell came from inside the temple. Silus reacted first, throwing the door open and charging through, Athaulf close on his heels.

Caracalla had his hand around the young priest's throat, shouting incoherently, spittle flying into the terrified man's face. Silus couldn't make out many of the words, and the ones he could discern were mainly curses and threats of violence. The Emperor's meaty hand squeezed the priest's neck hard, and as Silus stared, the priest's face turned from red to blue. Athaulf had his sword unsheathed, ready to deal with any threat to the Emperor's life, but there was none, and he didn't seem to know what to do.

Silus strode forward, gripped the Emperor's shoulder, and yanked him away. The priest dropped to his knees, clutching his throat and gasping air through his bruised windpipe. Caracalla's face was a mask of fury, and he raised his hand to strike Silus. Silus tensed to accept the blow, and prepared to force down the instinct to retaliate, which would likely be fatal, especially with Athaulf ready for action behind him.

The blow never fell, but Caracalla roared, 'You dare touch your Emperor! You will pay with your life!'

Silus quailed, but kept his voice steady as he replied. 'Augustus, I don't know what you seek here, but I know your wishes will not be served by murdering a priest of the healing goddesses.'

It seemed self-evident, but Caracalla's eyes shone with madness brought on by grief and rage.

'Who are you to question me?' he said, still furious.

'I am your bodyguard, your Lion. I am sworn to protect you against all threats. Even threats that originate from your own person. Augustus, I would not have the gods angry with you.'

Athaulf looked from Caracalla to Silus and back again. Silus had no doubt that the big guard would strike him down at a word from the Emperor, and for a moment, he realised, his life was being weighed on Fate's scales, balanced on one side by Caracalla's wrath and madness, and on the other by his reason, and Silus' past service.

Then Caracalla let out a shout, picked up the silver goblet and dashed it against the wall. Blood-red wine splashed out, and the goblet fell to the floor with a ringing sound, crushed and deformed. Caracalla shoved Silus out of the way, and stormed out of the temple.

Athaulf gave Silus an appraising look, then sheathed his sword and went after his Emperor. Silus glanced at the priest, gasping and sobbing in a heap, then followed.

Outside, in the peaceful countryside, Caracalla was gripping his beard in both hands, then shaking his fists at the heavens and shouting. Athaulf and Silus waited out the storm. Eventually, the rage subsided. Caracalla turned to the two Leones.

'Never speak of this.'

He untied his mount and leapt athletically onto his back. Then he dug his heels into its flanks, and set off at a headlong gallop, leaving Silus and Athaulf hurriedly mounting up and racing to keep their ward in sight.

When they arrived back at the marching camp the legions had erected as military tradition demanded for overnight protection, Caracalla made straight for the principia, the central square, and into the praetorium headquarters, Silus and Athaulf close behind. Inside, Julia Domna was waiting for him. Her lips were pursed into a straight line, her eyebrows drawn together, her hands clasped in front of her. Caracalla stood before her, and gave her a slight shake of his head. Her shoulders fell, her chin drooped, a small but noticeable gesture of resignation. Caracalla stepped forward and hugged her tightly.

-

Delicatus stood calmly at attention as Silus, mounted on his back, surveyed the unfolding battle scene. This was the big one. The culmination of all the smaller skirmishers and battles that they had fought in recent months. This would crush the last of the resistance east of the Danube, or alternatively inflict a crushing defeat on Caracalla that would dash his hopes of a campaign against the Parthians.

Silus was one of a dozen Leones accompanying and guarding Caracalla, their number including Maximinus Thrax and of course Athaulf. Others of Caracalla's intimate council were also on hand to provide advice if called upon, Oclatinius, Festus and Macrinus among them, but of course no Julia Domna – battle was no place for a woman. They sat on the crest of a small hill, looking out over a wide plain. Far behind them was the river Olt, which they had crossed three days before. The eastern limit of the province under Caracalla's father had been some ten miles east of that river, but Caracalla had pushed on a further twenty miles to bring the free Dacians and their allies to battle.

Dacia was an annoyance and inconvenience to the Empire, as far as Silus could tell. Conquered by Trajan to take the boundaries of the Empire to their greatest extent a hundred years previously, Dacia stuck out from the smooth north-eastern border like a blister ready to be popped. Yes, it had provided abundant gold and slaves at the time of its initial conquest, and since then had been slowly transformed with roads and colonial towns with all the civilising effects of baths and temples and fora that they provided. It also sucked up a lot of resources. Because of its shape, surrounded on three sides by barbarian tribes, it was hard to protect, and immediately on Trajan's death, his successor Hadrian had partially withdrawn to make the border more defensible. Since then it had been a constant source of strife, with multiple revolts and the temporary loss of the province during the terrible war Marcus Aurelius had fought against the Marcomanni and Quadi tribes half a century before. It was a measure of Caracalla's power and military success that he had restored one of the most insecure parts of the Empire, and victory today would consolidate that hold for a generation, as his victories in Germania and Caledonia had done. Silus reflected that a further success today would surely leave the Parthians trembling for their future.

Caracalla was leaning forward, watching intently. Messengers were at the ready to take his orders to any point of the field as necessary, but for now, they were not needed. Caracalla had set out his battle plan, and was relying on his legionary commanders and their subordinates to carry it out. He had full trust in his officers, just as they trusted and admired him. It was extraordinary how a man could be so loved by some portions of Roman society, the common man and the military, and hated by others, the elite senators and equestrians who were forced to bankroll him.

The forces arrayed against Caracalla today were vast. They were led by the Getae, a Thracian tribe with origins near the Pontus Euxinus, the so-called Inhospitable Sea, named perhaps for its dark water or the dangerous tribes on its banks. Certainly the Getae looked particularly fearsome, with vast numbers of spearmen, archers, cavalry and war chariots. They held the centre, but only constituted a part of the barbarian force. To the barbarian right was a large force of free Dacians and Sarmatians, and to the left were Bastarnae, Carpi, Roxolani and other minor tribes. All were no doubt filled with fury against the Romans, their subjugation and enslavement of the free, and probably no little jealousy about the perceived luxury of the way of life of those who lived within the Empire's limits.

They should spend a week in the Subura, Silus thought, and maybe they wouldn't be so covetous.

But Caracalla too had gathered an enormous army. He had brought most of the reserves, scoured from throughout the Empire, including the Second Legion and the praetorians, and large numbers of auxiliary and allied cavalry and foot soldiers drawn from provinces as far apart as Mauretania and Germania. To this he had added huge numbers of men pressed into service by his recruiters as they had progressed eastwards, gathered from Gaul, Macedonia, Greece and the provinces of the north-eastern frontier. Added to this were the speculatores acting as scouts and skirmishers, his artillery consisting of ballistae, scorpions and onagers, and the growing number of Leones, which were being formed into an elite cavalry unit as well as a bodyguard. The rest of the Leones were waiting near Caracalla, some hundred strong, comprising a heavy cavalry reserve.

The initial stages of the battle had already been joined. The artillery situated on the slope of the hill facing the battlefield hurled bolts and rocks down onto the approaching enemy. But though terrifying, and devastating where they fell, they were too few in number, too slow to reload, and too immobile to have a big impact on the battle ahead. On the Roman right, Carpi horse archers rushed forward to harry the Roman front lines, firing their arrows then whirling away to retreat as the Roman light auxiliary cavalry chased them away. They were little more than an inconvenience, though, most of their missiles fended off easily by the legionaries' shields.

The main event would be the clash in the centre. Both sides had placed their strongest troops here, Caracalla his praetorians and men of the Second Legion, the commander of the Getae his heavy infantry. The job of the left and right on both sides would primarily be to hold, and prevent the other side from attacking their vulnerable flanks, and if possible, to beat off the enemy so they in turn could attack the opposing flank. Silus could discern no subtle tactic here, no plan to retreat the centre and allow the wings to fold in and encircle the enemy, the way that Hannibal had at Cannae for example.

But Caracalla's tactics, though solid, were not his true genius when it came to military matters. His attention to planning, training, logistics, not to mention diplomacy and backstabbing, usually meant the battle was won before the first javelin was thrown. Silus wondered if today, against this huge confederation, it would be enough.

The centres approached to within a hundred yards of each other, then the Getae broke into a run. They had some discipline. Their lines remained straight, no individuals racing ahead of the others, where they would be easily cut down. But they had begun their charge too early. A hundred yards was a long way to sprint in armour. Silus wondered if their commander had known this, but had held them back as long as he could without risking them breaking and running like dogs sighting a hare, losing all coherency.

It was to the Romans' advantage, in any case. At thirty yards, the Romans let loose a volley of javelins which felled a large number of the onrushing Getae, leaving the front rank ragged. When they were twenty yards out, the Romans broke into their own charge, shields to the fore. It was enough distance to reach near full speed without being so far they would start to fatigue.

The impact as the two armies struck each other was like a crack of thunder that rolled across the plain. The roars of the opposing armies reached Silus' position of safety, and he thanked all the gods he was not down there, pushing and stabbing and fending off blows aimed at himself and the men to his left and right with shield and sword. He knew from experience that it was terrifying and exhausting in roughly equal measures. That as the battle wore on, extreme tiredness reduced your ability to defend yourself. That the muscles of your sword arm screamed, that your shield arm sagged under the weight. That your lungs burned and your heart pounded, that even though you knew your very life depended on your continued exertion, all you wanted to do was drop your weapon and sink to your knees gasping for breath.

As was often the case, the battle for the centre became a shoving match, the poor sods at the front thrust forward by their comrades behind them, trying to make the enemy take a step back, then another, until it became a retreat, then a rout. Silus watched as the advantage shifted back and forth, like two evenly matched teams in a tug of war. The wings engaged, lighter infantry and cavalry harrying each other. The screams of the wounded and dying began to dominate the cacophony of battle.

Caracalla pointed out a part of the battle to Macrinus where the praetorians appeared to be making headway, but even as Macrinus replied to praise his men, they were forced back, and the brief salient was flattened. Oclatinius moved his horse closer to Silus.

'Use your young eyes to tell me what's happening over there.' He gestured to the middle right, where lighter Greek and Gallic auxiliaries were confronting Dacians and Sarmatians. Silus squinted, trying to make any sense of the picture from such a distance.

'The enemy are getting the better of it, I think. They seem to be more heavily armoured than our men over there, and they outnumber them. There isn't much in it, but if I had to make a guess I would say our men are losing ground.'

Oclatinius nodded, and guided his horse to the Emperor's side. 'Augustus, we are weakening on the left. Maybe now is the time?'

Caracalla squinted in the direction Oclatinius had indicated. There was no need for a hasty decision, but it didn't take long for Caracalla to have assessed the situation enough to make up his mind.

'Do it. Send them in.'

Oclatinius called a command to a nearby bucinator, who blew a loud, clear pattern of notes on his horn. He repeated the phrase twice more. For a moment, there seemed to be no response. Then a low grumble came from behind Silus, from the reverse slope of the hill, getting louder and louder, until he could feel the shaking of the ground transmitted up his body via Delicatus' sturdy legs. He turned in time to see a score of war elephants appear at the crest. They paused for a moment, stamping their feet and trumpeting.

It was a magnificent sight. They were enormous, dwarfing even Thrax's huge steed. The lead elephant rider held his hand high, then gestured down the slope. The beasts lumbered into a trot, then a canter, gathering momentum as they raced down the hill. Horns blared out warnings, but the tremendous cacophony of the elephants could not be missed. The auxiliaries fighting desperately on the left turned to see the vast mass of meat and muscle bearing down on their rear. But instead of fleeing in panic, as instinct dictated, they formed quickly into neat files, opening wide channels down which the elephants could charge. It was another example of Caracalla's organisation – he had had the men and elephants train together for weeks so they did not fear each other, and this practice made their manoeuvres swift and precise.

The Dacians and Sarmatians attempted to flee as the elephants crashed into their front ranks, but the mass of their own men behind them impeded their escape. Men disappeared under giant feet, torsos and skulls crushed. Others were tossed aside by solid trunks or impaled on wicked tusks. The elephants trampled on through the barbarians, carving out bloody lines of carnage. Some resistance was organised, with spears and arrows striking home into the elephant flanks. At first the beasts dismissed them as irritants, but as the rain of missiles intensified, they became increasingly furious, ignoring their drivers' commands, lashing out at all around them, some turning in a circle to head back towards their own men. Several had to be taken down by their own drivers before they caused chaos and damage amongst the Romans – this was achieved by the brutal method of driving a spike through the back of their skulls with a hammer.

The surviving animals retreated, and the Romans pressed their advantage. But it did not last long, as the tough barbarians reorganised themselves, and soon the frontlines had reformed more or less where they were before the charge. Elephants were rarely seen in battle these days, and this showed why. They were unreliable, a danger to their own side, and enemies had often figured out how to deal with them. Their rarity meant they still had some shock value, but not much more.

The sun moved across the sky, morning heading for noon, and the air temperature increased. There was a light breeze that kept the watchers on the hill cool, but down in the battle, exertion and lack of ventilation within the crushed masses was taking its toll, and both sides began to weary. Caracalla grew more tense, and his horse, sensing its master's anxiety, fidgeted beneath him. He went to give a command, then countermanded it, cursing himself for his indecision. It must be an unfamiliar situation to him, Silus thought, to not be in complete control of the battlefield. He could see the Emperor was itching to be in the centre of the action himself, and suspected he was just waiting for his moment.

Eventually it came. Without warning, the right Roman wing crumbled. It wasn't obvious how it began – maybe the death of an important commander, or just a sudden collective loss of morale. It spread like fire through dry kindling, and in moments the German auxiliaries and the Quadi and Osroene auxiliaries were in full retreat.

Caracalla kicked his horse into a gallop, and sped off down the hill faster than any of his companions could react. Silus looked to Oclatinius, who was clearly too old to take part in the fighting. Macrinus and Festus showed no inclination to accompany their Emperor into the maelstrom either. But the Leones were Caracalla's men, to the death. Athaulf yelled a command, and the whole mass of Leones, the close bodyguard and the elite cavalry, raced down the hill in a wedge formation, Caracalla at the apex.

As they thundered down the slope, Silus clung to the reins, hoping no harm came to Caracalla as he put himself in danger once more, but wishing even more fervently that he didn't topple off Delicatus and make himself look like a complete idiot in front of the other Leones.

The Carpi and Bastarnae infantry had broken ranks and were pursuing the routed Roman right, waving spears and swords, hacking down any that were too slow in their flight. Caught up in the exultation of imminent victory, they didn't see the danger until it was too late.

Caracalla circled around to the right, and led the heavy cavalry into the unprotected flank of the barbarians. There was no organised resistance, and unlike the charge of the elephants, the armoured horses were highly disciplined, and mounted by the toughest of cavalrymen, armed with lances and spears.

Silus found himself just behind Caracalla, who was lashing out at all who neared him with his spatha. Silus hacked and slashed at the barbarian foot soldiers, many of whom, still focussed on the fleeing Romans, never saw the blows fall. The wedge of men hammered deep into the loose body of Carpi and Bastarnae, splitting them apart, and then it was every man for himself. Silus positioned himself on one side of Caracalla, fending off arrows and javelins and striking out at any that came near, while Athaulf did the same on the Emperor's other side. Maximinus Thrax appeared to have entered some sort of frenzied state, and had actually dismounted, the better to hack and slash at anyone within reach.

The thrill of victory turned to despair and the barbarians halted their pursuit of the Romans, first in confusion, then in terror, and it became their turn to about-face and flee. Officers among the routed Romans rallied all but the most panic-stricken, and goaded them with bribes and threats back into battle. But they needed little further encouragement when they saw their pursuers turn into pursued, and they re-entered the fray with enthusiasm, in an attempt to restore their reputation, and assuage the guilt of their temporary cowardice.

The collapse of the barbarian left was the beginning of the end. The Getae and Dacians had kept no reserves to counterstrike, and as the Roman right wheeled and assaulted the barbarian left flank, panic spread. Victory did not come quickly, but from that moment on it was inevitable, as more and more of the barbarian forces crumbled and retreated. The Getae chieftain fought on with a small group of cavalry to the last, and though Caracalla would clearly have loved to have fought him in single combat, Athaulf had by that time persuaded Caracalla to return to his command post on the hill where he could oversee the battle and ensure success was complete, and not unnecessarily costly.

When the Getae chief was finally felled by a Macedonian javelin, Caracalla held up his sword in salute, then cantered down the hill to commend his men.

The Romans and the allies and auxiliaries, though exhausted, wounded, overheated and dehydrated, broke into spontaneous cheers. Caracalla dismounted and walked amongst them, grasping shoulders, patting backs. His fine armour was thickly coated in blood and gore, and he bore wounds of his own. None could doubt that he had shared in the soldiers' hardship and peril. Silus and Athaulf stayed near, and once Athaulf was forced to kick away an overly enthusiastic soldier who had gripped Caracalla's leg and was weeping openly in praise and thanks. For the most part, though, the Leones kept a discreet distance, and allowed their Emperor to enjoy the worship of his men.

Silus wondered how long Caracalla's joy would last this time, before he once more retreated into depression and anger.

-

Caracalla's fine mood seemed to have persisted, at least for now. He had joined his rank-and-file soldiers in their celebrations, circulating amongst them, sharing their meat and wine, laughing and joking and even dicing with them. Silus and Athaulf attended him, but he never looked in any danger from his men, who adored him.

That was in stark contrast to those who attended the victory party in the praetorium. His senior commanders, his council, and invited representatives of the Senate joined him for drinks and food, but Silus could tell that many of them were disappointed with the fare on offer. Whether Caracalla was genuinely not interested in lavish banqueting, or it was an affectation designed to further endear himself to the common soldier, the result was a frugal feast. No nightingale tongue pasties, no oysters transported vast distances by express courier, packed in snow, no peahen eggs, and no delicately baked cakes in sight. Instead, the serving slaves brought out platters of dried dates, firm bread and salted nuts, with cups of water and diluted wine. Silus enjoyed the dismayed looks on the senators' faces as they reluctantly ate what was proffered and pretended to enjoy it, no doubt having expected a sumptuous spread, even here, in the field, far from Rome.

Maybe a score of notables were in attendance, reclining on couches arranged in the usual horseshoe shape, with Caracalla on the top couch, and Julia Domna to his right. Intriguingly, Macrinus was on his left. The praetorian prefect was clearly becoming more trusted by Caracalla, and more senior in his council. But Silus doubted Caracalla truly trusted anyone, except maybe Domna. Silus could put names to most of the other faces present. Ulpius Julianus and Julianus Nestor were seated near the

Emperor. Oclatinius and Festus sat together, further down the order, not speaking.

Among the senators were Dio Cassius the historian, and Helvius Pertinax. Silus was aware that there was a lot of resentment from the senators towards Caracalla's behaviour. He demanded they funded his expedition, but often treated them with contempt, summoning them and then leaving them standing outside in the heat for the entire day. Silus dreaded to think how Dio Cassius would write about Caracalla when he reached the present day in his great work of history.

The presence of the young Pertinax in Caracalla's council always intrigued Silus. In that year in which five different emperors ruled Rome, and Septimius Severus emerged as victor, Severus never fought against Pertinax senior, only entering the race to the throne after his death. Caracalla's father always honoured his memory, to the extent of adding his name to the extensive list of his own to become Imperator Caesar Lucius Septimius Severus Pertinax Augustus. Pertinax senior was deified and his son was made priest of his cult, theoretically able to style himself son of a god, though he was generally considered too politically astute to do something so dangerous. He was still a potential threat to Caracalla, though, and generally he was careful to offer the Emperor no cause for concern.

Which is what made what followed all the more surprising when Silus thought about it later. Maybe Pertinax thought that Caracalla was mellowing as he aged, in which case he was a naive idiot. Maybe he was aware of the rumours of conspiracies, or was even involved in one himself, and was emboldened by the thought of Caracalla's weakness or vulnerability. Though that still made him a naive idiot. Or maybe it was just because he was drunk.

Macrinus was giving a fine performance of sycophancy, drawing subtle sneers and eye rolls from Dio Cassius, though only when he was sure Caracalla wasn't looking his way.

'Victory after victory, Augustus,' Macrinus was gushing. 'Your successes surely surpass even the genius of your father.'

Caracalla narrowed his eyes. 'My father was a great ruler and a great general. The enemies he vanquished were many – Africans, Britons, Parthians...'

'Romans,' put in Pertinax.

Caracalla looked at him sharply. 'Traitors,' he said. 'Men who were responsible for the death of your father. Who my father avenged.'

Pertinax raised his silver goblet in salute. 'To the deified Emperor Severus, immortal companion of my father.' The words were slurred, and Silus was sure that it was not only to his ears that they sounded sarcastic. Caracalla paused, then raised his own cup, and everyone else did the same, mumbling a chorus of praise to Severus' memory.

Macrinus continued his flattery, as if the interruption had never occurred.

'Surely you will add to your own titles now,' he said.

'If the Senate grants them to me, I would of course accept any honours,' said Caracalla.

'There are many they could vote you. You are already titled Britannicus, Arabicus, Germanicus. Surely you could also be voted Sarmaticus, Dacicus...'

'Geticus,' said Pertinax.

The silence that followed was so profound, Silus thought he could have heard a feather land on a lake.

Everyone seemed to be holding their breath. Nervous eyes darted from Pertinax to Caracalla. It took Silus a moment to understand the tension. Pertinax had made a joke, referring with seeming innocence to Caracalla's defeat of the Getae people, while implying he could also take a title for the murder of his brother Geta. As jokes went, it wasn't bad, and was surely one of the most misjudged in history. Domna was white as marble, the back of her hand pressed to her mouth. Caracalla had turned somewhere between red and purple. Pertinax's smile at his own cleverness died as he realised the impact his jest had had. He opened his mouth to speak, but there was really nothing he could say or do short of throwing himself at Caracalla's feet, tearing at his clothes and hair, and begging forgiveness. As a son of a god, he clearly believed that behaviour was beneath him.

Caracalla breathed heavily, mouth closed, air snorting through his nostrils like he was a bull about to charge. Everyone waited for the dam to burst.

Domna put a gentle hand on Caracalla's forearm. 'Augustus, I feel tired. Would you escort me to my quarters?'

Caracalla stared at her, grinding his teeth. Then he took a deep breath, and let it out slowly.

'Of course, Augusta.' He rose to his feet, and all the guests did likewise, waiting respectfully as they left. Athaulf and Silus fell into step behind them. As Silus passed Oclatinius, they locked eyes. Oclatinius inclined his head subtly towards Pertinax, and Silus knew the spymaster well enough to receive the unspoken message. There was a dead man walking.

Chapter XI

Oclatinius' quarters held a wooden travel chest, a bed covered in standard legionary-issued blankets, and small desk and chair. Oclatinius sat at the desk, his face lit from beneath by a flickering oil lamp, the unnatural direction of illumination and the dancing flame making him look like some evil lemur, haunting the camp, unable to find rest. Or maybe Silus just needed some sleep. His day job guarding the Emperor had been passed to those Leones nominated for the night watch, but he had to make time for his other occupation, arcanus, assassin, spy. So now, rather than tucked up under his blankets, he was perched on the edge of the bed of an old man who just happened to be one of the most powerful and dangerous men in the Empire.

'What will happen to him?' asked Silus. They had been discussing Pertinax's disastrous blunder.

'Maybe nothing,' said Oclatinius. 'It depends whether he messes up again. Severus did genuinely respect Pertinax's father, I think, though he used his memory to shore up his own claim to the throne. And Caracalla honours his father, by and large. Besides, Pertinax has much sympathy and support in the Senate, and Caracalla cannot afford to treat him too rashly, however contemptuous he is of senators in general.'

'So he could be a conspirator?'

Oclatinius considered, stroking his chin. 'Of that, I'm not sure. He moves in circles I would consider anti-Caracalla, but whether he is an active participant…'

'So you do know who is plotting against the Emperor?'

Oclatinius shook his head firmly. 'Of course not. If I had evidence, don't you think I would take it to Caracalla?'

Silus wasn't sure he would, but he kept that to himself.

'So who do you suspect? Dio Cassius?'

'Again, he may be on the periphery. And he intensely dislikes Caracalla. But he is not the bravest of men, I can't see him being a man of action.'

'Macrinus and his followers?'

Oclatinius shuffled some papers on his desk. Silus waited.

'You know, Macrinus is a remarkable man in many ways. He came from a very poor background, humble origins in Mauretania. Somehow he managed to scrape enough money together to get a legal education. Some say he did it by being a gladiator, some that he was a prostitute, but people always say things like that. Whatever the case, he was a competent administrator, even though he was no genius compared to the Roman-educated lawyers. He was useful to Severus, and survived the execution of his friend Plautianus through flattery, bribery and a good dose of backstabbing. Since then he has been of aid both to Severus and Caracalla, hence his promotions. He is an ambitious man, but not a bold one. So. Maybe.'

Silus sighed. Considering the extent of Oclatinius' network of spies and informers, it was surprising he had not made more progress in discovering who was behind Marcellus' murder and who was plotting against the Emperor. Or was it? Again he felt the uncomfortable feeling of suspicion towards a man he respected, maybe even liked.

'And Festus?'

Even in the gloom, Silus saw a shadow pass across Oclatinius' face.

'Leave Festus to me,' he said, tone leaden.

'But I don't trust him. There is just something about him. I'm sure he is up to his neck in it.'

'I said leave him.' The words snapped out like a rebuke, an uncharacteristic loss of control from the usually impassive old man.

Silus pursed his lips and a long moment of silence passed between them. He wished Atius was here. The big oaf had little subtlety, but he was far from stupid, and was always a good sounding board when it came to this kind of thing. He wondered for a moment how his closest friend was doing, whether he was bonding with Avitus, and attempting to seduce Soaemias.

Nothing more was forthcoming from Oclatinius, so Silus stood.

'You don't have any more to report?' asked Oclatinius.

Silus hesitated. What was there to tell him? About the battles where Caracalla madly threw himself against the enemy? About the healing shrines, and his assault on the priest? They were nothing to do with conspiracies or assassins or plots. In fact, what evidence did he have that there was a plot against Caracalla at all? Maybe whoever wanted Marcellus dead had nothing against the Emperor. He sighed.

'Nothing.'

Oclatinius looked at him sternly, like a schoolteacher waiting for his pupil to confess to a misdemeanour. Silus found himself involuntarily shifting from foot to foot, waiting to be dismissed.

'Very well,' said Oclatinius eventually. 'Good night.'

A sense of relief washed over him as he left. There was no doubt things between Silus and Oclatinius were more strained than at any time since Oclatinius had recruited him, and he wasn't really sure why. Maybe his own suspicions about Oclatinius' behaviour were obvious to the canny spymaster. He seemed to have a knack of looking directly into people's minds and souls.

Silus stomped back through the camp, giving the password absent-mindedly when challenged by a pair of patrolling guards. The conversation had felt distinctly unsatisfying, like he had eaten half a meal – he was still hungry and there was food left on his plate. He walked past his own quarters and paced around the roads between the rows of tents and the more substantial wooden structures that made up the legionary camp. What was it about Festus that made Oclatinius close down the conversation that way? It wasn't the first time. Did Oclatinius know something about Festus? Were they in it together? Did Festus have some hold over Oclatinius? Too many questions whirled inside Silus' head. He stopped dead, then turned and strode back towards Oclatinius accommodation, determined to have it out with him.

Oclatinius' quarters were basically a large tent. Larger than the average legionary's, designed for sole occupancy, not eight sweaty soldiers belching and farting all night, with a proper bed instead of a thin papyrus rolled mattress, and a desk and lamp. But still just a tent. So when Silus marched up, ready to call out and pull back the tent flap, he was halted in his tracks by the sound of two voices. The first was Oclatinius, low, patient, sad. The second wasn't quite as familiar, and Silus took a moment to identify it. Then he realised, and his heart began to hammer in his chest.

Festus.

He crept away from the entrance, and around the side of the tent, out of sight of any passers-by, and listened.

'This isn't the first time I have had to warn you,' said Oclatinius.

'You aren't my master,' Festus replied.

'Yet who is it that gets you out of trouble every time? Like that nonsense with young Avitus and his crazy mother. I still can't understand what you were thinking!'

'You owe me, Oclatinius.'

'And at what point would you consider that debt repaid in full?'

'You tell me. How could what I did for you ever be repaid?'

Oclatinius sighed. 'Maybe you are right. But there are limits. There are some things I won't be able to protect you from.'

'You will. I know you take your debt seriously.'

'Festus, I have known you a very long time. You were my very first Arcanus. We have been friends and rivals. Our bond is strong. But if you make me choose between you and the Emperor…'

'Yes, Oclatinius. What will you decide?'

There was a long pause. Then Oclatinius said, 'I don't know.'

Silus couldn't listen any longer. He wandered away from Oclatinius' tent in a daze. Festus was the first Arcanus? Oclatinius was in his debt? Festus needed protecting from his own actions? And what was Silus supposed to do with this knowledge? Normally he would talk to Atius or Oclatinius. Atius was a thousand miles away, give or take, and Oclatinius was the problem. He could go to Athaulf, but the big German had no discernible subtlety, and Silus suspected he would either go straight to Caracalla and denounce both Oclatinius and Festus, or take matters into his own hands and slaughter the pair of them.

Silus wandered back to his own quarters, settled himself on his mattress roll, and stared at the side of the tent, sleep as far away as Atius.

-

The next day Silus had woken with a splitting headache. He didn't know how long he had slept for, but he knew it wasn't nearly enough. He had drawn a rebuke from Athaulf for his slovenly appearance when he reported for duty. Now he rode in Caracalla's guard, each thud of the horse's hooves on the road shuddering through him and making him wince. The Emperor was a dozen yards ahead, with Athaulf by his side. Maximinus Thrax rode beside Silus. Silus was relieved that Thrax didn't try to engage him in conversation, but when the column took a break, and they dismounted to pass horses to the grooms for water and food, Thrax approached Silus.

'Why do you look like shit, then?' asked the huge barbarian.

'None of your fucking business,' Silus spat back.

'Out whoring till dawn, no doubt.'

Silus gritted his teeth, trying to ignore the irritant.

'You're a disgrace. What are you even doing in the Leones? You are small and weak. You look a mess. And you are a Briton. You don't belong here.'

'And you do? A Carpi? I bet you're a spy anyway. A traitor, planted by the barbarians, ready to strike when the time...'

He didn't finish his sentence as the giant barbarian barrelled into him. Silus was knocked off his feet to land on his back, the wind knocked out of him. Thrax straddled him, drew back a fist like a mallet and punched down with all his weight. Silus saw the blow coming, and twisted desperately to one side. The impact of the blow on the sun-baked dirt sent up clouds of dust and he felt the shock reverberate through his body.

Silus wriggled and bucked. The weight of Thrax was crushing him, and he couldn't force air into his lungs. Panic rose within, the sensation of suffocation threatening to drive out reason. He fought it down, and as Thrax prepared another mighty punch, Silus struck with stiff fingers into the giant's throat. For an ordinary man, the strike might have been fatal. But Silus' fingertips struck solid neck muscle, which cushioned the force. Thrax grunted, sat back. Silus took the opportunity to heave the huge bulk off him and rolled away, sucking air down in deep gulps on hands and knees.

Thrax slowly got to his feet and advanced on Silus, great fists balled. Silus bounced up and leapt forward, jabbing Thrax on the nose and then hooking him in the ribs. Thrax didn't seem to notice. He threw his own punch at Silus, who ducked and countered ineffectually. The fight quickly became farcical, Thrax unable to land a blow on the agile Arcanus, Silus unable to injure the giant barbarian.

It ended moments later when Athaulf stepped between them. Though he said nothing, the fury on his face cowed both the combatants. Thrax bowed his head, and walked back to his mount. Silus looked at his feet, abashed.

'Pull yourself together,' Athaulf said, and strode away.

–

Festus met the slave in a temple dedicated to Artemis in the Thracian city of Philippolis. The slave looked understandably terrified, but the shrine was empty apart from an elderly priest cleaning blood off the altar.

'You are Acacius?'

The slave was of Greek ethnicity, though Festus knew he was from Alexandria. He swallowed and nodded.

'Good. I have a task for you. When we reach the Hellespont, you are to seek out a ship's carpenter by the name of Evaristus.'

'How will I find him?'

'I hear you are resourceful. You will work it out. When you locate him, you are to give him this.'

Festus handed a bag of coins to the young slave, whose eyes widened as he weighed them in his hand.

'We know how much is there, we will check with Evaristus that he receives the full payment.'

Acacius nodded.

'You will give him these instructions. Memorise them. Do not write them down.'

Acacius was a scribe for his master, one of those literate slaves that had a quality of life envied by the labourers, cleaners and prostitutes whose miserable existence kept the free people of the Empire in comfort. Festus described in detail what he required. Acacius nodded and repeated it back.

'And you understand what will happen if you fail?'

Acacius hesitated. Festus spoke slowly and clearly, as if he was talking to a child.

'Your father and mother who sold you into slavery to pay their debts are dead, Acacius. But you have a brother. A little older than you. He lives free as a papyrus maker in Alexandria. He has a wife and daughter. The little girl is what, five years old now?'

'How do you know so much about me?' gasped Acacius.

Festus ignored the question and continued.

'Your life as a slave is not a bad one. You have food and lodgings. No physical labour. I am informed your master is kind and never beats you. There are far worse lots for a slave. The farms in Sicily. The silver mines in Hispania. The brothels in the Subura. Fail me, and not only will you end up there, but so will your brother and his family.'

'You can't! They are free. They have been Roman citizens since Caracalla's decree…'

'Do you really think that matters to someone with my resources? Do you think, when they are abducted and enslaved, that anyone will believe them when they claim they have been wronged?'

Acacius stared at Festus, his eyes misting.

'I will do as you ask, master. Please don't hurt them.'

'There should be no need. If you play your part. Now get out of here and return to your master before you are missed.'

The young slave fled, clutching the bag of gold, tears running down his cheeks. Festus watched him depart and stroked his chin. The plan was in motion. But the conversation with Oclatinius had unnerved him. He didn't know if his old mentor had solid information about their plans, or was just fishing. He hoped he could rely on him, but who was truly trustworthy in this murky world of conspirators and traitors?

At least the slave would be dealt with. When he had played his role, his fellow conspirators had arranged for the lad to be done away with discreetly, so he couldn't identify Festus and his role. At least that was one detail he didn't need to worry about.

Chapter XII

Silus' listened to Oclatinius with his head cocked to one side, his weight on one hip and his arms folded across his chest. If Oclatinius noticed the defensive posture, he didn't comment.

'I have some intelligence that there is something imminent. I don't know what exactly, but one of my spies believes there will be an attempt on Caracalla around the time of the crossing. Before, after or during, he isn't sure.'

'What sort of attempt? Poison? Blade?'

'He doesn't know.'

'Funny, that.'

'What?' Oclatinius frowned.

Silus looked around Oclatinius' temporary office. The Arcani spymaster and praetorian prefect had the authority to commandeer decent quarters, but in the small Thracian city of Sestos on the European side of the Hellespont, the pickings were slim. The tablinum looked tired, the frescoes faded, the plaster cracked and peeling, and though someone had clearly sent the slaves in with mops and scrubbing brushes, there were odd stains on the floor and cobwebs in the rafters.

'Continue,' said Silus. 'What else?'

'Not much. I just want you to be alert. You can pass the warning on to Athaulf.'

'It's not much to go on, is it? Or are you holding back on me?'

'What's got into you, Silus? Do you have a problem?'

Silus hadn't meant it to come out like this. He didn't really know what he had intended. But suddenly he couldn't hold back, and it all poured forth.

'I trusted you! With my life! You are like a father to me, much better than my real one ever was. How could you do this?'

'What are you talking about?'

'I heard you. With Festus!'

Oclatinius blanched.

'I don't know what you think you overheard…'

'Festus is a traitor and you are covering it up. Or you are in it with him.'

Oclatinius took a step back, and Silus saw an expression he had never seen before on the old man's face. Was it shock? No, it was fear.

But it was quickly replaced by anger, and that, Silus had seen before.

'Get out.' His voice was quiet, not much more than a whisper.

'No, listen,' said Silus. 'I want to know…'

'If you make me say it again,' said Oclatinius, his voice no louder, but cutting through Silus' words, 'I will kill you.'

Silus looked into the old man's eyes, and did not doubt either his sincerity or his ability. He strode out. A memory came unbidden to mind, his father bending him over a table and beating him with a belt for some minor misdemeanour, a broken pot perhaps, or a poor performance in a grammar lesson. He hadn't cried then. Now, he wiped moisture out of his eyes angrily with the back of his arm, and cursed his own weakness.

-

'Are you Evaristus?'

The carpenter looked up from his cup of wine. He was seated at a table on the street outside a tavern, throwing knucklebones with a couple of other rough-looking men. His face was weathered and ruddy, and his hands were cracked and calloused.

'Who the fuck are you?'

'I'm Acacius,' said Acacius, then cursed himself. Shouldn't he have used a false name? Well, this was his first foray into the world of bribery and blackmail.

'And? What do you want?'

Acacius looked at the others at the table. 'What I have to say is for your ears only.'

Evaristus smiled. 'You can say what you like in front of these two. Like brothers to me, they are.'

Acacius turned his body to block the view of Evaristus' companions and showed Evaristus a glimpse of the coins in the bag. His eyes widened briefly, then narrowed in calculation.

'You two, leave us alone, will you. Private business.'

'Like brothers, wasn't it?' said one of them.

'Just fuck off, all right?'

'Fine, but you forfeit the pot.' The man scraped the copper coins off the table and palmed them, then he and his companion walked off down the street, grumbling and throwing dagger glances over their shoulders at Acacius and Evaristus. Acacius didn't care. Once his business was transacted, he would be out of there, and would never see any of them again. He took one of the vacated seats.

'What's all this about, then?' asked Evaristus.

'I was told you were the right man to approach about a job.'

'I've got a job.'

'Does it pay enough to service your gambling debts?'

Evaristus waved a hand dismissively. 'Those copper coins? That's just a bit of fun.'

'I was thinking more of the sums you owe to half a dozen bookmakers in Sestos. Bookmakers who have a lot of heavy thugs in their employ.'

Acacius hoped he was being sufficiently threatening. It occurred to him that this rough man could just beat him up and take the money. And where would that leave him? He doubted that Festus would accept any excuses. The same thing had obviously occurred to Evaristus, who was looking at Acacius' bag of coins speculatively.

'This is a down payment. There is another half to come when the job is completed.'

'You haven't told me what the job is yet.'

Acacius looked around to make sure no one was in earshot. He couldn't quite believe he was doing this. How had a senator's administrative slave got mixed up in this? He had no idea why Festus had chosen him. Surely there were lots of poor slaves with families he could threaten. But here he was.

He took a breath, and told Evaristus what was required of him. Evaristus stared at him.

'Are you fucking crazy?'

Possibly, thought Acacius. But he just closed his mouth and waited for a response. Evaristus breathed heavily through flared nostrils like a nervous racehorse, looking down at the tabletop as if the answer was there. Then he looked up.

'How much are we talking?'

Acacius put the bag on the table, and let Evaristus pick it up and heft it in the palm of his hand.

'It's enough to get those men off your back.'

'With the same amount again, yes, that would do nicely.'

'So you'll do it?'

'It won't be easy.'

Acacius waited, heart racing.

After what seemed like an eternity, Evaristus took the bag of coins and dropped it into his lap. 'Now get the fuck out of here.'

Acacius stood hastily, nodded, and hurried away, not looking back. There was an acid taste in the back of his mouth, and he wanted to vomit. His heart rate had not slowed an iota, and his legs trembled as he walked. But it was done. He was safe, and so was his brother and his family.

He rounded a corner, and collided with a stern-faced centurion. He bounced off the soldier's breastplate and staggered back a step. The centurion looked him up and down with a curled lip. His optio stood at his shoulder, and behind them half a dozen legionaries, all resplendent in their uniforms.

'Sorry, sir,' said Acacius, bowing his head submissively. He took a step to the side to go around the small patrol. The centurion stepped sideways at the same time. Acacius let out a weak chuckle, and stepped to the other side. The centurion matched him. He looked up, taking in the officer's insignia, a rampant lion. The badge of the Sixteenth Legion, Flavia Firma. And another badge that he couldn't immediately place.

'Your pardon, sir. May I pass?'

The optio stepped up level with the centurion, and one of the legionaries came up to his other shoulder. All three pulled solid wooden clubs from their belts. The centurion patted his weapon firmly twice, then drew it back.

Acacius threw up an arm to protect his head, and the first blow cracked the bones of his forearm. The pain was worse than anything he had ever experienced, so intense he couldn't even cry out. The second blow, from the optio, broke his ribs. The next smashed his shin and he crumpled to the ground. A sense of unreality overwhelmed him. As darkness closed in, a random memory flashed through his mind.

The other badge.

They were frumentarii.

–

Caracalla had assembled a fleet of boats and ships to ferry his vast army across the Hellespont. Some of these were triremes of the Imperial Navy, but most were civilian cargo ships commandeered for the purpose, with greater or lesser compensation for the ships' owners depending on the size and seaworthiness of the vessel, and the mood of the Imperial agents at that given moment. Of course, the senators and other elites of Rome would be footing the bill, but there was no point being overgenerous in payment. The rich could only be bled dry once, after all.

Caracalla's ship was emblazoned with Imperial emblems, so there could be no doubting which was his – an imposing quadrireme, with the usual four banks of rowers and two large square-rigged sails. Caracalla stood in the prow, his hands gripping the rail, the breeze ruffling his curled locks. Beside him, a little stooped, the white-haired Oclatinius stood, keeping his balance easily without holding on as the ship rocked beneath him. Domna was seated on a chair on deck near the stern, but in the centre of the deck, where the pitching and rolling were minimised.

Besides the sailors and rowers, there were half a dozen Leones accompanying the Emperor, among them Silus, Athaulf and Maximinus Thrax. They stood on guard, alert for danger, but there seemed little cause for alarm.

Silus could feel a ball of anxiety inside him, and suspected he had good reason to worry, not least because of the warning Oclatinius had given him. No threat had materialised on the European side of the crossing, and though his near-drowning earlier in the year made any sea voyage unsettling, the contrast with that journey was marked. These were fair seas in a favourable season, and there were armed, trustworthy men on board. And the crossing was short, too.

The Hellespont was one of the two crossing points of the strait that connected the Aegean Sea with the Pontus Euxinus, the other being the one between Chalcedon and Byzantium, whose steep cliffs made landings difficult. The distance between shores was only a couple of miles and the geographical fact that this was the only practical crossing from Europe to Asia meant it had been witness to some monumental moments in history. Xerxes, ruler of Persia, had ordered the Hellespont to be whipped when the bridge he had built had been destroyed by a storm. The Spartans had defeated the Athenians here in the final battle of the Peloponnesian War. Alexander the Great, whose Macedonian kingdom was at the time bounded by the strait, threw a spear into the water to announce his claim on Asia.

And now, Caracalla was taking his army across the strait, from Europe into the Roman province of Asia. The Parthian Empire, the ultimate target, was still over a thousand miles to the east. But even to Silus, a very small cog in Caracalla's war machine, and privy to only a fraction of the Emperor's planning, the event felt momentous. It might yet be two or three years before Caracalla had pacified the East sufficiently to launch his invasion, but now this huge army was in motion, it felt like it could not be stopped until it had marched into Babylon and beyond.

A gust of wind rocked the boat to one side, and the timbers creaked. Silus had spent enough time at sea to not be worried by those alarming sounds. He knew these vessels were constructed to take punishment far beyond what the weather could throw at them on that summer's day.

Then there was a loud crack, like a thunderclap, and Silus instinctively looked for a lightning flash, though he realised immediately that the light would have preceded the sound. As he sought the source of the noise, his eyes were drawn upwards by a long, drawn-out groan like the felling of a tree.

The lower yard, the horizontal spar from the mast of the largest sail, had split in two, and as Silus watched, it crashed into the deck, landing on a sailor whose scream was cut off as his chest was crushed. The ropes securing the sails dragged the mast sideways, and as this toppled, it thrust the yard arm further down through the deck, and with a mighty sound of splintering, the weighty timber smashed through the planks of the deck, and carried on through the bottom of the hull, punching out a hole the size of a horse.

The mast splashed into the sea off the port side, smashing through the railing, and sweeping two sailors and one of the Leones overboard, all of them broken and probably dead before they hit the water. The ship rolled heavily to port, pushing the hole in the hull deeper underwater.

Panic was instant and uncontrollable, spreading like a contagion throughout the crew. The rowers in the depths of the ship scrambled up ladders to escape the rapidly rising waters. The loss of the sailors and the oarsmen robbed the ship of any propulsion, making it impossible to manoeuvre to attempt to correct its roll, and the helmsmen, after a few moments hauling on the steering oars, gave up their efforts. The captain screamed orders at any within earshot, but was completely ignored by his crew who had lost their heads. Those who could swim were leaping overboard, while others were clinging onto anything that would support them as the roll accentuated.

Silus felt himself sliding sideways down the deck as the ship's tilt reached halfway to a right angle. He grabbed onto a rail, hooking his elbow around it, then looked around wildly, trying to assess the situation. Panic rose in his own chest, and the memory of being submerged in the cold waters of the Mare Nostrum threatened to rob him of his ability to act. He forced the feelings down, and looked forward, to where he had last seen Caracalla. The Emperor had taken a blow to the head, and was sitting on the deck, gripping onto a rope, dazed. Silus hauled himself along the deck, ignoring the crew scurrying for safety like the life beneath an overturned rock.

When he reached Caracalla, Oclatinius was by his side. The old man had the Emperor's chin in his hands, and was looking him in the face and talking slowly and clearly.

'Imperator. You must get to your feet. Do you understand me?'

Caracalla appeared to be having trouble focussing. There was another creak and crack, and the second mast, leaning at an angle it had never been supposed to reach, snapped and fell overboard. Its sails smothered several rowers and sailors who were splashing in the waves, bearing them underneath the surface, tangling them so they could not escape.

Oclatinius looked up as Silus arrived. 'There is a rowing boat, on the port side. Help me get him there.' They put their shoulders under his arms, one on each side, and half-lifted, half-dragged him to the tiny boat that Oclatinius had spotted. Athaulf and Maximinus joined them, hauling themselves between handholds. Athaulf's clothing was torn and bloody, but Maximinus appeared uninjured.

The boat was lashed to the side of the ship, and two sailors were attempting to untie the ropes so they could use the boat for their own salvation. Athaulf stepped forward and pushed them both overboard. Then he drew his knife and began to cut the bindings. Oclatinius helped Caracalla into the boat, then got in after him, stiffer than the younger men, but amazingly lithe for a man of his age. The boat came free, settling into the water and bobbing in the waves. Athaulf bid Silus to get in. The portside railing was now submerged, and Silus nearly lost his footing, but he jumped, landing heavily beside Oclatinius. Athaulf followed, and then Maximinus prepared to leap. Silus tensed, hoping the huge bodyguard would not smash through the bottom of the boat when he landed.

But before Maximinus could jump, the wind caught a stray sail, and whipped a loose spar to which it was attached over the deck and down towards the boat. Though it was only a small piece of timber compared to the main yards, it was big enough to smash the boat to splinters, and rob them of their only escape.

Maximinus turned to the threat and put one foot back, bracing himself for the impact. As it hit him, he heaved with his powerful legs, altering its course just enough. The sail whipped over Silus' head, trailing ropes lashing at the passengers in the little boat. Then the sail and spar disappeared over the side, bearing Maximinus into the water with it.

Silus stared after the giant, looking for signs of his resurfacing, and wondering whether he was brave or stupid enough to dive in after him.

'Where's Julia?' The voice was slurred, but unmistakably belonged to Caracalla. Silus turned to face his Emperor. Blood streaked down the side of his head and coagulated in his beard. His eyes did not seem to be focussing. But his voice became louder and firmer. 'Where is Domna?'

Silus looked back to the ship. They were drifting away from it now, six feet, nine. No one had thought to pick up an oar yet, but the little boat seemed stable and seaworthy. Many heads were in the water, but none near enough to imminently attempt to board the boat and topple it or overwhelm it. They seemed safe.

The ship, on the other hand, was listing violently. The prow was underwater, and the stern was raised in the air. Was it possible that Domna was still on board? If not, she was surely drowned. And if she was, then the same fate wasn't far off.

'Get her,' said Caracalla, addressing Athaulf and Silus. His voice brooked no argument. This was a command from the Emperor. Still, Silus had no desire to get into the water after his previous brush with death under the waves. He looked at Athaulf, hoping that his commander would volunteer. Athaulf looked helpless, for the first time.

'What is it?' mouthed Silus to Athaulf.

'I can't swim,' he replied quietly, so only Silus could hear the words and the pitiful tone in his voice.

Caracalla, stunned as he was, noticed their hesitation.

'Save the Empress,' he said to his guards, his voice dripping with menace, 'or I will kill you and everyone you love.'

Silus looked at the sinking ship, the waves lapping at the side of the boat, and said, 'Fuck.' Then he kicked off his sandals, pinched his nose, and jumped.

He had braced himself for a similar experience to his previous involuntary immersion. But this time there was no cold shock. The summer water temperature could have been pleasant under different circumstances. The sea was calmer too. And this time he was in control.

He wasn't a strong swimmer, but the distance back to the sinking ship wasn't far. He was in fact in greater danger from the hazards on board than those of the water.

When he reached the side of the ship, the deck was half-submerged, the port side completely under the surface, the starboard side rearing high above him. What remained above the waves was sinking fast.

A few sailors and rowers remained on board, clinging to timbers. They stared at his return with expressions of wonder that suggested they either thought he was insane, or that he had come back to rescue them. He avoided their eyes. He wasn't here for them. No doubt these were the crew who had been unable to swim or too paralysed with fear to act. Either way, they would likely drown when the ship went down, sucked under by the powerful forces that the sinking mass produced. Silus realised he had precious little time to avoid sharing their fate.

He was near the bow, and the last time he had seen Domna, she had been near the stern on her little wooden chair. He recalled that the legs of the chair had been nailed to the deck to stop it sliding around. Would that have given her something to cling to? He didn't want to think about the possibility that she was dead. He suspected it would drive Caracalla to a fury and madness that no one had yet witnessed. For a moment it occurred to him that if Domna had drowned, the only way to save Tituria might be to kill Caracalla himself.

He cursed, then prayed aloud to Neptune to spare the Empress.

The side of the boat slipped further underwater, and he forced himself into action. The wet boards were treacherously slippery, and he had to haul himself from handhold to handhold, using whatever was within reach to drag himself slowly forward.

A splintered plank gave him something to grip, though the little shards of wood ripped at his palm. He reached out and grabbed a rope attached at one end to the rigging, the other flailing loose. That enabled him to make it a dozen feet further forward, to where some torn sail flapped in the breeze. He yanked on the linen sailcloth, testing its weight, then clambered along it like a spider rushing across its web to catch a newly trapped fly.

There was a loud rip, and the cloth tore down its middle. With a yell, Silus slid down the decking towards the waiting brine. Desperately, he pulled himself up the sail, even as it tore further, so he felt like a man running uphill on ice, making no progress no matter how fast his legs pumped.

The ripping stopped abruptly when the linen was torn in two, and Silus found he was clutching a narrow strip that was still fortunately attached fast to a sturdy beam. Planting his feet on the deck, he used the sail like a rock climber uses a rope. His bare feet slipped and slid on the greasy planks, but he made it to the firm beam and clung to it, catching his breath for a moment.

Something grasped his ankle, and in his heightened state of anxiety, he pictured some sea monster rising from the depths to grasp him in its tentacles and drag him down into the depths, to consume him at leisure in its lair. He looked down, and saw a pitiful face, a tough-looking rower with tears streaming down his face. The oarsman gripped Silus' ankle tight.

'Help me, please,' cried the rower. Silus looked around, but there was no obvious place of safety he could direct the man too. The ship lurched, and they both slid sideways along the decking, the rower dangling from Silus' leg like the lead on a plumb line. The weight of the body was too much, and Silus felt his hold loosening. He looked away from the poor man's terrified gaze, and stamped down.

Cartilage and bone crunched beneath his heel, and the rower howled, but hung on tight. Silus stamped again, and he felt the grip ease. Another stamp, and with a despairing cry the rower slid down the decking and into the waves. He tried to grab the edge of the decking, but there was no purchase, and his screams were cut off as the waves broke over his head. He emerged only once more, waving frantically but with no air left to cry out. Then he was gone.

The ship was three-quarters submerged now, the prow and entire port side beneath the surface, and Silus knew his time had almost run out. He scrambled and leapt from spar to rope, from splintered decking boards to the rowlocks of the uppermost oar.

Then as he clambered over the sodden rags of the hindmost sail, he found her.

Domna was clinging to the starboard railing. Her legs dangled down the decking, which was rapidly approaching the vertical. Her immaculate hairstyle was a soggy mess, her carefully coiffured locks smeared across her shoulders and face. Her fine stola clung to her body, outlining every curve in a way that almost made Silus avert his eyes, rather than stare at the Empress' form.

But her face was serene. Though she had not yet surrendered to her fate, Silus could see she was prepared to accept whatever Fortuna decreed.

'Augusta!' he shouted above the cacophony of groaning, cracking timbers, the cries of drowning sailors, and the wind whipping through the tattered sailcloth. She didn't seem to hear and he yelled louder.

'Augusta! Domna! Keep hold. I'm coming.'

Now she saw him, and a faint smile crossed her face. He worked his way up the decking to the starboard rail, and dragged himself along until he was level with her.

'Silus. What an unexpected pleasure.'

He had always respected the Empress. She had conducted herself with dignity throughout all the hardships and tragedies she had experienced, and she was thoughtful, cultured and intelligent, not to mention beautiful. But he had never admired her more than now, so composed, with her life hanging by the slenderest of threads.

'The pleasure is all mine, Augusta,' said Silus, her calmness and poise infectious. 'But I'm afraid we don't have much time.'

'I'm in your hands, Arcanus.'

Silus looked around him. Reaching Domna was only the first challenge. He could not yet feel relief that she was still alive, given the danger that they were in. The ship was sinking fast now, the stern rising as the bow and midship plunged downwards. In moments, their part of the ship would be underwater and if they were near it at that moment, they would be sucked down with it.

'We need to jump, Augusta.'

'I'm afraid I neglected my swimming lessons, Silus. I will be no safer in the water than staying here.'

'I will keep you afloat,' he said with more confidence than he felt. But what choice did they have? 'Climb up onto the railing. We are going to jump feet first into the water over the side. I'll help you.'

Domna hesitated, maybe wondering whether she shouldn't just accept her fate. Then she nodded.

'Very well.'

Silus clambered onto the railing and reached down to take both her hands in his. She looked at him and nodded, and he hauled hard, pulling her up so they were seated on the edge of the railing. Behind them was the near-vertical decking. Before them, twenty feet down, was the water of the Hellespont. Silus reached over and took Domna's hand in his own, and squeezed.

'We need to get as far away from the side as possible. Jump as hard as you can. We go together,' he said. 'On three.'

Domna swallowed, nodded.

'One. Two. Three.'

They pushed off at the same time, Domna's leap understandably feeble given she was a privileged middle-aged woman who took minimal exercise. But Silus' grip gave her extra impetus. The wind whipped at Silus' hair and Domna's dress, and then they splashed into the water a few feet from the side of the ship.

The height of their jump meant they hit the surface with some force, their legs and knees taking the impact before they both disappeared under the water. Silus felt Domna's grip on his hand loosen as terror and panic set in, but he squeezed harder, and kicked for the surface. The boundary between water and air, death and life, seemed incredibly distant. Silus stroked with his free hand and paddled frantically with his feet, and though he had a chest full of air, his head told him it wasn't enough, that he was going to drown. Every instinct told him to release the Empress, leave her to the depths and save himself.

He clutched her tightly and heaved her upwards. They broke the surface together, sprayed out brine and breath, and sucked in sweet air.

Immediately Domna started to thrash. Her previous poise and equanimity vanished as the terror of water of one who couldn't swim took over. Silus trod water, bobbing up and down in time with the waves, and with difficulty kept hold of her arm.

'Domna, calm down. I'm with you.'

'Silus, help me,' she spluttered.

'I know it's hard, but you must relax. I'm not going to let you drown.'

Whether his voice was sufficiently reassuring, or Domna simply got a hold of herself, Silus wasn't sure, but either way her thrashing movements relented. He took a quick look around and spied some floating wreckage twenty feet away.

'We're going to swim over there. Lie back. I'm going to come behind you, and put my arm around you. The waves will splash over you but stay calm. It isn't far.'

With an effort, she did as she was told. He manoeuvred himself behind her, so his front was to her back, then he slid his arm around her chest. The waves buffeted him, and he adjusted his hold to secure her.

Suddenly, with a feeling of absolute mortification, he realised that he was holding a handful of her breast. His immediate instinct was to let go, but that might see Domna disappear underwater again, with no certainty he could bring her back up. Despite the terror of the situation, he felt his cheeks flush red, and was relieved that at least Domna was not looking at him as they shared this compromising position. He decided there was nothing for it but to press on, so he tightened his grip, getting ready to kick out for the relative safety of the flotsam.

What the fuck was that?

Something large and solid and irregular was pressing into the palm of his hand. Something beneath the skin of Domna's breast.

A tumour.

Julia Domna, Empress of Rome, had cancer of the breast.

For a moment, he almost forgot his peril. So many things made sense now. Caracalla's fluctuating mood, his frequent visits to healing shrines and his anger when the priests failed him. Caracalla wasn't ill. His beloved stepmother was.

Silus forced himself to concentrate on their predicament. He struck out, swimming steadily with one arm and both legs, focussing on keeping Domna's mouth and nose out of the water. It was much harder than he'd expected, and he fought against waves and currents and the drag of the dead weight of the Empress. The distance between them and safety didn't seem to change, and he even wondered for a despairing moment if the wreckage was drifting further away from them. But slowly, inch by exhausting inch, they drew nearer, until, just as Silus thought his burning arms could hold Domna no longer, his outstretched fingers touched the wood.

He used his remaining strength to pull the wreckage to them, and helped Domna to take a hold. There they sat, bobbing up and down like gulls, gasping for breath. Silus looked around him. There were few men struggling free in the water now, though one or two had found spars and planks to hang onto. The shore seemed impossibly distant, but he prepared himself to start paddling towards it, using the wood as a float.

'Silus.'

Domna was looking earnestly into his eyes.

'Augusta, I…'

There was a sound like a whale breaching, a spout of air and water escaping from a gash in the hull, and the ship finally sank, disappearing completely, the cries of those still on board abruptly cut short. A minor tsunami radiated out, and when it reached them it tossed them about like they were ants on kindling sticks. Silus wrapped one arm around a timber, and the other around Domna's waist, and they held on until the buffeting subsided.

Domna wiped her straggled hair from her face, cleared her eyes. She still seemed to want to speak. She opened her mouth.

'Julia! Julia! Where are you?'

Caracalla sounded hoarse, as if he had been calling for her until his voice gave out. Silus turned. In the distance, the tiny rowing boat, tossing up and down, appeared in sight now it was no longer obscured by the ship. Athaulf and Oclatinius were hauling on the oars, a rather lopsided arrangement given their respective muscularity, so that Athaulf had to continually alter their bearing. Caracalla knelt in the prow, clutching the sides, staring desperately ahead of him.

Silus raised an arm which suddenly felt ten times as heavy as it ever had.

'Over here!'

The wind, the cries for help, the water lapping at the timbers, seemed to swallow his feeble shout, but Caracalla's eyes whipped round. He pointed, yelled at the rowers to redouble their efforts.

'Julia! I'm here. I'm coming!'

Julia adjusted her grip on the timber so she could rest her hand on Silus' forearm. She spoke quietly, but Silus heard her clearly. 'Say nothing to anyone about this. We will talk privately in due course.'

'Yes, Augusta.'

The boat arrived quickly after a few minor course corrections, and when Caracalla reached them, he grabbed Domna and hauled her on board, clutching her and showering her head with kisses, crying over and over that he thought he had lost her and that he loved her. The others averted their eyes at this overt display of affection.

Athaulf and Oclatinius helped Silus climb over the side, and he lay in a puddle in the bottom of the boat, water pouring off his soaked tunic, breathing heavily and looking up at the sky, marvelling at the feeling of being alive, breathing cool air, with a solid surface beneath him.

Athaulf and Oclatinius took to the oars once more, and when Silus found the energy to sit up, he saw a large trireme was approaching. Its flag flew the colours of the prefect of the fleet. When it was in earshot, Athaulf bellowed, 'We have the Emperor. I command you in his name to bring us on board.'

A cradle was hastily constructed from thick ropes and lowered over the side. Athaulf pressed Caracalla to go first, but he wouldn't hear of it, and helped Domna in instead. Once she had been hauled up, Caracalla grabbed the ropes and climbed the side athletically, unaided. Athaulf followed suit, and then, to Silus' surprise – though he realised nothing about the man should surprise him at this point – Oclatinius did the same.

Silus would have loved to have been carried up in the makeshift seat. His efforts in the water had left him drained, every muscle emptied of reserves. But the sailors looking expectantly down made no attempt to help, and with a resigned sigh, Silus grabbed the rope and climbed, using his feet to walk up the side, feeling like he would lose hold and crash back into the sea. When he reached the side rail, and strong hands pulled him over, he felt like he would black out from exhaustion. He fell prone, face to one side, mouth opening and closing, for all the world like a landed fish.

A hard kick in his ribs made him yell in surprise and anger, and he raised himself onto one elbow, preparing to curse his assailant. The fierce, bearded face of Caracalla looked down at him. Silus swallowed the words on the tip of his tongue, and struggled to his knees. He bowed his head.

For a moment, Caracalla said nothing. Then he laid his hand lightly on the top of Silus' head and said, 'Thank you.'

Chapter XIII

The four conspirators sat around a small table lit by a single oil lamp. It was the first time Festus had had a chance to meet with the chief conspirator since the shipwreck the day before, and unusually, the man had brought his lackeys with him.

Caracalla's procession had continued, undelayed by the near-death of the Emperor and Empress, and many of the common soldiers were celebrating his seeming invulnerability, going as far as to declare him a victor over Neptune. Now, they had reached Nicomedia, the capital of Bithynia in north-west Asia Minor, and after the troops had found themselves quarters, they were let out in shifts to enjoy some leave exploring what the city had to offer.

Festus had found his fellow intriguers a small private backroom of a tavern to meet in at night, and they had all arrived, separately and alone. The dim flame of the lamp gave the unhappy faces around the table the appearance of an even deeper gloom.

'It was a stupid idea,' said Festus.

'You seemed fully behind it before it failed,' said the heavily bearded man opposite him. The other two, subservient, nodded agreement.

'Nero didn't think it was a stupid idea. He used the same tactic to attempt to kill his mother.'

'And that failed too! I mean really, what were we thinking?'

'It nearly worked. The saboteur did exactly what he was told. And he did it very well. He half-sawed the yard with perfect judgement so it failed when they were in the middle of the crossing, not before or after. And his other adjustments, loosened nails and weakened hull fittings, guaranteed the ship would go down. It's just bad luck that the Emperor and Empress survived.'

'Bad luck, and that cursed Arcanus, Silus,' said Festus. 'I really need to do something about him.'

'And what other options did we have? We are all agreed that Caracalla must go, for the good of Rome. His past deeds shame us, and his madness grows for all to see.'

Festus reflected that the need for Caracalla to be deposed had more to do with the ambition of the man sitting opposite him, and if Festus was honest with himself, though the glory and safety of the Empire was his main motivation, his own promotion was almost of equal import. Always in Oclatinius' shadow. Well, not for much longer. If they could just find a way to be rid of this egregious Emperor.

'We can't poison him – he has food tasters. We can't attack him with soldiers – these new Leones are loyal as wolfhounds and twice as dangerous. And if a blatant attempt on his life is made, and it turns out unsuccessful, then Caracalla's fury will be apocalyptic. We would have no guarantee of surviving it, even if he didn't have evidence against us. As it is, this wreck looks like an accident, and we can gather our resources and consider what our next move will be.'

'And if he finds something to link us to the attempt?'

'How can he? Only you spoke to the slave who acted as an intermediary – Acacius, wasn't it? – and we have done away with him. There is no trail leading back to us, and no evidence that this was anything other than an act of an angry deity.'

'No evidence, maybe,' said Festus. 'But Oclatinius was there. He isn't stupid. He isn't likely to let this go.'

'Even with his obligation to you?'

'If he becomes convinced of my involvement, I don't know if our past will be enough to protect me.'

'I see.' The bearded man glanced at his colleagues to his left and right, a look passing between them that Festus couldn't interpret. 'Well, thank you, Festus, for your efforts. Let's reflect on all this, and meet again soon.'

Festus realised he was dismissed, and he stood and nodded. He left through a back door that led onto a quiet alley. He looked up and down the street, but could see no one lurking, no one surreptitiously observing him, and he could detect no one following him as he headed back to his quarters. But he couldn't shake the anxious feeling in the pit of his stomach, an impending sense of doom.

Back in the dim room in the tavern, the bearded man shook his head. 'He worries me.'

'And me,' said one of the other conspirators.

'But we have our insurance,' said the third. 'If the Arcani get too close, we can throw Festus to the beasts.'

They all nodded agreement and then sat in contemplative silence.

–

'I haven't had a chance to properly thank you,' said Domna. Silus reclined on a couch, eating small honeycakes and sipping a fine wine. Domna's couch was at right angles to his, and she was lying so their faces were close, and Silus felt uncomfortable at such proximity to the Empress. He hoped Caracalla didn't walk in on them. He didn't want a jealous Emperor on his back.

'There is no need for thanks, Augusta. I did only what duty required, what any true Roman would do for his Empress, mother of the Emperor.'

'Stepmother,' she reminded him, and he was sure she had a little twinkle in her eye when she said it. 'Nevertheless, you saved my life, and I am not ungrateful. If you need a favour in the future you may call on me.'

He wondered whether he could get her to remove the assassin in Tituria's household, who was ready to slaughter the young girl if her orders required it. But he wasn't sure whether Domna had that much influence over Caracalla, and it seemed insulting to bring up the matter of her stepson and lover's planting of a killer in the household of a Roman maiden. It was strange; he could face down a screaming, axe-wielding barbarian in battle, but being alone with Domna made him tongue-tied and red-faced, like a schoolboy finally given a chance to speak to his older crush.

'I hope I never need to presume on you,' he said. Well, that was true. If he was ever in the situation of having to call in favours from the Empress, things had probably got pretty dire.

'Will there be an investigation into the cause?' She didn't have to elaborate on what she was referring to.

'There isn't much left to investigate, Augusta. The ship is at the bottom of the Hellespont. But I'm sure some enquiries will be made, for appearances' sake, as much as anything.'

'Do you believe it was an accident?'

Silus hesitated. Even without Oclatinius' warning of an attempt on Caracalla's life, any event that nearly killed the Emperor had to be treated with some suspicion. But given his doubts about some high-ranking intimates of Caracalla, it would be foolhardy to discuss his thoughts with the Empress. Powerful men did not like others casting aspersions on their loyalty to those above them – understandably, since those sorts of rumours could lead to a swift execution.

'I have no evidence to suggest otherwise.'

Domna nodded, and didn't pursue the topic. She was wise enough to know when someone wasn't prepared to enter further discussions.

'There is something else we must talk about,' she said instead.

Silus swallowed. He figured this was the real reason he was here. And he desperately didn't want to have this conversation.

'During the rescue, you were touching the Imperial person.'

Now Silus really blushed. 'I'm so sorry, Augusta. There was no other way...'

'I'm not looking for an apology. I already told you how grateful I am. But, I believe as you manhandled me, you may have noticed something unusual.'

'No, Augusta, I didn't...'

'Don't lie to me, Silus!' she snapped.

Silus pursed his lips, then inclined his head. 'How long have you had the tumour?'

Domna regarded him steadily, apparently satisfied that the subject was now in the open.

'Perhaps half a year. Maybe longer before I first noticed it.'

'And the Emperor knows.'

'Don't be naive, Silus. How could I keep it from him?'

Silus wished the ground would open and the ghosts of Hades would bear him away. This was worse than when his father had tried to explain the facts of life to him.

'What do the physicians say?'

'You have heard of Galen of Pergamum? He is a friend of mine. An old man now, but still the best. He said it was due to an accumulation of black bile. He offered to attempt to cut it out, use a hot blade, lead and arsenic pastes. But he said it felt like it was too deep to get it all out, and that the karkinos, as he called it, was incurable. A lot of pain, not to mention the disfigurement, and for no gain.'

'There are no herbs, no medicines?'

She shook her head. 'It continues to grow, regardless of ointments and potions. Slowly, but inexorably. There is no hope. Only prayer.'

'Caracalla hopes. It's why he visits the shrines, isn't it?'

'And why he gets so frustrated when nothing seems to work. But he hasn't given up. I don't think he's surrendered to anything in his life.'

'I believe that.'

'So. You know. That makes three. Antoninus, Galen. And you.'

'That number need not get any larger, Augusta.'

'Not even your superior, Oclatinius?'

'Not even him, Augusta.'

A tension seemed to go out of the Empress, a release around the shoulders that Silus hadn't noticed until it was absent. She had genuinely been concerned about his keeping her secret. And her solution to that was to talk to him in private. When she could, with a word in the right ear, simply have had him killed. His respect for her climbed even higher than its already elevated position.

'I think we should drink a toast. To Harpocrates.'

Silus paused in the act of lifting his cup.

'Sorry, who?'

Domna smiled. 'The second son of Isis.'

Silus still looked blank.

'The god of silence.' She took a sip from her cup.

–

'I can't believe Maximinus survived,' said Silus. The giant bodyguard had swum ashore, using a beam as a flotation device, and had straight away reported for duty to Athaulf.

'That man is indestructible, I suspect,' said Oclatinius. They sat together in the spymaster's temporary office.

'So what do you think? Was it sabotage?'

'Of course it was sabotage.' Oclatinius' tone was that of a disappointed schoolteacher. 'I was there. Which brings me on to another point.'

Silus' guts clenched. He had been waiting for this.

'Do I seem suicidal to you, Silus?'

'No,' he said, voice not much above a whisper.

'No, what!'

'No, master.'

'Do I look like I am so devoted to a cause, I would throw my life away?'

'No, master.'

'And do you have any more accusations you would like to throw my way?'

Clearly Oclatinius had not been involved in the assassination attempt on Caracalla. It would have been easy for him to make some excuse, feign an illness, invent a duty, so he did not have to be on that ship at that time. However, Silus still had questions. Did Oclatinius have information that Festus was involved? Did their relationship go deeper than former master and apprentice?

But Silus was no more suicidal than Oclatinius. The look the Arcani commander had given him when Silus had first brought Festus up still made him shiver. So he bit down his queries, and mumbled, 'No.' Then he hastily added, 'Master.'

'Well if you're sure, maybe we can get back to our work. I want you to go back to Sestos and track down the craftsmen who worked on the Emperor's ship. Find out who did what, and on whose orders.'

Silus bowed, and hurried away from Oclatinius' glower as quickly as was polite.

-

It took Silus a surprisingly short amount of time to track down Evaristus. But then, maybe he shouldn't be surprised at all, he reflected. People's capacity for overwhelming stupidity was a constant in life. So it just took a few conversations and a few coins in the palms of some dock workers and shipwrights for them to point him in the direction of the ship's carpenter who had suddenly come into money, paying off all his gambling debts in one hit, and then blowing a cartload more in the cock pits and dicing rooms, not to mention the taverns and brothels.

Silus found him arguing with a bookmaker, gesturing loudly at the spurs on a proud-looking cockerel, who was standing on the bloody corpse of another bird. Silus could smell strong wine on the man's breath, and his inebriation made it easy for Silus to take his arm and drag him away. He shouted apologies to the bookmaker for his friend's behaviour, and ignoring some ineffective protests from Evaristus, led the carpenter down a narrow, quiet alleyway.

As soon as he was out of sight of the main road, he shoved the surprised man up against a wall, his forearm pressed against his throat, and with his other hand drew a blade that he pressed against Evaristus' groin.

'We need to have a little talk.'

There was a sudden warm feeling against Silus' middle, an acrid smell, and he looked down to find Evaristus had released a large puddle of urine. A full bladder from too much wine and sudden terror did not mix well. Silus grimaced, but didn't loosen his grip. This was one of the lesser hardships he had suffered for his work.

'You came into some money recently.'

Evaristus was a big, rough, well-built man, but he babbled like a toddler.

'My aunt died. I inherited it. It's all legal...'

Silus cut off his words by pressing his blade more firmly between Evaristus' legs.

'Someone paid you to sabotage the ship. I want to know what you did, and who paid you. If the next words coming out of your mouth are not an answer to one of those questions, I'm going to cut your tiny cock off.'

'Wait, no, I...'

Silus grabbed a handful of genitalia. Evaristus shrieked.

'His name was Acacius.'

Silus paused.

'Continue.'

'That's all I know about him. Scrawny little thing, slave I think, but well-spoken. One of those educated Greeks.' The words came out in a rush.

'And what did you do?'

Evaristus hesitated, and Silus pushed the tip of the blade into Evaristus' scrotum deep enough to draw blood.

'He had me saw halfway through the yard arm, and loosen some nails in the decking and hull where it would fall, to make sure the ship went down when the beam collapsed.'

Silus nodded and considered the information. It fitted with what he had witnessed. And he had the name of the intermediary now. He could tell that was as much as he would get from this terrified fool.

So what to do with him now? Letting him go was not an option; men had died because of his greed. Should he hand him over to Oclatinius or even Caracalla? His fate would be horrific – torture, then a drawn-out and brutal execution. Which would serve no purpose since he had nothing more to tell.

Silus rammed the blade deep into Evaristus' inner thigh, then pulled it out with a flick that whipped the wickedly sharp tip through the deep vessels there. Evaristus gasped in shock. It would not even have been that painful, and it would take a few moments for the carpenter to realise the severity of the wound. By which time consciousness would already be fading.

Silus stepped back, his tunic now drenched in blood from the spraying artery, as well as urine. Time for a new one, he supposed. He waited until Evaristus had collapsed to his knees, then his side, then left him there to bleed out.

-

When Silus was admitted into the Emperor's presence, Oclatinius by his side, he immediately noticed the difference. Caracalla was deep in discussion with Macrinus, head bowed, but it was unmissable.

He had shaved.

Silus looked at Oclatinius, who shrugged, just as nonplussed. Ever since Silus had known Caracalla – in fact, as far as he knew, ever since the Emperor-to-be had first sprouted whiskers – his stern face had been framed by a thick beard of tightly curled dark brown hair. It was not the only change. He was dressed in a kind of beret, a flattish cap with tassels at the rear, calf-length leather boots and a linen cuirass. The overall impression reminded Silus of someone he had seen in numerous statues and busts before, but for a moment he couldn't place it. Caracalla's conversation with Macrinus soon reminded him.

'I want to recruit sixteen thousand men. They must be Macedonian. They will form a phalanx. I want them equipped with ox-hide helmets, linen breastplates and bronze shields. They will be armed with long spears, short spears and swords.'

'Yes, Augustus,' said Macrinus in a tone that Silus hoped didn't sound as obviously like he was humouring a child to Caracalla as it seemed to Silus.

'The officers will take new names. Ptolemy, Cassander, Seleucus, and Antigones. The unit will be called Alexander's phalanx.'

'It shall be as you say, Augustus.'

Silus swallowed nervously. Had the Emperor gone completely mad? There was some logic to having a unit of spearmen to counter the Parthian cavalry, but why equip them like an army from five hundred years ago? Maybe because Caracalla had decided he was the new Alexander, on his way to conquer Persia. How would he react to

Silus' news, if he was genuinely considering himself the new coming of the God King who conquered the world?

Caracalla looked up, seeming to notice Silus and Oclatinius for the first time.

'Yes? Something to report?'

Silus waited for a moment for Oclatinius to speak, then realised his boss was leaving it up to him. *Thanks for that*, he thought.

'Yes, Augustus. I have grave and disturbing news.'

'Out with it.'

Was Silus imagining it, or was the Emperor affecting a Greek accent now? This couldn't be good. Silus took a deep breath, then spoke.

'I am afraid that the shipwreck was no accident.'

Caracalla leant forward on his marble throne, his attention abruptly focussed on Silus. Silus ploughed on.

'I tracked down a shipwright who worked on your ship. He confirmed he sabotaged it, for money.'

Caracalla's face reddened, the hue more visible now on his bare cheeks. 'And where is that man now?' His voice was tight, but Silus could sense the pressure building within, ready to erupt like Vesuvius.

'He did not survive the interrogation,' said Silus truthfully. 'But he gave me a name. Acacius.'

Caracalla gave him a blank look. 'This name should mean something to me?'

'No, Augustus, nor to me, but I found him anyway. Or at least his household. He is a slave. But he has vanished.'

'And this Acacius was the one who paid the shipwright to sink the boat?'

'Yes, Augustus.'

'So? To whom does the slave belong?'

Silus looked at Oclatinius beseechingly.

'Acacius is a clerk,' said Oclatinius. 'Owned by Helvius Pertinax.'

-

Publius Helvius Pertinax knelt in the courtyard of the villa of the Governor of Bithynia, stripped to the waist. Caracalla was seated on a tall chair, so he was looking down on the man from a great height. His full council had been commanded to attend: Oclatinius and Macrinus, Festus, Ulpius Julianus and Julianus Nestor, Theocritus and Epagathus the freedmen who had been made supreme praetorian prefects, as well as the senators who had accompanied Caracalla on his expedition such as Julius Alexianus, father of Julia Soaemias, and Cassius Dio, the perpetually discontented historian. Armed Leones, uniformed and at attention, lined the courtyard perimeter. Caracalla obviously intended this to be an exemplary punishment, a warning to all of the consequences of treason. Caracalla clearly preferred to be feared and hated than loved, Silus thought. And many of the senators really did hate him, for his bleeding them dry of cash, for the way he favoured the soldiers over the noble elite, the contemptuous way he treated them, summoning them and leaving them standing for hours outside his palace, ignoring their demands and pleas and generally marginalising them.

The sun beat down, and sweat ran freely down Pertinax's back, mingling with the streaks of blood where his back had been whipped raw. The young senator looked up at Caracalla with terror in his eyes. Silus could see the poor man was trying to keep his dignity, but a man would need to be made of stone to hide his fear at a moment like this.

'Augustus,' said Pertinax, speaking loudly for the benefit of the audience, managing admirably to keep the tremor out of his voice. 'I swear by all the gods, by my father's deified shade, I am innocent of this charge. You have treated my father's memory and myself with nothing but respect. I have always done the same for you.'

'Is that right?' said Caracalla. 'Would you care to repeat your suggestion about which titles I should be awarded?'

Pertinax blanched. 'Augustus, I am sorry. It was just a joke. A tasteless one, I admit. I will take any punishment you decree for that. But please believe me. I am part of no conspiracy. I am not a traitor.'

Caracalla gestured to Athaulf. For once, Silus wasn't being asked to be the Imperial executioner. Athaulf had insisted on taking the task on his own shoulders, maybe to atone for his failure as head of the Emperor's bodyguard to prevent the attempt on Caracalla's life. Athaulf drew a long, sharp spatha, and stood behind Pertinax.

Now the young man started to shake, and tears ran down his cheeks.

'You can't do this. I am the son of an Emperor. I am a consul. I…'

The sword flashed, a swish through the air, and the blade momentarily reflected the bright sun into Silus' eyes. He blinked, and when he opened his eyes, Pertinax's head was rolling to the left, and his body was falling to the right.

The audience was silent. Some closed their eyes. Some bowed their heads. Some moved their lips in inaudible prayers.

Caracalla rose, and stalked back inside the villa.

Chapter XIV

'He died for a greater good,' said Festus, raising his cup of wine. 'Poor innocent Pertinax.'

'I'm sure that will comfort his shade,' said the conspirator seated opposite him drily. 'And, let us hope, pacify his deified father.'

Festus looked at the other three in the room. He had expected their praise, now that the plan had gone so well, and their apparent displeasure rankled.

'Listen, I have played my part. It isn't my fault that Caracalla didn't perish in the wreck. But I have limited the damage.'

'By sacrificing a noble member of the Senate, a consul.'

Festus narrowed his eyes. 'We knew there would be bloodshed. You cannot overthrow a man like Caracalla with flowers and kind words.'

'It's easy for you to say,' said the man to Festus' left. 'Your head is still on your shoulders.'

Festus felt irritation building within him.

'And where do you think your conspiracy would be without me?'

'Probably exactly where it is now,' said the man to Festus' right. 'Nowhere. We have made no progress. All we have done is alert Caracalla and his loyalists to the threat. It will be a long time before we can make another attempt. Maybe years. And in the meantime, he grows ever more mad.'

The first conspirator, seated opposite Festus, nodded agreement. 'This obsession with Alexander, this crazy new Alexandrian phalanx, all these visits to healing shrines, his mood swings. He becomes more and more dangerous and unpredictable. Anyone who is close to him must fear for their safety if he takes against them. More than that, I fear for the safety of the Empire. We have a madman leading us into war against Rome's most powerful current enemy, maybe our toughest enemy since Hannibal. And we have lost our chance of ridding ourselves of him because of your incompetence.'

'My incompetence?' It was supposed to be a clandestine meeting, but Festus couldn't help speaking louder. 'You are nothing without me. I am the one with the resources. I am the one with Oclatinius in my pocket. I am the one with the brains and the cunning and the daring. And you three? What do you bring? Not even a noble birth between you. Let me remind you, there are other figureheads I could put on the throne. You aren't the only ones with ambition. In fact, there are plenty of others more qualified by birth and experience, and who are a lot more competent.'

Festus wondered if he was going too far, but Pertinax's execution had unsettled him more than he cared to admit. It had been too easy to picture his own head rolling across the courtyard.

The other men glanced at each other, and the man opposite Festus spoke.

'I think we should disband.'

'You mean… give up?' Festus was taken aback. He hadn't expected so easy a surrender, even given the supine character of the man who supposedly led this conspiracy.

'I mean, let us take our time, keep our noses clean until things die down. We can reconvene in the future, when the timing is more opportune, and the omens are better.'

Festus looked around the three closed faces, then rose slowly.

'Fine. If that's how you feel. But don't be surprised if events proceed without you, and you are left behind.'

When he was gone, the three conspirators sat a while in silence. Then one said, 'It's not unexpected.'

'It's why we took precautions,' said another.

The leader sighed. 'He has to go.'

-

The cat lay on her side with one hind leg raised, so her three kittens could access her nipples. They suckled greedily, while their mother rested in the shadows cast by the buildings on the south side of the street. Silus sat on the north side, at a table outside a tavern, picking at a bowl of dates unenthusiastically, the full glare of the late morning sun in his face. The mother and her little ones reminded him acutely of his lost family. Years had passed now, and at times he managed to forget them, to find pleasure in his life, but that made him feel guilty. And when he did remember them, the pain was as sharp as ever.

He didn't even have Atius to distract him, to say something stupid, or do something reckless that would require Silus to intervene. There was Oclatinius, but his relationship with the old man had never been comradely, and even though Silus now knew that Oclatinius was loyal, their relationship was strained. He felt lonely.

He wondered if he should drink something stronger. Gamble. Find a woman. Start a fight. All the things Atius would have done in his place. But he had no will to do any of that. He just wanted to go home. But he didn't have a home.

A cart drawn by an ass rumbled down the street, a tarpaulin covering the contents in the back. Silus' eyes followed it idly. As it passed him, the driver reached behind him and pulled away the tarpaulin, revealing an object wrapped in a blanket. The driver gave the object a push and it slid out and landed in the dirty street with a thud. The driver hit the ass with a stick, and it broke into a brisk trot, and the cart tumbled away.

Curious, Silus put his cup down. As he approached, he realised the blanket concealed the shape of a human body. He knelt down and gave the edge of the cloth a tug, and with a groan, a man rolled out.

At least, it resembled a man. The figure had an arm and a limb that stuck out at crooked angles. The naked skin was covered with welts of black, blue, yellow and green. The nose was flattened and out of alignment. Shards of broken teeth protruded from swollen lips.

Silus looked down the street wondering whether he should pursue the carter, but the man before him needed his help more urgently. He stared for a moment, unsure now what to do. The man was breathing stertorously, little bubbles swelling out of one nostril then bursting. His eyes were squeezed shut, but he was moving feebly, waving his unbroken arm in the air as if he was drowning and signalling for help. Silus was suddenly reminded of the sailor he had kicked overboard during the sinking of the ship, and the sharp pang of guilt made him determined to aid this stranger.

He knelt beside the man, and took a hold of his hand. The man's eyelids cracked open a fraction and he squinted up at Silus, his expression rigid with pain.

'Don't worry, you are safe now. You're injured, but I will make sure you get the best doctors. The medici in the legions are rubbish when it comes to curing the flux, but they are experts at fixing broken bones.'

The man coughed, a wet sound, then rolled onto his side and retched. Silus cradled his head until the dry-heaving had finished. He saw that the poor wretch had at least one broken rib. The pain of vomiting and coughing must have been excruciating. Silus fetched his cup of water and put the rim gently to the man's mouth. He took a tiny sip, suppressed a cough with an effort, then drank more in small gulps.

The tavern keeper had come out now to see what was going on outside his establishment, and when he saw the badly injured man, he wrung his hands and began to complain about bad omens and curses being brought down on his establishment.

'Get your cart,' snapped Silus. 'We are taking him to the legion barracks to get him medical attention.' When the tavern keeper hesitated, Silus said, 'I will pay you.'

The offer of money overcame the businessman's reticence, and he hurried away to fetch his donkey cart.

'Everything will be fine,' said Silus. 'I'm Silus of the Leones, and of the Arcani. You are safe with me. Can you tell me your name?'

The man's mouth worked, and at first Silus thought he was letting out another incoherent moan. Then he realised what he was trying to say.

'A...a...Acacius.'

Oh. Shit.

'Don't upset him,' said the medicus. 'And don't take long. He is in a very fragile state.'

Silus looked down at the badly injured slave, stretched out on the valetudinarium bed, one arm and one leg splinted and bandaged, bruises and cuts covered with pungent ointments and unguents. He seemed barely alive, but when Silus laid a gentle hand on his shoulder, he opened his eyes and gave a half-smile.

'Thank you,' he half-mouthed, half-whispered. Silus wasn't sure if he should be thanked, given Acacius' crime. What had been done to him so far would be nothing compared to the punishment a slave would receive for his involvement in the attempted assassination of the Emperor.

But Acacius was remarkably cooperative, seemingly oblivious to his danger, or maybe resigned to his fate, and he needed no coercion from Silus or Oclatinius to answer their questions.

'Who did this to you?' asked Silus, when the medicus had left to attend other patients.

'Soldiers,' said Acacius. Every word he formed took an effort, and Silus had to listen carefully to make sure he understood.

'Could you tell which legion? Which unit?'

'Sixteenth. Frumentarii.'

Silus shot a querying glance at Oclatinius, who shrugged. 'There is a detachment of the Flavia Firma based in Syria with Caracalla's army. The legate is still in Syria. It doesn't seem significant.'

'And what exactly did you do?' Silus asked.

'Paid the shipwright. Gave him instructions.'

'You told him to sabotage the ship. Told him how to do it?'

Acacius nodded stiffly.

'Why?'

'Family threatened. Brother in Alexandria.'

Oclatinius looked puzzled. 'Why would your master need to threaten you? You are his trusted secretary. If he ordered you to do it, surely you would obey without the need for intimidation?'

Acacius mumbled something.

'What? Speak up.'

'Wasn't… master.'

A cold feeling settled over Silus like a dump of snow. 'Not Pertinax? Then who was coercing you?'

'F…Festus.'

Silus looked at Oclatinius. The old man's shoulders sagged, and his face fell. He let out a long sigh. 'Damn.'

Acacius started to cough, expectorating phlegm flecked with blood, clutching his broken ribs as if he could defend them from the agony as his chest heaved. The medicus hurried over.

'Leave him now. He must rest. Out, out!'

Oclatinius could have overruled the junior officer, of course, but they had heard enough. They walked slowly out of the valetudinarium together, reflecting in silence on what Acacius had told them.

Silus spoke first.

'I'm sorry.'

'For what?' Oclatinius' tone was sharp.

'For Festus. I know you aren't complicit, but I know too that you are friends with him.'

'Not friends,' said Oclatinius, and Silus waited for him to elaborate. He was not forthcoming, though, so Silus spoke again.

'Pertinax was innocent. And his death is on me. I was the one that led them to him.'

'Pertinax was on borrowed time after his Geticus joke,' said Oclatinius. 'Even if he had survived that, Caracalla would have been rid of him eventually. He believed he was invulnerable because of his father, which just showed how incredibly naive he really was. In any case, Pertinax was set up, that is clear now. To throw us off the real conspirators.'

'Festus.'

For a moment, Oclatinius didn't reply. Then he said simply, 'Yes. Festus.'

'But why wasn't Acacius just killed? Why has he shown up now?'

'I'm not sure,' said Oclatinius. 'Maybe he was rescued. Maybe there was a falling-out among the traitors. But we can't escape the fact that Festus is in it up to his neck. It's the end for him, for sure.'

'What do you want me to do?'

'Do nothing. Leave him to me.'

Silus had grave misgivings about that. This should be taken straight to the Emperor. But he had doubted Oclatinius once, and he wasn't prepared to do it again. He put a hand on his commander's shoulder in what he belatedly realised was an overly familiar way. Oclatinius covered the hand with his own, and squeezed.

-

'It's over,' said Oclatinius. 'You must run. You have the contacts, the resources, the wealth. Disappear. Never be heard of again.'

'I don't know what you are talking about,' said Festus.

'Don't insult me. We found Acacius.'

Festus' face remained neutral, though he couldn't hide the lividity of his cheeks as the blood drained away.

'Is that name supposed to mean something to me?'

'Really, Festus? Is this how you want it to be?'

'How I want what to be?'

Oclatinius clenched his fists, relaxed them with an effort.

'Tell me the names of those working with you. Or who you are working for. I'm not sure where you fit in the hierarchy.'

'Oclatinius, if I was working in some shadowy conspiracy to assassinate the Emperor, with a group of powerful people, do you think I would live long if I gave their names away?'

'I can protect you.'

'No you can't. Your power only reaches so far.'

Oclatinius looked deeply into Festus' eyes, his focus switching from one dilating pupil to the other. Festus was scared. He wondered if it was a new feeling for the self-confident former Arcanus. He made to leave.

'Wait!'

Oclatinius turned back, one eyebrow raised.

'Will you... give me some time?'

Oclatinius considered. 'We will be in Ilium in two days. Caracalla is walking in Alexander's footsteps. He has been obsessed with Arrian's *Anabasis of Alexander* for some time now. In the city, he will honour Achilles, like his hero. At Ilium, I will tell Caracalla everything I know. I hope you can make all your arrangements by then.' He gave Festus a long, hard look. Then he shook his head and said, 'Fortune be with you,' and left his former protégé to contemplate his ultimatum.

Chapter XV

Rome had an ancient connection with the city of Ilium. The Trojan prince Aeneas, immortalised in Homer's *Iliad* and Virgil's *Aeneid*, descended from the goddess Venus, was the legendary ancestor of Romulus and Remus. Ilium itself had suffered a turbulent history. Destroyed by the Greeks in a time so remote that the events were passed on by word of mouth, only much later being written down, it had suffered destruction time and again. Earthquakes, fires, war and urban planning had flattened its homes and temples over and over, yet it continued to rise. The current iteration had been founded around two hundred years previously by Emperor Augustus, and had grown to a decent-sized, flourishing city, sporting beautiful temples and theatres and thriving markets and fora. But its main attraction remained as a tourist destination for those seeking out the origins of Rome, and the legendary places of the *Iliad*.

Alexander himself had come to the city in order to visit the tomb of Achilles, whose fortune in being heralded for posterity by Homer he bemoaned, wishing someone would do the same for him. Caracalla had announced to his entourage that he would emulate Alexander with sacrifices and games to honour Achilles. His council had enthusiastically embraced the idea, though Silus had seen the looks on their faces, the subtle shakes of their heads and sucking of teeth after Caracalla had left the council meeting.

Silus spent most of his time in attendance on Caracalla in his role as bodyguard. He had not yet spoken to Athaulf about Festus, nor had he had a chance to get alone with Oclatinius to see what steps he was taking to bring the former Arcanus and Head of the Sacred Bedchamber to justice. Festus seemed to have made himself scarce, and Silus hadn't set eyes on him since they had left Nicomedia. But no one had remarked on his absence, so Silus presumed that none were yet aware of his guilt, or thought his remoteness suspicious. He was after all a spymaster, like Oclatinius, albeit of a parallel and rival organisation, and for him to be away on intelligence gathering duties was not surprising.

On the day before the games that Caracalla had decreed, the Emperor visited Achilles' grave. The tomb was a short distance from the city, marked by a simple marble column on a small tumulus. No doubt the mound had once been bigger, but centuries had weathered it. Achilles' mortal remains were buried somewhere deep beneath the earth, and the marble monument was a more recent addition. But it gave a focus to visitors wishing to honour the great Greek hero.

Caracalla, as had become his habit, was dressed in full Macedonian style, the smooth chin, the beret, the boots. He had even discarded the caracallus cloak after which he had been named. The Emperor stood before the tomb, attended by priests of both the Roman pantheon and the local cult of Achilles, and placed a wreath of laurel on the column. He poured libations of expensive wine into the earth. Then he sacrificed a pure white calf, holding it firmly while blood from its cut throat watered the ground. Then he dismissed everyone but his bodyguard. The priests and council members shuffled away, heading back to the city, to shade and wine and comfortable couches. When they had departed, Caracalla knelt and then put his face in his hands and wept.

Silus wasn't sure of the source of this emotion. Grief? Guilt? Fear of loss to come? It was clearly not affectation. Only his private bodyguard remained to stand witness. When the sobs subsided, the heaving of the shoulders ceased, and the Emperor remained there in silent worship for a lengthy period.

Silus stood at attention with Athaulf and Maximinus and a handful of other selected Leones. Silus had taken care to clean and polish his uniform to a rare shine – he didn't want to attract Caracalla's wrath for seeming disrespectful. The sun beat down, and sweat trickled down his back. His mouth dried out and he started to daydream about immersing his head in one of the crossroads fountains, or plunging into the frigidarium of the legionary bathhouse.

A movement in the distance caught his eye and snapped him back to the present. A dust cloud, from the direction of the city. The drum of distant horse hooves. A delegation? A messenger? He tapped Athaulf on the arm and pointed.

The cloud drew nearer until Silus could resolve individual horses, and their riders. A dozen men in full armour. No standards, no insignia. All bearing spathas, the long, sharp cavalry swords.

'Augustus,' said Athaulf, voice low but clear. 'Trouble.'

Caracalla stood slowly, turned to face the oncomers. He nodded, as if he had been expecting it.

'Pass me a sword.'

One of the Leones handed Caracalla a long sword, hilt first, head bowed respectfully. Caracalla took it and swished it in a wide circle, made a couple of feinting thrusts, then looked down the length of its blade.

'This will do. Now a spear.' Athaulf gave him a long wooden spear with a barbed iron tip, which he hefted in his free hand. He stepped forward so he was at the front of his guard. Leading from the front, as his martial instincts dictated. Athaulf moved to stand by his side, not able to eclipse the Emperor's senior position, but ready to protect him. The other Leones formed to either side of them, a V shape with Athaulf and Caracalla at the point.

Silus looked around him. The horses that had borne them to the tomb were tied up a few hundred yards away, where their snorting and farting would not disturb the ceremony. They were too far to reach – even if they ran, these riders would be upon them before they had untied the animals, let alone mounted them. There were six Leones in Caracalla's honour guard, big, tough, experienced fighters. But they were on foot, and outnumbered two to one. Silus wondered if there was any chance that these newcomers were friendly.

At a shout from their leader, the riders broke into a canter, then a gallop, swords raised high. That removed any doubts from Silus' mind about their intentions. As he waited for them to arrive, he wondered briefly who had sent them. But the answer was obvious. Festus. He cursed Oclatinius for his delay in dealing with the traitor. They would be having words when this was over. If Silus made it out alive.

The foremost rider was a dozen yards away when Caracalla gave the order to plant their spears. As a body, they hadn't practiced this move. This wasn't a situation they had ever expected. But as individual experienced soldiers, they knew what to do. Each man placed the butt of the spear firmly into the ground and angled the shaft so the tips pointed forward and up.

The momentum of the onrushing horses was too powerful to check or even redirect. The lead horses slammed into the spears. Wooden shafts snapped, mounts went down with iron deep in their hearts, or reared up in pain and panic, tossing their riders off. Caracalla and the Leones dived, rolled, or were swatted aside. All but one rose again, the exception lying on his back staring at the sky, his chest caved in with a hoof-shaped print impressed into the ribcage.

Only four of the attackers remained mounted. Four were on their feet, swords at the ready. Two more raised themselves unsteadily, one of them hobbled by a shattered ankle, the other with his arm across his chest like he was protecting a broken collarbone. Two were dead.

The four mounted men were carried past by their inertia, and yanked on their reins to wheel about.

'Forward!' yelled Caracalla, and ran at the dismounted attackers. This was no legionary battle. They had no shields to hide behind, so tactics of 'step forward, thrust, withdraw blade, step forward again' were useless here. They were fighting as a pride of Lions, with iron tooth and claw.

Silus was confronted by a short, broad man with long blonde hair and a droopy moustache, a typical Gaul. He held his spatha with the tip pointing down and to one side, his stance that of an expert swordsman. Around him came the clash of metal on metal, and the roars of fury as the two sides came together. Silus tried to block it out as best he could, leaving just the faintest awareness to be alert for any other threats. But all his focus was on the man before him, the one who was at that moment trying to kill him. He watched his eyes carefully, searching for any sign, any warning that an attack was coming. He bided his time, waiting for any opportunity to launch his own assault.

The Gaul struck first, lulled in by a deliberate dipping of Silus' sword tip. He lunged forward, his arm fully extended, the thrust aimed directly at Silus' liver. Silus whipped his own sword up, and it deflected the attack safely over his shoulder. At the same time, the Gaul's middle was unguarded, and Silus kicked hard, the side of his boot thumping into his midriff. The Gaul was shoved backwards by the force, letting out an explosion of air, but his stance was solid and he kept his footing. Without pause he rushed back into the attack, swinging a cut diagonally upwards towards Silus' chin. Silus parried again, once, twice, then saw an opening and drew his sword back to strike.

A widening of the Gaul's eyes alerted Silus to the danger before the sound of horse hooves registered in his consciousness. He dived one way, and the Gaul dived the other, and a rider galloped through the space they had been in just a moment before. Silus felt the breeze from the rider's spatha on the back of his neck, and cursed himself for his carelessness.

He rolled to his feet to find the Gaul a few feet away but already charging towards him. Silus allowed the thrust to come, but this time twisted and grabbed the wrist of the hand that held the sword. He pulled, and the Gaul was yanked off balance. As he toppled towards him, Silus jerked his head forward, so he butted his opponent full in the face. Cartilage and bone crunched and blood sprayed and the Gaul fell back with a cry. Silus didn't hesitate and rammed his blade into the Gaul's guts, slashing and withdrawing. Ropes of bowels spilt out through the rent, and with a despairing cry, the Gaul sank to the ground.

Silus spun to assess his immediate surroundings. As he watched, Athaulf whipped his blade through his opponent's throat, then threw a knife at a passing rider, toppling him. Another rider skewered one of the Leones from behind, but his sword caught, and ripped out of his hands. He aimed his mount at Maximinus, but the giant stood his ground, and the intimidated horse swerved at the last moment. Maximinus grabbed the horse's neck and heaved, hauling it to the ground. It rolled over its shoulder, and its rider was crushed beneath its weight.

Silus looked for Caracalla and saw him kneeling astride the chest of his attacker, repeatedly pounding him in the face with his mighty fist. The man beneath him was clearly already dead. But Caracalla, lost in his blood lust, had not seen one of the assailants marching purposefully towards him, sword raised high. Silus was the nearest of the Leones to the Emperor, but he was ten yards away. Athaulf saw the danger and cried out, but he had lost his knife and had nothing to throw.

Silus did still have his dagger at his belt, as yet unused. It was a pugio, a chunky blade like a miniature gladius, designed for a short, sharp, fatal stab. It was not meant for tossing like a throwing knife. But it was all he had.

Silus held the pugio by the tip. Inhaled deeply, aimed.

The sword raised, descended towards Caracalla's unprotected neck.

The pugio flew.

Struck.

Caracalla cried out in surprise as his unseen attacker toppled onto him, sword clattering to the ground, clutching at the pugio lodged in his throat. The Emperor shoved the dying man aside and struggled to his feet, looking around until his gaze lighted on Silus. His eyes narrowed, and he nodded once.

Athaulf rushed past Silus, clapping him on the back in perfunctory congratulations, and took up guard beside Caracalla.

But it was no longer necessary. The attack was over as quickly as it started. Only one of the assailants remained mounted, and he turned tail and raced towards the city. But one of the other Leones, a skilled horseman from Scythia, grabbed a spear and leapt onto one of the uninjured mounts, then rode after him. He quickly got into range, and let the spear fly. It hit the fleeing rider square between the shoulders. He fell and his horse rode on alone.

The remaining attackers were all dead, or were being rapidly dispatched by the Leones. Silus considered calling out for them to take a prisoner for interrogation, but the furious Leones, incensed by the assault on their beloved Emperor, were in no mood for mercy. In any case, Silus knew who was behind the attack. And it was time the Emperor knew too.

But it had to be Oclatinius who gave him the news. The Emperor's anger would be great, and if there was any suspicion that Oclatinius had tried to cover up Festus' betrayal, he would be dead. Silus owed Oclatinius the opportunity to prove his loyalty to Caracalla by revealing the plot. He approached Caracalla and bowed his head.

'Not a bad throw, Silus,' said Caracalla. The rage had left him, for the moment, though Silus knew it would return.

'I'm very relieved it flew true.'

'As am I. Your services to me seem to keep mounting up.'

Maybe one day the old bastard would start repaying him, he thought, though he was not stupid enough to give voice to the sentiment.

'Augustus, I have two roles in your service. I guard your person, a duty I hope I have discharged with honour today. But I am also an Arcanus, part of your intelligence service. I must report this disgraceful attack to my superior as soon as possible. With your permission, and of course, the permission of Athaulf.'

Caracalla looked to Athaulf, who nodded.

'Very well, Silus. Go and report to Oclatinius. And tell him I want to know who was behind this within a week.'

Silus hurried over to where Delicatus was hitched with the other Leones' mounts. *Oh, it will be a lot quicker than that*, he thought.

–

A heat haze shimmered over the field before Achilles' tomb and the early afternoon sun blazed down from a cloudless sky. Wooden seating had been erected, layered in full circles to create a temporary amphitheatre. As with all such venues, the front row was occupied by the elite, the senators, senior army officers and council members not invited to sit with the Emperor. The second row was filled with local dignitaries, and the remaining rows with any free citizens – all free men in the Empire were citizens now – who were able to leave their labours to attend the complementary entertainment. Patrolling up and down on the lookout for custom were the usual entrepreneurial sellers of fast foods and drink, and outside jugglers and acrobats performed in the hope of coin, and the lenos looked for customers for their girls and boys.

The Emperor's box, of course, had a prime view of the arena, and Caracalla sat on a beautifully carved wooden throne, looking down on the festivities. With him as usual were Domna, Athaulf, Oclatinius and Macrinus. Silus on the other hand was standing in the centre of the arena, dressed as a Trojan warrior. The bronze armour – a two-piece cuirass held together by leather hinges, greaves of beaten bronze sheets padded with thick linen, a horned bronze helmet and a round bronze shield – felt bulky and ridiculous in equal measures, and though it weighed more than iron, he knew that it was weaker than the modern metal. His sword, held loosely by his side, had a sharp bronze blade, but it would blunt easily. He hoped that wouldn't be a problem.

It was hot too, and he sweltered under the layers of cloth that protected his skin from abrasions from the unforgiving bronze. Sweat ran freely down his neck and the backs of his legs, and he wished Caracalla would give the signal to begin, before heat exhaustion weakened him too much.

The crowd too was getting restless, despite the fact they had been treated to a gladiators-against-beasts contest, a chariot race, and even a foot race in which a naked Emperor Caracalla had raced against some of his fittest warriors. Unlike Emperors of the past such as Nero and Domitian, Caracalla's pride would not allow him to insist his opponents let him win, and in fact he had come an impressive second, behind a fleet young Macedonian auxiliary. Caracalla had made a big fuss of the victor, and promoted him to commander in his new Alexander-style phalanx.

But the crowd knew that the big event was the last one. A recreation of one of the critical moments of the Trojan war, the battle between Hector and Patroclus. Silus remembered his father telling him the story, how the Greeks' greatest warrior, Achilles, had refused to fight because of an argument over a woman, and how his best friend and lover Patroclus had donned Achilles' armour to lead his Myrmidons against the Trojans. It hadn't ended well.

Now Silus stood in the middle of an arena, gods knew how many hundreds or thousands of miles from Britannia, the country of his birth, surrounded by jeering crowds and playing the part of Hector, the Trojan hero. Funny what a difference to a life hacking the head off a barbarian chieftain can make.

Caracalla had himself ordered Silus to act out this part. It hadn't surprised Silus in the least. He had resigned himself now to his role as Caracalla's go-to when something unpleasant needed doing. Murders, assassinations, executions, dressing up as a Trojan prince. It was all in a day's work. Silus wasn't sure if Caracalla kept picking Silus because he trusted him or hated him.

The wooden gates at the other side of the arena opened, and a figure emerged, shoved out into the daylight to stand blinking and looking at the crowds. Here was Patroclus, dressed in a facsimile of Achilles' legendary armour, the bronze shining like a mirror in the bright sun. The crested helmet enclosed the face of his opponent, only the eyes visible. The shield had been faithfully reproduced from Homer's description, with imagery of the constellations, of city and country scenes and the great Ocean. The cuirass and greaves were inlaid with gold. The appearance was every bit as spectacular, Silus suspected, as the armour created for the original Achilles by the crippled god Hephaistos.

Patroclus took a few unsteady steps forward until he was in the centre of the arena, and the crowd roared his name. 'Patroclus! Patroclus!'

Silus walked up to him, and stood a couple of arm's lengths away.

'Festus,' he said, quietly.

'Silus,' replied the Commander of the Sacred Bedchamber in a voice of resignation. 'This isn't how I envisaged our final meeting.'

'Strange how things work out,' agreed Silus. He noted that Festus spoke clearly, without slurring. In the *Iliad*, Apollo took Patroclus' wits from him, leading directly to his death, and Silus had wondered if Festus might be drugged to simulate this. He wasn't sure if he was pleased or concerned that Festus was fully in possession of his faculties. After all, this man was once an Arcanus, and though he might be rusty, Oclatinius had warned Silus before the fight that he had been a formidable fighter when he had picked him to be his first Arcanus.

'Why didn't you give up the names of the other conspirators?' asked Silus. After the failed ambush, Silus had ridden straight to Festus' quarters, taking with him a couple of burly Leones. The traitor had been waiting calmly for them, seated on a comfortable chair, a cup of wine and some dates on a small table before him. He had decided to wait for the outcome of his final gamble rather than flee, and accept whatever Fortuna brought him.

Festus' torture had not been overly vigorous – Caracalla had wanted him in good health for this spectacle – but Oclatinius and Silus had questioned him thoroughly nevertheless.

'Whatever you think of me,' said Festus now, his voice calm, 'and however motivated I was by personal advancement, I still believe in this cause. Caracalla will lead the Empire to ruin if his ambition is unchecked. Someone needs to end him. Maybe you will realise this, in time.'

Silus was unable to disagree with him. In that moment, privately, despite the sea of baying humanity that surrounded them, Silus wondered if he didn't have more in common with Festus than he cared to admit. After all, it was his ambition that had started him along the trajectory of his career path, and personal considerations had warred with loyalty to Emperor and Empire ever since.

'Patroclus! Hector!' Caracalla's booming voice cut through the noise, and the crowd hushed. 'Here, before the tomb of the greatest warrior the world has ever known, we will witness your epic contest. Only one of you will survive. There will be no quarter. Will it be as history told, or will Patroclus this time be triumphant? Begin!'

It was to be a genuine contest. Silus didn't know what fate awaited Festus if he killed Silus. Feted as a victor, then quietly done away with by poison, probably. It wouldn't matter to Silus, though, since he would be dead.

Silus raised his sword in salute to the Emperor. He had better play his part well – the Emperor was watching in rapt excitement, and he would not be pleased if the spectacle was spoiled by bad acting. Festus did likewise, and the crowd cheered the name Patroclus even louder. Silus realised that he was the bad guy in this scenario. Although the Romans claimed descent from the ancient Trojans, the story of Patroclus' heroic and tragic death firmly put the reader on the side of the Greeks.

Festus lunged.

He was quick, despite the weighty armour, and Silus was forced to dance back, swinging his sword back at the same time to deflect the thrust. Festus followed up with a flurry of attacks, feints, thrusts, swipes high and low. Silus defended desperately, using blade and shield to keep his attacker at bay. Eventually Festus' attack lost impetus as the first signs of fatigue set in. Silus took the opportunity to counterattack, and now it was Festus' turn to retreat, parrying and blocking as he went.

The battle moved back and forth this way for some time, with neither offering the slightest opening. The clash of sword on sword or sword on shield and the grunts of the combatants filled the air, mingling with the jeers and cheers of the crowd.

Combat of that intensity could not last. The physical activity was exhausting, even before factoring in the heat and the weight of the armour. Silus' sword arm burnt, the shoulder muscles of his shield arm protested, his heart thumped, and his chest heaved as he sucked warm dry air into his lungs. Festus was much fitter than Silus had expected, and he was amazed that the older man had so much energy.

Age told eventually. Festus' shield dipped, little by little. His sword came up slower. His blows lost force. Silus suffered the same, but to a lesser extent, his relative youth and his exertions over recent years giving him an edge in condition. Silus found more opportunities, and managed to draw blood, a slash to the thigh, a stab that grazed Festus' arm.

But the first Arcanus had a wealth of experience to draw on. When his shield fell too far, Silus took his chance to commit to a strong attack, realising too late it was a ruse. As his sword pushed over the top of Festus' shield, Festus whipped the shield upwards, knocking Silus' blade away, and countering with a thrust to Silus' abdomen. Silus twisted to avoid the killing blow, but this unbalanced him. Festus stuck out a foot and hooked Silus' standing leg around the ankle, flicking away the support.

Silus crashed to the sand, in a clatter of armour, sword flying from his hand in the impact. Without hesitation, Festus stabbed downwards. Silus fended off the blow with shield gripped in both hands, but Festus, drawing on every reserve, rained down attack after attack. Silus had no chance to regain his feet, and soon, something would penetrate Silus' defence.

But Silus was not without his tricks as well. Even as he rolled from side to side, angling the shield so the attacks slid harmlessly away, he hooked one foot around Festus' ankle. Then, before Festus could react, he slammed the heel of his boot into Festus' kneecap.

With a howl, Festus fell backwards, and Silus leapt up. Festus tried to bring his sword round, but Silus stamped on his wrist, shattering the bones. He tossed away his shield, then gripped Festus' shield, and after a brief tussle, ripped it out of Festus' hands and threw it to one side.

Oclatinius' protégé, his first Arcanus, lay supine below Silus, unprotected, whimpering in agony. Silus looked up to Caracalla in the Imperial box. The Emperor was standing, gripping the railing, watching intently. Silus held up a hand in the traditional gladiator's salute, awaiting the Emperor's judgement. It was a formality. There could be no doubt about Caracalla's decision.

Still, the Emperor milked the moment, gesturing to the crowds to voice their opinion. The onlookers showed their fickleness. Despite moments before cheering Patroclus to the heavens, they now shouted 'Hector, Hector!'

Caracalla held out his thumb parallel to the ground, held it there for a long, theatrical moment. Then he rotated his hand.

Death.

The crowd went wild, screaming and shouting, tearing their clothes in their bloodlust. Silus turned back to Festus and looked down at him apologetically. Festus returned the stare with resignation. Through teeth gritted in pain he said, 'Get it over with.'

Silus nodded and lifted his sword high.

'One day,' said Festus, 'you will come to think like me.'

The sword fell, the point thrusting through the neck, between chest plate and helmet, the blow carrying such force that the blade cleaved the spine and carried on to lodge in the sand. Silus stepped back, leaving the upright sword wobbling gently in the breeze. Without looking back at the Emperor, he walked slowly out of the arena.

-

Festus' funeral was held the next day, but it was no celebration of his life, or commendation of the late spy to the afterlife. In fact, no mention of his name was even made, since even in death, he continued to play the role of Patroclus. His body was cremated on a huge pyre, while Caracalla played the role of Achilles, weeping, beating his breast, throwing a lock of his hair onto the fire, which drew some surreptitious sniggers since his hair was now cropped so short, the tuft was a little pathetic. More sacrifices and prayers were offered, and a further day of games was decreed. None of the locals, the council nor the senators, the legionaries nor the camp followers, seemed to know what to make of the Emperor's behaviour, but apart from some snide comments in private and in confidence by some of the senators, everyone accepted the entertainment on offer and made the most of it.

Oclatinius and Silus walked away from the funeral together in silence. Silus had not yet found the right words to say to the head of the Arcani. *Sorry I killed your friend? Why did you protect that traitor?*

It was Oclatinius that broached the subject first.

'What must you think of me?'

Silus opened his mouth, then closed it again. It was a complex question.

'That might take some time to answer,' said Silus eventually.

Oclatinius let out a brief snort of amusement. 'Fair point. Though of course, I meant in particular with regards to Festus.'

Silus shrugged. 'You don't owe me an explanation. Festus is gone, and you did your duty.' *Eventually*, he added to himself, but didn't speak the word aloud.

'I had a son,' said Oclatinius. Silus stopped in surprise. All these years, and Oclatinius had never mentioned him. Oclatinius turned to look at Silus, searching his eyes, gauging his reaction. Silus waited for him to continue.

'His name was Marcus. He had talent. He was strong, brave, clever. He could have been whatever he wanted. A career in the military, in politics, in law. He would have excelled in whatever he chose.

'When he was nineteen years old, he was killed by bandits on the road from Napoli to Rome. I was with him. I fought, so hard, to save him. He fought too, so courageously. They killed him, and left me broken, in body and spirit. I had just created the Arcani. It was a brand-new organisation, and Festus was my first, and my right-hand man, just like you are now. I was too injured to avenge my son. Festus did it for me.

'He spent weeks infiltrating the bandit gangs in the Campanian countryside, and he tracked down each one who had been involved in the murder of my son. At my request, my command, he killed each and every one. And their families. Women and children. I was not satisfied until the murderers had paid in blood with everything they cared about. Festus did that for me. And never spoke of it to anyone.'

Silus rubbed his face, not daring to speak.

'So, you see, I did owe him. And I wish, wish with all my heart, that I could have saved him. But he was too stubborn. I warned him that I could protect him no longer, but he went ahead with his stupid plans anyway. What a waste. All in the name of ambition.' Oclatinius swallowed, eyes full of water.

'Not just ambition,' said Silus. 'He had more than that. He told me, at the end. He believed in necessary change, that Caracalla is leading the Empire to ruin. In his way, he was a patriot.'

Oclatinius looked at Silus for a long moment, then nodded. 'Then I shall remember him thus.'

Together, the two Arcani walked back towards the city, as the smoke from the funeral pyre drifted into the clear sky.

Epilogue

Juik gently combed through Tituria's long hair, teasing out the tangles. When the comb caught, she held the strand near the scalp, so she could ease it through without hurting the young lady. She had started her bleeding the month before, so she deserved the title 'lady' now, but there was no coming of age ceremony for girls the way there was for boys, when they discarded their bulla and their toga praetexta and donned the pure white toga virilis of a grown man. Her next transition in life would be when she was wed, but there was no hurry for that. Tituria was cared for in a well-off household, so she did not need to be married off for money, and she was not a blood relation, so there was no gain in marrying her for an alliance. She could continue in that odd, responsibility-free time of life between child and woman for a while longer yet.

'I'm very jealous of your hair, mistress,' said Juik as she continued her grooming. Tituria, seated at her dressing table, dressed in a simple nightgown, glanced into the mirror and made a face, one corner of her mouth twisted in doubt.

'Don't joke with me, Juik. You have beautiful hair. You are the envy of every woman in the household.'

'I'm not joking, mistress. It has length and body, and wonderful shine. It seems a shame to truss it up in the modern fashion each morning.'

Tituria let out a light laugh, like the babble of water over stones. 'You are funny, Juik. I do love you. I've been so happy since you came to the household. I mean, it was very sad when Aristomache died. Run down by a cart when out buying vegetables from the market for our stew. Such a waste. But she was a bit dull, and she was quite heavy-handed with the brush. Am I dreadful for saying that?'

'Of course not, mistress. Aristomache's bad fortune was my good fortune. I am very pleased to have been chosen to serve you and the master and the rest of his household.'

She gathered Tituria's long, dark hair and tied a ribbon around it, then used a damp flannel to cleanse the make-up from her cheeks, preparing her for bed. Her eyes were drawn to the girl's neck, exposed by the drawing back of her locks. A delicate blood vessel throbbed steadily beneath the pale skin.

She liked Tituria. It was hard not to. She was bright, intelligent, easy-going, and she treated her slaves with respect. Juik really hoped she wouldn't have to cut her throat.

–

Atius lay on his back as the woman explored his naked body with soft kisses. When she reached the wound on his side, he winced, even though the touch of her lips was light as a feather.

'It still hurts, after all this time?'

'It was deep. I don't know if it will ever be right. It's why Silus sent me out here – to recover, away from the dangers and politics of Caracalla's court.'

'You think Syria has no dangers or politics?'

Atius laughed, and his wound gave a dull ache. In truth, it had healed quite well, enough that he could run and fight, though he suspected it would give him pain for the rest of his life. He snaked an arm around the woman's waist and drew her on top of him so he could kiss her full lips. Her breasts felt soft against his chest, and he liked the feeling of her warm skin against him. He stroked her hair gently.

'Aren't you supposed to be watching out for Avitus right now?'

'As are you.'

'He is with Gannys right now. He is fine.'

Atius reflected that it wasn't so long ago that Gannys had been part of a plot to sacrifice the boy to the god Elagabal, but times had changed, and he had to admit that Gannys had become something of a father figure to young Avitus since the death of Marcellus. Atius was fond of the strange lad himself.

'Gannys must not find out about you and me,' she said. 'He would be furious.'

Not half as furious as Silus, Atius thought, if his friend discovered Atius' latest love interest.

Julia Soemias' fingers stroked across his chest. 'There is a storm brewing, you know.'

Atius was only half listening, enjoying her touch.

'My mother and aunt tell me what is going on in Rome, and in the Emperor's inner circle. He angers too many powerful men. I worry for what will come. If Caracalla succeeds in his Parthian war, his power and fame will be immense, but so were Caesar's, and that didn't prevent his murder. If Caracalla dies, will my son be safe?'

Atius murmured something placating. She kissed his cheek, his neck.

'Will you be there for him? Will you be his shield?'

'Of course, Julia, of course.'

Her fingers stroked his belly, moved lower. He closed his eyes, and put Caracalla and Silus and Avitus, and war and murder, from his mind.

Historical notes

Most of the events of this novel are based on contemporary historical accounts of Caracalla's reign, and as always, I try not to contradict the accepted facts, but rather fill in the gaps with my own inventions. Sextus Varius Marcellus was a real person, a close confidante of Caracalla's and the putative father of Varius Avitus Bassianus, later the controversial Emperor who history came to know as Elagabalus or Heliogabalus. Marcellus died of unknown causes while Governor of Numidia, and his tombstone still exists, which can be seen here: www.livius.org/pictures/italy/velletri-velitrae/velitrae-tomb-of-varius-marcellus-inscriptions/

The inscription reads:

> *To Sextus Varius Marcellus, procurator centenarius of the water supply, procurator ducenarius of Britain, procurator trecenarius of the private purse, acting as praetorian prefect and praefectus urbi, senator, prefect of the military treasury, commander of the Third legion Augusta, governor of Numidia, has Julia Soaemias Bassiana, daughter of Gaius, with her sons,* [dedicated this] *to her husband and dearest father.*

Interestingly the tombstone refers to sons, but we have no other evidence that Avitus had a brother, so I have omitted him from the story. Perhaps he died young, since he was never mentioned in connection with accession to the throne after his brother's reign ended. The exact Praetorian prefect succession after Marcellus' death is unclear, but ultimately Oclatinius and Macrinus were made joint prefects, although this was complicated by Theocritus and Epagathus being made Supreme Praetorian prefects, suggesting that at one stage there were actually four Praetorian prefects instead of the usual one!

Domna's cancer and Caracalla's visits to healing shrines are also attested, although not connected – it was suggested that Caracalla was looking for healing from his own impotence and mental health problems, although how these private, or "secret" maladies were common knowledge is not explained. Caracalla's eccentricity did seem to increase as his reign continued, with his constant desire to imitate Alexander the Great in armed forces, dress and career path. Always ruthless, his bloodthirstiness also seemed to increase in inverse relation to the length of his temper. Maybe it was guilt and mental instability after the death of his brother, or maybe his father and his brother had actually been keeping his worst excesses in check.

The cause of the shipwreck in the Hellespont is unknown, but Festus was put to death after the event which may have been due to failure to prevent sabotage being ascribed to one of Caracalla's trusted spymasters, or to active involvement in the disaster.

The Leones were as described, a newly formed bodyguard, separate to the Praetorians, which Emperors had good reason to mistrust. Maximinus Thrax, another future Emperor, was a member of the Leones. He was also reputed to be eight feet tall, and while this is undoubtedly a vast exaggeration, he nevertheless sounded like a very impressive individual. Caracalla really did have a pet lion as well.

It can be hard taking the known facts and turning them into an exciting novel with all the peaks and troughs we subconsciously expect from a fictional story arc. On historical fiction author fora, accuracy versus story is a frequent discussion point, and it is often argued that as we are writing fiction, accuracy should take second place to plot. While this is certainly a valid argument, it is not my preferred approach, and I hope my readers will forgive me if at any point where I have tried to preserve historical accuracy, the plot of this novel seems disjointed or implausible. That's life and as it often said, the truth is stranger than fiction.

Contemporary Source material

Herodian Ch VIII 1-5

Adapted from "Herodian's history of the Roman Emperors Containing Many Strange and Wonderful Revolutions of State in Europe, Asia and Africa, also their most remarkable embattles, speeches, antiquities etc, together with the most solemn ceremonies used at the deification of the Roman Emperors with a character of the Ancient Britains," Translated from the Greek by a Gentleman at Oxford, John Hartley, London, 1698.

> After he had reviewed his army on the Ister, he passed over into Thrace where it borders Macedonia. Here he became Alexander the Great and endeavoured by all means to revive the memory of that King. He commanded his images and statues to be erected in all the cities – Rome itself, the Capitol and all the temples were filled with them. These honours were paid him in consideration of an alliance to him which the Emperor pretended to. I have seen ridiculous pictures with one entire body and head and two half-faces, one representing Alexander, the other Caracalla. He appeared abroad in a Macedonian habit, with a turban on his head and

slippers fastened to his feet. He had a regiment composed of the flower of his army, which he called the Macedonian Phalanx, and he commanded his officers to take on the names of Alexander's generals. He also sent for young men to Sparta, and called them the Laconian and Pitanite bands.

After he had done this, and put all things in the cities in as good order as they were capable of, he proceeded to Pergamum in Asia Minor in order to have the benefit of Aesculapius' healing influence. After he arrived, and followed his own whimsy for as long as he wished, he set out towards Ilium. Here he surveyed the ruins of that city, and visited Achilles' tomb, which he adorned lavishly with garlands of flowers. He became a second Achilles, and being at a loss for a Patroclus supplied the want by this means. Festus, his favourite freedman and keeper of the Emperor's diary, died while he was at Ilium. Some say he was poisoned, so that he may be interred in the same manner that Patroclus had been, but others say he died naturally.

His dead body was ordered to be brought out and a funeral pile to be raised of wood. The corpse was laid upon the middle of the pile, and beasts of all kinds were slain, after which the Emperor set fire to the pile and holding a bowl in his hand, sacrificed wine and prayed to the winds. His hair was extremely thin, and it was ridiculous to see the Emperor cut it off and cast it into the fire, and very much diverted those that looked on. He extolled the Roman Sulla and African Hannibal above the Generals of all the ages, and to demonstrate his high opinion of them, commanded their statues to be erected.

Cassius Dio Book 77, 15-16

Adapted from an English translation of Cassius Dio, Roman History, Book 77, 15-16 by Earnest Cary PhD, 1914, taken from Lacus Curtius website. http://penelope.uchicago.edu/Thayer/E/Roman/Texts/Cassius_Dio

He likewise published outright to the world some of his basest deeds, as if they were excellent and praiseworthy, whereas others he revealed unintentionally through the very precautions which he took to conceal them, as, for example, in the case of the money. Antoninus devastated the whole land and the whole sea and left nothing anywhere unharmed. The enchantments of the enemy had made Antoninus frenzied beside himself; at any rate, some of the Alamanni, on hearing of his condition, asserted that they had employed charms to put him out of his mind. For he was sick not only in body, partly from visible partly from secret ailments, but in mind as well, suffering from certain distressing visions, and often he thought he was being pursued by his father and by his brother, armed with swords.

Therefore he called up spirits to find some remedy against them, among others the spirit of his father and that of Commodus. But not one of them spoke a word to him except Commodus; as for Severus, they say that Geta accompanied him, though unsummoned. Yet not even Commodus said anything to help him, but, quite the contrary, so that he terrified him all the more; for this is what he said:

'Draw nearer judgment, which gods demand of thee for Severus,' then something else, and finally:

'Having in secret placed a malady hard to be cured.'

For publishing these facts many were treated with gross indignities. But to Antoninus no one even of the gods gave any response that conduced to healing either his body or his mind, although he paid homage to all the more prominent ones. This showed most clearly that they regarded, not his votive offerings or his sacrifices, but only his purposes and his deeds. He received no help from Apollo Grannus, nor yet from Aesculapius or Serapis, in spite of his many supplications and his unwearying persistence. For even while abroad he sent to them prayers, sacrifices and votive offerings, and many couriers ran hither and thither every day carrying something of this kind;

and he also went to them himself, hoping to prevail by appearing in person, and did all that devotees are wont to do; but he obtained nothing that contributed to health.

While claiming to be the most pious of all mankind, he indulged to an extravagant degree in bloodshed, putting to death four of the Vestal Virgins, one of whom he had himself outraged – when he had still been able to do so; for later all his sexual power had disappeared. Consequently he satisfied his lewd desires, as was reported, in a different manner; and his example was followed by others of similar inclinations, who not only admitted that they were given to such practices but declared that they did so in the interest of the emperor's welfare. A young knight carried a coin bearing his image into a brothel, and informers reported it; for this the knight was at the time imprisoned to await execution, but later was released, as the emperor died in the meantime. This girl, of whom I was just speaking, was named Clodia Laeta; and she was buried alive, though protesting in a loud voice, 'Antoninus himself knows that I am a virgin; he himself knows that I am pure.' Three others shared her sentence; two of them, Aurelia Severa and Pomponia Rufina, were put to death in the same manner, but Cannutia Crescentina hurled herself down from the top of the house.

In the case of adulterers, also, he acted in the same way; for, though he had shown himself the most adulterous of men, – so long, that is, as he had the power, – he not only detested others who were charged with the same thing, but even slew them in violation of all law. And though he hated all good men, he affected to honour some of them after their death. Antoninus censured and rebuked them all because they asked nothing of him; and he said to them all: 'It is evident from the fact that you ask nothing of me that you do not have confidence in me; and if you do not have confidence, you are suspicious of me; and if you are suspicious, you fear me; and if you fear me, you hate me.' And he made this an excuse for plotting their destruction.

Antoninus, when about to kill Cornificia, bade her choose the manner of her death, as if he were thereby showing her especial honour. She first uttered many laments, and then, inspired by the memory of her father, Marcus, her grandfather, Antoninus, and her brother, Commodus, she ended by saying: 'Poor, unhappy soul of mine, imprisoned in a vile body, fare forth, be freed, show them that you are Marcus' daughter, whether they will or no.' Then she laid aside all the adornments in which she was arrayed, having composed herself in seemly fashion, severed her veins and died.

Antoninus came into Thrace, paying no further heed to Dacia. After crossing the Hellespont, not without danger, he honoured Achilles with sacrifices and with races in armour about his tomb, in which he as well as the soldiers took part; and in honour of this occasion he gave them money, just as if they had gained some great success and had in truth captured the very Troy of old, and he set up a bronze statue of Achilles himself.

Bibliography and further reading

As usual, I have consulted too many texts in the research for this novel to list here, but some of the principal books I have relied on are listed here:

Bowman, A. K., Garnsey, P. & Cameron, A. (2005) *The Cambridge Ancient History: Volume XII, the Crisis of Empire AD 193–337*, 2nd edition. Cambridge University Press, Cambridge

Carroll, M. (2001) *Romans, Celts and Germans, the German Provinces of Rome*, Tempus, Stroud

Goldsworthy, A. (2011) *The Complete Roman Army*, Thames & Hudson, London

Grant, M. (1996) *The Severans, the Changed Roman Empire*, Routledge, Abingdon

Matyszak, P. (2020) *Forgotten Peoples of the Ancient World*, Thames & Hudson, London

Southern, P. (2001) *The Roman Empire from Severus to Constantine*, Routledge, Abingdon

Swain, S., Harrison, S. & Elsner, J. (2007) *Severan Culture*, Cambridge University Press, Cambridge

Syvänne, I. (2017) *Caracalla, A Military Biography*, Pen & Sword Military, Barnsley

Acknowledgements

Thanks as always to the team at Canelo – especially Michael Bhaskar for continued support and editorial comments and Kit Nevile for general organisation, and Steven Mulcahey for another beautiful cover. Thanks to Elodie Olson-Coons for a thorough copy edit. Thank you to Antonio Mosca for being a fantastic and knowledgeable guide through Pompeii and Herculaneum this February. Thanks of course to Naomi and Abigail for putting up with the Roman obsession. And last but not least thanks to all my readers, without whom this would all be pointless!